The Wall of Hope

The Wall of Hope

A NOVEL

Kathleen L. Martens

BYZANTIUM
Sky Press

Byzantium Sky Press
Ellendale, DE, 19941

The Wall of Hope is a work of fiction. Any reference to historical events, real people, or real places are used fictitiously. Other names, characters, places, and events are products of the author's imagination, and any resemblance or similarity to actual events or places or persons, living or dead, is entirely coincidental and not intended by the author.

ISBN 978-1-955872-18-8 (paperback)
ISBN 978-1-955872-19-5 (ebook)

Library of Congress Control Number: 2024930650

First Byzantium Sky Press paperback edition, March 2024

Interior design by Crystal Heidel, Byzantium Sky Press

Manufactured in the United States of America

Body of book is typeset in Adobe Caslon Pro
Dotunder and some foreign accents typeset in Minion 3
Chapter Numbers are typeset in Liza Caps Pro

Cover Photographs:
Golden Gate Bridge, Maarten Van Den Heuvel, Unsplash.com
Painting (back blending to front), Geordanna Cordero, Unsplash.com
Various Watercolor Images blending over images, Unsplash.com
Image of Woman, Min An, Pexels.com
Cover Map image courtesy of Vectonauta, Freepik.com

"Let There Be Peace On Earth" song by Jill Jackson Miller (1913-1995)

While suffering from late-stage Lyme disease at sixty-three-years-old, I took a bold chance to do something new. I wrote a memoir with Margaret Zhao, a woman who'd grown up under Chairman Mao's tyrannical rule and escaped to America in the 1970s. The new paperback book arrived from the printer at 12:12 p.m. on 12/12/2012.

I shared the happy news with my parents the day before I left California to visit them in Tampa, Florida.

Entering their living room, I handed Mom *Really Enough: A True Story of Tyranny, Courage, and Comedy.* She was an avid reader. Why did she look confused?

"What's wrong, Mom?" I thought she'd be thrilled.

"This is a book." Her incredulous look confounded me. She ran her finger over the gold first-place medallion on the cover. "First Place?"

"Yes. Crazy, right? My first book won the Best Biography/Memoir award in a contest. I was so surprised."

"You wrote this?" Mom's shoulders rose.

I worried. In her late eighties, she'd always been mentally sharp. "Yes, I wrote it."

"Wait, Kathleen, this is a real book." Mom turned it over as if she'd witnessed a miracle.

I laughed. "Yes."

"But it's a *book* book—like you'd buy in a bookstore."

That was the most memorable, comical, touching moment in my life with my mother that I long for today. She couldn't believe someone from our family had risen from our modest circumstances to write a book. Despite my international career, business successes, and master's degree, I'd written a book.

My name and photo on the cover made Mom shake her head in disbelief. She sat on the sofa reading non-stop, delaying dinner. More than once, she paused her reading, looked up, and said, "Really, you wrote this?"

I wasn't insulted. Mom was delighted; I was an author.

Everyone who came to the house was subjected to her enthusiastic required reading. I wouldn't be surprised if she'd announced it at Sunday Mass from the pulpit.

In the years following her death, something was missing each time I published another book and held it in my hands. She'll never have the chance to read it. I'll never see that astounded look again, I'd thought. I long for my mother to reappear and say those wonderful words, changing "book" from a noun into an adjective. I long for the chance to see her awestruck expression again. I ache to have her there for that fleeting moment each time I'd hand her one of my publications—*Wanderlust: A Wartime Search for Hope and Home*, *Under a Jungle Moon: A Novel*, or *Rising Women, Rising Tides: Stories of Women, Water, and Wisdom*, and now my newest novel, a sequel to *Wanderlust*, called *The Wall of Hope*.

To have my mother say those words to me again would be a loving, eternal embrace.

"Kathleen! It's like a real book. A *book* book."

One of the challenges authors and all creative people face is finding the time to pursue their craft without neglecting the people close to them. Art is never a nine-to-five job.

I dedicate this book to my husband Steuart who helps to clear the space for me to create when I'm inspired. What a blessing to live beside a person who knows how to translate love into life. I admire his dedication to the well-being of others as a board certified health coach, and I'm grateful for his dedication to me and my passions.

ACKNOWLEDGMENTS

No book comes alive without a team. My heartfelt thanks to:

Judy Catterton, Story Editor/Copyeditor who dedicated endless hours to provide her incisive insights and logic. Her ability to find the inconsistencies and identify the improvements that make a difference was uncanny. What better experience could she have than a career as a successful prosecutor of the law?

Stefani Tran, Authenticity and Developmental Editor who enlightened me about the Vietnamese cultural traditions and intercultural issues, helping me to ensure authenticity. Her developmental edits for the substance and arcs of the story were invaluable.

Abby Hale, Proofreader who kept me on good terms with the Chicago Manual of Style while respecting my own rule-breaking style on a record-breaking timeline.

Nancy Powichroski Sherman, Proofreader for the front matter and beyond.

Maribeth Fischer, Executive Director of the Rehoboth Beach Writers Guild, my superb teacher who guides and inspires me as a Kathleen-come-lately novelist.

Rehoboth Beach Writers Guild for providing unparalleled support, encouragement, and writing opportunities to its fortunate members.

The sisterhood of women writers who have been endlessly generous with their irreplaceable support and inspiration for the books I've written and curated.

My friends, Alpha and Beta readers and brainstorming wizards who provided honest, on-target feedback, viewpoints, and advice:

Maryn Arnett

Jean Aziz

Sarah Barnett

Christy Briedis

Jane Klein

Jane Knaus

Fran Mossberg

Kristen Janine Sollée

Nancy Walker

Judy Wood

Crystal Heidel and *Byzantium Sky Press, Publisher,* for her faith in my work and her support and outstanding creativity in designing the interior and cover for *The Wall of Hope.* Who wouldn't want a publisher who is an author and talented graphic designer?

1

BLADES OF SUNLIGHT flashed between the buildings along the Boston Harbor waterfront below. Hope's first job at her father's new headquarters sent a sizzling high through her. In the penthouse reception area, she admired the new sign on the wall, *Uplift Children's Foundation.* Years of studying through the night, endless classes, papers, and tests at Boston College and Harvard Law School had led Hope to this moment.

How could she resist seeing the newly renovated sky-high offices alone with no distractions? Hope's father wouldn't mind; he'd given her the keys. Sunday afternoon was the perfect time. Things would be hectic when the foundation officially opened at 9:00 a.m. tomorrow in its impressive downtown location. Hope would be busy meeting the new team members, settling in, and practicing legal strategies for aiding in the adoption process for war orphans.

A new daily calendar with a Kelly-green bow greeted her on the shiny wooden reception desk. The attached note read, *Welcome*

Aboard, Hope! Love, Shiloh. Yes, that was the Shiloh Hope knew, the woman who'd guided her through her life to this moment. Tearing off the cover of the six-inch-square pad, she found the right page—Sunday, September 3, 1995.

Photographs of children rescued from war zones around the world hung throughout the hallways. Their enchanting, innocent eyes and fragile smiles reflected twenty years of touching, foundation successes. It was the perfect introduction to the soul of the organization.

Peeking into the large conference room, Hope loved how the soft blue walls blended into the blue sky and the expanses of water below. The scent of the freshly painted walls said, *new* beginnings. She imagined the space could easily accommodate one hundred staff members as they continued to grow the organization. Such a change from the start-up offices over the coffee shop on the other side of town.

Continuing down the hallway, Hope was moved to see her name etched into a brass plate on the second mahogany door on the left—Hope Lê James. She'd always had trouble with her Vietnamese surname, Lê. Some people spelled it Lee, thinking it was a typo, leading them to misunderstand her ethnicity. She was glad the plate couldn't hold her hyphenated, legal American surname, Ketchum-James. She'd deleted *Ketchum.* Too much. A mouthful, and she'd never wanted the attention that last name would bring. From high school through law school, all Hope had heard was, Oh my God, you're Kate Ketchum's adopted daughter? She's so awesome. Wouldn't that spotlight distract everyone from the person Hope really was?

The differences between the Vietnamese and American naming structures caused confusion. Placing the given name at the end after the father and mother's surnames in Vietnamese was something her father had settled by Americanizing her name. Instead of Lê Ketchum-James Hope, she would be Hope Lê Ketchum-James. Even that string of names was confusing enough for Americans, but at least her first name came first.

Hope greedily drank in yet another stunning view through the all-glass wall with awe when she opened her office door. A wide eye, open to the city. She set her briefcase on the desk, dropped into her leather office chair, and admired the skyline. Did she look like a child with her petite body ensconced in the oversized high-back chair?

Taking three photos from her briefcase, she set them on her new desk. The first showed her tall, all-American handsome father, Michael James, with his silver blond hair still shining at forty-five, receiving an award for his charitable works from Vice President Al Gore. A larger four-generation Ketchum family photo of thirty-seven relatives included her dad's mother, Grandma Christine, who'd become part of the clan. Only Kate was missing. She was on tour, as always. The third framed photo was a close-up of Hope with Ernie and Mary, her two adopted American siblings with disabilities. Hope remembered the day her adoptive mother had brought them into the family when Kate had been a special education intern—before Kate's singing career had skyrocketed.

An easy swivel of her chair changed Hope's view from one end of the boat-filled harbor to the historic buildings along Back Bay—a scene she felt compelled to paint. Hope's father had encouraged her to learn piano from him. Still, when she wanted to express her emotions, Hope turned to her hobby, sketching and painting. She smiled, remembering her childhood portraits of Ketchum family members she'd scribbled on the inside of cardboard cereal boxes.

Taking out her sketch pad and watercolor paints, Hope prepared to capture the stunning view outside her new office window. The sunlight sliced through the clouds, painting unexpected streaks of pink and yellow across the sky. Capturing nature scenes had always enchanted Hope—it was her secret escape from the stress of exams and the pressures of school. Whenever she'd experienced a micro-aggression from a stranger, or worse, a racist comment from a boyfriend's family member for being a brown-skinned girl in a white world, she would turn to the healing arms of Mother Nature. Hope couldn't deny it; she'd always been a nature girl. Had she ever made an important decision in life without walking by a river or the ocean, waiting for the reflections in the rippling water or the applause of the waves to give her the answers she needed? She hugged herself. Then, a heavy feeling interrupted.

Was it the faces of the refugee children along the hallways that had propelled her back to her beginnings? Images she'd long ago locked away. The ones she'd learned to compartmentalize after her young years of therapy.

On a fresh page, Hope sketched the military rescue plane. She could see it in her mind, buzzing and frightening, landing in the distance on the dirt road.

At three-years-old, she'd had no idea what the other children were cheering about when they'd heard the thundering sound of the plane overhead. Why would they run toward it? Wasn't it the same threatening sound that had dropped the explosives, devastating the orphanage where they'd lived? Why would they have run toward the starlit red, white, and blue rectangular image on the side of the plane? Later, Hope understood. The other kids were older and wiser. That American flag signaled their rescue. A bigger girl had taken her by the hand. Swept up in their excitement and contagious squealing, Hope had run through the smoke toward her future.

At twenty-five, memories of her days in the orphanage were faded and vague. Lightly rubbing the side of the pencil over the scene on her sketch pad, Hope tried to capture the image of smoke. She remembered crying and gripping the frame of the plane's window when the other children were dropped off to be cared for by the American Red Cross at a military installation nearby. She remembered crying when the plane took off again, as the only one who didn't get to stay. Hope would never forget the hum of the engines and the hand of a Marine pilot named Jeremy patting her shoulder to calm her as they flew to some secret remote landing strip in Thailand.

She remembered being hoisted by Jeremy into the arms of a stranger, her father. Little Hy Vọng must have smiled at the stuffed bunny she'd found on the front seat of his car as he took her to her future Bangkok home, Hope thought. As an adult, she still snuggled that bunny for comfort.

Hope had little memory of being called by her birth name, Hy Vọng. The English translation *Hope* suited her. Easier to blend into a new world in America. She imagined her Marine dad finding the word *hope* in his Vietnamese-English dictionary before naming his newborn infant. It was strange to use Hy Vọng for a child's name, a Vietnamese college acquaintance had told her. It was like calling a child *perseverance*. Her colleague had laughed at her father's innocent mistake. Yes, *hy vọng* translated into the word *hope* in English, but he'd said it would be very unusual to use an abstract noun for a given name in Vietnamese.

Now, she would be bringing hope to other children in danger. She didn't want to be a woman crying in the workplace with her coworkers around. Albeit, weeping with gratitude. Hope would do that now, alone, looking out over her future.

Wiping her eyes, Hope searched for a parallel. Something to make sense of the crazy, fateful changes in her life. The Butterfly Effect, part of the Chaos theory she'd studied in college, came to mind. She was fascinated with that theory. Small causes can have significant unrelated effects halfway around the world. Scientists theorized that one butterfly fluttering its wings could cause a hurricane thousands of miles away.

One older woman, a stranger from another village, entrusted by Hope's Marine father to deliver his newborn child to her grandparents' nearby village, had delayed the baby's delivery by one day—one fateful day, the woman had waited. Hope's father had told her the story. It was a rare occasion for the close-to-the-vest man to share his memories. On that same day, Hope's grandparent's village had been decimated by bombs with no reported survivors.

That one military man, a stranger willing to break the rules, forge documents, and enlist a Marine pilot to save her, had shifted the trajectory of Hope's life—her father, former Marine, Michael James.

Hope's life truly had transformed like a butterfly—from searching through rubble to find food for herself to providing planeloads to needy children in her new foundation job, from her life in an orphanage to living in her parent's mansion with the affluence to give back to a needy child in a country she'd never seen. She was grateful to that butterfly wherever it was.

Hope began to sketch a Blue Morpho Butterfly and its complex design. And didn't the life cycle of a butterfly have some parallel to the good fortune of her life? From larvae to creeping caterpillar to cocoon, emerging from its chrysalis to become the majestic, winged beauty floating free in the blue sky.

These unexpected blessings had led Hope from an infant in a devastated orphanage to a toddler with a father, cocooned in the safety of a new family, where she'd transformed and had taken flight with her Harvard education. Now, she'd taken wing with a job as an attorney in a prestigious foundation high above the city in the blue sky. Didn't she owe a debt of gratitude?

Why was she thinking in metaphors today? That fantasizing phenomenon often happened to Hope when she'd sketched or painted. Her beautiful escape. How had she been so fortunate? Chaos theory—one stroke of fate—one rule-breaking Marine pilot, Jeremy, had spotted her running by the edge of the rice field with five other orphans who'd survived the explosion. One embassy official who'd risked his career and lost his job to rescue a love child he hadn't seen in three years.

Since her current job was helping connect refugee orphans to a new life with a loving adoptive family and finding missing children for families who'd lost them during the chaos of war, could Hope use her job to learn about her own past? Find the missing pieces? Was that what had driven her to join her dad in his passion for helping children in war zones? Hadn't she once been one of those homeless wartime children who'd lost her family? Even though her blood relatives were gone, she'd always ached to know more.

It was clear her father resisted looking back. Given his suffering from *Combat Fatigue*, as they called PTSD back then, she had to respect that, didn't she? And wasn't her birth part of his trauma?

Had she not had her childhood therapy, Hope surely would still suffer from that same shell shock that had caused her constant nightmares and fears. After all, she was her father's daughter, Hope thought.

He'd never discussed his Post Traumatic Stress Disorder from the war. It sometimes turned the light in his eyes off and then on as his haunting memories pressed in and retreated. Clearly, her father couldn't bear to share what he knew about Hope's biological, Vietnamese mother—his lover during the war. Exactly what war traumas and history had caused her father to withdraw behind his wall? Who was Hope's mother and what was her name? Was she still alive or had she left her American Marine boyfriend amid the chaos of the war? What was her mother's story? Hope was compelled to learn more.

Had it been two decades since her anxious father had illegally brought Hope through the Boston airport US Customs with forged documents?

Now, she regretted not knowing anything about her own culture of origin. It was as if half of her was missing. Ironically, the half she knew little about had caused her the most pain, suffering, discrimination, and prejudice. But the subject of her past was always off-limits with her dad and her stepmother, the world-famous singer, Kate Ketchum. Maybe this place and this job would hold the key to her mother's story and Hope's early years. She released a shallow sigh.

Stretching her arms wide, Hope took in the ever-changing view over the harbor. Then she finished sketching herself in her father's arms on that fateful rescue day. If her father hadn't wrapped her in his Marine T-shirt with his name imprinted inside the collar, if she hadn't become so attached to that tattered rag that carried some irresistible scent of the past, if she hadn't inherited her father, Michael's blue eyes, she would not have been identified as his daughter. She would not belong to her loving Ketchum-James family. She would never have been a Harvard grad, an attorney working for a prestigious foundation in the penthouse of a spectacular skyscraper on the other side of the planet.

There would be no Hope.

2

THE ENDLESS RIDE on the elevator down to the parking levels gave Hope time to think. As she drove home in her sentimental blue VW Beetle, she was surprised the visit to the high rise had evoked so many thoughts of the past. She wanted to stay in the thrill of the present.

Her commute was a mere ten minutes. The only traffic she'd encountered on the sunny Sunday was the temporary flood of people exiting the Ketchum family's Catholic church three blocks from her family home. Parking in the driveway of the three-story Georgian mansion, she again shook her head at her good fortune. Only last night, she'd come home from the airport after a summer living in Paris. Hope enjoyed traveling alone. Or was that what she'd told herself since she had no traveling companions? It was hard to form close relationships commuting to college from home. In law school, everyone was riveted on studies and interviewing, and Hope lived alone in her apartment off campus.

Hope climbed the sweeping, curved stairway to her bedroom and headed for the wine bar in her sitting room. She'd always preferred hanging out in her bedroom suite when she was home alone rather than the central area of the house downstairs. Like being back in her small apartment in Cambridge at Harvard Law School, her room on the second floor had a sitting area, kitchenette, and private bath.

Glancing across the room, she saw something new on the wall—her Harvard Law School diploma. It was sweet of her father to have framed it while Hope was in Paris.

Without considering any other options, Hope followed in Auntie Shiloh's footsteps. She was now officially a lawyer, Harvard Law Class of 1995. Hope had been so focused on studying and succeeding that she hadn't stopped to take it all in. Passing the Massachusetts bar in July before she'd departed for her vacation in France had been a relief. Hope's throat tightened, remembering the entire family cheering from their stations in the shoe factory when her Grandma Cecelia had announced the good news.

Shiloh was coming by to chat. She said she'd felt bad that no one had been free to pick Hope up at the airport. Hope understood. She shared her father's priorities. When he'd called to say Grandma Christine's lake house roof had leaked, Hope had insisted he go. Her dad was good at rescuing people, and he was close to his mom. He said he would see Hope at the offices tomorrow. After their opening celebration, he would take her to a family dinner at her grandparents' home an hour away.

Hope propped her sketch on the dresser of her dad holding her when she was a three-year-old refugee. Those old fears and memories hadn't resurrected in so long. After two decades since the Vietnam War, there rarely had been reminders to trigger those images until today, she thought.

The familiar sound of Shiloh's signature knock, tap, tap-tap, tap brought Hope out of her thoughts. A smile broke through her blues. Shiloh had a way of doing that. She could always pull Hope out of her down times as a child. Her stepmother's best friend from college had always been there for Hope like family should. Did Shiloh call herself *Auntie* to make Hope feel a more profound sense of belonging when she'd arrived as a frightened toddler?

"Come in, Auntie Shiloh."

With that distinctive jingle jangle of Shiloh's ever-present silver jewelry, she entered Hope's bedroom. "Hi, sweetheart. I used my key so you wouldn't have to do those stairs after your travels. How was your flight? Was Paris wonderful? We've missed you."

Was there any prominent lawyer in Boston like Shiloh? Her black and gold paisley bandanna imprisoned an explosion of dark corkscrew curls. Her treasure chest of silver spangles and bangles that danced from her ears, fingers, wrists, and neck contrasted her serious, skirted, black lawyer suit. Like Cher dressed for her classic skit, Kate had always said. With her Cherokee heritage, even Shiloh's name had intrigue. She loved to say it came from a Civil War battle. And she was a true warrior when it came to advocating for children in danger or need.

"Paris was indescribable, Auntie Shiloh. In six weeks, I fell in love. The best graduation present Dad could have given me."

"I need to hear about this. What's this lover like? When will you see him again?" Shiloh sat in one of the ivory brocade wing-back chairs and leaned forward as if waiting for the juicy news. Then she took a book from her satchel.

"Paris, silly. I fell in love with *Paris.*" Hope laughed, hugged Shiloh, and sat in the chair next to her. "What's the book you're holding?"

"I've just been lost in memories reading a bit of the past, and I think I should give you this to read."

Fluttering the pages of the worn leather diary, Hope recognized her adoptive mother Kate's handwriting. Tilting her head and lifting her shoulders was enough to express her confusion.

"I know, maybe I shouldn't give you that journal. But you know Kate. Since our college days, she's always on the road and has no time to pause and reflect on where she's been. But there are memories here that are precious to her, nonetheless." Shiloh shifted her bandanna. "I suppose that's why she gave me this for safekeeping a few years ago, so she wouldn't lose it on some tour bus or in a dressing room halfway around the world."

Heading for the wine bar, Hope poured another glass of Pinot Grigio. "Would you like a glass of wine, Auntie Shiloh? We both might need it right now."

"Sounds good, sweetheart."

Hope stared at the diary as she set the two glasses on the end table next to their chairs. Why did Shiloh give Hope her adoptive mother Kate's private diary *now*? Guilt shivered through her as she fingered the thick, black, and gold, weathered book. Hope hesitated.

"I know. It feels strange. Kate entrusted it to me. Let's talk." Shiloh took more than a sip of her wine. "I battled with that question myself. I thought maybe it would help you to understand why Kate sometimes is, well, often, not here. I was hoping to build a bridge so you could start fresh. You need to read the whole thing to understand, honey."

Hope sighed and closed her eyes.

"Look, I know it's confusing, but she does love you."

"I know she does. I feel that, Auntie Shiloh. But she couldn't even make my law school graduation in May."

"Out of her control, right? Plane delay. But sad for you *and* Kate." She patted the aged journal. "Maybe her words will help to heal your heart, Hope. It's one thing to hear it in hindsight, another to read it written from her perspective, back when it all happened. When your stepmother, I mean, Kate, was your age."

"I'll tell her that I let you read it. I promise. And I know it seems odd, though I don't always play by the rules when there's a higher cause. When Kate entrusted her diary to me some years ago, she looked at it and said, I wish Hope could read this someday. Maybe she'd understand my choices better."

"Maybe now is the time." Shiloh reached out and took Hope's hand.

"I don't mean to whine, Auntie Shiloh. I know I'm blessed. And I know how much Kate's career means to her."

"I understand living with other people's life choices can be challenging, honey. My parents were hippies who took my brother and me touring in an RV to do political, outdoor theater. They homeschooled us until high school. But you never know what good can come of a challenge, right? Political injustice inspired me to go to law school."

But then it had inspired Shiloh's twin brother to enlist in the Marines and lose his life in the Vietnam War, Hope thought.

"Never mind, stand up and let me look at you." Shiloh scanned Hope up and down. "I think we need to do some clothes shopping." Throwing her head back, Shiloh let loose her characteristic echoing laugh. "Honey, you and I share one thing besides our

Harvard Law degree. I had to give up my hippie garb back in the day when I turned lawyer. You'll have to give up cropped tops and embroidered jeans. Adult-up a bit."

"True. I need to go a little more corporate, Shi." Hope looked in the full-length mirror. There was more than a hint of her mother's genes in Hope's heart-shaped face and light brown skin, Kate had once said in a rare moment of openness. But how did Kate know? She'd shut down and refused to continue the conversation.

Trying to imagine what her Vietnamese mother looked like, Hope squinted in the mirror. Her sky-blue eyes and warm natural highlights that streaked her shimmering dark hair were clearly from Hope's fair-haired father.

"Or at least dress a little more *nonprofit*. Did I lose you there for a minute, Hope?" Shiloh laughed.

"No, I'm here. But to be fair, you did keep your signature bandanna and bangles with your serious suits, Shiloh."

"Funny. We deal with people from so many different cultures at the foundation. I guess we can have a little latitude. But find something benign for your signature *thing*, Hope. Make them focus on your brains, right?"

"How about a nose ring?" Hope pinched the base of her nose. She loved their silly banter.

"Are you sure you have no Ketchum blood in you? You're too funny. Speaking of cultures, we've hired our new Overseas Operations Manager. I think you'll like him. Very impressive. He's from France. His name is Dominique. A graduate of the Sorbonne. He's the son of a family friend of ours." Shiloh took a break to drain her glass of wine. "Your dad loved him. Hired him right off. And along with him, I think we might have inherited a major donor. Our *most* major donor. His mother already notified us she wants to contribute to our cause. We hired him before we knew. Of course."

"Very cool. Can't wait to start work tomorrow and meet him." Hope engaged her knowledge of French. "By the way, his name means 'of the Lord.'"

"We'll see how holy he is." Shiloh winked. "When he sees the gorgeous face and knock-out petite body of our adorable new attorney."

"Auntie Shiloh!" Hope knew about Shiloh's free love philosophy formed in the '70s and her leadership in the Students for a Democratic Society orchestrating anti-war protests at UConn. It was no secret she had a wild side. She always had a new lover in her life. Kate had repeatedly teased Shiloh about that when she was home from touring, saying, "Did you catch his name this time, Shi?"

Hope's only two romances had been disasters. Both families had found it difficult to accept a half-Vietnamese war baby girl-friend for their sons, even if she was the adopted daughter of a famous performer. She couldn't face that discrimination again. She'd thought Steve would be the one, but he'd folded under his family's pressure. His ex-military father's prejudice had become contagious. Hurtful. A life lesson.

Shiloh's mood shifted. She adjusted her bandanna.

Hope could read it in her face. She knew what that meant. Something serious was about to come.

"Honey, don't make the joy of tomorrow's celebration at the office contingent on Kate showing up. Just in case. OK?" Shiloh shifted her bandanna. "I called Kate. Her European singing tour will be over tomorrow, and she says she'll be here a day late, but she'll be here. Your dad asked me to pick her up at the airport.

And he wanted to be here when you arrived, but your Grandma Christine needed some help at her lake house."

"I know. I talked to Dad, and he said we'd leave after work tomorrow for our special dinner. You're coming, Auntie Shi, right?"

"Of course. Would I miss a night with the Ketchums? OK, Hope. Great to have you back. I'm thrilled you're finally on the Uplift team. I'm off. See you tomorrow, honey. So exciting." Shiloh stood to leave.

"See you."

A familiar pause hung in the room before Hope could express her feelings. "I . . . appreciate you, Auntie Shiloh." Hope would never leave her family like Kate had, she thought. Always one more night, one more performance. The anger tried to take control, but Hope's thoughts of seeing her Ketchum family after so much time pushed it away.

Shiloh seemed to read Hope's thoughts. "Kate wanted to be here for *you*. I promise that. We'll all go and have a good time with the family. I'm going to head out. See you at the office, OK? Maybe, until then, you'll read a bit with those gorgeous blue eyes you inherited from your father." She pointed to Kate's diary.

"Sounds good. I've missed everyone."

Shiloh hugged Hope, touched her cheek, and left the room.

Hope stripped and tried on a colorful print baby doll dress with her red ballet flats. It would have to do until she could shop for an appropriate business wardrobe. She slumped into the antique chair and flipped through her adoptive mother's journal entries.

As she sipped her wine, Hope thought about Kate. She wasn't unkind or unsupportive. And she'd undoubtedly been generous with the financial rewards of her overnight fame. Without memories of her biological mother, Hope had always wanted to capture every detail of her good memories of Kate. She could hear Kate's award-winning voice crooning behind her father at the piano, her hands lovingly on his shoulders. She could see the gold flecks in Kate's green eyes, the pull of her earrings on her soft earlobes, her striking long red hair, the pride in her pursed lips when Hope had tried to play the piano as a child.

A hundred little memories, she'd collected them like precious gems. Sadly, when it came to the critical milestones, the big moments in Hope's life, there were very few memories to cherish of the woman who could have been like a mother to her. Kate wasn't there.

Hope scanned her luxurious bedroom decorated with priceless mementos from Kate's round-the-world tours with her band Riverrun. The silk bed coverlet, famed artwork, crystal lamps, and Louis the Fourteenth settee had transformed Hope's room and their eight-thousand-square-foot home into a mini-European palace. Hugging a raggedy stuffed bunny in each arm, Hope felt the comfort of those two lifelong friends. Maybe it was silly at her age, but she didn't care.

Hope's move to their new home in Boston to attend a good Catholic elementary school at six-years-old had been so exciting. Now, she was conflicted. The beauty of the big eight-bedroom mansion and living alone with her dad, except when Kate came home for brief respites from her tours, often felt empty. Things could be different now with Hope's new connection to the Up-lift staff. Still, nothing could compare to the warmth and love of the big Ketchum family gathered in their old three-bedroom row house.

She remembered Kate trying to get her parents to move out of their aging brownstone to a lovely five-bedroom house only a brief car ride from their factory jobs in Glynn after Kate's success brought more money than she could spend. But why would Grandma Cecelia and Grandpa Kevin want to leave their home, their walkable neighborhood filled with relatives, the factory, their church, and O'Leary's pub—where they'd spent their entire adult lives only two blocks away from anything that mattered, they'd said. They preferred the rowhouse like Hope preferred the old familiar bunnies to the precious antiques.

Her first memory of the bunny returned. Dad had given her the one that was now worn out from love. Hope could see it awaiting her on the front seat of his car when she'd first arrived in Thailand on the plane from the bombed-out village in Vietnam. Back then, she'd thought her dad was just a kind stranger. The matching stuffed animal was a gift from Kate to celebrate the day she'd arranged for Mary and Ernie's release from that terrible institution, Rolling Hills, to join Hope as a part of the Ketchum family. The two-decades-old-scruffy pair of rabbit friends held Hope's history.

She only had flashes of her early childhood memories of Kate when Hope had toured with her dad. Always in the intense spotlight, there was too much glare to see her newly adopted parent—the press, the fans, hotel after hotel. Kate's visits to Grandma Cecelia's house between tours, TV shows, and Grammy awards left little time to form a deep bond with her adoptive mother. Hope felt closer to Kate's mother, Grandma Cecelia, with whom she and her dad had lived for three years in between tours and now visited regularly for Sunday dinners and special occasions. Those infrequent times when Hope felt she belonged made Kate's absence more hurtful. Kate belonged to the hundreds of thousands of fans around the world.

Everyone always commented on Hope's unusual blue eyes. The one speck of proof beyond the T-shirt that Michael was her father. Another anomaly—the warm highlights in her dark hair—a stray gene from her father and grandmother Christine's silver blonde hair. Hope was grateful for any evidence beyond his Marine's T-shirt that Michael was her father in the 1970s before there were DNA paternity tests. Now, in 1995, it would have been easy to prove.

Scanning the journal, Hope spotted an entry that made her pause. She ran a stuttering finger along the enlightening words.

November 12, 1974,

Stroking the luscious velvet always calmed me in those agitated moments when I questioned everything just before I'd launch onto the stage. The feel of the heavy, soft, front-of-house curtain quelled my self-doubts, regrets, and guilt and melted them into joy. The one thing I could always count on, whether in Paris, Bangkok, Sydney, or New York, was the silky, retractable border that separated my two lives—reluctant wife and mother on one side and singing superstar on the other.

Nothing had changed. Kate was all about her singing. Hope didn't expect Kate to give up her spectacular Grammy-winning success for her family, but wasn't she powerful enough to strike a balance somehow? It was hard to understand. Kate came from such a close-knit family that was always there for you. And yet, Hope's father, Michael, seemed to accept his wife's passion and supported her constant absences. Hope would try to follow suit.

She couldn't help but read one more line.

Singing to an audience with glowing faces arched up, swaying to my music, is thrilling. Their joy is my joy. On the stage, I'm home.

Home? The statement gave Hope more insight. She read about Kate's whirlwind life as the warm-up act for the Grammy-winning Keys band. Then, decades of being on the road with her own band, Riverrun. The temptations of fame. The joy of the crowds.

How many times had Hope been riding in the car, and Kate's powerful, bell-like voice would come on the radio? Some of Hope's favorite songs were written by her adoptive mother. But Hope would turn off the radio in a flash whenever she heard Kate's first and biggest hit, "Too Precious to Leave Behind." Too precious, maybe, but Kate did leave Hope behind. But wait—was Kate referring to her child or her career? That thought had never crossed Hope's mind.

Who wouldn't admire Kate's success in rising from a laboring shoemaking factory family to a world-renowned performer? But Hope still needed and wanted Kate in her life more. Even now, as Hope launched into her new job and adult life, she needed guidance. Hadn't Hope been busy, away at school, or traveling? It wasn't the time apart, she realized. It was the emotional separation. Kate had always kept things on the surface. No matter her age, in some ways, Hope still sometimes felt like that orphan baby inside.

Why did Shiloh give this diary to her? Hope wanted to read it; she didn't. She picked up her sketch pad and tried to lose herself in another pencil portrait of her dad. The diary was too tempting. Did it contain any hints about Hope's mother?

As much as she resented Kate's choice to prioritize her touring, Hope admired her famous adoptive mother's success. But somehow, she needed and wanted a closer relationship with Kate as Hope launched into her new job and future adult decisions in her life. Could it change? It was unlikely. There had been little change in their friendly but distant relationship in two decades.

Glancing across the room at the photo of her father holding Hope and Bunny when Hope was a toddler, she pulled the journal from the end table. She'd never experienced a passion like Kate's. It was hard for her to understand Kate's choices, having been raised among passionate nonprofit workers and philanthropists who put others' needs first. Hope had never thought to explore her other options. She felt like a Prairie dog who'd just popped up out of the ground and saw the landscape of her life for the first time. Hope had been underground, riveted on her education for as long as she could remember. Hiding out in school and travel, she'd always looked outward without time for introspection.

Hope had never questioned she would be a part of the family foundation working with her father. Wasn't that her passion?

3

HOPE WAS THE first to arrive at the new offices. Inspired to do something special to celebrate the new staff and the grand opening, she'd filled the elevator twice with two dozen colorful balloons and two bags of gifts by seven o'clock. The surprise would add to the festivities. Each ride to the penthouse had been dizzying. As the numbers rose, so did her excitement.

With the decorations unloaded and in the conference room, Hope tied a balloon to the twenty-four chairs around the table. Opening the shopping bags, she placed a custom logo mug personalized with the name of a new staff member at each seat. The white ceramic coffee mugs matched the ones she'd given her Auntie Shiloh and Dad when they'd been a small start-up charity.

Last, Hope opened the bag her adopted brother Ernie had left at her door to surprise her when she arrived home from Paris. There were twenty-five small, gift-wrapped packets inside. Hope opened one. She ran her fingers over the supple, handmade, black Italian leather wallets and admired the foundation's logo stitched onto the outside corner. Was there anyone more thoughtful than Ernie? He had the most loving heart, her family had always said. Imagining his skilled, gnarled hands working in the shoe factory with her grandfather to fashion the wallets from scraps, Hope placed one at each seat and slipped the unwrapped one into her briefcase for her father.

Walking back to her office, Hope thought about her dad's inheritance of the business and its towering reflecting glass building. It had allowed him to take his small charity to the heights. He'd sold his father's investment business to a prominent firm and dedicated every dollar of those proceeds to the works of Uplift Children's Foundation. Hope admired that.

There were no remnants of her deceased grandfather's former multibillion-dollar investment business that her dad had rejected all these years. With the interior renovation, Shiloh had turned a serious money-making business office into a warm and welcoming suite of offices suitable for a children's charity. Her father had said the top two floors offered a spacious workplace for the team, and the rentals on the other floors provided a steady stream of income for operations and missions. Finally, her dad had the inheritance his mother, Grandma Christine, had said he deserved.

Returning to her office, Hope sat and watched the city come alive. In the distance, colossal construction cranes began to awaken and yawn, opening their earth-moving jaws to the sky. Starting their work for the day, the dinosaur-like cranes dangled see-sawing steel beams in mid-air over a building in progress. Scaffolding hugged a new skyscraper, blossoming from the ground below. Another high-rise building added to her childhood Lego-like memories of the rising profile of Boston's skyline. *You and me, Boston.* She was giddy with her good fortune.

The wind blew in sideways from the harbor, and beads of rain clicked like cat claws against the wall of glass in her office. The click-clicking mimicked the sound of Hope's fingers as they flew over her computer keys. Hope opened the letter from Harvard she'd tossed in her briefcase at the last minute this morning before she'd left home.

As a graduate of the class of 1995, she felt compelled to add her opinion to the Harvard Coalition for Civil Rights survey about diversity among students and faculty. The fact that there had never been Asian Americans, Native Americans, African Americans, gays, lesbians, Latinos, Latinas, and other women minorities on the faculty was a major concern, the survey introduction said. She agreed. There were only two Asian students in her class of more than five hundred. They didn't even distinguish Southeast Asians from other groups of Asians. Hope had never been able to be invisible and blend in. She'd been met at worst with prejudice or at best with curiosity in her all-American white neighborhood. Her big, connected family had rarely left the familiarity of the streets of their factory life.

She finished the survey and printed it.

Tucking the survey into the envelope, Hope remembered moving to Boston at six-years-old from her grandparents' factory town, Glynn, just an hour away. With over one hundred thousand Vietnamese refugees settling around the city, Hope wasn't such an anomaly. She remembered seeing the first girl who looked like her holding her mother's hand, standing at the bus stop on the way to Hope's new school. It provided her with an unexpected awakening, a realization that other Vietnamese girls like her were out there.

Hope imagined her little face peeking out of a limousine when

Kate returned to Glynn. It must have been a rare sight for the Ketchums' working-class neighbors, too.

She closed her new Power Book laptop and gazed out the window. But here in this diverse group of liberal-minded employees dedicated to helping children worldwide, wouldn't she fit in? Her only concern was being the Chairman of the Board's daughter. There could be two sides to that. Would she be treated with kid gloves as Michael's daughter? Or would she be held at arm's length, suspect, and untrustworthy? She wanted to be treated just like everyone else. She would call her dad, Michael.

Shiloh had been the foundation's lawyer and second in command since the beginning. Hope would surely drop the *Auntie* title for Shiloh while at the office.

Hope checked the clock—seven-thirty. She looked forward to meeting the new team when they arrived at nine and was excited about the reception at the close of the day. It will loosen everyone up, her dad had said.

Centrifugal Force, she thought, as she pushed off the glossy hardwood floor and rotated around in her chair again. If a train was running at high speed on a track around the equator, in the opposite direction of the Earth's rotation, the train would remain stationary. True. So, was it really happening if her life was moving this fast in the opposite direction from what she'd ever expected in her early years with the Ketchums? She laughed. Crazy mind, always looking for answers to explain the inexplicable.

A double tap at her door brought her back into the room.

"Come in, Shiloh." Who else would be here so early? Wait, Hope thought, that wasn't her signature knock.

Hope's door opened a crack. "Bonjour, Mademoiselle." A young man peeked in. "Oh, excuse me, you were expecting Director

Shiloh Miller?" He leaned into the partially opened door. "May I introduce myself? Dominique Bellamy Bonchance. The new Overseas Operations Manager for the foundation."

Remembering Auntie Shiloh's romantic prediction, Hope bit her lip and swallowed a laugh when the clicking of the rain stopped, and the sun lit up the room. "Oh, Dominique, please come in." She felt a rush of heat in her cheeks. He was beyond attractive with his fine features, shiny dark hair, and engaging smile. There was no other way to describe him with his blue cashmere sweater over his shoulders, wearing gray slacks and a pink dress shirt with its collar open, no socks, and loafers. Not the usual corporate garb. Hope liked it. Classy but casual.

She pulled herself together. "*Bonjour*, my name is—" She wasn't used to having such an electrifying attraction like this so soon. And she wasn't used to being at a loss for words. "Sorry, honestly, I was deep in thought. I'm Hope." Rising from her desk, she reached out to shake his hand.

"Hope, yes—" He pointed to the nameplate on her door. "I've been looking forward to meeting you. Shiloh has spoken so highly of you." He became distracted, gazing out the window at the sun as it swept the storm clouds away. "Beautiful. Can I get any work done with this view across from me?"

Hope took advantage of the moment to study her new colleague. Shiloh had told Hope he was kind, intelligent, and impassioned for their cause. And she'd teased Hope about his irresistible attractiveness. She wasn't kidding.

"Oh, excuse me, Miss Lê Ketchum-James. I was taken with the changing sky."

"Please come in and sit down." And a nature boy, too, Hope thought. They had one thing in common already. Hope became self-conscious. Smoothing down her long hair, she straightened her jacket and pulled at the skirt of her new serious, gray suit Shiloh had suggested she buy. The notched lapels seemed a bit too masculine. Too late now.

He crossed the room and sat across from Hope.

Wasn't it nice that he wasn't a Jolly Green Giant? She cringed thinking of the words she'd shouted at the tall, teasing, mean boys at school when they'd made fun of her petite size, calling her an elf or a midget.

No, Dominique was a comfortable five-foot-nine or ten, she estimated. Lean and athletic. And yes, his accent charmed her. It was so good to hear French again after her summer trip, the official language of her country of origin for so many years. French was the second language her family would have spoken. She'd studied it for years for that reason.

The Vietnamese language wasn't offered at school, and Dad didn't want to speak it once Hope had learned English. Too many painful memories. It was a connection to her mother and the family Hope had never had the chance to know.

Hope launched into her best French. *"Avec plaisir. J'ai hâte de vous rencontrer, Dominique."* Yes, it was a pleasure to meet him and to see his look of surprise at Hope's French, polished in Paris all summer. There was an immediate magnetism she'd never experienced before.

A fluttering in her stomach.

Yes, it was a pleasure.

SHILOH HAD said the team was a hodgepodge of twenty-four cerebral, passionate, beautiful optimists. All different sizes and colors, but all dedicated and brave humanitarians. As the multi-cultural group stood amid the multicolored balloons sharing stories in the conference room that afternoon, Hope immediately relaxed at the celebration. Feeling like she would fit in, she joined in the conversations.

Dominique, who'd helped Michael hire the new employees for the expansion, could obviously tell a good soul the minute they'd walked in the room, she thought.

After college, Hope had always assumed she would be in a small cubicle, meeting with social services clients and being helpful to single mothers who had fallen on hard times. But the foundation was already world-renowned by the time she'd finished law school. Now, with the overseas teams in place and the newly expanded staff in Boston, they could work with their in-country representatives in warring countries to arrange for a full range of support for children—food, rescue, adoptions, future education, a chance for a good life.

"Impressive," she whispered to Shiloh as they sipped wine and scanned the room. Dominique Bellamy Bonchance. Even his last name had elicited a smile from Hope. *Bonchance*, when you said it out loud, it sounded like the French words for good luck, *bonne chance*.

Shiloh pointed to the balloons and mugs and whispered, "This is so you, Hope."

Just before the team arrived in the conference room, Hope had hors d'oeuvres and a globe-shaped cake delivered. She'd designed and made name tags to accommodate the new staff. She'd planned it for days.

"I don't know what you're talking about." She wanted anonymity, but there was no getting anything past Shiloh.

The group gathered against the blue walls of the conference room with their champagne flutes in hand.

Her father began. "Shiloh Jackson, you're an inspiration to the team and an advocate for every woman and child alive. I am sure there are six families today and countless others who are deeply grateful for what you did these past weeks in Bombay and beyond. Here's to your bravery and your dedication."

"Well said, Michael." Dominique led a toast, and the clink of glasses filled the room.

"And thank you, Dominique, for building this amazing team."

Hope noticed Dominique's look lingered, focusing on her as she congratulated Shiloh.

"Dominique comes to Uplift from Paris, where he worked at several major nonprofits. He's a master of organization and operations and quite a talented writer. That skill will come in handy for our promotions going forward. Just what we need as we grow. Thank you for putting together this team of experts. I think about the impact we'll have with a dedicated group like ours. Would you like to say a few words?"

Dominique put his hands in his pockets, shuffled his feet, and stood straight. "I come here to honor my father who gave his life for human rights. It is my purpose in life to carry on for him." His deep breath was audible, and his sincere and emotional tribute made Hope put her glass down and cross her hands across her chest. Another thing in common. Wasn't Hope's experience in the war just as connected to her dedication to serve?

Dominique introduced all twenty-four impressive team members, paying tribute to their skills and experience.

Michael thanked him and retook the floor. "Thank you so much for this great celebration, Shiloh. Balloons and a globe cake. Is she great, or what? Best friend, best lawyer, best backup anyone could have."

Hope smiled and winked at Shiloh. She reminded herself not to call her "Auntie" at work.

Clearing his throat, Michael introduced Hope. "And now I want to introduce our newest Uplift Children's Foundation team member, Hope Lê Ketchum-James. A recent Harvard Law School grad. Top of her class, I might add, at the risk of embarrassing her. To give her the best introduction to the broad spectrum of our endeavors, I'm assigning Hope to be Uplift's Director of Intake."

Hope's eyes darted from person to person to see their reactions. They applauded and smiled supportively. There was no mention of her family connection to Michael. She was glad. Everyone knew, but everyone understood, it seemed. Shiloh must have been behind the smooth transition.

"As the point person for our US headquarters for the next ninety days supporting Dominique's role as Operations Director, Hope will be able to meet each client and coordinate their services. This will allow her to become familiar with each staff member, our roles, and the kinds of overseas connections we make. She'll also be the one to see for legal document reviews, her future permanent position. Congratulations, Hope."

Had Shiloh had a hand in this plan? A broad shaft of late afternoon light cast a sunburst around the colored balloons that floated over them. Hope thought she was floating, too. Dominique was a master at eye contact. Hope was not. There was promise in his blue eyes. Working together would require balancing on a razor's edge, she thought.

Michael continued telling the story. Shiloh had not only done the cultural research, but she'd prepared the maps and briefings and put together all the details from the informants on the ground that had kept the Uplift team safe. And Shiloh herself joined the team in Bombay and planned the hit on the brothel, personally rescuing the six young girls from the despicable hell hole on the sordid side street. All under twelve. The children stood with Shiloh's arms wrapped around them in the photo Michael had framed as a surprise. How had they managed to smile?

Hope's chest ached at the sight of their young faces. They'd expected young women in the sex trafficking sting, Shiloh had said, but these six little ones were much younger than they'd imagined. Hope wondered how many others were still out there. Could she endure hearing about these tragedies even with their happy endings? The rescued girls were now in a good, safe, private school in another part of their country, and the team would be finding in-country family placements.

Would every success bring her back to her own painful beginnings? What would the next story be?

THE FIRST day couldn't have gone better. But the time difference between Paris and Boston left Hope exhausted. Her dad said he needed a little more time to organize the foundation's next mission before they left for the family celebration. Hope had plenty of time to be tempted. Was it a good thing that Shiloh had given Hope the diary? Could it really change things? She picked up her sketch pad and began to lose herself in a pencil portrait.

She sketched her Hollywood-handsome dad at his baby grand piano playing backup for Kate's gorgeous voice in college, where it all had started between her parents. Her art didn't provide its usual escape. The diary was like an alluring cobra tempting her from her desk. She picked up the book, crossed the room, and looked to see if Kate had written about first meeting Michael. Hope found the right passage.

I remember it like it was yesterday. The moment I first met Michael. I'd just auditioned for a voice major at UConn and failed. I didn't meet the requirements. I couldn't read music. I dragged myself to the church for choir practice. At least Father Sullivan had seen something in my talent. He'd let me join the award-winning choir. The church was empty except for one blond guy kneeling and praying with his head in his hands in the front row. I was still trembling from my audition failure as I climbed the steps to the choir loft. I was the first to arrive. My new life had all started wonderfully—then the most essential thing had gone wrong. I was crazy to think I could compete in music just on raw talent and desire. Shiloh had said I should find another way to pursue my singing. What way? Singing at the protests, she'd said.

It was comforting to see Father Sullivan. Paging through his sheet music at his organ, the afternoon blotches of colored lights flickered through the stained-glass window as clouds passed overhead. I told him about my problem. How could I learn to read music?

He led me down the stairs to the front of the church. The young man was just rising to leave. I couldn't help but notice his chiseled profile, his biceps fighting to burst out of the sleeves of his blue cotton dress shirt, and his strong hands with slender long fingers jutting from his rolled-up sleeves. Then, his shoes, circa 1960, penny loafers. They were from Owl & Shamrock.

Father Sullivan introduced the blond student as Michael Edward James. He stepped aside and chatted with Michael. I remember this gorgeous guy glancing at me.

The confident way Michael stood there talking—his formal posture, attentive to Father Sullivan, yet humble, his hands folded in front of him—was nothing like my unpolished home-town, Glynn guys. Michael's sophisticated way about him spoke of quiet class and a privileged upbringing. His demeanor, dress shirt, blond hair, and cornflower blue eyes, the whole look of him, said class.

Father Sullivan said Michael was a classically trained pianist, and he'd be happy to volunteer to teach me to read music.

Michael smiled, kept his eyes on Father Sullivan, and made no eye contact with me.

I offered to pay him, but Michael said no payment was necessary.

I can see the splash of colors from the stained-glass window, lighting him from above. "The Lord has answered," Father Sullivan said, turning his hands over in the flashing lights.

We all laughed.

"It seems you have an angel, Ms. Ketchum." Father Sullivan clasped his hands behind his back.

"Oh, I wouldn't say I'm an angel," Michael said. I can still see him shuffling from one foot to the other.

"Oh, no, I was referring to myself." Father Sullivan smiled.

The priest's sense of humor made me feel more at home.

I agreed to meet Michael at the Student Union the next day at 2 o'clock. I told him how much it meant to me, and I connected with his arresting blue eyes for the first time. He cast them downward.

It seemed he wasn't there. What had just happened? Like a light went out in his eyes, like a wall had dropped between us. I remember thinking it was better that way. I promised myself I'd keep my mind off his square jaw and alluring smile. I would keep my eye on the ball like I always had.

I remember thinking, could I?

Hope tossed the journal on her desk, grabbed her coffee mug, and headed for the break room. There was a similarity between Kate and Michael's first connection and Hope's first meeting with Dominique. As she opened the door, Hope literally fell into Dominique's arms. "Oh God, I'm so sorry."

They both laughed with embarrassment.

"Everything is timing, Hope."

He had such a charming and gentle way about him, she thought.

"Michael asked me to tell you he'd be another hour. Would you like to get acquainted and walk in the gardens across the street? We won't have many more warm fall evenings. I've reached my limit on being indoors for today."

Glancing back over her shoulder through the window at the lovely sunny afternoon, Hope couldn't agree more. The afternoon sun and drifting clouds were enticing, and Hope had always loved the Boston Gardens. "Why not? We have so much to learn." It was clear her words had two meanings. Was her blush a giveaway? And his words, *everything is timing.* Was he flirting?

"Yes, our jobs will be so intertwined."

They left the building, and Hope walked Dominique to the orderly French gardens that dotted the landscape of her beloved Boston Park. She wanted to show him the early April faces of the daffodils and crocuses and the promises of the pansies and tens of thousands of tulip buds that would fill the beds throughout the park in the spring. She was getting ahead of herself. "Did you know tulips have grown in this Victorian-era park since the mid-eighteen hundreds?" Hope imagined reading the brochure the first time she'd wandered through the meandering paths of the familiar flower scenes.

"I look forward to seeing the flowers unfold, but I love experiencing the famous fall in New England."

Unfold? Fall? Did everything they said to each other have an underlying meaning, or was she imagining it? Hope turned the conversation to their work relationship as they walked along the path beneath the trees with russet and multicolored maple leaves swirling around their feet.

They discussed her role as the point person for every request or assignment that came to the organization. She would interview all contacts to determine their needs and concerns, whether it be someone looking for a lost child, potential adoptive parents, government representatives, or leaders from related nonprofits. They shared the same perspectives on working to keep the children safe in their own countries when possible. His accent put a soft edge around the serious subjects. She needed that.

By the time they returned to the office, Hope had a comfort level about working together and more than a bit of discomfort around her ability to remain simply his coworker. She knew the dangers that lurked in workplace relationships. She would not let that happen.

Would she?

4

MICHAEL PARKED IN front of the Ketchums' home with Hope sitting silently beside him. Things were so familiar, Hope thought. The subtle scent of smoke that permeated the factory town, the unraveling wicker chairs on the front porch, and the squeaking green door that would announce their arrival as they entered her grandparents' home. The Ketchums' family security alarm, Kate had joked once when they'd walked through that creaky door together years ago.

Hope wanted to see her Grandma Cecelia, Grandpa Kevin, and the whole gang to celebrate the foundation's new digs. Still, she was reluctant to leave the car. After reading parts of Kate's diary, she needed to know more. That one line lingered. *I felt betrayed that Michael didn't trust me enough to tell me about Hằng.*

Hằng, her mother's name was Hằng. What did it mean in Vietnamese, Hope wondered.

Could Hope finally feel comfortable enough to ask him about her mother?

Hope's father squeezed her hand. "Good to be back, huh?"

"So many memories, Dad." The fifty-five-minute drive from Boston to Glynn had been filled with reflections on the Ketchum clan. Her childhood quickly came alive for Hope as they'd driven through the old factory town—past the Catholic church, the Owl & Shamrock handmade shoe factory, and O'Leary's pub—the center of their lives that humorous Great Grandpa K had dubbed "The Holy Trinity."

Her father sat gripping the steering wheel, sharing her silent and contemplative mood. He stared up at Kate's childhood bedroom window.

"Dad, can you share?"

He glanced at Hope.

"Please?" She engaged his eyes and didn't look away.

"I just remembered the first time I visited the Ketchums for Thanksgiving. Kate invited me as a friend since my parents were visiting Paris without me." He pointed to the upstairs righthand bedroom. "That was the night I first slept in that room. Alone, of course. As their guest." Dad snickered. "Surrounded by that citrus scent of her half-empty bottle of Shalimar." The memory made Michael smile, and his face reddened.

"Tell me more, Dad." She wanted to fill in the details. He rarely talked about his early days with Kate and had never shared when it came to her biological mother and his Marine days in the war. He believed in living in the present, he'd always said. Hope had felt that was an excuse to bury his memories and not talk about anything personal or traumatizing from the past. She'd never wanted to risk triggering his PTSD.

"Junior year in college. We were standing by the Student Union at UConn after we'd performed for a room filled with foot-tapping students. I told Kate my parents were going to Paris without me, and I'd planned to stay on campus alone for the break. From Kate's expression of surprise, I don't think she meant to ask me home for our Thanksgiving vacation. It surprised us both. We'd been singing together but not much else."

"What did she say, Dad?"

"Her exact words were, *Not as long as the hinges on the Ketchum front door work, you won't.* It's become an inside joke."

They both laughed. "That's Kate for sure, Dad. What did you say?"

"It had taken me a minute to process what she'd said, but I answered right away. I said, *You know . . . sure. I'd love to go.*" He gazed out the window and told the story in a low voice as though he were talking to himself. "It wasn't like me, but then there was her face, those green eyes, and the whole package. I'll tell you honestly, her singing voice had shot down my spine when I'd played the final tune on the student union piano that afternoon, Carole King's 'You've Got a Friend.' Those lyrics Kate sang were so right on. Honey, I'd never been so low and troubled, and I realized I'd never needed a friend so badly."

"She was right about that, Dad." Hope loved her dad's baritone voice and how he got carried away singing the lyrics.

"Honey, Kate's voice was like velvet, a bell, like a smooth glass of fine wine. You've heard her, Hope. That voice changed my life. No exaggeration. And that window up there reminds me of that Thanksgiving with her family and singing with Kate at O'Leary's pub. Sometime that night, alone in her room, I realized I'd just fallen in love."

Hope welcomed the memories and filed them away. She scanned the familiar bedraggled buildings along the street, and in her mind, she, too, was back in her childhood days in the warmth of the Ketchum family.

His hands gripped the steering wheel tighter.

She wanted to ask her father, '*What are you thinking?*'

Michael hesitated and looked at Hope with moist eyes.

"Dad, I love when you share these stories of you and Kate." She took his hand. "Please? I need it."

His head dropped, and she hesitated. Hope didn't want to cause him pain or ruin the mood for the night ahead of them with the family. But somehow, she knew this was leading to her real mother.

He glanced at Hope and sighed. "I was remembering the terror and the shame that I'd felt thinking of another woman that way so soon after—"

Hope sat frozen, afraid to move, afraid to break the spell.

"It had only been months since I'd arrived home. After my second tour of duty had ended, your mother and I had planned to get married and move to the States. And you, young lady, were quite a surprise." He smiled.

She knew his smile belied his pain.

"Your mother—" He shifted in his seat and turned to look out the window. "It feels strange telling you this, Hope."

His fragility was contagious, but she pushed on. "Dad, I'm a grown woman. Please, it's time. I know so little."

"Your mother was so . . . so special."

A squirrel scurried up the tree next to the car, stopped, and stared at them, drawing her dad's attention.

She didn't want her father to stop.

Then, it wisped up to the branch above the car. Her father watched the creature's antics and got that faraway look that meant he was shutting down. He looked into Hope's eyes, and then he dropped his head. "It was different. The war . . . and—"

"What was she like, Dad?" Had Hope gone too far?

Her father gripped his face with his hands.

"I'm sorry, Dad. You're right. We need to stay in the present."

"Hằng? She was like you—charming, witty, intelligent, and obviously beautiful." He glanced at Hope. "Your mother said, *My name's pronounced Hahng, so don't let me hang.*"

Hope smiled, and her dad let out a puff of laughter.

"I'd only been back in the States for a few months when I met Kate. Believe me, I was still embroiled in the memories, in the guilt of—" He covered his face with one hand, shook his head, and sighed. "How can I put those images in your mind, honey? I've never been able to . . . it seems wrong, selfish."

"I understand." Hope did understand the terrors of PTSD and the pain of repeating torturous memories. "You don't have to go on, Dad."

"Are you OK, honey?" He lightly stroked her hair.

"Yes, I'm fine, Dad." She wasn't OK, but there was so much Hope wanted to finally know. He was avoiding not just the tragic part but the good parts, too—her mother's personality, her thoughts, and her dreams. Hope waited, then touched his face, wanting to plead for something she wasn't sure she wanted to hear.

"If she'd only kept to the plan. I would have been home in a month. We would have been married, moved to the States, and you'd be with her today. God Dammit!" He crashed his hands down on the steering wheel.

He turned to Hope, his face red and damp. Her father's words tumbled out. But not the story she'd hoped for. He repeated

Hope's childhood story. The one she'd already learned from Kate and Jeremy.

"I can still remember your innocent scent as I kissed your forehead. I had no idea how to feed you. Coconut water at first. That's all I had. Then that goat, that wonderful life-saving goat. I wrapped you in my T-shirt. It had my name in it in case I could come and find you when the war was all over."

"And Dad, you did." Hope held his hand to her face.

"These hands." He pulled away. "These hands gave you to an old village woman. I'd called you Hy Vọng, meaning hope. I asked her to bring you to your grandparents' village right away. She'd waited. Why, I don't know. Maybe the Vietnamese I'd remembered from your mother's lessons back then was wrong. Maybe I misspoke, but it saved your life, Hope."

"You don't know how I got to that orphanage. You don't know anything else?"

Her dad shook his head. "Nothing, until three years later. I asked my Marine pilot buddy, Jeremy, to find the old woman in the village. Locals said she'd taken you away. And he checked in at that nearby orphanage on a hunch. Your grandparents' village . . . well, I told you it was devastated. No survivors. No longer there."

"I have only vague memories of those early years, Dad. Only when Uncle Jeremy's plane came after the bombing of the orphanage, those sounds I remember, the whine of the incoming bombs, the buzz of the planes, the confusion and screaming. Then running along the rice field with the other kids who'd survived." Now, it was Hope's memories that were haunting her.

"I love that Jeremy asked you to call him Uncle Jeremy." Her father leaned forward and looked at the sky as the squirrel scampered down the tree. "And I know those sounds well, honey." Michael turned the key to quiet the engine of the silver Jaguar. "Hope, I swore I'd never share those memories of Hằng with our child. Having those violent images of your mother's death in the war in *my* mind is enough. I just can't add that to your traumas. Do you understand? It would be so wrong. But it's true, you are a grown-up woman, and I know you've been waiting to learn more. I just can't. It was enough you'd experienced three years in an orphanage and its devastation. I carry a lot of guilt for that. I was sure your mother would want you to be with your grandparents rather than start a new life in a foreign country with me. I only meant for Jeremy to ensure the old woman had brought you to your home village and you were safe with your family. Kate was the one who inspired me to find you, to make sure that the old woman had followed through."

Her father sighed. "Kate went through a lot with me back when we first got together. I had a complete breakdown during a campus protest. I called Kate . . . I called her Hằng when I'd kissed her and—"

Her father's body tensed, and he put his head against the steering wheel. "Imagine telling Kate I'd never gone to look for you. I mean, how could I? An ex-Marine living in the States, and during a war? Kate said, *That's not the man I know.* Her words haunted me until three years later when I was in my new job at the Thai embassy. I cooked up that crazy plan with Jeremy, my old Marine buddy, to look for you on his missions back to the area. I was so fucked up back then. Oh, sorry, honey."

"I know you won't believe this, but Dad, I've heard the word before." She tried to lighten things a bit.

He grunted a little laugh.

Hope scanned the handmade shoe factory two blocks up the road. She thought how painful it must have been for her father to hold his memories inside for over two decades. "Dad, I'm glad you told me what you could. It helps me understand you and your suffering, too." She looked up at his strong, handsome profile. She wanted to ask more. Not about Kate. Not about Hope. About her mother. What did she look like? How did they meet? How exactly did she die? Knowing couldn't be as hard as not knowing, Hope thought. It distanced her from her mother somehow, to not be able to grieve properly.

The late light shone through the car window on the thick scar that encircled her father's neck. It was always there as a reminder, just inside the open collar of his dress shirt. Kate had explained the near miss on his last day before his tour was over in her journal.

Who could be alert to the enemy with the terror of losing his true love and having just given away his newborn child so fresh in his mind? The surgeon had said one more fraction of an inch, and he wouldn't have survived.

Hope wasn't alone with her own war trauma, she thought. It had bonded them in a special way. She snuggled in, put her head against her father's shoulder, and held his arm tight. "Thank you, Dad." She just couldn't ask him anymore. She felt ashamed.

He was quiet.

Had she brought him to the edge? Hope let out the breath she'd been holding. "Now we'll do our work in my mother's name. We'll stop some other child from suffering in some war out there. Lots of children. Right?" For a moment, she felt the parental role shift to her. "Now, let's go in and have some Ketchum fun." She saw his flicker of a smile. "What, Dad? We could use a smile."

His stone-serious face came alive again as he seemed to shake off the sorrowful memories. "I'm thinking of Kate's face when Grandma Cecelia met us at the door in her flour-dusted apron and hugged me. *Michael James! Mrs. K!* we'd called out at the same time." Michael closed his eyes and released a one-note laugh. "Kate was confused. I knew them as Mr. and Mrs. K, not Ketchum. They'd seen me annually for my new-shoes trip with my mother. It was fate. Who would have guessed my ritzy, fine, handmade shoes would have brought me to my—" Her father stopped, glanced at Hope, and sighed. "Sorry, sweetheart."

"Dad, it's OK. You were going to say 'true love'. Life goes on, doesn't it? I want you happy, Dad. *I* want to be happy."

"The Ketchums embraced me as their own. Like they do you."

"Thanks, Dad." It was painful, yet in some strange way, it's healing to know even a little more of her mother's story. Even to know her name. "Dad, you lost your embassy career and everything for me."

"Yes, well, misappropriation of government property and forging your papers. I was lucky my Marine buddy's father, Mr. Harrington, was Ambassador to Thailand. He kept me out of prison. Enough of that. You're here safe and sound now. I love you, Hy Vọng." He kissed her forehead and opened the car door.

"Wait, Dad."

Halfway out of the car, he stopped, suspended over the seat.

"Thank you for the chance to give back, Dad. And I love that you didn't succumb to the pressures of your family to be someone you weren't so that I could become who I am. Hey, I should write that down." This is who I'm supposed to be, isn't it? It was a thought that had never invaded her mind before. She forced a smile and opened the door, wanting to know more, but she wouldn't push. Kate's journal might have what Hope was looking for. They had to shake it off and enjoy the evening with the family. There was no sense in dragging them back into the sorrow. She'd had enough. They'd had enough.

5

HOPE WALKED UP the sidewalk and spotted Kate's mother, Cecelia, through the front window. "Dad, don't you just love Grandma Cecelia?"

"More than I can tell you. If you ever need advice, she's the one." He took Hope's arm. They climbed the gray-painted stairs, scarred, cat-clawed, and cracked by decades of the family's comings and goings.

Hope pulled open the old gray door. "The hinges are still working, Dad."

He laughed and hugged her as they went inside and hung their jackets on the brass hooks in the hallway. They were met by the classic scent of Grandma Cecelia's corned beef and cabbage.

"Michael! Hope!" Her grandmother, Cecelia, was a magnetic and loving redhead like her daughter, Kate. "Come in, darlings. Kevin, look who's here."

Kate's father, Hope's Grandpa Kevin, hobbled up from his Barcalounger. Wearing his classic corduroy pants and plaid shirt, he kissed Hope's forehead and patted Michael on the back. That Ketchum kiss was their signature greeting. It made her sentimental. Two sets of Ketchum grandparents, Michaels's mother Christine, and Kate's parents, siblings, cousins, aunts and uncles, and the whole lot huddled around Hope. Except for Grandma Kendall, who wore her typical frown. Who knew why? That's just the way she's always been, Kate had said.

The usual fun and banter began with Hope's three uncles, Kevin, Keith, and Karl. All in their forties. All three were born within three years. They were Irish triplets. Muscular and handsome, they shared matching, telltale tummies from their daily stopovers for a few beers at O'Leary's pub on the way home from work at the Owl & Shamrock shoe factory.

"Congrats, Hope. What can I get you? A Guinness?" Uncle Keith put his arm around her.

"Hey, here's the man who saves the world." Uncle Karl shook Michael's hand.

"How are the new offices? Congrats, buddy." Uncle Kevin Jr. chimed in.

They huddled around her father and thunder-patted his back. In their classic style, they commented one after the other, talking about their favorite subject, sports.

"How 'bout those Patriots beating the Browns yesterday?" Keith said.

"Nipped 'em by three points. That field goal was dead on." Karl added.

"Did you bet secret money on it, Michael?" Kevin Jr. elbowed Michael, a teasing gesture that said he knew her father never gambled.

The "double K" Ketchum family was in its usual happy mood

at Hope's grandparents' home tonight. Hope loved that all of Kate's siblings' names started with a K—Keith, Keven, Karl, Kendall, Karen, and Kelly Ketchum.

Cecelia chimed in. "Are you hungry? You must be hungry." She winked and guided Hope to the kitchen door and opened it.

Hope knew what to expect behind that door. "Surprise. Happy thirty-ninth birthday, Ernie!"

"Woohoo! Hope! You're my best gift." Ernie released his distinctive cheer as he high-fived Michael. His cleft palate and hair lip caused his distinct lisp and high-pitched teasing voice. With childlike humor wrapped up in all thirty-nine inches of the thirty-nine-year-old guy, Ernie was the joy machine in the family.

At eighteen, he'd been the first to break through to Hope when she'd arrived at three-years-old, traumatized from the devastation in Vietnam. He was the only one who could lure her out from behind Grandpa Kevin's Barcalounger. The one who came right out and said Hy Vọng should be named Hope so people wouldn't make fun of her like they'd made fun of him for being different. She was grateful for that. Ernie thought the name would prevent her from fitting in. Little did he know the name Hy Vọng would also be strange in Vietnamese. A double blessing.

Everyone cringed whenever Ernie called himself *ugly*. Hope could hear Kate's voice. "Ernie! It's nineteen ninety-five. Better to say you are a person with special needs or disabilities."

Well, I *am* ugly, he would say. Even my parents had to leave me. His laugh was unconvincing. Kate had said Ernie's usual clowning around about his differences and Down's Syndrome had a sadness hidden behind it.

Hope would never forget her stepmother Kate's stories of her student Ernie at the Rolling Hills Institution during Kate's college internship for special education in the 1970s before her singing career exploded and took her in a different direction. But she'd cringed every time he'd used the word *retarded*, even though back then the word was commonly heard. *She's not too retarded. See that girl banging her head against the wall, she's retarded, but that girl Mary, she ain't retarded, she's just pretending. Yeah, true, Mrs. Ketchup.*

If not for her informant, Kate said she would never have discovered that Mary was faking her disability to avoid being sent back to her abusive stepfather. Now, Mary was adopted by Hope's aunt and lived a few houses away, just as Ernie was brought into the family by Kate after she'd decided against grad school and left for her first European singing tour. Such complicated stories were behind all the rescued children in the Ketchum-James family.

"OK, I won't say I'm ugly. I'm a handsome dude." Ernie laughed. "Hope, I wanted to surprise you because Kate said when she lived in Bangkok, people *gave* gifts to people on their birthday instead of getting them. Remember? And I have one for you."

"Yes, I remember Kate saying that about Bangkok. Ernie, you're too much."

"This is to celebrate your new job, Hope." He handed her a new black leather jacket. He and Grandpa Ketchum had made it for her for Boston's crisp fall weather, Ernie said.

Who else had leather craftsmen for grandparents? Their specialty may have been making shoes, but they could fashion anything from that fine Italian leather the factory imported.

"Try it on, Hope." Ernie clapped. "Woohoo!"

Hope slid her arms into the fine leather jacket. The stylish padded shoulders made her petite body look even smaller than her five-foot stature.

"You're too young to be a big-shot attorney for a world-renowned nonprofit," Ernie said in his unique way. "That's what Kate called it."

He'd been like a beloved brother to Hope for two decades, ever since Kate's family adopted Ernie and Grandpa K took him under his wing to join the family working in the Owl & Shamrock handmade shoe factory. Ernie's loving heart was her anchor, she'd always said. Hope leaned over and hugged Ernie's short body. "Thank you, brother. I love it." Buttoning up the jacket, Hope spun in a circle in the kitchen. It had been her favorite room as a child, with Grandma Cecelia's spaghetti sauce or corned beef and cabbage scenting the air. The room, with the pantry filled with goodies, was where her Cheerios were kept. She ran her hand over Grandma Cecelia's gray linoleum kitchen table.

Shiloh joined them in the kitchen and reminisced. "Hope, remembered making circles, trails, and designs with the cereal when you were little?"

"And eating those round treats by the fistful when her artwork was done." Grandma Cecelia filled in the story, smiling. "And now you're a lawyer." She shook her head. "Hard to believe, yet not."

It was hard for Hope to believe, too, she thought.

Caught up in the memories, Hope could hear the squeal of the kettle and the scent of the tea Grandma had served her dad while they'd talked, sitting on the shiny red chairs with silver legs. She remembered the sound of the neighbors' screaming arguments and her father slamming the window closed. No wonder he'd immediately bought that house next door when the couple divorced and put the house up for sale. Hope and her dad and Kate would use it as a vacation home when they visited, he'd said. Grandma had always laughed at the memory of his comment to think of the smudgy old factory town of Glynn as a tourist spot.

Nothing had changed except the silver threads that had appeared over the years in her grandma's scarlet hair. Hope's grandparents had remained who they were despite the fame and amassed fortune of their daughter, Kate. Hope admired that, but at least they no longer had to worry about mortgages and groceries. For that blessing, they were grateful. Kate Ketchum was the picture of success for her factory-working family. The closeness of Kate and Grandma Cecelia was warm and enviable, and her grandfather Kevin had given Kate total acceptance for her career choice over time spent with family.

They all moved to the living room. Grandpa Kevin let Ernie sit in his off-limits Barcalounger. A special occasion.

Smiles swept across the relatives' faces at Ernie's excitement when Hope handed him his birthday present. "You'll love it, Ernie."

"Can I open it now?"

"Sure," the family said in unison.

He tore open the green plaid wrapping paper. Pulling out the gift, Ernie admired the T-shirt with Hope's Kelly-green custom-designed logo—a pair of red twinkling shoes over the Owl & Shamrock logo and the title *The Official Shoe Elf.* Everyone clapped and laughed. Although the name he'd bestowed on himself had initially made the family uncomfortable, it was a good call on Ernie's part—it had charmed the little children. They squealed with joy when he measured them for their shoes. The words, *'Mommy, Daddy, the Shoe Elf is making my new shoes,'* could be heard daily at the factory. Hope was once one of those children; she still had those red shoes.

Ernie was inundated with presents from his big family.

"OK, everyone, before we light the candles, it's time for Ernie's 'I remember.'" Grandpa Kevin quieted everyone for the traditional taletelling at a Ketchum birthday celebration.

The first story was told on a tape sent by Kate from Dublin, where she was performing. It was a classic. "Happy Birthday, Ernie. Sorry I couldn't be there, buddy. I remember when you first called me Miss Ketchup." She told the classic story about how Ernie had surprised Kate the first day in class, hiding his compact body in her big oak desk drawer. The family laughed at the image of her shocked face when he'd slid the drawer out from inside and called her Miss Ketchup instead of Ketchum to make the kids laugh. The name had stuck.

Michael stepped away and threw Kate's sisters Karen and Kendall's babies up in the air to hear them squeal and giggle as Mary sat smiling in the corner.

Ernie's birthday salute continued.

Hope reminded him of her first years in Glynn and the red shoes he and Grandpa K had made for her. "I remember when Ernie gave me the first dress shoes I'd ever had. I remember, Ernie, you taught me my first sentence in English when I said, 'Pitty wed soos.'"

"And now you're a lawyer in pretty, red shoes." Ernie pointed to Hope's flats.

Michael spoke up next. "Kate asked me to do this one. She remembers the day she was taking you back to Rolling Hills after you'd had a two-week respite with the Ketchums. She remembers you two were driving down the road, and she decided she would not let you go back to that dreary place. Remember Ernie? You'd said, *Pull over, pull over,* and you reached for the car door handle. Kate thought you were going to be sick. She remembers saying, *Hold on, I have to find a place.* She remembers skidding onto the crunching gravel at a country store. You leaped out of the car and celebrated with that hysterical dance of yours—hands on hips, elbows bent, with your cowboy-bowed legs, a kind of clog—your wild Irish jig, as Kate had always described it."

Ernie nodded and put his face in his hands, laughing. Then he jumped up from the chair and did his classic dance.

As Great Grandpa Ketchum told his 'I remember,' Shiloh took Hope aside. "Have you read any of Kate's diary? I think the insights will start your new life off right. There's a lot you need to know."

"Yes, there is a lot and—"

"Everyone," Grandma Cecelia called for the family's attention, lifting her glass of sparkling water. "Before dinner, I want to congratulate Hope on her new job! Here's to Michael and Shiloh and the new foundation offices. May you change little lives everywhere! And as I said to my daughter, Kate, may you follow what lights you up."

6

THE GRAY, STORMY October day hugged the penthouse office windows. Hope turned on her desk light to finish writing the letters of gratitude to their partner organizations in Bombay. Up all night, she'd sketched and painted in duplicate. It had become a new standing tradition for Hope over her first months at her job.

She added the pencil and watercolor portraits of each rescued child to the shipping package.

The first time she'd sketched a picture of Ernie sitting at Grandma Cecelia's kitchen table with a number two pencil inside a Cheerios box came to mind. Why is it that some memories stick and return over and over? Hope had only been five. The portrait had drawn amazement from her father and Grandma Christine, who was visiting. She's a natural artist, they'd said.

Her habit of drawing things she loved in nature had evolved into charcoal, watercolors, and acrylics when Hope went to law school and had her own space to indulge in her hobby. Anything she'd learned about painting or art was from either a book or observing famous artists' works at galleries. She sipped her coffee and swiveled to look at the harbor. A lone gull jetted along the skyline and took refuge on her windowsill. Hope quickly outlined it in her notebook.

Hope's love of capturing nature scenes as she grew up and traveled was her favorite escape. She'd no longer done portraits but had naturally returned to her childhood origins in portraiture at the foundation when the frightened and fragile faces of the rescued children arrived from the team after a mission. It, too, was her means of escape.

She knew not all those children had the fantasy lives she'd found with the Ketchums. Many of them were deeply scarred by their terrorizing war experiences. Even if she'd matched them with new families, some rescued children would not adjust and were still in war zones. And not all adoptive parents had their child's best interests at heart.

She'd ensured that the children were always smiling in her renderings. Was it her way of reminding the liberated victims that their futures were hopeful? Was it a technique to soothe them? To pay tribute to their adoptive families? She hadn't realized how much it would mean to them.

Dozens of letters from the overseas staff, families of rescued children, or parents of adopted kids saved by Uplift from war zones arrived after each overseas operation. Dominique and Hope had read them together in his office daily, with the ever-changing weather decorating the scene through his windows. They shared their love of nature, even from their offices forty-five floors above the ground. Hope felt they were becoming close, but they'd kept their professional boundaries so far.

As though he'd caught her in the act of thinking about him, Dominique knocked and peeked around the door in his usual coy way. "Hope, can I ask you to join me in the reception area for a moment?"

"Of course. Is something wrong?" She straightened her suit jacket, shimmied down her skirt, and followed him.

"Why would you assume something was wrong?" His smile was suspicious.

"I'm a lawyer. I know guilt when I see it." Hope loved their comfort level, and Dominique was beginning to get her teasing Irish humor.

As Hope entered the reception area, she stopped, drew a sudden breath, and held it. Dominique had framed and hung the letters of gratitude and the duplicates of Hope's portraiture on the reception area wall with a large sign that read, The Wall of Hope. She was surprised and touched by his thoughtfulness. "Oh my God, Dominique."

She stopped herself from throwing her arms around him by tucking them behind her back.

"Now, everyone at the office will begin each day with your paintings of sweet children's faces from around the world."

Hope studied the portraits of children with their arms wrapped around a parent, volunteer, or another child.

"It will inspire the team to launch out again to reach more children in danger or need," he said.

"Dominique, I—" How do you respond to such thoughtfulness, such creativity? The Wall of Hope?

He placed his hand on her arm. "You, my dear, are an extraordinary woman to add your portraiture work at night to a full day's work. Touching."

His gaze unnerved her. Hope bit her lip to prevent her emerging grin. "Shall we have a coffee?" Hope recognized her familiar yet awkward strategy of avoidance. Her plan to keep things professional was unraveling by the minute. "Thank you, Dominique." It was all she could muster.

They headed to the break room to post the reports and artwork and get a good dose of the caffeine she desperately needed.

Dominique stepped into the break room behind her, as he had every morning since her first day with Uplift. She'd worked hard to keep her attraction for him under control. Hope was no Shiloh, and an office romance felt threatening. But the velvet ropes on her emotional stanchions were fraying fast. She was only human.

They'd gotten into the habit of business lunches to discuss projects. Often, the conversation went beyond work. Hope had become aware Dominique was trying to get her icy professionalism to thaw. A touch here and there on her arm or shoulder was innocent yet not, as they'd entered a restaurant. Those friendly touches lingered longer with each day. He'd chosen private booths instead of tables in cafés. And with his mother in France, Hope thought there was no family on his side to interfere. Maybe it could work.

"Where are you, Hope?"

She awakened from her thoughts of the evolution of their relationship. "I'm here."

"Would you consider another nice walk in the park after work before winter is upon us? It's a beautiful fall day. I thought we could discuss the Dunn and Marino adoptions."

Here we go, Hope thought. She tried to sound casual. She worked to keep up the façade of friendship. "Yes. Stop by for me when you're ready."

"Oh, and by the way, I have some news. I believe my mother, Jolie, is visiting Boston next week for the first time and would love to meet with you and Shiloh regarding a donation."

Timing, Hope thought. She'd no sooner had the thought, and Dominique's mother would enter the picture. Hope stopped pouring her coffee mid-stream to listen.

"Since Michael's in Thailand for Kate's concert, would you be free on Saturday? Perhaps a meeting at my home here in Boston?"

The timing was ridiculous. Hope's inner child's dialogue revved up. A half-breed, love child certainly wouldn't be a wealthy Parisian mother's dream for her son. Hope hadn't been enough for the parents of her past love interests. A Harvard education doesn't cover up your past, doesn't erase your insecurities, she thought. Especially when they had their roots in hard-learned lessons. Her love affairs had been painful failures. Was this the beginning of a love affair? Or was he just being kind and thoughtful—a close friend?

Dominique had never spoken of his mother except to say she disliked flying, and they weren't close. Hope was glad she'd held herself back with him. If there was potential for something between them, her mixed race and past could be a liability for their future together. When would she stop vacillating between being proud of herself and feeling inadequate? The two Hopes. Would they ever get along?

"And Shiloh has already accepted the invitation to meet my mother on Michael's behalf." Shiloh's mother is a dear friend of Jolie's. Dominique put his hands in his pockets, looked down at the polished, Brazilian hardwood floor, and paused. His entire demeanor changed. A serious look. A hesitation. "Well, truthfully, I wanted her to meet you, Hope."

"Meet me?" The new attorney in charge of intake, or me, the young woman whose eyes Dominique was engaging, Hope wondered. Stop! She chastised herself for creating trouble where it didn't exist. Yet. "Sure . . . I'd love to meet your mother. Regarding the donation, I mean. How wonderful." Her repressed smile joined the chill that showered down her back. She'd unconsciously repeated her father's words when he'd answered Kate's first invitation for Michael to go with her to Thanksgiving dinner at the Ketchums' home. With her history, it was no surprise Hope would be concerned that Dominique's mother could be prejudiced when it came to her son's love interest.

Still, Hope felt the professional wall she'd built between them start to crumble. It was only a matter of time for Hope and Dominique to become an item, as Shiloh had predicted. Or was she misreading the charming man's kindness and attention?

COMMERCIAL BUILDINGS led to residential luxury brownstones on streets lined with mature trees. Historic Beacon Hill. Hope had been to the lovely neighborhood once for a birthday party for a classmate in her early years.

Maneuvering her Mercedes, Shiloh sang, "Just my Imagination running away with me." The Temptations' lyrics were meant to tease Hope about the apparent magnetism between Hope and Dominique.

"Hilarious, Shi." Hope tried to follow the written directions to Dominique's home, where his mother was staying.

Shiloh shared some details about Jolie's background with

Hope. Shiloh's mother and Jolie had been college roommates at the Sorbonne. Jolie's activist husband was killed in the '68 Paris riots fighting for worker's rights. Four-year-old Dominique was Jolie's only child when her husband died. When he was old enough to understand his father's fate and dedication, Dominique had always said he wanted to do something in his father's honor. And now Dominique had left France to do that through Uplift. His mother was against him participating in any dangerous activities, Shiloh explained. "She'd already lost her husband. She and Dominique had quite a rift, I understand."

"I can understand that, and now I understand why he never wants to talk about her," Hope said.

"I think he has another motive to mend fences with his mother now." Shiloh fluttered her eyes at Hope.

"Shiloh, I get it. You want us together." Hope laughed. "You're incorrigible."

"I just want you to be happy, that's all. And there's that look in his eyes when he studies you during staff meetings. And you're already spending every waking minute together." Shiloh adjusted the rearview mirror.

"True." Hope thought about Dominique's loss, which he'd never mentioned since the opening day when he first acknowledged his father's death in the 1960s Paris riots fighting for workers' rights. "Too much for a family to bear," Hope said. She watched through the car window as the neighborhood became more affluent, the landscaping more beautiful. Nature's colorful gift before the winter white arrived.

The brands of cars in courtyards and driveways shifted from utilitarian to elite, from Toyota Corolla to Rolls Royce, and Chevy truck to Mercedes sedan. Twenty-two McPherson Street wasn't one of the upscale brownstones they were passing. It was a mansion tucked back between the rows of beautifully maintained, high-end semi-detached homes. Like the king's castle in a fiefdom, the home made the beautiful row houses seem like the simple hovels of the peasantry.

"OK. We're here." Shiloh pulled into the open gate. "Money doesn't guarantee anything, does it?"

As she exited the car, Shiloh's remark struck Hope. "True. Suffering knows no dollar limit."

Affluence did cushion you through the tough times in life. She thought of the Kennedy family. Their wealth couldn't prevent the loss of their two sons nor soothe their suffering. Hope knew when you had no money, it seemed like people with financial security had it all. And certainly, when trouble came along, money didn't hurt, but money didn't prevent life from delivering tough times, she'd learned.

Hope rang the doorbell, straightened her navy linen straight skirt, buttoned her blazer over her silk blouse, and pulled her black wool coat around her. Wearing heels was still uncomfortable.

"Don't worry. You look gorgeous, and Jolie's a very cool person. I guarantee she's ready to donate something, but if she likes what she hears, maybe enough money that it could change everything. A new division at Uplift, maybe?"

Shiloh hugged Hope.

7

DOMINIQUE OPENED THE enormous double doors. *"Bonjour, mon amie."* He kissed Hope on both cheeks, and she answered in French. "And Shiloh, thank you for coming. My mother is in the drawing room. Let me take your coats." He moved behind her, lifted Hope's coat from her shoulders with a gentile politeness, and hung it in a nearby closet. "Shiloh, may I take your coat?"

Hope's stomach dropped. He was gorgeous with that boyish smile. Seeing him outside work and their café rendezvous, dressed in a suit and tie, made Hope even more aware of Dominique's charm and allure. What was it about him? It was his calm, kindness, insights, intelligence, and their never-ending conversations. Oh, and the accent. She'd never get over that accent.

Hope looked around the grand foyer, knowing she shouldn't assume Jolie and Dominique's indulged life meant they were shallow, unprincipled, or snobby. But with both worlds in her mind, her life in Boston where she'd often been shunned, and her loving, warm factory family of acceptance in Glynn, Hope was ashamed to discover a slight prejudice inside her, a reverse discrimination. It wasn't the affluence; she'd experienced that at home. It was the sophistication, the worldliness that Jolie exuded. It reminded her of the wealthy families of her former boyfriends, who'd shunned her for her differences. The environment made Hope feel as though she were meeting royalty.

As Shiloh engaged with Jolie, sharing her mother's best wishes and updating Jolie on what was happening in her best college friend's life, Hope put things into perspective.

Dominique's father had led strikes for the working class and died for his beliefs. Dominique was formed by his father's tragic fate, just as Hope had been formed by her mother's death and her father's children's foundation. Dominique's money hadn't protected his heart nor saved his father's life. It was errone-ous to believe wealth gave you some kind of shield against the pain and losses in life. Hope's humble beginnings and laboring relatives hadn't made her noble, either. And Kate coming into millions as the daughter of factory workers didn't change her character suddenly. She was generous, loving, and kind. Kate didn't abandon her values. And though Hope's dad came from money, she'd never experienced that world by the time she came into his life. Her father had detached from his father's privileged life. Her father was so down to earth and had values like his mother. Grandma Christine came from an upper-middle-class family. She'd married into that privileged existence when she became pregnant with Michael as a young woman. Yes, they lived a life with money, but it was new money. They didn't have the sophistication and heritage that Jolie naturally wore like a crown. Hope was wealthy by circumstance; Dominique was rich by culture and ancestry. He came from Louis Quinze furniture;

she'd started life on an orphanage floor. No. Hope knew financial means didn't necessarily translate into elite, overindulged, or spoiled people. Why was she experiencing this feeling? Was it prejudice or feeling inferior?

Kate had described the first time she'd visited Hope's father's family home in Nantucket. She'd experienced the same thing. Kate was the daughter of skilled laborers and had a college education. Hope had no excuse not to accept herself as worthy. Still, there was something about old money that made Hope uncomfortable.

As Shiloh and Dominique stood chatting in the gracious space, it was hard for Hope to decide what to focus on—his engaging face, the curved staircase behind him, or the original artwork that graced the thirty-foot walls.

"Please shall we go in? Perfect timing. My mother has just arrived." Sweeping his arm toward the archway, Dominique led Shiloh and Hope down the hallway to the parlor. He seemed serious, maybe out of sorts.

Hope took in a quick breath. It was like walking into a Paris Museum. A gold-trimmed glass clock with visible mechanisms that spun around inside sat on the marble-top entryway table. Priceless shield-backed chairs with celadon silk upholstery seemed an impossible place to sit. Their shiny, bowed wooden legs ended in elegant feet that disappeared into an inches-thick Oriental rug. The paintings were sized to dwarf her—dark, ancient, from the hands of the masters like she'd seen while wandering through museums when she'd traveled.

Velvet drapes the color of a fine burgundy begged to be touched. So elegant. Hope recalled Kate's diary description of stroking the velvet stage curtains at her concerts. Hope discreetly ran her hand down the drapes. With all the changes in Hope's life lately, she missed having Kate's sage advice even more.

"Gorgeous décor, huh, Hope?" Shiloh said.

"Mother, this is Hope." In French, Dominique told his mother about Hope's interests, skills, character, and accomplishments as though she were being interviewed for Woman of the Year. It was so awkward, but it wasn't done disrespectfully. He was swooning over her, she realized. Was he sharing these compliments and her background with his mother, or was he indirectly talking to Hope? Was he telling Hope how he felt about her? How he viewed her?

From her openness, Hope was confident that Jolie had no idea Hope spoke fluent French. "I hear you are quite an artist," Jolie said against the backdrop of million-dollar masterpieces.

Shiloh threw Hope a guilty grin and a shrug. Had her auntie already laid some groundwork, or had Dominique?

"Well, just some little sketches and watercolors, really." Hope wanted to lighten things up a bit, as she'd seen her Irish relatives do when things got too serious. "The Metropolitan Museum of Art has been hounding me for more, but . . ."

"How wonderful."

The humor was lost on Jolie.

Hope flushed, realizing her joke didn't translate across Jolie's culture of affluence and possibilities. "Oh, I'm sorry, Jolie, I was just being—" She hated to admit her silliness to the gracious woman. Ketchum family humor. When nervous, make a joke. "I apologize. I felt so humble about my artwork that I overstated for humor." Hope rolled her eyes at Shiloh, embarrassed. She was already blowing her chances to be accepted by Dominique's mother, she thought, yet Hope wanted to be herself.

Shiloh's laugh erupted. "My funny friend."

Jolie finally got the joke. "I love a person with a sense of humor, Hope. Forgive my delay in catching on. Few of my friends and associates indulge in such clever repartee. Very charming, dear."

Dominique seemed so comfortable in his formal surroundings.

"God, Hope, that accent. If you don't grab him, I will. Half my age or not." Shiloh whispered while Dominique and his mother were catching up.

Hope gave Shiloh a look of warning. "Please, she might hear you."

Jolie said words in French about Hope to Dominique like *ingénue, très charmante, intellegente, belle jeune femme*, woven into their private conversation as Jolie set the Proust tome she was reading on the gilded desk.

Translating for Shiloh on the side was fun. "She says I'm a charming, intelligent, and beautiful young woman." Dominique's mother approved of Hope. But what was she being assessed for?

"I wish I knew more about her plans as a donor. I only know she mentioned wanting to contribute to the foundation," Shiloh said.

"I wish we knew too." Hope felt out of her league, yet intrigued, flattered, and confused. She'd lived a high-class, indulged life in Boston, private schools, Boston College, and then Harvard, and neither Dominique nor his mother had done anything but admire her.

"Jolie has flown in from Paris to meet you," Shiloh said, nodding to Hope to cross the room and talk to the refined woman.

Hope's thesis on culture shock, written for her sociology class, took on a different meaning. She understood that the discomfort people felt being introduced to a foreign culture where all the rules changed would make them feel overwhelmed, inadequate, and fearful. She never thought she would experience it in her own life in Boston. Culture and class were lost in the chaos on campus, but maybe not in the business world or in high society. Jolie had come to meet *her*. Today, Hope was being double-cheek-kissed by an heiress and her knock-out son. Why?

Jolie Bellamy Bonchance. Her perfect posture made Hope shift around, imagining a book balanced on her head. She was entranced by Jolie's soft voice, the charming French overtones to her perfect English. Jolie, holding an ivory cigarette holder in elegant hands, to avoid something as base as tobacco from touching her perfect rose-lined lips. Jolie's angelic features, perfectly coiffed hair, dressed in her sheer ivory blouse, short linen skirt, jewels, and high heels.

"Please, my dear, won't you sit down?"

On command, Hope perched on the edge of an antique chair decked out in her blue business suit, lip gloss, and shiny, clean hair. Should she have pulled her long hair back or let it flow free around her shoulders like she'd done? It was a business meeting, wasn't it?

The light scent of Chanel No. 5 on Jolie made Hope relax a bit; it was Shiloh's fragrance.

Classical music came on in the background. Maurice Ravel, Hope identified it. The sound added to the elegance of the room.

"So, *mon cherie*, I will share my ideas about the foundation soon. May I first get a chance to know you better? Although, perhaps Shiloh's judgment and my son's smile and approval say enough."

Hope was taken aback by her openness. Jolie's words emerged with a tone that matched the texture of the drapes, velvet. Hope was flattered one minute and suspicious the next for being left in the dark. A counselor had once told Hope that emotional vacillating was PTSD like her dad had. And was being the daughter of a world-renowned singing superstar a part of it? Get over it, she told herself.

A butler appeared from nowhere, balancing a tray, crossed the room, and handed glasses of ruby-colored wine to Hope, Shiloh, Dominique, and Jolie.

"Thank you, Charles." Jolie kissed her glass to Hope's with a light clink. "*Mademoiselle* Ketchum-James, I am curious to know one important thing about someone to whom I will entrust my future legacy," Jolie said.

Had Jolie purposely omitted Hope's Vietnamese family surname, Lê? Was she indirectly exposing her prejudice?

"Jolie, I go by Hope *Lê* James professionally to honor my Vietnamese heritage."

"Yes, of course. My apologies. And what of your mother's name, Ketchum?"

"I prefer not to bring such attention to myself."

Jolie smiled. "I can understand that. The notoriety might cloud one's existence."

Dominique moved to the other side of the room by the window, arms crossed, and looked out, giving them privacy.

The afternoon sun angled through the windows, casting an angel glow around Jolie's head, making it harder for Hope to face her. Her future legacy? What did Jolie mean? Hope shifted in her seat and swallowed. Fine moisture emerged on Hope's forehead, and she wondered if Jolie could see what Hope could feel—tiny beads popping out in slow motion across her head and down her cheeks. Had she ever felt so completely clueless and uncomfortable? Hope resisted, wiping them away.

"Since my darling husband Marcel left us in the nineteen sixty-eight protests. Well, he passed away. No, he was murdered, to be truthful. I need to be able to say that word. I no longer stand on formalities. It seems there is no time." She took an audible deep breath. "It has broken me open to my truest emotions, so to speak. Do you understand? The need to go deep and not wide? With friends, family, and lovers. By being open, I've learned I can more likely access the hearts of others." Jolie's gaze drifted out the window. "Sometimes suffering is a blessing in the end. There was a time when I was furious at my husband. His choices left me a widow. To the point that—"

Hope's frustration melted with her compassion for Jolie. She waited patiently.

Jolie looked across the room at Dominique, who stood by the window, lost in his own thoughts, seemingly unaware that the focus was on him. "To the point that I marginalized my own son. A double loss. So, what is the thought that most resides in your fine mind, even haunts you, *Mademoiselle* Hope? For me, the answer is—the moment my beloved husband died and my not having been there to hold him, to close his passionate eyes. I think that our passions are to be followed, even if it means loss. Yet another loss I could not bear, I confess."

Hope crossed her arms, uncrossed them, and searched for a place to store them as if the unfamiliar appendages had newly joined her body. Dominique had said his mother had been angry with his father, arguing daily about his leadership in the protest activities. How had she come to some peace with his sacrifice? It was a model for Hope. Anger only destroys the angry one, she thought.

Reaching out from the adjoining chair, Jolie grasped Hope's

hands between hers. Her touch was warm, tender, and maternal. Her misted brown eyes widened, waiting. "What is the single thought that lives and breathes in you, my dear?"

Jolie's words made Hope want to get up and run. She wanted to know everything about Hope, but Hope knew nothing about anything that was happening around her. She didn't dare remove her hands. Intimacy wasn't a skill Hope had honed or even practiced at all in her world. She'd been starved of touch in her early years in the orphanage. Hope often wondered if that was what made her uncomfortable with expressing affection.

She'd grown up in a combination of sophistication, formal private schools, and a close-to-the-vest, full-of-humor Irish family. No-touchy-feely, as her father had described Kate's family, but don't let anyone do you wrong, or they'll be right there for you. They had your back and loved you deeply. Hope knew she was always in her head and constantly accused of that. She'd openly shown love for the inner circle people of her life through actions. No problem. But reveal her soul? And verbally in public? Rarely. Never to a stranger. Maybe her emotional wall had been at the core of her failed relationships.

Her Irish grandma, Cecelia, expressed love and affection primarily by doing, not by intimate openness. Lots of laughing, rare crying, but few words, and only at poignant moments to share life advice.

Even her intimates didn't fully see the true Hope. The few friends and acquaintances in Hope's life only knew the funny, smart, or kind Hope. She fought to leave her hands in Jolie's.

Remembering Shiloh's words, that she suspected Hope would love what Jolie had to say, she took a breath and tried to trust. This was a moment, a turning point. Not only was the game a mystery, but so was the prize. Hope felt the gravity of it as she searched for the answer, her truth.

Jolie's eyes were warm, not threatening. Hypnotic. Hope's compassion for Jolie's loss made her let go a little and trust. It was something she understood. One random explosion that had stolen a person from your life. Hope tried to find the answer. What was the thought that most captivated her? Was it thoughts of her mother's death that was still a mystery? Her dad? No. One was a memory, and the other a person she cherished and loved. Jolie was asking for something bigger, something inside, something personal about Hope. Something she'd thought over and over that drove her and directed her choices. What was it that Hope repeated? What was constantly running through her mind? It required such self-awareness to answer the question. Hope was nearly always looking outward, not inward. Thinking about what? Her *one* thought? Had Dominique shared Hope's early childhood story with Jolie? "In light of your own intimacy and loss, Jolie, I can hardly . . . be generic, can I?" Hope needed to buy time to run through her list of important things so she could focus on that one thing.

"Please, yes, that is the idea, my dear. Before I entrust my future to you, I must know your one thought . . . if you will excuse the word—that holds your *soul*? And yes, there is no place for superficiality. Trust it." Her eyes entranced Hope.

"Yes, I agree." Hope wished she knew what the surprise plan was. She imagined Jolie's husband sprawled out on a Paris sidewalk. The explosion that had taken his life was something she understood in a way. The terror of the sounds, the sky falling around him.

Except, Dominique's father had died like Hope's mother.

Dominique hadn't run along a rice field and been saved by a cavalier Marine pilot to share a love-filled life.

Emotion erupted inside Hope. The truth came to her mind, but the words stuck. She wrapped her arms around her stomach to keep her words from spilling into the room. Her reaction confirmed her truth. Hope forced her words. "That there is a child somewhere out there who desperately needs help right now like I once did, and I am helpless to reach that little soul—the millions of those little souls." The words were squeezed through her tightening throat.

Jolie's tears spread along the edges of her eyes and sent rivulets of rouge down each cheek, staining her ivory blouse. She was silent. "Beautiful, my dear. Perhaps that child will not be helpless for long. You have the heart I was seeking."

"Jolie, are you alright?" Shiloh stooped in front of her mother's friend.

"I am moved to meet a young woman with such compassion, just like my husband was. Wasn't he Dominique?"

Dominique nodded and moved next to Hope, encircling her with his arm. Hope couldn't interpret what was happening. She could only see herself running along the rice field, terrorized by the frightening plane above her.

"She is perfect, Dominique." Jolie dipped her linen handkerchief in a glass of water and dabbed the stain on her blouse.

Stepping behind his mother's chair, Dominique rested a hand on Jolie's shoulder. She covered his with hers.

With everyone seated, Jolie laid out the plan. She prefaced it with an introduction, explaining she'd wanted to put her entire fortune to good, start a new life, and repair her relationship with her only child. "I wish for you to design a meaningful special project to make good use of my estate for the benefit of needy children."

Hope wanted to put her arms around Jolie. It was the children, Hope thought, regardless of social status, each vulnerable child. It wasn't about Hope. So many thoughts were battling inside her, vying to take control, but the one thought Jolie had pushed her to reveal remained centered. Everyone in the room was on the same page. It wasn't about Hope's losses in the past. It was about this moment. They cared passionately about the same thing. Different reasons, same passion.

A child out there somewhere. Lifting one child.

8

"YES, WE ARE birds of a feather, my friends, when it comes to prioritizing that one child." Shiloh broke the heavy silence. "Will you all forgive me? I do need to leave. I have an unexpected conference call with the Bombay staff. Thank you, Jolie, for your generous support for Uplift." Shiloh smiled at Hope. "Maybe Dominique would consider driving Hope home?"

Hope knew a strategy when she saw one. Shiloh knew Hope was open and vulnerable after her exchange with Jolie. The perfect night to be alone with Dominique. And, of course, Michael was overseas with Kate, so Hope had the house to herself. Shiloh was playing matchmaker.

"My pleasure, *mon amie*. I'd be happy to escort you home."

Jolie double-cheek kissed Hope and Shiloh, then touched Dominique's cheek. "My darling son, it's so wonderful to see you again. But I'm going to rest a bit after my long trip."

"Of course, Mother. Your room is ready, and your luggage is there."

"And Hope, it was a pleasure getting to know you, dear. We will continue discussing the details another evening. I'll give you a chance to gather your ideas. I look forward to many years working with you."

MANY YEARS? Jolie's words still inhabited her mind as Hope opened a new bottle of Pinot Grigio. "Dominique, are you OK with Italian wine? I don't have any French in the house."

"Italian is fine, in fact, my favorite. Don't tell my mother."

"Ha, my lips are sealed." Hope was still shaking her head over Shiloh. She had been setting them up to be alone. Of course, Hope had been the one to invite him up for a drink. After his mother's loving reception and acceptance of Hope, maybe she could take a chance to move things forward with Dominique. It was such a pleasant surprise. No other parent of her dates had welcomed her as Jolie had. And Hope had never allowed herself to be so open. But was the deletion of Hope's Vietnamese surname a telltale sign of underlying prejudice? Or a lack of understanding of Hope's complex name? A concern remained. Maybe it was the past lingering where it shouldn't, but it set Hope on high alert.

"Your home is lovely. And a Louis the Fourteenth settee. Did you know you would someday host a French *colleague* in your boudoir?"

"Very funny. I like it here in my *sitting room*. It's better than being downstairs in the living room where the ceiling is so high you hear everything twice." Why did she react to the word, boudoir? Act your age, Hope, she told herself.

"Sometimes hearing things twice can be pleasurable."

"Are you flirting *Monsieur* Bonchance?" She poured the first glass. And the windows downstairs were floor to ceiling, she thought. She imagined jumping up and breaking the mood to pull all those heavy drapes closed.

She didn't want to be the one to initiate, but Hope wanted to be in the right place just in case. What if she'd misread the entire thing? What if this was classic French charm? A simple flirtation. Hope wasn't sophisticated regarding relationships, especially with someone from another culture. Still, she ached to become closer to Dominique.

And if things went too far, she had a secret she would have to share.

"Are you hungry? I can put out some cheese and crackers and fruit."

He wore a grin she hadn't seen before. "You know the French are known to move fast."

"Very funny, *monsieur*." She sat on the sofa with proper space between them, took a sip of her wine, turned, and gazed at him over the rim.

She thought he returned an intense flirtatious look—something out of a French film. "You have thoroughly charmed my mother. That is not easy to do. Because of you, she seems to have accepted me back into her good graces along with my passions. I'm grateful."

"Dominique, were you in the same room with me? The way I saw it, you sold *me* to your mother."

"Perhaps both, but she's been bitterly angry at me since I followed in my father's footsteps, taking on a job in a war-related nonprofit. When I told her about us working together in Boston and my contributing but not going out into the field on missions, suddenly, she was on my doorstep."

Hope was caught off guard. What had she to do with Jolie's arrival? The foundation, yes, but Hope herself?

"I understand she's afraid to lose me to some accident or tragedy like she lost my father, but it was no reason to cut me off. I felt motherless."

"Motherless, I understand." Hope rested her hand on his arm. "We seem to have something excruciating in common. The loss of a parent."

"Yes, and I still feel the darkness come over me sometimes." Dominique closed his eyes.

"Anger is just a costume for hurt, I've learned, Dominique. When things get dark, you can turn to me. I understand." Hope shared what little she knew about her mother and her suspected violent death in the war. Or had she survived and abandoned Michael? That was a new possibility. "Anger, like love, often has no logic," Hope said.

Dominique put his glass down on the coffee table and shuffled closer.

Hope had to know. She couldn't help herself. "I know this is an awkward moment to ask this, but Dominique, is there any prejudice behind your mother leaving out my Vietnamese name, or am I being overly sensitive?"

"*Mon cherie*, she had just traveled from Paris. I think she just got confused, as do many with foreign names and traditions. She is the president of the international club in our enclave in Paris, darling. I doubt there is discrimination."

"Ah, that's good. I couldn't take one more dismissal for my ethnicity."

Dominique kissed her. "You are understandably self-protective, darling." He stroked her hair.

"One more thing." She took a deep breath.

"Only one?" Dominique mimicked Hope's habit of biting back a smile after she knew she'd made a humorous comment.

"Funny French boy. What did you say to Jolie about me that made her come running?"

He took Hope's glass from her hand and set it next to his. "I told her I wanted to do this." Tucking Hope's hair behind her ear, he studied her eyes. Then he kissed her—a sensuous and slow kiss.

She kissed him back. Oh yes, the reputation is well-deserved, Hope thought. A French lover. Was she imposing a stereotype of the French lover on Dominique? If so, this man fits. He knew how to kiss slowly, exploring her tongue. He knew how to touch her. Hope felt he was making love to *her*. Not just trying to *get some*, like she'd felt with other guys.

Dominique took his time with each button, folded her clothing over the end of the sofa, and then disrobed himself.

She forced herself to watch.

He didn't devour her, then rip off her clothes, throwing them around the room like some ridiculous American romance movie. He was with her, only her. He cared, letting the passion build, waiting for her responses.

Hope ran her hand over his tight, muscular shoulder.

He shifted her under him.

He was ready; she was not. Her breath shuddered, and she stopped. "No, wait."

"Hope. Have I done something wrong?" Dominique sat up and held her shoulders.

"Dominique—" Oh God, this is so embarrassing, she thought. It was so perfect, but she had to tell him. And they had no birth control. She had to be responsible.

"*Cherie*, I have protection. No need to worry. I would never put you in jeopardy. And there are other ways to—"

"It's my first time." Hope felt a blush of humiliation. Nearly twenty-six and a virgin. It wasn't that she was a prude. Determined to earn her place in her world, Hope had been dedicated to her education. She didn't want to get sidetracked. The closeness and the trust with the guys she'd dated were just never there. It sometimes seemed from their comments that they just wanted to try out this Amerasian girl for curiosity, for kicks, or bragging rights. Besides, with his mother involved, a breakup would be disastrous this time. It struck her. Wasn't vulnerability at her core from the very start as a child?

"Are you not ready?"

"I don't know, I feel so awkward. Clearly, you know what you're doing, Dominique, and honestly, I do not. I'm not without experience, but it's . . . well, incomplete." Hope released a quiet chuckle. "And yes, I'm ready. Yet not."

"Darling Hope, all the more precious. There is more to love than sex." He reached for his shirt. "We'll discover it together. I will patiently wait until you're ready. We'll go slowly. I suspect it will be worth the wait."

"Dominique, there's so much at stake here." She reached for her blouse, plucked it from the arm of the sofa, and held it to her chest.

"Do you mean losing my mother as a major donor?" His eyes went wide.

"No, of course not, Dominique. Losing *you!*"

He smiled with relief, pulled her into his arms, and kissed the top of her head.

She listened to the slowing of his breath until the rhythm calmed. Hope had no words to describe the tenderness of the romantic man. He'd said *love*.

9

TONIGHT, HOPE WOULD see Kate for the first time in four months. Her stepmom had been on tour since her performance at O'Leary's for the opening ceremony for the new Uplift headquarters. For weeks, her father had been touring with Kate on her fundraising concert tour while he made the rounds of the countries Uplift was assisting. A win-win, he'd said.

Shuffling through her reports as Hope sat at her desk, she wondered if she should tell her dad about Dominique. Not yet. Yes, they'd been officially lovers for months since Dominique's mother had returned to France. Still, the office romance thing made her reluctant to share just yet. Dominique had agreed. Only Shiloh was in on the secret. There was no way Hope could keep anything from Shiloh and keep her sanity. But Shi was right, wasn't she? Hope and Dominique belonged together.

Thanksgiving was here, and Hope's ninety-day assignment as Intake Director was nearly over. Michael's idea for Hope's first temporary position with Uplift had benefited her. She'd met all the players and learned so much about politics, logistics, and the subtleties of international relations and law by being the organization's point person. However, working on the adoption and legal documents would be rewarding. More her skillset and close to her heart, as Dominique had said. Uplifting one child's life and placing one child in the arms of someone who would love them inspired her. The perfect name for their new division: Uplift One Child.

She called Shiloh. Hope needed to talk to someone about her changing feelings. With the war in Bosnia and all the ethnic cleansing by the Serbs, so many children were at risk. The Uplift Children's Foundation, One Child division, funded by Jolie, would set up private schools in refugee areas to give orphans a new, safe start until the Uplift team could arrange adoptions. The Uplift One Childe Division was Hope's idea, and Jolie had loved it. They were working with a NATO peacekeeping force to help the children. Assistance was needed in the Balkans, in Macedonia and Kosovo too. Never-ending. Through the staff's daily reports, Hope had an up-close look at what "ethnic cleansing" meant. She would never understand the need for groups of people and governments to render an area ethnically homogenous. The force and intimidation used to clear an area of all people of a different ethnicity or religion made no sense to her. It was at the core of so many violent conflicts.

Hope picked up the phone, and Shiloh's special knock made her smile. Was she an intuitive? Shiloh was always there when Hope needed her.

"Come in, Shi."

"Hey, Ms. Lawyer. How goes the transition? Do you miss him, even though he's just up the hall?"

"Truthfully, yes. Auntie Shiloh, I mean, Shiloh, I need your advice." Hope explained her feelings about her work and the dark clouds forming over The Wall of Hope in the Uplift headquarters' lobby. "How can things change like this? When I first arrived, this brought me the most joy I could ever remember feeling. Now I'm—"

"Hope, you've already captured the faces of over one hundred diverse children for The Wall of Hope through your amazing art. That must be rewarding."

Dominique's loving gesture didn't greet her with inspiration every morning like he'd predicted, she thought. For Hope, the expansion of The Wall of Hope reflected how intense things were in the world's war zones. "Yes, Shi, only one hundred children were saved, and millions more are still out there." Hope needed to envision thousands of portraits of smiling faces ten years into the future, on hallway after hallway of The Wall of Hope. How many of their smiles would Hope also have to falsify, painting over their fragility, fear, and tears?

Hope explained to Shiloh how it was both gratifying and depressing. "Now Michael has invited me to meet some of the children I've sketched in one of the safe zones. He thought it would be gratifying for me."

"Wouldn't it be?" Shiloh leaned on the desk.

"I've found excuses not to meet the children before." The truth was she needed to keep her distance from the children. She needed to keep them as symbolic portraits with smiles on their faces. It was too real, like looking in a mirror as a terrorized toddler. There was no way to explain her fears after a life growing up in a loving family. "Shi, I realized I don't think I want to have children. There would be no painting a smile on their faces in troubled times. I can't face the unknown, raising a child in an unpredictable world. I don't want the responsibilities for things I would have no control over. Wouldn't I be the classic, nervous helicopter mom?"

She remembered that phrase from a book Hope had read in college by Dr. Haim Ginott in 1969, *Between Parent and Teenager*. Hope wouldn't want to cripple her children by hovering over them like a helicopter. She had real-life experiences with the thundering sound of helicopters overhead and the devastation their bombs had caused.

"Oh honey, I don't know what to say. I don't have a stable relationship, so children aren't on my mind." Shiloh flickered her eyes, seemingly searching for answers in the floating clouds outside. "This must mean you two are getting pretty serious. But that's off in the future. Whenever I fret, I find that taking a few breaths and focusing on what's happening *now* can help balance the insanity of our buzzing brains."

Tonight, Kate and Dad were performing at O'Leary's for the holiday, and tomorrow would be the traditional holiday dinner at the Ketchums. It had been a long time since Hope had been with her Ketchum clan for a night at their favorite pub. She looked forward to seeing everyone. And Hope had done a risky thing and invited Dominique. Should they keep their secret much longer? Could they? Every time he'd said, I love you, the guilt rose that she hadn't shared that love with her family. Jolie was thrilled. Didn't Hope's family deserve to share in their happiness, too?

"Why not keep your mind on tonight's Ketchum family fun?"

"Good idea. I know you have lots to do, Shiloh. Thanks for talking me off the ledge in my unknown future. He's never even mentioned marriage or having children. I'll cross that bridge later."

Kate had bought out the house for the private event and would perform with Michael like in the old days. Wouldn't it be the ultimate test to see if Dominique could fit in? Hope bit her lip and held back a laugh. If she could fit in with Jolie, he could fit in with the shoemaking Ketchums. Couldn't he? She would take him by the factory first to give him the full impact.

Dominique entered Hope's office with a file in his hand. "Oh, Shiloh, hello. Hope, sorry to disturb but we have a client that needs help, and you're the perfect person to do it. They're Vietnamese. An older couple looking for a grandchild who was taken during the war twenty years ago. They'll be here next week to visit family. Do you have time on your schedule?"

"I'll leave you two to deal with what's happening right now." She winked at Hope and left.

"What was that about?"

"Oh, nothing for now. What's the assignment?"

"Friends of Jolie's. Sorry for the late notice. Here are the notes they gave us." Dominique handed Hope the folder, making sure that his hand touched hers. Hope winked and sent him a slow and sensuous air kiss—their playful dance that went on all day at the office. She felt the familiar heat rise on her face. Hope was getting bolder, and the conflict was a battle of love and fear.

Hope flipped through her calendar. "Of course. I can do Thursday at three o'clock. Can you let them know, or shall I?"

"I will contact them to confirm and let Jolie know it's been handled. See you for dinner."

It was rare to have a case from that era anymore. Hope may have been the perfect person to do it, but she thought they weren't the ideal clients for her. She wasn't looking forward to resurrecting all her memories of those times. Hope had over-heard her therapist from childhood talking to her family in the kitchen. She'd warned them that it was important not to expose Hope to traumatizing events and violence in movies or TV, for example. She needed that cocoon to feel safe and prevent triggering PTSD. Was that a reason that Kate wanted Hope in private school? Away from the rougher public schools in her factory town?

Snowflakes were already fluttering down across the harbor, as predicted. The roads had a light dusting. Hope and Domi-nique would have to leave the city and go to Glynn before any accumulation. Still, she had time to do some basic research on the inquiry.

She would leave her car parked in the building where the team wouldn't see it in the morning before she arrived. Dominique could stay with her again. Hope loved it when he held her at night. Her touch-starved self was changing in the glow of this complex and compassionate guy. She was finally in love. Hope was accepted, no, adored by his mother. Nothing was in their way. It was a first.

Reading the clients' notes, an unexpected dark mood descended on Hope. It was rare for the team to find a child separated from her family over two decades ago. Many children had become em-broiled in court battles between their birth parents and adoptive parents. Such pain for both sides. All good intentions, different viewpoints. Hope had read that after many years and lawsuits, only twelve children who were not orphans were reunited with their Vietnamese parents after the war. Damn war. When would the world learn? So sad.

Pulling out her file, she researched all the flights during

Operation Babylift in April of 1975, when the Nguyen couple said their granddaughter had been spotted being taken away. Hope was touched that the name her father had chosen for the foundation was a play on that operation's moniker, *Uplift* Children's Foundation.

Nguyen Thi Am. Searching for a child with one of the three most common surnames in Vietnam would be a nightmare, especially during those chaotic times when the paperwork was scattered, mismatched, or often lost in the turmoil.

She studied the mass evacuation of children from South Vietnam to the United States and other countries like Australia, France, West Germany, and Canada at the end of the Vietnam War when Saigon fell. April 3-26, 1975, the time frame in which their granddaughter had disappeared. How would Hope identify one child out of several thousand infants and children who'd been airlifted out of Saigon on over thirty planned US military aircraft flights? Not to mention the many private aircraft sponsored by compassionate individual Americans. One American civilian had mortgaged his home to pay for a flight to evacuate three hundred infants and children he didn't know. That was touching to Hope.

Hope scanned the photos of babies in cardboard boxes and children huddled in blankets. Such a chaotic time. One article said those thousands of children were adopted by families all over the world, the majority, nearly two thousand, in the US.

Shivering at the thought of her own fate had Hope's father not been that rule-breaker, Hope recalled Kate's fateful words: *That's not the man I know.* Those words softened Hope's feelings about Kate. Her judgments wavered between blame and disappointment now. Being in love for the first time provided some insight into her father and Kate's relationship, an understanding she'd never had before. She'd do almost anything for Dominique, Hope thought.

Swiveling in her chair, Hope watched the snow as it stuck to the glass, blocking her view of the harbor. She knew from her research that Operation Babylift was controversial. Not all those children were orphans. Many of them were taken without consent, like the Nguyen's granddaughter. She'd read that the military in charge, at the command of President Ford, thought that with the war in full force, it was in the children's best interest to be adopted in America. This older Vietnamese couple and many others who'd lost their beloved children, and many Americans, thought otherwise. They believed the children belonged in their own country. We should have focused on their safety and reuniting them with their families in Vietnam.

Hope ran her finger over their notes. It might have occurred in mid-April of 1975, they'd said. Such a relief. Thank goodness it wasn't April 4th when the first plane to escape with orphans crashed twelve minutes after take-off.

Hope thought there was a chance, a slim chance in time, they could find the child.

Pulling a group of photos from her file cabinet, she set them on the desk. When years later, someone had told the couple they'd seen their granddaughter embarking on a plane outside of Saigon, they were impassioned to follow up, they'd said. They'd thought their granddaughter was dead like her parents and siblings, their only daughter's family. Their notes said she would be their only surviving relative if they could find her. The child's given name was Am.

Hope had called her only Vietnamese friend from college and discovered that Am meant lunar girl. It struck her. Hope's mother's name, Hằng, also had a moon name, meaning *angel in the full moon*. In Vietnamese culture, the moon represented prosperity, he'd said. The moon name could signify the good fortune a daughter brings to your life.

Vietnamese names were confusing to her. The father's surname was sometimes combined with the mother's surname, and sometimes not. The combination could be different for boys and girls. There were many given names used for both males and females.

Hope thought of her first emotional and revealing conversation with Jolie—uplift one child out there, somewhere. She had to try.

10

THEY RODE THE elevator down to the first floor, where Dominique's car was parked.

"All right, my love, let's see if my petite blue French hegg is up to the New England challenge?"

Hope loved his little foreign compact car he called his little blue "hegg." Dominique knew he was mispronouncing "egg" as he would be expected to had he been a Frenchman first learning English. The extra consonant added to a word that began with a vowel always made Hope smile. It seemed charming.

The windshield wipers worked overtime to push the heavy snow away. And the snow tires helped get them out of the city and through the crunch on the main road into Glynn. They'd made record time by driving behind a plow.

Whenever she'd heard Dominique's last name spoken out loud, the sound reminded her of the French words for good luck, *bonne chance*.

Dominique had brought good luck into Hope's life. Would

she have that good fortune moniker someday? The thought of adding another surname made Hope laugh.

Hope pondered if she should have told the family about her relationship with Dominique. They knew he was coming, but she'd told them Dominique was her coworker—the truth but not the whole truth. That phrase seemed to be coming up often in her life lately.

The Ketchums were no fools. Would the truth about their connection be revealed tonight at O'Leary's? Could she and Dominique hide the electricity between them any longer? And maybe there wasn't a need. A permanent connection was likely if things continued to go in the direction she'd imagined.

Hope would have to tell her father first. She couldn't let him be caught off guard. Once Auntie Shiloh told the romantic tale, their love affair would no longer be seen as some racy, office hook-up. Hope couldn't imagine doing this repeatedly like Shiloh had done. But then, for Shiloh, it wasn't about true love, she'd said. If that came along, Shi would stop. Until then, it was full steam ahead. Here she was in her forties and still a free spirit. You had to love her. Shiloh was her true self.

Maybe Dominique would understand Hope's background more fully once he'd met the family. She'd only met his mother and only in Boston without seeing Dominique in his other worlds in Paris and Spain. Her past love relationships had both collapsed the more she'd gotten to know them.

They arrived at the factory. "It's only five o'clock. Shall I show you the shoe factory, Dominique? You can meet the whole gang in one fell swoop."

"Of course, that sounds fascinating."

"Just pull up and park in the customer lot there, OK?" She

pointed to the side of the old brick factory, its mortar crumbling from the century of the non-stop shaking and thundering of the machinery inside. It would certainly be a different experience from Hope meeting Jolie in Dominique's mansion in Boston.

"It's quite old, isn't it?" Dominique ran his hand along the dusty brick wall.

They climbed the stairs and stopped on the landing. "So darling, Hope, we must pretend we don't love each other passionately for the next few hours. Is that the idea?"

"Yes. Sorry."

"Then, one last kiss."

She was still woozy with his kiss when Dominique pulled on the old rusty door handle. It didn't bring him much success. "Is it locked?"

"No, try this." Hope wedged her foot against the crumbling brick wall, as Kate had first shown her, and tugged open the heavy, gray door. The gunshot boom of the creaking door slamming behind them was a familiar sound from her childhood. It drew no attention from the sea of workers on the basement level below, but it made Dominique jump.

Removing their heavy coats and scarves, they left them on the hook at the top of the stairs.

The deafening din of the shoemaking machinery rebounding off the century-old factory walls met them at the door. "All these people you see below are cordwainers, mostly family, five generations now." Hope imagined how those syncopating sounds of metal stamping and punching leather had filled Kate's life and threatened to swallow her future, as her journal had revealed. For a moment, Hope had sympathy for her adoptive mother.

Dominique yelled over the machinery noise, "What is a

cordwainer? And how do they stand the noise? And what is that smell?"

"I think it's kind of exciting. The shoes are all handmade by the Ketchums. No machine-made shoes here for years now. That business mostly went to China. The aroma of dye, leather, Lysol, and grease keeps those irreplaceable hundred-year-old machines running." Hope had to yell over the clunking and clanging noise of the old machinery. "That scent is so you can always tell a Ketchum is coming." Hope nudged him. There were times her humor didn't resonate across their cultures; there were times it did. "OK, remember, you're not my lover." She could see that the charade was not to his liking from his posture, lowered eyelids, and arms crossed in front of his chest.

Hope's experience meeting Jolie for the first time had been so accelerated and open. It had been awkward at first, but then she'd felt accepted and appreciated for who she was. They'd skipped the formalities in his affluent culture in which she'd expected the unfolding of their relationship to be very measured. Did he feel Hope was embarrassed or ashamed of their relationship? Her American culture called for discretion; his did not. "Not your lover, for now. Until later tonight." Her bold words were beyond her usual reserved self. Hadn't she been encultured by a close-to-the-vest Irish Catholic family, full of jokes and with their way of demonstrating their love through *doing*? Hadn't he grown up in a freer Parisian society where sex on the first date was the norm and relationships cast off from shore like speedboats? Finally, she'd lured a smile from Dominique.

"I looked forward to celebrating our relationship, not being ashamed of it." He reached for her by habit.

Hope drew away. "Let's go. Grandma Cecelia is looking."

Scanning the massive buzzing room for her Grandpa K, her uncles, and cousins, she strategized the sequence of introductions and explained what a Cordwainer was. A crafter of handmade shoes. Watching Dominique's reaction to the chaos was entertaining, but Hope was getting nervous about their exposure.

He scanned the room, shook his head, tilted it, and squinted his eyes ever so slightly. Hope could almost read his mind. *Why would your aging family with a wealthy superstar daughter want to continue leading this life?*

Grandma Cecelia caught sight of Hope and waved. She waved back.

"Shall we meet everyone?"

"Hope, darling, I'm not sure I can tolerate this commotion. It's been a long week. Can we just meet everyone at O'Leary's? Where we can at least hear each other think. They seem to be very busy."

Hope was shocked. A little hurt. "Sweetheart, you won't hear anything in O'Leary's either when things get going with the conversations and music with Kate's voice and my dad's piano."

"Then, *you* go, darling. They assume I'm just a colleague. My phone's in the car. I'll wait outside for you. Tell them I had a call to make, and I apologize. I'll see them later, *mon amour*. I look forward to it."

Hope knew her jaw-dropping look of surprise and disappointment couldn't be missed. This was not the Dominique she thought she knew.

She turned away to walk down the steps.

"Sweetheart, wait." He looked down at the workers two stories below. Several had begun to look up at them. "Why not, darling? It isn't as if I'm going into a war zone. This is your family, and you faced Jolie. Why would I not do anything for the love of my life?" He acquiesced with a nod and a smile.

Love of my life? His words erased her concerns. It was beyond anything he'd ever said to her. "Sometimes love is painful, Dominique. Let's go meet my family."

He laughed on cue.

She resisted taking his arm and took the lead down the metal stairs.

The red-haired Ketchum clan stood out like a dozen red roses scattered among the hundred dark-haired domes below. Hope remembered Kate describing the view from the stairs that way.

"Half of these workers are Ketchums," Hope said in Dominique's ear. In her periphery, she spotted the shop foreman, Mr. Donohue, spying down on them with his vigilant eye from his glass loft. With hands on his hips, he forced that familiar twitch of a smile. Kate said she'd always counted him among the villains in the stories she'd read as a child—evil pirates, slave drivers, or cruel stepfathers. He'd always sent a shiver down Hope's back when she'd visited her family. She hated the condescending look he sent down on the hard-working Ketchums. "Ignore him. Without my family, there wouldn't be those beautiful shiny shoes on some of New England's most affluent and famous people. Even the governor wore Owl and Shamrock shoes to his inauguration," Hope said as they reached the bottom of the stairs.

"Then why is your family, as skilled as they are . . . how should I say this—"

"Working-class poor?" Hope helped finish Dominique's thought. "Because, as my Grandpa K says, the money doesn't trickle down to the floor. Ask him that, and he'll answer with his favorite clever saying, Our souls for their soles."

They passed three machines manned by her three uncles. Uncle Karl bent over the antique apparatus that punched the holes along the channels to stitch the soles to the uppers. He looked up. "Baby doll! I'll be damned. Keith, Kevin, look who's here!"

Her two other uncles jumped up from their machines. "Hey, baby doll," they chimed in with their affectionate nickname from her childhood that, somehow, she hadn't outgrown, literally, with her petite stature. Their towering, muscular physiques were distinguished by their enlarged bellies that told the tale of a family tradition—a nightly stopover after work at O'Leary's for a pint or two.

She leaped into their arms, hugging them, one, two, three. "This is my coworker, Dominique."

Her three uncles and Dominique exchanged hellos. Dominique's accent elicited an "Oo la la. A Frenchman. Welcome, buddy."

Hope repressed her laugh as her uncles patted Dominique's back. "Yes. Michael told us all about you. He's very impressed, and that's good enough for us. These are my brothers, Keith and Kevin. You know, we're the K-to-the-third-power brothers. Will you be joining us at O'Leary's?"

"Yes, he's coming. Michael invited him. So good to see you. I'm going to see the cousins, Uncle Jack, and Grandma Cecelia." Hope didn't have much of a relationship with the youngest generation since she'd lived in Boston and had been away at school as they grew up. She blew a kiss to the six young workers gathered around Grandpa K, his new generation of apprentices.

"Those are my two aunts, Kate's sisters, Kelly and Karen, at the sewing station, Dominique." Hope waved, and the women mouthed "welcome home" then nodded and dropped their heads to focus on the line of stitches they ran down the toe box of men's black wingtips.

"Are those two women identical twins? Amazing." Dominique pointed at her Great-Uncle Jack's twin daughters across the high-ceilinged room. They were nestling the pairs of shoes into tissue paper in boxes imprinted with the famous winking Owl & Shamrock label.

Hope filled in the story. "Glynn used to be one of the shoemaking capitals of the world back in the day." They moved through the room, stopping at the different stations, Hope hugging or not, and Dominique shaking hands, asking questions, and admiring the work of the Ketchum relatives.

Dominique ran his hand over the soft leather of a woman's high heel on Uncle Jack's table. "I'm fascinated with the process and the skill. Feel this, *mon amour.* He held it out for Hope to touch the fine leather."

Mon amour. Hope was glad no one in her family spoke French. Great-Uncle Jack smiled. His usual stack of books was on his table. She rarely saw him without a book at his workstation held open by a shoemaker's hammer. He was always passionate about wanting to self-educate. When Hope was in college or law school and visited, Uncle Jack had encouraged her in a way that made her feel a little guilty that she had such an extraordinary opportunity and he had not. She introduced Dominique as her colleague at the foundation.

"Our old Owl and Shamrock shoes were a family tradition for the *well-heeled* of Massachusetts and beyond. *Well-heeled,* get it?" Uncle Jack put his hand on his hips. He seemed to be testing Dominique.

Dominique laughed. "Yes, sir, I get it. Very clever."

Then Uncle Jack shocked Hope. "Well, *mon amour*," —his shoulders popped up and down with his laugh— "*comment est ton nouveau travail?*"

"My job? I love my new job." She felt the truth closing in around her. "But how did you—"

"How did I what? Learn French?" Uncle Jack winked. "Michael told me he hired a young French guy, so I thought that would be fun, a new learning endeavor. You know *me*."

Her eyes followed his, and she spotted the title of the top book in his pile on the table. *Fast French in Ten Lessons*. He took Hope aside. "Honey, you know I read lips, right? And body language," he yelled over the chaos. "And I now speak the language of lovers. *Vous êtes amoureux je vois? Il et vrais?*"

"Oh, Uncle Jack, yes, we are lovers. No, *in* love, I should say. But please, we haven't told my dad yet. Or Kate. Or Grandma Cecelia. It's only fitting we tell my parents and grandparents first."

"So, it's not just an office romance? Some family that's going to disrespect you again? I admit I feel protective."

Dominique joined the conversation. "*Monsieur, tu es très intelligent, nous te prions de garder le secret.*" He looked over his shoulder at Hope. "Sir, I love her very much, as does my mother. My father is no longer. Given our work relationship, we waited for the right time to tell Michael. It's delicate." Dominique looked at Hope. "Although we haven't spoken of it directly. We have a future together, I believe. Hope?"

It was the strangest way to learn of Dominique's view of the future. He's only hinted at it until now, saying, *I'm not going anywhere.*

"Hope, darling?"

She saw the pleading in his eyes from her hesitation. Finally she said, "Uncle Jack, I'm in love with Dominique. You know, I've never said that before."

Jack nodded his head as if he were considering the news. "Does he know about your hot temper and mean streak?"

Dominique's jaw dropped, and his eyes flashed from Jack to Hope and back.

"Dominique, he's just giving you the Ketchum humor test."

"Ah, be my guest, Uncle Jack." He pulled Hope close and laughed.

Hope slipped her arms around Dominique. She couldn't help giggling.

Patting Dominique on the back, Uncle Jack laughed. "Sorry, buddy. I'll guard *le secret*, but I suggest you two share your news soon. If I could read that you two were an item, so will everyone when we meet at O'Leary's tonight." He glanced over at Cecelia, who was putting away her burnishing tools and finishing her work for the day.

Hope took a deep breath and nodded. She took Dominique's arm and crossed the room to greet her grandmother like they were walking to the guillotine.

"Grandma Cecelia."

"Hope. How wonderful to see you, honey. And this is your coworker, Dominique?"

"No." Hope was caught in a velvet trap.

Her grandmother put the shoe down on the long, metal table. The women around her glanced up and turned their eyes to the upper-level glass window where old Mr. Donohue stood above them, with hands on his hips, as usual. They rolled their eyes, smiled, waved at Hope, and returned to work.

"No? But, Hope, I thought you said—"

"No, Grandma, I—" Hope looked up at Dominique. She needed his support. There would be no joking this time.

Dominique took Hope's hand. "Madem Cecelia, I'm Dominique Bellamy Bonchance. *We* have something to share with you."

11

HOPE AND DOMINIQUE bundled up and left the factory to walk the two blocks to O'Leary's. They were early and hungry. A plate of the pub's famous Corned Beef Cabbage was on Hope's mind. "I've never seen these sidewalks and streets clear like this. There are benefits to Kate Ketchum coming to town." Hope laughed. The glow of Uncle Jack's inadvertent discovery had made her joyful and relieved. She would tell the world. Squeezing Dominique's arm, she looked up into his eyes. She knew they were both thinking the same thing: Who would have expected a relative in the depths of the old shoe factory to speak French? Who would have imagined how our truth would be revealed? "See, I told you the Ketchums would catch on somehow."

"Everyone sees it in our eyes." Dominique stopped and turned her toward him. "And thank you, Hope, for preventing me from being ridiculous about the thundering machinery. To be honest, I think I was nervous. Out of my element. I apologize."

Hope was always surprised to see him tear up when things got tender or emotional. No one she'd ever dated had such openness. It was unnerving in some ways, yet endearing. "Oh, I understand perfectly. At least they didn't ask you for your *one thought* with all the chaos around like Jolie did to me."

"Your humor lifts my world. It teaches me to think in metaphors and to turn my perspective around. To lighten up."

No boyfriend had ever spoken to her that way. "How is it you're so open and expressive? I thought the Parisians were more formal, courteous, and reserved. And you cried at one of my photos of a child from Bosnia. And just now—" Trying to read Dominique was like reading a foreign language. "From what I've read—"

"So, you are studying my culture, *mon amour*. I suppose I was different because we spent so much time in our home in Spain after my father died. It took Jolie many years to return to Paris, where she was forever reminded of him. I had a Spanish nanny and went to school there, as well. On many occasions, I witnessed male teachers let go with tears. Do the Irish cry? Show their emotions?"

"What would you guess?" She lifted her shoulder flirtatiously and smiled.

"I'd say the strict Catholic element makes the Irish less likely to express their emotions in *certain* ways."

"But then we do have that charm and wit. And we're flexible since I did break the rule against sex before marriage." She didn't want to tell him that two of her aunts had gotten pregnant out of wedlock in their teens. Hope fluttered her eyes at him. "Well, OK. I broke the rule after twenty-five years."

They shared a sputtering laugh.

"Then there's our kindness and tolerance for man's weaknesses. That will benefit you, my love," Hope said.

As they approached, they saw an excited crowd had filled the sidewalk and lawn beside the old converted Victorian mansion. They were being herded behind wooden barricades.

Hope tightened her green scarf, took Dominique's arm, and headed toward the steps. "Amazing."

"Just a minute, miss. Your tickets?" Two gentlemen in suits blocked the entrance to O'Leary's.

Tickets to O'Leary's? Hope laughed, thinking it was a joke until she saw the two security guards in uniform behind the ticket-takers. "I don't have—" She imagined the envelope on her desk she hadn't opened in her rush to leave. It must have been the tickets.

"Step aside, please." The guard held his arm out, encouraging Hope and Dominique to blend back into the mass of fans. Clearly, the word about the private party and concert in Kate's hometown must have gotten out. There were more people than Hope had ever seen at the Glynn Memorial Day parade, let alone in the middle of a snowstorm.

She should have thought of this. Her dad had been out of the country in some remote place, so she hadn't received his usual daily contact.

"Sir, I didn't realize . . . no one told me there were *tickets*. This is a private family event."

"Yes, exactly. A private *family* event." He put his hand on his billy club.

This was the pub where they'd eaten lunch regularly, where Uncle Jack bartended at night, where Grandpa K brought homeless people from the street to make sure they had a meal, and where Kate had grown up singing on the one-step-up stage handmade by her cousin, Hope thought.

"Sir, it's OK. I'm Kate Ketchum's daughter." Hope went to move up the splintering steps.

"OK, I've heard some good ones, but I don't think Kate Ketchum, the Irish queen of music, has a Chinese daughter. No offense, miss."

Offense was taken. It was a punch to Hope's stomach, and her anger raged like a fever.

Dominique stepped in with his exotic accent. "The lady speaks the truth, sir. Hope is the daughter of Michael James and Kate Ketchum-James."

"Excuse me, officers, gentlemen. Please let Ms. Ketchum's daughter in." Uncle Jack opened the big green door to the pub and waved Hope and Dominique in.

"Sorry, miss, I didn't—"

"You should take manners classes, sir." That was not what she wanted to say, but she restrained herself. It was Kate's special night.

Dominique put his arm around Hope, pulled her close, kissed her cheek, and led her up the stairs. "Proud of you."

"Thank you. I don't know why I'm quick to stand up for someone else, yet I'm reluctant to stand up for myself."

"Not anymore, my darling. *Merci*, Jack." Dominique threw his words back as they entered the pub. "And by the way, the lady is *Vietnamese American*. But I wouldn't expect anything but ignorance from you."

"OK, easy, guys. So sorry, but don't let one idiot ruin the night. I should have asked if you'd gotten Kate's tickets." Uncle Jack put his hands on their shoulders. "I was too distracted by your *belle nouvelle de ton amour*."

Yes, the news of their love and the thought of the crazy way it had all come out. Hope relaxed when Jack changed subjects in French. She needed a strategy to inform the Ketchums. She should have known; you could never carry out a secret plan in her big, tight-knit clan.

"Now, *that* is an aroma I can enjoy." Dominique dramatically breathed in the scent of the Corned Beef and Cabbage, O'Leary's traditional dish that permeated the old pub.

The place was empty, but soon it would be packed, Hope thought. They should order.

Dominique said, "This is much bigger than I imagined from the outside."

"Yes, once they'd stripped the interior rooms, it made a great space."

They stood leaning against the forty-foot glossy oak bar, watching Kate's band set up on the one-step-up stage where Hope had seen Kate perform before her fame took hold, before the Grammy's and Riverrun's world tours. She loved the diversity of the band members—a Japanese drummer who'd let Hope bang on his drum kit backstage when she was young and touring with her dad, two Riverrun Thai guitarists who tried to teach her Thai, and a Filipino keyboardist with a harmonizing voice like an angel who sang to her. Tonight, Hope knew her father would sit in and play some of their original favorites from their old college-days song list when they were playing for tips. What would her life have been like if her dad had felt the same passion for performing as Kate? No job, no foundation, no father around.

Now, she had to tell her parents and relatives about her relationship with Dominique. She wanted him to feel the same belonging, acceptance, and, eventually, love she'd felt with Jolie.

"What are you thinking, Hope?" Dominique remained riveted on the musicians setting up their instruments.

Hope scanned the dance floor, the large dining room with tables for eight with green tablecloths, and the private booths for two along the wall. Everything green at O'Leary's, the shamrock cocktail napkins, the décor, and the Kelly-green painted dance-floor. "Just memories and thinking about how Kate had gotten her start here. Let's sit in that booth. It's my favorite. Great view of the stage."

As they dined on the traditional Corned Beef and Cabbage, Uncle Jack served up two mugs of Guinness. "There you go. Stick with tradition, right?"

The family and invited friends filtered in and sat at the tables and the long bar. The two waitresses buzzed in and out of the kitchen, balancing plates of food.

Hope tried to carry on a conversation with Dominique in the din of excited chatting and laughter. "Honestly, I'm also thinking about how to best introduce you to my parents and my family, so you feel their affection as I did from your mother. The circumstances are so different. I want you to feel comfortable with my big old Irish family."

"They're here!" Uncle Jack called out from behind the bar.

HOPE RUSHED to peek through the green drapes with a shamrock print that covered the front windows. The limo was parked out front, and a river of fans flooded in around Kate, guarded by four suited gentlemen. One held the door for Kate, and the other three allowed her the space to drift along the wooden barriers to sign autographs. The admirers had photos or personal items awaiting the signature and a written message from the famous woman. They chanted, *Kate, Kate, Kate!*

"Dominique! Come see this scene."

He joined Hope at the window. "How must that adoration feel?" He pulled the curtain open wider. The cheers were contagious. "Look at the fans wearing green for Irish Kate, these drapes, and everything at O'Leary's."

"I'll have to wear the green plaid kilt Kate brought me from her stop in Dublin."

"Here comes Kate, and look, Michael's arrived as well." Dominique kissed Hope on the temple.

Kate looked all put together as always. In her mid-forties, she'd kept her figure and could still pull off her signature short black leather skirt and high-heel boots made by Grandpa K. Her gorgeous long red hair was still vibrant. There were barely any signs of aging in her beautiful face. She looked just as Hope had remembered her from childhood. And her expansive personality could still send engaging energy across any room.

Michael approached the bar, greeting the family and friends who'd arrived.

"Dad, over here." Hope realized that at home in Boston and in Glynn were the only places she could call him Dad. "Dominique, why am I so nervous?"

Her father held up two fingers, requesting two minutes as he pointed, providing directions to the band members.

"I admit that I'm nervous too, darling. I'm being assessed by some daunting protectors of Hope—the K-to-the-third-power uncles. And I am just a gentle, French, only-child date with Spanish tears behind his eyes."

She laughed. The more Hope learned about him, the more

she loved him. He was picking up on her humor. She'd never experienced such tenderness and sincerity.

"We will do it together. It's unfolding as it should. But give me credit now. You only had to please Jolie. I have a clan of thirty-seven," Dominique said.

"You only have one person to please, well two—you and me."

The reunion with her father was warm and loving as always. He called Kate over, and they all hugged. And Kate planted the Ketchum kiss on Hope's forehead.

"Hope, honey, you look so professional," Kate said.

"Yes, I'm all grown up, Shiloh re-styled me. She said I needed to adult-up my fashion for work."

"That's Shiloh, alright. But then there's always her jingle jangles." They laughed together.

Then the time came as Dominique flashed his eyes at Hope. "Kate, this is Dominique. We're a team at the foundation, as Dad probably told you. He handles overseas operations, and I support him as Intake Director."

"They make a great team, not a glitch in any project since they teamed up. But I'm anxious to get Hope into her legal work, Kate. That's your passion. Right, Hope?"

Hope squeezed Dominique's hand and whispered, "Here goes." Please don't be too protective of me, Dad, she thought, especially after the previous two breakups, which infuriated both Kate and her dad since it was all about racism and externals—her color, her culture, and her past. Having spent her entire life in the Ketchum family, wasn't she culturally more Irish American than she was Vietnamese? After three years of being Vietnamese and twenty-two years in an American factory family, what was she? Which had more influence, genes or family?

"Well, Dad, Kate, I've developed another passion."

Her father looked from Kate to Dominique. "Did I miss something?"

"Dominique and I—" Hope looked at Dominique but couldn't find the right words. A serious relationship but no commitment yet. What should she call it? Why did it have to be so dramatic? And so public?

His words came just in time. "It's a pleasure to meet you, Mrs. Ketchum-James."

"Please, of course, you can call me Kate." Kate took Michael's arm and leaned closer as the noise level rose with the influx of family members. "It's so wonderful to be home, but if you'll excuse us. We have a show to put on." Kate nudged Michael and moved toward the stage.

Even at this special moment, Kate didn't prioritize Hope's good news over starting the show. A show she had control over. Dominique flashed a questioning look at Hope. She wasn't alone in her assessment.

Grandma Cecelia stepped up to join the conversation. "Wait, Kate, sweetheart, before you go, how do you like Hope's new boyfriend? We've had such a wonderful time getting to know each other. Haven't we, Dominique?"

Shiloh arrived just in time to share her story of Hope meeting Jolie. "You would have been so proud of your daughter. She charmed Jolie right into funding an entirely new division of our foundation. We called it Uplift One Child."

"And she charmed herself right into my heart." Dominique pulled Hope close. "I want to be open and honest since Hope has suffered insincerity and insensitivity in past relationships. I love your daughter without prejudice, of course, and always will."

His words stopped all conversation as Uncle Jack's booming voice filled the room from the mic on the stage. "Ladies and gentlemen. Our entire family is here to celebrate Kate Ketchum-James and her two decades of Grammy-winning success. Please welcome our Kate and Michael and their band, Riverrun."

In the din of applause, Hope watched her stunned parents head to the stage.

Shiloh laughed. "Well, everything is timing, right? Congratulations, you two. It's all downhill from here."

"I will kick off the evening with a traditional limerick performed by *moi*!" Uncle Jack smiled in Dominique's direction.

"There once was a girl in the choir,

Whose voice rose higher and higher,

Till it reached such a height,

It went clear out of sight,

And they found it the next day in the spire."

The applause welcomed Kate and Michael to the stage. As Kate hitched one hip onto her old wooden stool and Michael settled himself next to her at the piano, the whining of Riverrun tuning up, plucking notes, and tightening strings began.

Kate flipped on the mic, and Michael led in on the piano.

"Welcome, Ketchums, Kellys, and Callahans!" Kate called out as the applause and whistling quieted. "And thanks to Uncle Jack for the limerick tribute to my mother. She is the one who inspired my singing. I heard her gorgeous voice echoing in the rafters every Sunday in the church choir. Thanks, Mom. I owe you so much."

Cecelia waved and covered her face with her hands.

"My first song is dedicated to my daughter Hope and her new love, Dominique. 'My Cherie Amour.'"

Hope pulled her head down into her shoulders like a shy turtle.

Michael was caught off guard but played the first few notes of the song they'd performed when he'd sat in on Kate's Paris concert on their foundation tour.

Kate's voice filled the room with the lovely lyrics of "My Cherie Amour."

Hope felt Dominique's arm slip around her shoulder. She nodded her head as he leaned over and whispered, "I guess this means I've officially been accepted."

12

AT 3:00 P.M., the Nguyen couple arrived, escorted by Domi-nique. He introduced them and left. "I will see you at our meet-ing tonight, Ms. Lê James." His formality protected their secret relationship when they were at the office.

Hope explained the issues in finding their granddaughter to the well-dressed couple, who appeared to be in their sixties. "I see you heard through the grapevine that your granddaughter was seen leaving on a plane sometime in April nineteen seventy-five, and—"

"Yes. Excuse me for interrupting. We now know it was April fifth," Mrs. Nguyen said. "The neighbor who saw our grand-daughter remembered because it was her husband's birthday. Who would have guessed? Her sister visited our neighbor in Connecticut, where we now live. The news came out when she realized who we were."

"That helps a lot, ma'am. I'll investigate the flights that left that day. Oh, and does she have any distinguishing marks?" Hope poised her pen. She'd kept a private journal on every case, nothing that could be found on a computer, for the client's privacy, and in case Jeremy provided information from government documents.

"I don't think so." Mrs. Nguyen looked at her husband questioningly. "Wait. Yes. A scar from a cooking burn from childhood. On her left hand just here." The woman rubbed the top of her hand beside her thumb.

Gathering information about the missing child, Hope continued to look through the newspaper articles and shots of planes that had left during that timeframe, searching for one that had departed on April 5th.

"Mr. and Mrs. Nguyen, I will do everything I can to find *Am*. Let's schedule a meeting in two weeks to give me time to do some in-depth research. Of course, I'll call you if I find anything before then. Once we have a lead, we can do some DNA tests for verification."

"Thank you, Miss Lê James. We are so grateful."

Hope tossed an unrelated blow-up of a photo aside. It showed a long line of Vietnamese civilians climbing wooden stairs with rope guide rails. The stairway was suspended below a helicopter perched on a tower with its blurred rotor spinning. A classic scene from those days.

"What is this photo?" The white-haired gentleman asked. He pulled in closer and showed it to his wife.

"These were Vietnamese civilians who supported the Americans during the war or some lucky people who got out on some of the last military helicopters to leave Saigon," Hope said. "Why do you ask?"

He tapped the faces of a couple who were halfway up the stairs. "These are old friends from our village."

"Yes, with three of their children." Mrs. Nguyen pointed to each child. "This is their second eldest daughter, Linh, a beautiful girl. And here on the step below are their two sons."

"How wonderful. The Lê family was fortunate," Mr. Nguyen said.

Hope wanted to move on. It was getting late. "So, I will continue to explore the departing planes from that date. I have a contact who might be of assistance, and I'll be in touch."

"It's good to know the Lê family escaped." They said in unison.

It was a common name, Hope told herself. Still, it sent chills down her spine. If only that had happened to her family. She stood to signal the time was up.

"Such lovely people. And their daughter Hằng's Marine boyfriend, he was so kind. I wonder what happened to him."

"Marine?" There were thousands of Marine boyfriends like her father, Hope thought. In fact, her research showed an astounding fifty-thousand children had been fathered by American soldiers with Vietnamese women during the Vietnam War.

"Yes, it's them, Lê Van Ahn and Lê Thi Lan. What was that American boyfriend's name?" Mrs. Nguyen continued tapping on the photo with one finger. "I cannot remember."

Mr. Nguyen turned to his wife. "Ah yes, Michael."

HOPE SPENT the rest of the afternoon researching with a strange trembling in her stomach. She was afraid to believe her family had survived, yet she couldn't help fantasizing about the possibility.

"Darling, how did the meeting go?" Dominique closed the door for privacy and kissed her. "Where are you? Thinking about the child?"

"Yes." It wasn't a lie. She was thinking about the child and the shocking find. Hope's mind ping-ponged between the lost child and Hope's family. Could they be alive? "Sweetheart, can we delay our dinner for an hour? I need to make a few phone calls and do my report."

"Of course, I'll call the restaurant and make it seven. Does that work?"

"Perfect."

It took all the control Hope had to not tell Dominique of the possibility that she had family that had survived. Not yet. She had to talk to Jeremy first. Hope didn't want to distract Dominique from the current project he was focused on. There were hundreds of babies' lives at stake in Bosnia.

She stood in front of the fog-covered window. Where did that helicopter go, and what flight did it connect with? To where? Her family—grandparents, one aunt, and two uncles could be alive. After two decades, maybe she had cousins now, another generation of Lês.

She'd immediately thought of her rescuer, Jeremy, to help with the Nguyen case. Now, he was essential for another search. He'd overseen that operation's departures. If anyone could find out where that helicopter was headed, it was Jeremy. And like her father, he would bend a rule to do the right thing.

Hope remembered the story her father had told her about Jeremy. Hadn't he once taken a homeless boy at the last minute on his final evacuation flight out of Saigon? He'd sat him on his lap as he piloted a plane filled with embassy officials, refugees, and Vietnamese civilians who'd worked for the Americans. The boy was a child alone on the streets that Jeremy had been feeding for years while assigned to Saigon. If left behind, he doubted the boy would have survived the bombings.

Hope had met the young man when she'd visited Jeremy and his wife and five children with Michael last year. He was the same age as Hope now and had become a pharmacist.

If not for Jeremy sharing that story with her father, he would not have had the idea to ask his Marine buddy to check in on Hope's location. And Jeremy would never have spotted that little girl running along the side of the rice field carrying a US Marine T-shirt.

Jeremy patting her shoulder as he lifted off with her and flew away from the devastated orphanage was the most dramatic moment of her life. That and being hefted into the arms of her father.

Call me Uncle Jeremy, he'd said when he'd visited Hope for her 6th birthday. Picking up the phone, Hope dialed his number. He still worked for the military in Washington, DC, and had access to old files. You could always count on Jeremy Jones to be there for you.

With every ring, Hope became more nervous. She couldn't let go of the image. Like a big burly teddy bear, Jeremy had hoisted Hope onto his broad shoulders and walked down the steps from the plane. It was a brief memory. How much of that picture was filled in by Uncle Jeremy's recounting the poignant moment when Hope was delivered to her father on that remote, secret airstrip in Sriracha, Thailand? Startled by the circle of cheering Thai village children, you climbed onto your father's shoulders and wrapped your arms around his head, he'd said.

"Jeremy Jones here." His unforgettable, deep, growling voice belied his warm and friendly nature.

"Uncle Jeremy. It's Hope." She looked at her notes and the photo of the helicopter.

"Sweetheart. How are you? No need to tell me your name. I'd know that sweet, soft voice anywhere. There's nothing wrong, is there?"

"No, no. Uncle Jeremy, I need some help. With a case. Well, two cases. I know it's unnecessary to ask you for your confidentiality."

"Hey, this is me you're talking to, honey. What's up?"

Hope ran her fingers through her hair and took a deep breath. "There's a couple who have reason to believe their granddaughter, whom they thought was killed in the fall of Saigon, got out during the evacuation in nineteen seventy-five."

"Wow, and they only found out now. How?"

"A neighbor had spotted her embarking on a plane. They'd been separated and never saw the Nguyens until recently in Connecticut. The flight took off on April fifth in seventy-five."

"Well, that narrows it down, but I'll have to check out how many went out that day. Can do. How's Dah-Dee?"

Jeremy's laugh made Hope shake her head. "I love you, JJ." Hope's first word in English, her version of Daddy, was a story often told and a name often mimicked in good fun, especially by Ernie. "Dah-Dee is doing great. Michael was just on a whirlwind trip for the foundation with Kate. She's raising money through a special tour called Uplift for the Children, while he was meeting with key government people in the countries we're focusing on right now."

"Sounds great. Kate is one amazing woman. Always liked her. Best thing that ever happened to my buddy. Oh, except for you, of course." He barked out a laugh. "OK. So, what is the best you held for last?"

Hope looked closer at the helicopter photo and read the ID numbers. "Uncle Jeremy, if I gave you the numbers on a helicopter involved in the evacuation, could you find out its destination?"

"Hmm. Technically, no. The records were sealed, and the judge told the people handling the adoption cases they couldn't contact any Vietnamese families and let them know where their children were. But I have a workaround. So, for you, yes."

Hope read the ID of the chopper and hesitated. "I sent you the photo. Check your email." The new electronic messenger system still fascinated Hope. Her father had ensured they were equipped with the most modern means of communication to support their efforts.

"Got it. This shouldn't be too hard. Where those passengers went from there depends on where they landed and what plane connection they took. I've got everything on a hard disk. Is this a rush? I can get to it right away."

"No problem. My follow-up meeting with the couple is next Thursday afternoon."

"Imagine if you can find their grandchild? But what's the helicopter bit all about?"

"Uncle Jeremy, I haven't shared this with anyone." Why did she feel she should be discreet? It was a miracle to share, wasn't it? But could she handle another loss if the end of the story wasn't happily ever after? "That couple searching for their granddaughter, they'd identified a family on the stairs in a newspaper photo back then. I need confirmation."

"So, another dusty search. Whose family?"

"Hopefully, mine."

13

THE DOOR OPENED, and Hope jumped. She'd been like that all week since she'd spoken with Jeremy.

"Sorry, darling, I didn't mean to startle you." Dominique said. "You seem nervous lately. Is it this Viet Nam case?"

"I'm fine." She wasn't fine.

The assignment was resurrecting old memories of those terrorizing times. Nightly nightmares. Nothing she saw any purpose in sharing.

"Come here." He held her and gave her a Ketchum kiss on her forehead. "I have exciting news. But I need your advice."

Hope took her seat, and Dominique rested one hip on the edge of her desk. "I have decided to join Shiloh on the next trip to Bosnia."

Hope jumped up out of her office chair. It was not a reaction that was in her control.

"No, Hope, honey. I won't be there during wartime. Don't worry. The peace negotiations are underway in Dayton, Ohio.

They'll be signed in Paris soon, just a formality. Over two million displaced refugees. I want to help."

"Yes, I know wars. The worst is often at the end. I thought you loved working stateside of these wars."

"I love my job, and I love this gorgeous woman lawyer who works here, but I've never been in the field to see how we make a difference up close. I haven't seen the looks on the children's faces when the food arrives or when we evacuate them to safety. This is the perfect time with the war over."

Hope went to the window and stared down at the traffic below. Miniature vehicles, like trails of ants, moved through the city on the late sunny Friday afternoon.

Dominique wrapped his arms around Hope from behind, tucked his chin into the crook of her neck, and sighed. They were silent, looking out at the sun, flashing on the glass buildings and glowing with the red of the imminent sunset behind them. "Sweetheart, numbers are coming over daily. The Serbs have raped thousands of Bosnian women since it all began in ninety-two. So many babies. So much heartache. As you say, 'uplift one child.' I can move forward if I do this in my father's name. My mother has mended fences, but I have not yet challenged myself to leap that fence. You understand."

That unnerving sound of incoming bombs played in her head. Her constant reminder of the threat of the places where they did their good work. He'd never heard that sound, never run along a rice field with the roar overhead. She was naïve when she'd decided to take this job, to go into this field, thinking only about romantic images of rescuing and helping the children and families, but not the risks. They'd become all too real now from Shiloh and the team's stories at the roundup meetings.

Somehow, when it was Bosnia or Croatia or someplace that she had no stored images of, Hope could feel like a part of the heroism of their meaningful work. The reality of the horrific backdrops was blurred by the portraits of those smiling faces she'd created. A naïve fantasy. Now, with the Vietnam project, it was all coming back.

"Darling, your thoughts?" he whispered in her ear.

Hope knew her reaction to his news was not causing the thrill Dominique was looking for. She would miss her sense of belonging when he was near, his warm skin against her back at night when they tucked in together, if only for two weeks. But could Hope compare that hunger to a hungry child? And wasn't that what they both believed in? Of course, she should support his dreams. She thought of her Grandma Cecelia's words. The ones she'd told Hope she'd always said to Kate when she was at a crossroads.

"Hope? What are you thinking?" He turned her toward him and grasped her shoulders.

"Follow what lights you up. It's who you are." Cecelia's words had helped her understand Kate. Now, she would use those words to help her understand Dominique. "Yes, I know you need to do this." But he was a gentle soul, not a tough and hardy one like Shiloh, Hope thought. Why had she never worried about Auntie Shiloh? She seemed invincible, worldly. Nobody put one over on Shiloh. Dominique was so . . . what was the word? Tender-hearted, an intellectual, a writer. He'd already captured the descriptions of the projects they carried out on the ground in several countries in his articles for the foundation. He had a way with words, translating the foundation's work into emotional stories that brought donors running to support their efforts. Not that he wasn't strong with a deep sense of integrity. These thoughts were not what a man wanted to hear who was about to embark on a dangerous journey. "I want you to be true to yourself, Dominique."

"Thank you, darling. Michael and Shiloh have approved my plan to join the mission team. I knew you would understand. Just this one trip and I will have memories for a lifetime to inspire my articles based on the teams' experiences." Dominique dropped his head. "My dilemma is, do I tell my mother? I will only be on site for two weeks, helping Shiloh with food distribution. Jolie would never know I was gone. I don't want to worry her. Yet, I don't want to lie to her either." Dominique took Hope's shoulders and engaged her eyes in his usual way. A loving gaze that melted her resistance.

"I think it's wrong to lie to her, Dominique. It can only destroy the new bond you have. I won't lie to her if she calls. I'll downplay it, but that's all."

"She is vacationing at our home in Spain. She's not likely to call when she's entertaining. So, shall we celebrate my new opportunity tonight with a nice dinner out? There are other things we should discuss." His smile was enigmatic.

"How about the restaurant at the Omni Parker House?"

"I've not been there. We never seem to have time for just us, do we? Grabbing our meals in between project meetings."

"It opened in eighteen fifty-five. You will love its old charm. It's one of Boston's best." Hope didn't feel her supportive responses were a charade. She did want him to follow his instincts. Still, she didn't want him to go to a war-torn country where over one hundred thousand people were reportedly killed, and some two million refugees were in need. Even if it was a post-war food mission. She now understood Jolie's fears about Dominique being on the overseas assignments.

Without him . . . Hope couldn't let her thoughts go there. It was too real, not just an unfounded fear. They had his father's and her mother's deaths to support that fact.

The fax machine delivered a document, and Hope jumped back. She had freaked every time the phone rang, and a fax came in, waiting for Jeremy's information.

"Hope, are you OK?"

Hope was silent. She recognized Jeremy's official letterhead from across the room. Was it right to withhold something this colossal from your lover? She couldn't say it out loud, not until she knew. It would be too devastating a loss again. Or maybe a joyful find.

"You're somewhere else. By the way, what happened with the Vietnamese couple? Can we help?" He popped the cork from the bottle of *Chateauneuf du Pape*. One glass to wind down. An end-of-day tradition in their offices.

"It will be mission impossible, but one never knows. Finding one Nguyen is like finding a Smith in the US, but Jeremy has some intel on the woman. She would be my age if she was lifted at five. Jeremy knows she landed in the Presidio of San Francisco. He'll send me some viable contacts who might be able to help." Hope wouldn't share the intel she had about her own family. Dominique needed to stay focused while he was in the fray. She knew that. No distractions. And it would be unfair to use the news to derail his plan to go to Bosnia. She couldn't take on that responsibility that could lead to long-term regrets for Dominique, maybe resentment toward her.

It was the first time she'd hidden the truth from Dominique. If her family members weren't alive, she would not want the mistake to be resurrected repeatedly in conversation. The perseverating images of them climbing the stairs to the evacuation helicopter would be enough.

"Let me finish planning and make a few calls, and I'll stop back when I'm finished. Does that work?" Dominique opened her office door to leave.

"Wait. Actually, no."

"You've changed your mind about dinner at the Parker House?"

"No. I'm tired of spending my entire day in a men's style suit. Can you pick me up at home so I can feel like a woman about to dine with a sexy Frenchman?"

Did she see his face flush as he stood gripping the open door? It made her laugh to be the aggressor, a job he'd almost exclusively filled.

"Now I confess to being even more hungry, darling." Dominique shook his head at her surprise role change. "I'll pick up the princess at seven; does that work?" He waved and left.

As soon as Dominique left her office, Hope grabbed Jeremy's fax. He'd found a contact—a journalist on the same flight with the Nguyen's grandchild—a valuable clue.

Before she left the office, Hope had to soothe herself with a painting. It's what she did to comfort herself, to get lost in a moment of happiness, escape the frightening realities of the foundation's work, and bury herself in its successes. It was her drug of choice.

She spread a plastic tablecloth, placed a piece of paper made of linen and rags on her desk, and pulled out her watercolors. Was there any sight more lovely than the flow of watercolor seeping into the pores of a fine, handmade paper? Hope captured the dramatic sunlit scene of the day's end on the harbor below, adding blues and reds. The clouding of color as it flowed across the textured rectangle, blending with another hue, had always thrilled her. It was an adventure not unlike *life*—some outcomes intended, many uncontrollable.

14

TURNING AROUND, HOPE viewed the dress in the full-length mirror. The outfit was perfect. She was tired of those serious suits for work and her embroidered jeans on her days off. She wanted to dress up to feel grown up dining with her lover. Hope loved to call him that. It erased the seriousness of the day. She yearned for an evening to just be Hope and Dominique. She ran her hand along the elegant Bateau neck of the blue satin dress.

The style had a French flair, elegant with its off-one-shoulder, folded, slanted neckline, and a knee-length fitted skirt that showed off the curves of her petite body. Hope pulled at the three-quarter-length sleeves. Had it been decades ago, it would have called for a pair of long white gloves, like a Hollywood movie star from the nineteen fifties. The sash at the waist and ribbons of crystal woven through the bodice added that extra wow! Spritzing her neck with some of Shiloh's Chanel #5, Hope put on her fur jacket and was ready for a relaxing night with the only guy who'd ever made her feel special and truly loved.

"I WILL never forget our first days in Boston. How many times on our lunch break did we ride around the lake on that swan boat? Remember, darling?"

"I remember." There would be no forgetting the moment she'd fallen in love with this intriguing gentleman in the Boston Gardens. She was on emotional lockdown back then, after her failed relationships. "Dominique, I love you."

"*Je t'aime*, my darling." He took her hand.

It was easy to say, having been tutored by the romantic Frenchman.

Culture was always a fascinating mystery. A factor that would be so important should she ever find her Vietnamese family. Hope wanted to learn about her heritage.

"A lady dressed as elegantly as you shouldn't walk from the parking garage." Dominique dropped her at the front door of the hotel.

The doorman helped her from the car. Did she notice his questioning look? What is this Amerasian little thing doing with the handsome man in the Mercedes? Or was it her paranoia?

Dominique joined her inside the entrance dressed in his blue suit and silk tie, his coat over his arm, looking like someone she'd never dreamed would be her . . . what was he, her boyfriend? That word didn't suit the seriousness of their world.

"Do you realize we have spent almost every day together since we've met—twenty-four hours a day, between work and . . . let's just call them our *evenings* together?" He dropped his head at an angle and glanced away. A shy gesture she'd never observed before. "If you add the hours, it would be equivalent to the time some couples spend over many years, perhaps."

What was he getting at? Hope thought of the workdays sitting for hours together reviewing adoption documents and writing the histories of the children the foundation had helped. They'd read the letters of gratitude from adoptive parents and stories of the children's new lives. She'd edited the moving articles Dominique wrote to promote the organization. He had a way of capturing the essence of what they did—communicating with government officials, arranging complicated logistics, and coordinating with other international organizations for overseas missions. Yes, they'd bonded in a way she never had with a man—they were friends, partners, coworkers.

Hope studied his face, but there was no clue.

Then his thought seemed to evaporate.

"Are you hungry? I'm looking forward to a lovely dinner with my lover." He guided her through the bustling lobby to the restaurant.

The meal *was* lovely, the setting even more so, as though they'd transported back in time with the carved wood ceiling trim and Waterford Crystal chandeliers. She read the description on the menu aloud to Dominique. "The ornate hand-carved woodwork of this Grand Dame restaurant serves as a reminder of the days when Charles Dickens, Ralph Waldo Emerson, and other literary greats dined here as members of the 'Saturday Club.'"

"Well, we are members of the *Friday* club. Shall we make history?" Dominique had a distant look she couldn't read, as though he were holding back something important.

After a delicious meal of the restaurant's signature Boston Scrod, the traditional Boston crème pie was delivered. "Wait, dear, before dessert, something even sweeter." Dominique reached into his pocket. "Darling Hope." He took her left hand. "Before I leave for what will soon be a thing of the past, let's make this our most memorable moment." He opened the little black velvet box.

"Yes, Dominique, yes. I will." She covered her mouth with her hand, suppressing her laugh, a burst of pure happiness. Had she just preempted his proposal? "Oh, I'm sorry, Dominique."

"But how did you know what I was about to ask? I thought I'd have to beg, plead, get on one knee to capture that answer from a woman like you." He slipped the ring on her finger. They'd nearly knocked their chairs over trying to get to each other. Laughing together and hugging, they elicited a muffled clap from the waiter's gloved hands.

"CONGRATULATIONS! OH, I knew it." Shiloh spun Hope around the office. "Tell me every detail of the night . . . well, not every detail. You'll make me jealous. Have you told your family?" Shiloh looked down at her watch and froze in place. "Oh, Hope, Dominique leaves with me and the team at four o'clock. What timing. Look, he doesn't have to go. If you want me to—"

"No, Auntie Shiloh, I would never ask him to cancel. He needs to do this, though I'm not exactly happy about it. In fact, I'm terrorized by the thought. You are the first and only one that I'm telling."

"Oh honey, this assignment isn't going to be like that. There hasn't been any fighting in that area. We're delivering supplies at the border to the refugees. Michael and I wouldn't have agreed if there was conflict near there. We know he's not a rough-and-tumble kind of guy. But you're right. It's not the best way to start a relationship." Shiloh lifted Hope's left hand. "But the ring is stunning. Antique?"

"A family heirloom from his great-grandmother. I'm nervous wearing it, knowing it's priceless, and I wonder if his mother even knows he's given it to me?" Hope had to let go of her fear. And she had work to do. It was the perfect time to make her trip to San Francisco, she realized.

"Honey, that has to be at least three carats, and it's eye-clean, as my mother used to say." Shiloh let out one of her classic cackles. "I love the single-cut diamonds all around the main stone. And honey, this is platinum for sure. And the delicate carving around the band, like lace. Amazing."

"Anyway, you'll all be home in two weeks. I just have to avoid Jolie until then," Hope said.

"Dominique doesn't want Jolie to worry. I get it. And no need." Shiloh adjusted her bandanna, and a shiver of jingles from her jewelry made Hope shudder.

Was there really no danger? Now her fiancé and her mentor were going into a war zone with only a fragile peace agreement. Yes, it was not in the hot zone, only on the secured border, Hope told herself.

"I want to tell my family face to face, but I'm leaving for San Francisco on Monday. I'll wait until we can tell them together. My docket's clear, and if I sit around here waiting and worrying, that won't do anyone any good." Hope shuffled some files and put them in her briefcase.

"What's in San Fran?" Pouring a glass of water from the pitcher on Hope's desk, Shiloh sipped and waited.

"I need to do some research on the Nguyen Am case. Jeremy gave me some leads. A journalist, Maggie Miller, was on the flight. Her sister was the nurse on duty for the children, too. Maybe they know something. It's a start. Or an end. She lives in Sausalito."

"That name is familiar. I think she became an advocate for Vietnamese parental rights when our government took them away." Shiloh huffed down into the leather loveseat by the window. "Seems like a lifetime ago, that war. I led protests over the Vietnam War in college, and Kate sang for the events. I remember that Babylift. I wasn't exactly in favor of those decisions President Ford made. The poor Vietnamese families who lost their children and couldn't get them back. Do you know the US government canceled the Vietnamese parental rights?"

"I've read about that." Hope felt impassioned about these things, but at the same time, the subjects made her heavy with sadness.

"You were lucky, Hope. If your father hadn't sent Jeremy to find you, you would never have known your father or the Ketchum-James family . . . or me! And, of course, Michael was your biological father."

"I wouldn't have Ernie or Uncle Jack. I can't imagine my life without Grandma Cecelia." Hope engaged in the soothing view of the expansive harbor and skyscrapers. "But looking back, it was complicated for those children who weren't orphans and were taken away. Stay and be in life-threatening danger or go and lose your family. And the orphans, too, looking down through those foggy airline windows, being swept away, not knowing where they were going. The babies were better off. They didn't know what was happening." Hope's voice was monotone as she battled to remain unemotional.

Shiloh cast her eyes down, then looked up and smiled. "I love that your father believes in finding homes for orphans and lost kids in their own countries or nearby. At least they could be repatriated when a war was over."

"True. That makes a big difference. Love Dad for that—and my mother who inspired my dad that way. And now there's Jolie. Her money is building the new Uplift schools and pays to reunite kids with their families and funds their education and support." Hope was used to falling into these serious philosophical discussions with Shiloh, but excavating this subject after two decades was haunting. Hope had never studied the political details of the times until recently; her own story was enough.

"So much of it was all political image and illusion. For the US, it was about strategy and image, instead of soul." Shiloh stood. "Americans even changed Viet Nam to one word. Even the UN still uses two words, and the country of Viet Nam does, too. Don't get me going about our politics and motives."

"But Shi, there were good intentions too on the part of adoptive parents, right? And the social workers and medical teams? It was tragic and complicated at best." Hope had felt both ways. She liked to think about the loving people who adopted those children sight unseen. But yes, it was sad the children were uprooted from their cultures. It's so confusing being a dual-culture kid. No one knew better than she. Most of the time, Hope would forget she looked different until someone gave her that look—sometimes just curiosity, sometimes condescension. A look that said, what are you doing here? It was a wake-up call after being so loved and accepted by the Ketchums.

"OK, honey, lecture over. Sorry to say, I've got to go. Good luck in SF. You'll have fun telling your family about your engagement when we return. My lips are zipped." Shiloh made the appropriate gesture across her mouth. "But I hope I can be there. They'll be thrilled. They love Dominique. And speaking of loving Dominique, we're leaving in fifteen minutes. One more thing. I want this to be a surprise, I sort of 'know' one of the editors of the Boston Globe, shall we say *intimately*."

The statement made Hope shake her head and grin. "Yes, and?"

"He's read some of the articles Dominique has written and wants to do a feature on him and his stories of our work with kids. I'll introduce them when we get back."

"Fantastic, Auntie Shiloh."

WHEN HOPE entered his office, Dominique wasn't there. "Dominique?" She felt that old familiar anxiety rush to her throat, and her breathing became shallow. There was no valid reason for her response, she thought.

"Down here, darling."

She found him bending over his luggage. "All set, honey?" Hope lifted her voice to add a touch of normalcy.

"Yes, just had to take you with me." He slipped Hope's photo from his desk between his clothes, stood up, and rubbed his back. "I'll miss the real you."

Why was she being silly? It was only two weeks. But it was their first time apart since they'd met. Had it only been three months? Every day, working together, celebrating together, loving each other. And he would be her husband someday.

With Shiloh and the entire team going abroad, only her father would be in the office. Unless he decided to join them over-seas—something he did often and spontaneously. Hope hadn't seen him in weeks. The word "team" had fallen short of what she'd expected when she'd first arrived at the foundation. They were her daytime family. In their absence, when they all went on assignment, Hope missed the joy of belonging. She longed for their return. Thank goodness Hope would leave for San Francisco after the weekend. She twisted the beautiful ring on her finger. Please, God, keep him safe. "I love you, Dominique. Two weeks will fly by."

He stroked her hair. "My love, when I return, would you be ready to make plans for our life together? I don't think I can spend another night without you."

"Me either. And I know you are French, so things will go fast. Like wanting to make love on the first date."

He nodded with a sheepish grin. *"Aimer, ce n'est pas se regarder l'un l'autre, c'est regarder ensemble dans la même direction.* I like that old French saying by Antoine De Saint-Exupery. Love does not consist of gazing at each other but looking outward together in the same direction."

"But for now, can we look at each other, Dominique? Let's tell everyone together when you return. About the engagement." She flashed the ring in front of him. "I love the ring, Dominique."

"I agree. We'll tell them together. That ring has a history I need to share. We will add our story to its history. *Je t'aime*, Hope." He kissed her in his tender way that reached every part of her.

Watching him walk down the hallway to the elevator, she felt weak. Why did their relationship feel like one of her childhood fairytales? It was almost embarrassing how perfectly romantic their connection had been. That could be why she didn't trust it.

Maybe that's why she was so afraid something would go wrong. In fairytales, something always did. Even Jolie had laid her entire financial legacy at her feet. Was anything that good? It had just unfolded and blossomed like a flower. There she went again, sounding like Dominique.

How much fun would the Ketchums have at Sunday dinners as Uncle Jack and Grandma Cecelia took credit for unleashing the news of Hope and Dominique's love to the family? Everything would be fine.

While Dominique was gone, she would focus on finding the girl who would now be a woman exactly her age. Given the history of finding lost children from the war, she didn't have much confidence. Hope was three-years-old when she came through Boston Airport in 1972. Am was five when her flight brought her to San Francisco in 1975. Hope prayed the journalist Jeremy had identified would have some knowledge of the child with the scar on her hand. Such a small clue to find a child twenty years after her landing in the Presidio in San Francisca amid a mass of refugees. Why had this case come Hope's way? Why did Dominique have to go just when she had reason to put her pain behind her?

Dominique waved and sent a kiss from the other end of the hallway. The ding of the elevator took him away.

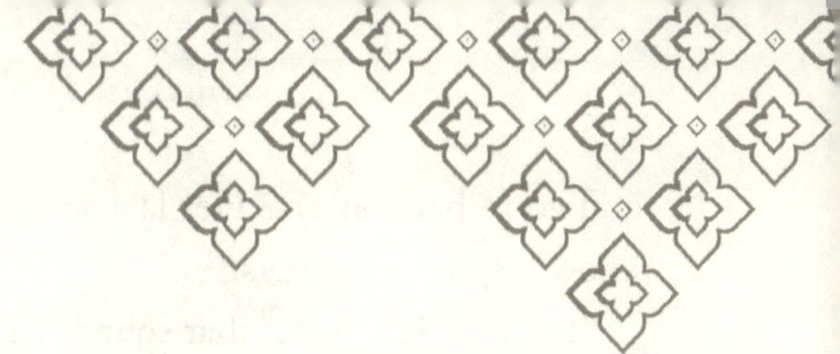

15

THE MORE HOPE researched, the more helpless she felt about finding Am on her own. She could have enlisted their professional investigative team, but Hope needed a distraction with a purpose. She'd sent emails to three nonprofits that had dealt with reuniting Vietnamese families. After so long, many of them no longer focused on the issue, but a few organizations had kept old records.

She would wait and see. What did people do before they could write a letter, and it would instantly appear electronically at the other end? She would light up all channels to find the woman, just to see the light in her grandparents' eyes. Hope planned to book her flight to San Francisco for a Monday departure so she could prepare and pack over the weekend. The phone rang, interrupting her thoughts.

"Dad, what's happening? Are you back yet?"

"I'm home. Honey, I have an idea. Kate is playing at Madison Square Garden tomorrow night. Why not take a private plane and go to her concert? Her last stop on the US tour. I think I know how to get tickets."

"Funny, Dad. Sure, that sounds like fun. Just a typical Saturday night with the family." Hope loved hearing his laughter and enthusiastic voice. She had the weekend to pack and study more. Why not?

"How about we steal Cecelia away with us? I know Grandpa Kevin won't go. He works Saturdays unloading supplies. So, you're in? I'll get our driver to pick me up first, then swing by for you around two, OK?"

"Can't wait to see you, Dad. Seems like forever since we went to a Kate concert together."

THE RING was in the safe, and she was ready to go. A concert would be fun and sentimental. At moments, Hope was disappointed that Dominique had planned a hit-and-run engagement, leaving her alone with the secret. Although, she was thrilled about their future. They would have a future, wouldn't they? Don't assume the worst, she told herself. There had never been a loss or injury yet on their team, through all the work they'd done in war-torn countries for two decades.

With an hour to kill, Hope read more of Kate's journal. Reading it still gave Hope a wormy feeling. She flipped through and found an interesting entry.

The spotlight hit me, stabbing my eyes and blackening out the audience, and the raucous applause was deafening. This was no O'Leary's crowd; this was no factory floor. The walls were solid teak from the floor to the vaulted ceiling. Massive portraits of the King of Siam flanked the stage with Thailand's red, white, and blue flags that were fluttering from all the excitement in the hall. How can I describe my feelings as I hit the bridge of the song, and applause built from a few hands clapping to the crowd, calling out "Kate, Kate, Kate"? The volume rose to a level like I'd never heard. Thousands of simultaneous hands together, voices in synch, blending my chanted name, their applause grew into a roar like a full-on locomotive. No, like the deafening machines of the shoe factory at full tilt. The sound pushed me back on the stage. It filled me up. How had I come to this place halfway around the planet from Glynn?

The screams, frenetic bodies, and fists punching the air surrounded me. I could hardly breathe. My face hurt from my perpetual smile. My joy wasn't just about the audience's adulation; I loved knowing I'd touched them with my voice and the lyrics. As I ended the set, I shifted to the side of the stage, feeling humble. My knees gave out. I hung onto the mic stand and planted one hand on the pebbled surface of the Fender speaker. It was bigger than any emotion I'd ever felt; how could I contain it? This was a sound I could hear forever.

Was Kate exaggerating? What had ever lit Hope up like that? She searched her memories.

Outside, everything was covered in frost. Hope had trouble tolerating winter. Spring was her favorite time of year. The Crepe Myrtles lined the street outside their home—the lavender kind that determined themselves to blossom ahead of the others as if they couldn't wait to be admired. As a habit, Hope focused on nature. It calmed her. She and Dominique shared that tree-hugging mentality, he'd said.

Why had she never thought to paint outside and capture her favorite season in watercolor or acrylics? No time.

Waiting for the limo to appear, Hope sat on the porch, thinking about Kate and the journal entries she'd read. As a child, she'd always thought Kate was out there having the time of her life, never thinking of Hope and her father. But it was more than that. Lately, thoughts of Operation Babylift and the complexities of adoptive families made her realize Kate's situation was more complicated than Hope had ever considered. Kate had dreams. She had an exceptional talent that couldn't be denied. And she hadn't had a say in becoming a mother. Dad just showed up one day and said, *guess what?* Hope had never looked at it that way before. How would she feel if Dominique did the same?

Maybe Hope disagreed with Kate's choices, but perhaps she didn't know what it felt like to pick between something you chose and something that chose you. After touring with Adam Anderson and the Keys, six-time Grammy winners who'd launched Kate's true passion into the stratosphere along with her band Riverrun, how could she not keep going?

Hope had never considered anything but following in Shiloh's footsteps and working for the foundation. She'd kept her head down and focused on her academics. It made everyone so proud and happy. Didn't she owe her dad that? Wasn't Hope his "one child?"

Grandma Cecelia's words of advice lingered and spun around in Hope's mind. Follow what lights you up. The only time she'd felt joyful or lit up, besides when she was lit up with Dominique, was when she was painting. The brush sounds against the hand-made paper, the rough sound of the charcoal, the flow of seeping colors—watercolor and charcoal—a fascinating combination—the fluidity of one, the assertiveness of the other. And seeing a child's happy face captured for The Wall of Hope had always lit her up from the first day. It had given her hobby a purpose. But her art at work at the foundation was never a creative outlet or play for her. It had always been connected to the horrors of war, the loss of children and families, and the din of destruction, despite the painted-on smiles.

Hope read more entries about Kate's travels and inner doubts. One paragraph stopped her.

> *The battle between two weeks basking on a beach on the French Riviera with Adam and his band and rushing home to Michael to introduce Hy Vọng to my family surged inside me. So much travel, but I imagined the warmth of holding Hope in my arms when the child was afraid and having Michael's arms around me. I had to laugh. I'd worked so hard to escape Glynn, and now I'm conflicted. Some cosmic joke. Did I ever dream I'd have to choose between such extremes, Paris or Glynn? Family or career?*

Kate's choice began to have a different dimension. Hope had a new compassion for Dominique's decision to go to Bosnia, and Kate's world began to make more sense. But Hope's support of Dominique's choice had a profound cost for her.

The limousine arrived with Grandma Cecelia's warm smile peeking through the window. Hope hopped in the back seat with her. "Are you excited, Grandma?"

"Honey, I haven't seen one of Kate's concerts since Ireland when you were nearly four, and my red had no gray. I'm thrilled. Michael, this is so sweet of you."

Michael sat across from them, twisting the corkscrew into a bottle of champagne. "Shall we? So, what's new, Hope?" He handed them each a flute and began pouring.

"Yes, tell us what's happening, dear. Shiloh tells me Dominique decided at the last minute to help in Bosnia. He's such a love."

Too late to change the subject. With a bit of luck, this trip would take Hope's mind off the news of her engagement that sat repressed like a jack-in-the-box. Whenever she spoke with someone or thought about telling someone, the crank would turn and turn, creating more and more pressure to release the truth. Wasn't withholding the news a kind of lie? Was the clown about to spring forth from the box to share the excitement with her dad and grandmother?

HUGS AND kisses in Kate's green room were over quickly, and they were hosted to their first-row floor seats in front of the stage. Kate waved and threw a kiss to them as she started her first song.

For the first time as an adult, Hope experienced the energy of the crowd of nearly twenty thousand people and their reaction to Kate's charming introductions to each song and her enchanting voice. Captivating a sea of fans in Madison Square Garden had to be a fantasy for a singer from a factory family. Kate's journal descriptions of the sights and sounds of one of her concerts came alive in the room. She hadn't exaggerated.

With college, law school, and internships taking up Hope's time these past years, she hadn't been able to travel overseas when Kate was performing in large venues.

And maybe Hope's underlying hurt had played a role, too. She squeezed her grandmother's hand. "She's awesome, Grandma. Thanks to you."

Hope watched the tears hanging to the edges of Cecelia's eyes and her wide smile.

Michael leaned forward, rocking his head to the beat of the music, his fingers tapping to the imaginary piano keys on his thighs. There was a moment when Hope physically experienced her feelings toward Kate softening. A lifting of the tension in her chest. Disappointment, yes, but no longer so angry. Shiloh was right. Reading Kate's journal had begun to put salve on the wound. As much as Hope still felt uncomfortable with the invasion of privacy issue, Shiloh had insisted Kate would be OK with it once she saw the outcome.

Shiloh had promised she would tell Kate when the time was right. She'd never given Hope bad advice. Hope would trust Shiloh and swallow her guilt.

The show ended with deafening applause, three encores, and Kate's touching dedication. "Tonight's concert is dedicated to my mother, Cecelia, the inspiration of my life; my husband, Michael, the love of my life; and our precious and brilliant daughter, Hope, the highlight of my life. Thank you for being here for me. I love you." Kate shaded her eyes and looked down at them in the front row.

The words *daughter* and *highlight* had their effect. How could Kate say these touching words in front of a crowd of thousands and never have said them to Hope in person, one-on-one, stepmother to stepdaughter? Still, Hope was moved. It was a first. She jumped up and joined the crowd, clapping until her hands hurt, hugging Cecelia and her dad.

KATE JOINED them in the limousine for a farewell toast and chat before departing for the airport.

"Let's have a toast to my wife and the love of my life. Kate, you were amazing, as always. Congratulations on your twenty-year success." Michael kissed Kate, and they all clinked and sipped.

"Thank you, honey. Let me catch up here. How's Dominique? The last time we were together, you had fallen in love. Don't tell me. You eloped." Kate laughed. "Those French men."

Hope took a breath. The clown had to explode out of the jack-in-the-box, she thought.

"Dad, Grandma . . . Ka . . . Mom." The word came awkwardly from Hope's mouth. It was a choice—to feel like a liar withholding the life event or disappoint Dominique by telling them without him. But hadn't it been her idea to wait? She couldn't. "Dominique and I got engaged just before he left. We'll plan our future when he returns and announce it to you. And I'm telling you before Uncle Jack finds out and forces me to confess."

They laughed together.

"I'm so happy for you both but, I must say, like father like daughter. Wouldn't you agree?" Kate looked at Michael with the sweetest teasing look.

Michael smiled. "Yes, Hope, you are the secretive one . . . I've been known to do that on occasion. So, you have an excuse. It's hereditary."

"Let's not skip over this wonderful news. I'm so happy for my granddaughter to have found true love. And Dominique seems to be a man of character, like our Michael. Not to mention handsome and kind. We're keeping it all in the family—he's part of the foundation, too. Just wonderful." Grandma Cecelia made the sign of the cross.

"Dad? You haven't said much." Hope leaned toward him.

"Well, I'm the one who picked him, but I didn't expect him to steal my only daughter." Her father's pause was disconcerting. He quickly lifted his glass and smiled. "Oh honey, I shouldn't tease when it's so important. Congratulations! Cheers to you both. Of course, I approve."

16

THE LONG FLIGHT to San Francisco would finally give Hope time alone to read more of Kate's journal. She'd kept it on her nightstand for months. She'd been distracted from sleeping with a *French lover* every night, as she'd come to teasingly call Dominique. Reading the diary still felt wrong, like sneaking through someone's private mail.

Hope's mind was still possessed by the revelation of her engagement to Dominique. Sharing the news had been awkward and laughable, and the result was fantastic. But Dominique hadn't been in touch for her to share it with him. She wouldn't let her unfounded obsessive fear of losing Dominique in some war diminish her happiness. Hope comforted herself; he was probably just busy. Maybe she should call to tell him. Or would he be disappointed? Would sharing the stories make him feel left out? Distract him from his work? He needed to focus on the fragile border situation and the complicated logistics. But he'd be home soon, and they could continue their life together.

Wouldn't he? Hope would wait and share the story with him in front of the family so he could feel their love and acceptance as she had with Jolie.

FLYING FIRST class had always awakened Hope to her blessings. Kate had insisted her daughter have the best. Hope's inheritance was Grandma Christine's gift, and Kate's generosity came in gifting Hope money on every special occasion. And why couldn't Hope just rejoice in it? She'd been able to pay for her entire education with those gifts. She wavered between gratitude and the thoughts of all the children wandering through cities and the countryside seeking food and safety. But wasn't she dedicated to their cause?

"Can I get you anything, miss?"

Hope looked up at the flight attendant and read her name tag. "Yes, Susan, but as my flirtatious and naughty fiancé said to me, unfortunately, what I want is not on the menu."

Susan hesitated. "Oh, that's too cute."

"Seriously, Susan, just coffee, thank you."

"Cream and sugar?" She suspended the full pot over the paper cup on her tray. It vibrated with Susan's repressed giggles.

"Just black, please."

The flight attendant set the cup down in front of Hope. "*Not on the menu.* I have to remember that one next time I see my boyfriend."

Uncle Jack had always said that sharing a light moment created an instant micro-connection with a stranger. A win-win.

He was right. Making someone laugh was a gift that gave back, Hope thought. Her mood changed as she sipped her coffee and opened the journal.

Admiring Kate's familiar rhythmic handwriting perfected under the eyes of the Catholic nuns, no doubt, Hope flipped past the entries about Kate's career she'd already read. It began with interning at Rolling Hills Institution, that dreary place for people with disabilities, where Kate had first met Ernie and Mary. Kate wrote about how she could not just leave them there. She'd arranged for The Ketchum family to adopt them.

The diary shed light on the part of Kate that Hope already admired. And didn't Kate's passion and the Ketchums' open hearts welcoming Ernie and Mary into the family give Hope two people in her life who were like siblings to her? But then Kate had just left and gone on tour again.

The story of the luck-of-the-draw in singing with The Keys and for superstar Adam Anderson himself, no less, when his opening act got food poisoning, was typical of Kate's adventuresome life and luck.

Shiloh was right. Hope's perspective was changing about Kate with every turn of the page.

I longed for that feeling when my new sleepy daughter would curl into my lap. I wanted to repeat that tender, heart-clutching emotion I'd felt when Hope had snuggled close to me that first night together after her dramatic rescue—singing to her in the rocking chair in our bedroom in Bangkok with the pink Bunny tucked under Hope's chin. I can almost taste the irony. I'd spent my entire time in Glynn trying to avoid becoming a mother. How often had I denied myself with some cute boyfriend and prayed for it not to happen? After being away for the Keys tour,

I ached for this little girl to come closer. Having her alive with Michael and me was such a dream. Imagining the orphanage collapsing around the child, I wanted to put my arms around Hope and never let go.

From the glider across the room, I could see into the bedroom where our daughter was asleep on her pink quilt on the floor. "Our daughter," would I ever get used to that? We had an instant child.

I hear Michael's baritone voice, "Hy Vọng, sweetie?" She hadn't stirred.

I remember telling Michael to leave her be. I was insanely excited, having just arrived from Paris after a three-week tour, but she might wake up cranky, I thought. Don't expect some romance at first sight, I told myself. Mother was a word Michael's daughter would grow into.

That made Hope stop. She put the open book face down on the empty seat beside her. Watching the display of clouds shimmering in the early morning pink sky through the plane window, Hope embraced her reality—life was good—a first-class seat. And she had reservations at the Four Seasons on the Embarcadero, overlooking the water close to the ferry terminal. Hope imagined the view with the Bay Bridge span stretching out in the distance. In the morning, she would take the ferry to Sausalito to meet with the journalist from the Babylift flight.

Why go back to the past? No, she had to read it all, Shiloh had said. Hope had to finally take the time to understand Kate.

I can still see Hy Vọng stretching and rubbing her eyes. I couldn't wait for her bright blue eyes to open. That beguiling twin reflection of Michael and his mother. I remember when Hy Vọng ran out of the bedroom toward me.

"Sweetheart?" I used my softest voice and held out my arms.

I'd anticipated some reticence, but I hadn't expected the child would push me away. It was nothing like that first day together.

"Oh, honey, it's OK. It's Mommy." The word mommy came clumsily from my mouth, I admit.

Hope gasped at the parallel. Hadn't addressing Kate as *Mom* after the concert felt just as clumsy? Hope continued to read.

I remember that moment so clearly, like a metaphor for how I felt. The room had gone dark from the passing of an afternoon cloud that swallowed the sunlight.

"Không, không!" Hy Vọng held her head and shook it.

I remember asking Michael to translate. I can hear his words. "She's saying . . . no, no. Just waking from a dream."

"Dah-dee, Dah-dee," she'd wailed. Hy Vọng ran across the room and climbed up Michael's leg. I watched Michael soothe Hy Vọng. Wrapping his arms around his child, he held her tight, rocked her, and started a humming chant. Hy Vọng whimpered until she was caught up in the rhythm of Michael's sounds, and the hum began to soothe her. Her sobs subsided into little wounded chirps and sniffles.

That's when my college memory surfaced. I buried my face in my hands, remembering Michael during the UConn campus protests, his body wrapped around me, rocking me on the quadrangle grass, running his hands down my body, calling me Hằng. I can hear myself pleading in his ear to let me up. That first experience with his torturous PTSD had been terrifying. A chill spasmed down my arms thinking of it so many years later. Now, the child from his deceased lover was my daughter. Be patient, I told myself. Isn't this what you learned about at Rolling Hills—patience and acceptance of differences?

I could almost feel my mother-in-law's eyes riveted on me with sympathy. Christine moved to sit on the striped glider, put her arm around me, and pulled me close. "Honey, I'm so sorry. She'll be OK. It happened when I got here, too," she'd said.

"She let me rock her that first night," I'd told Christine. For the first time, I let down my guard and leaned into Christine for comfort.

Michael returned and sat in a chair beside me, holding Hy Vọng. He tried to pass it off as what always happens with someone new, and she'd just awakened. "She'll come around. Sorry." I can hear his sympathetic voice. "Sorry, honey."

I wanted to put my arms around my new daughter, to feel the soft skin of her sweet face. I remember thinking the arms that had always comforted me were now engaged. Of course, the child should come first.

Hy Vọng pointed at me and muttered something in Vietnamese. Michael answered, "That's Mommy, remember?"

She didn't.

Hope held the diary to her chest. Its contents continued to create a new perspective on Kate. Maybe Hope was growing up, stepping from her childhood into maturity. Still, as a woman, Hope couldn't imagine leaving her child behind.

17

THERE WAS SOMETHING about an elevator ride Hope liked—a metaphor for her life, she thought, as she finished her morning walk and returned to her hotel room for breakfast. Magically, you're lifted to a higher place with a view you'd never imagined, empowered by an unseen force. She could view her life that way, figuratively and literally. Hadn't an unseen plane plucked her into the sky from the devastation below, she thought, as she dined on her room service breakfast overlooking the expansive San Francisco Bay? And hadn't it made her a bit dizzy rising so high in her life, ending up as a Harvard grad attorney working in one of the tallest skyscrapers overlooking the Boston Harbor? It was still new and magical, and her good fortune crossed her mind with her daily ground-to-sky trips. She snapped the ivory linen napkin and lay it on her lap. When would she fully believe in her privileged, cloth-napkin life? She was blessed.

Savoring the poached eggs, prosciutto, her favorite rye toast, and coffee, she admired the view from the top floor of the forty-five-story, mixed-use building that housed the Four Seasons Hotel. It struck Hope that she'd made the same forty-five-floor rise to her office every day. Four plus five equals nine. Hope drifted back to her college days. Nine was the luckiest number. She'd learned that from her college roommate, Leila who'd studied numerology. The significance of nine still lingered in Hope's memory—completion, fulfillment, and achievement.

When Hope kept running into the number four in her Boston College days, just for fun, she'd asked her friend what it meant. Leila explained that four symbolizes our role in manifesting positive change in the world. Four symbolized creation, strength, practicality, and hard work. That suited Hope's world right now. She smiled at the memory. Four was still following her through her days. And now, nine. What luck was coming her way?

Last night, the view from her lounge chair by the window was uplifting, too. The expanse of the San Francisco Bay changed colors. The pinks and reds floating in the sky with streaks of yellow and blue sinking into the horizon predicted the sunny day that had spread out before her. Red sky at night, sailors delight, she remembered her old boyfriend Steve saying when they'd launched out on his sailboat in the Boston harbor.

She finished her meal and put on a blue sweater, jacket, and multi-color scarf for the sunny, crisp December day. A high of sixty-four and the bright sun was the best weather she could expect this time of year for her ferry ride to Sausalito. She slid her sketch pad into her briefcase with a few art supplies so she could create her way through the day.

Meeting Janine Mills, the journalist Jeremy had identified was on the flight with the Nguyen's granddaughter, provided Hope with a flicker of optimism about the mission impossible.

Refusing a ride from the concierge, she walked down California Street, cut over to Market Street, and around Steuart Street to the Embarcadero and the Ferry Building. Hope bought her ticket and sat in the terminal building, sketching the scenery, and glancing at her fellow passengers to complete a few quick portraits.

A family of three with a chubby-cheeked toddler drew her attention as she waited for her 10:10 a.m. departure. The family looked Vietnamese, and they were conversing in their native tongue. Hope recognized a word here and there. She regretted not learning the language, never expecting to be working on a Vietnamese missing person's case two decades after Operation Babylift. And she'd never wanted to make her father speak the language he associated with his pain. But now Hope wished she could communicate with Am in her native tongue, should Hope find her. Of course, Am would speak English after all these years, but wouldn't speaking Vietnamese elicit trust?

The thirty-minute ride would put Hope on shore in Sausalito at 10:40, with time to see some sights on the way to Janine's houseboat and still arrive by 11:30. Hope opened Janine's note to check the directions. The journalist's father was a veteran and artist and had been given the old houseboat by a wealthy man who'd taken pity on the homeless soldier. Janine's father was one of many veterans, hippies, artists, and musicians who'd set up home on old boats on Richardson Bay after World War II. Now, after her father's death and a widow herself, Janine told Hope on the phone that she was using it as a home base on the West Coast when she wasn't on one of her international assignments or at her primary home in Washington, DC.

The view on the ferry trip was breathtaking, with Alcatraz

floating off in the distance like a miniature mountain with a castle on top. The Golden Gate bridge spanning the water at the other end of the Bay must have brought tears to the refugees who came by boat to the charming city like the Statue of Liberty had welcomed emotional immigrants on the East Coast.

Hope sketched two children about five-or-six-years-old holding onto the blue and gold ferry railing. They faced the wind, giggling and jumping up and down with excitement. One was light-skinned, and the other had darker brown skin. It touched Hope to see the children blind to their differences.

When Hope reached the Sausalito terminal, she was delighted to see the string of restaurants and art galleries along the waterfront. It was only a mile and a quarter to Janine's houseboat. The locals preferred the expression "floating home." She'd told Hope to use that moniker if she were to ask for directions.

Walking well over a mile up the Bridgeway, the first wooden walkway led her to Janine's dock. Her wooden floating home showed its age but was charming. A porch built off the back had a magnificent view of the Bay. Over the hillside peeked the towers of the Golden Gate Bridge.

"Miss James, please come in."

It was common for people to skip over the cumbersome "Lê Ketchum" middle names and jump right to James as her surname. She didn't blame them. "Please, let's be Hope and Janine."

"My pleasure. Coffee?

"Sounds good. Thank you." A wisp of a woman, Hope guessed Janine was in her forties. So young to be a widow.

"Please have a seat. Be right back."

Hope smiled when she felt the first slight sway of the boat and the sound of an engine passing by. It was such a different lifestyle living on the water at sea level. The inside of the floating home was modernized with all the conveniences of a house with one significant benefit—the view. Through the windows that had been expanded, she could see the beautiful Bay and the hills of Marin. She took her sketch pad from her briefcase and did a quick pencil sketch of the view.

Janine returned with the coffee. "Oh, may I see?" She walked behind Hope's chair. "I didn't know you were an artist. That sketch is so good. Lots of scenery for you around this town."

"Would you like to keep it since it's your view?" Hope tore the page from her book.

"Love it. Thanks. I'll have it framed." Janine propped it on the fireplace mantle. "And by the way, today is the ICB's annual open house. Opening night at six tonight if you can stick around, or all weekend if you're staying in San Francisco."

"ICB?"

"That's the big old Industrial Center Building. There are maybe one hundred artists' studios there now. If you have time, you might enjoy it. Here's the brochure. It's not far from here." Janine pointed to the map on the brochure.

Janine sat and sipped her coffee as she explained that she was only a young cub reporter during the mid-70s and, by chance, had an assignment in Saigon when Operation Babylift took place. It was terrorizing for her second overseas assignment, she said. Her older sister Ginny, a nurse engaged by the US military, assisted the children on that flight.

"As I mentioned, I'm seeking to reunite a woman who was a five-year-old child on that flight with her grandparents." Hope shared the details and mentioned the clue, the scar.

"There were only a few older children on that flight, but boxes and boxes of infants. I can't say I remember a child with a scar, but I wasn't working directly with them."

No news was what Hope had expected. She rose to thank her host.

"Wait. Let me call my sister, Ginny. She's just home today from an overseas volunteer trip. I couldn't reach her before. She did a health check on each child and kept in touch with some of the families." Janine left the room and called behind her. "It's a long shot, but she recently helped to organize a twentieth-year reunion of the passengers on that flight. She did a lot of research."

When she returned, Janine's face worried Hope and confirmed her fears. Staring out the window, Janine shook her head. "I find this to be impossible . . . but my sister remembers the scar and the child."

"What?" Hope shared that "seen-a-ghost look" with Janine and sprung from her chair.

"And she'd kept in touch with the adoptive parents. They were both doctors from Rhode Island, a pediatrician and Obstetrician named Rachael and Brian Carlisle. And she had the name of their adoptive daughter. Of course, as was the way of the times, adoptive parents gave new names to their Vietnamese children right away." Janine looked down at the sticky note in her hand. "Her given name is Frances Anne Carlisle. That's the good news."

Prepared for the worst, Hope sat down again.

"Ginny tried to contact them for the reunion; they didn't answer her invitation. They'd lived in Warwick, Rhode Island, just outside of Providence. Ginny guesses they must have moved or were traveling on an extended overseas mission, maybe. But they never responded."

"Still, this is good news, Janine. Thank you. Researching two doctors in the US who worked a short drive from Boston narrows things down tremendously! But no knowledge of Frances Anne's whereabouts?"

"No, Ginny didn't have a direct connection to the daughter, unfortunately."

"Janine, I am so grateful, and I'll keep you in the loop. I know you have a lunch appointment, so I'll be going. Thank you, thank you."

"Yes, well, now there's hope. Oh, in more than one way, I guess." Janine smiled and handed the note to Hope. "I'm so happy we could help. Good luck."

HOPE WAS tired from a long afternoon wandering through art galleries and having lunch on the waterfront in downtown Sausalito. She would take the 4:30 p.m. ferry back to the Four Seasons and return tomorrow to ICB art building's annual open house. She didn't want to miss the waterfront scenery at night from her hotel room and, more importantly, the chance to share her exciting breakthrough with the Nguyen couple. With the three-hour time change, she could call them at five, West Coast time. Hope assumed they would have finished their dinner by eight. It was a huge breakthrough, not a guarantee, but yes, there's *hope*, as Janine had said. There were times she was grateful for the name her father had chosen for her in the middle of the world exploding around him, Hope thought as she rode the elevator to the sky.

Opening the drapes to her magnificent view, Hope sat on the

loveseat and called the Nguyens. She was careful not to be too confident, but weren't the odds in her favor that she would find Frances' parents now? And eventually, Frances. Ginny had told Janine that both the Carlisles regularly volunteered for Doctors without Borders. Who knew why they hadn't responded to the reunion invitation? It didn't mean they couldn't be traced. She had top investigators volunteering for the foundation, and she'd already left a message with Angie, Uplift's receptionist, to put the word out.

"We are so grateful. It's wonderful to know that Am had a loving home. We'll hold our breaths until we hear from you."

The Nguyen couple's words filled Hope with both joy and anxiety. The pressure was on. She would follow up in person. It was the best way for Hope to understand her work. There was so much at stake.

18

THERE WERE NO words for the spectacle Hope was watching through the window walls of the Four Seasons rooftop dining room. One hundred eighty degrees of moving art, five hundred feet above the Bay. The city's lights came on as nature's light show went out.

Was her watch moving slower than usual, or was it the excitement of sharing her news with Dominique? Hope took the final bite of her seared scallops. She signed the check and went to her suite. Hope hadn't had a single PTSD dark spell since she'd arrived in this magical city and immersed herself in the art galleries and nature's scenery. She'd heard no sounds of explosives and planes overhead, had no flashes of children's bodies strewn along the rice field near her devastated orphanage, no images of Hope running from the terror of the sounds of war around her. There had been peace in her mind.

She'd booked a flight home Sunday early afternoon. Hope thought that would give her all day Saturday to luxuriate in the arts of Sausalito. The time change and the excitement of the day were taking their toll. She pulled the ivory satin cover back, slipped into the silky sheets, and tucked herself into bed.

Hope wished she could share her news with Dominique, her father, Shiloh, and the entire team. She missed them all. But with a little more research, she might have more satisfying news to share, and according to their itinerary, the Uplift team was in transit with more supplies to the Bosnian border. Anyway, she kept telling herself she'd be in Dominique's arms in three days. If she were to be able to handle the fears, she had to push them away and not let her worries overtake her life. She couldn't emotionally survive his being overseas if she didn't cling to the positive. Right now, good things were happening, Hope thought. She would spend every waking moment sketching and painting the irresistible, dramatic scenery of the city.

The phone rang as Hope was sketching her memories of the day. Who would call her at ten o'clock? It would be 1:00 a.m. on the East Coast. She picked up her new Nokia 9000. A generous donor had given them a dozen of the amazing portable phones before they were even on the shelves for the public. Wouldn't technology change things in the field now that phones were becoming more portable? She pulled up the antennae and answered.

"*Bonjour*, Hope."

"*Bonjour*, Jolie. How are you?" Hope did the math. It must be 7 a.m. "Is everything alright, dear?"

Jolie's words were broken on the crackling line.

"Jolie? Can you say that again? I missed that. We have a bad connection."

The message came through loud and clear. Dominique was not answering Jolie's calls, and she was in a panic.

What should Hope say? She couldn't lie.

Jolie told Hope she'd planned to surprise Dominique with a visit, arriving Sunday evening in Boston.

It was a double concern for Hope. Would Jolie find out he was overseas on a mission? More importantly, had something terrible happened to Dominique? After losing her husband so tragically, Hope didn't want Jolie to assume the worst. She was right where Hope had told Dominique she didn't want to be—torn between the truth and compassion for his mother.

Hope shared the news that she was in San Francisco on a case. She would pick Jolie up on Sunday and send a message to Dominique. With the time change, she would arrive in time to meet Jolie's flight.

"You have not heard from him either? I assumed you two lovers spoke every night. He has never ever not answered my calls immediately."

Gazing out at the sparkling night cityscape, Hope made a difficult decision. "Jolie, I'm happy for him. He's taken a long-deserved respite in nature for the weekend." The lie came easily; she was her father's daughter, but only when it came to covering up for a good, compassionate reason, she thought. "A strategy conference at a spa with a group from one of their partner charitable organizations." Hope gave the story a noble cause. Where did that come from? "I think they weren't supposed to take their phones." OK, there was the lie she didn't want to tell, swore she wouldn't, but she couldn't leave Jolie with any doubt that Dominique was fine. And she needed to buy time. Was he fine?

Hope distracted Jolie with the story of the missing girl and her progress in the investigation. Jolie seemed to relax. "I'll see you Sunday, Jolie. Have a safe trip."

As Hope hung up, she could feel the shift to her worrier-self. Her jaw clenched. Running her hands through her hair, she took tension-cleansing breaths and dialed Dominique's phone. It would be a little after 7 a.m. in Bosnia. He should be just getting up. No answer.

She called her father's line. No answer. Shiloh was a dead end, too. Don't panic, Hope told herself. It wasn't uncommon to have trouble getting through to them when they were in the middle of an overseas assignment. She would have to wait until dawn to check in with Angie at the office.

THE INDUSTRIAL Center Building at Gate 5 Road in the Marin ship district was easy to find. Hope's eyes scanned the high-arching roofline of the enormous metal building. It was daunting. First in line to enter the annual Open House of the ICB Artists Association, she was handed a brochure by a fashionable woman with telltale speckles of blue paint on her long denim skirt. The brochure said the ICB building housed over a hundred artists' studios—a place where Bay area artists could rent gallery space and immerse themselves in the work they loved under one iconic roof.

Hope could feel the energy of the ICB artists as the visitors flooded in. Three stories of artists' studios to explore, she was in heaven. She'd had no response from her team since last night. This was the perfect distraction.

Her little pencil sketches and charcoal and watercolor works seemed like something created by a kindergartener compared to the art pieces she'd admired. Maybe Hope's naive works were just the beginning. As she wandered and wondered, she overheard snippets of conversations about commissioning works, the artists' creative processes, lessons, and purchases. Hope was captivated. Something important was taking root inside her. She'd always craved more time to focus on her art.

The brochure explained that the building was part of a large shipbuilding complex during WWII. She laughed at its old nickname, the "Mold Loft." It had been where templates and mock-ups were made to fabricate the raw steel for the Liberty Ships, she read. When Hope passed a sculptor doing a demonstration at the entrance to his studio, she thought it was still the "mold loft" as his hands pressed the clay into the shape of an old ship. Such history, from war to art.

On the second floor, Hope stopped to admire landscape paintings reminiscent of her country of birth. Rice fields, dramatic mountains ensconcing ancient temples, colorful and captivating countryside scenes of winding rivers and villages. Sometimes, Hope had vague memories of a thatched-roofed house on piles in a rural village. She'd assumed they were remembrances of pictures she'd seen in a book. Her father had only shared some of his recollections on that one precious night parked in front of the Ketchums' house in Glynn.

Hope wished he could be more open, but she understood he was protecting Kate . . . and himself. Moving closer, she read the description on the wall beside the painting. *Scenes of my homeland. Vietnam.*

"May I help you, miss? Do you also have fond memories of Vietnam, perhaps?" The slender woman stared at Hope and then gazed at the painting in silence.

Hope wondered what she was thinking. "I assume these are yours." Hope waited for the woman to respond.

The artist took in a quick breath. "Oh, sorry, you look so much like someone I know. Yes, the artworks are mine." The woman glanced up and was clearly stunned by Hope's blue eyes.

"I was just admiring your work." Moving inside the studio, Hope studied the portraits on the far wall. "These are wonderful. Did you start out in nature scenes?"

"Yes, I began painting these scenes from memories of my homeland but turned to portraits for my customers here."

Wandering through the gallery, Hope was fascinated with the artist's technique of blurring the background. "I've recently started doing charcoal and watercolors. I mean, as a hobby, of course. Your technique makes the faces come alive."

"Thank you. I'm humbled. So, you're an artist, too? From your briefcase, I would say you wear two hats?" The woman then launched into Vietnamese.

Hope thought it was natural the artist would assume she would speak her language.

"Oh, I'm so sorry, I don't speak my native tongue. I was raised by my American family in Boston since I was three. And truly, I'm just an amateur, a doodler. I work for a charitable foundation."

The conversation, the exquisite scenery, and the faces in the portraits reminded her of Hope's search for her Lê family. She'd been so focused on the Frances Carlisle case that she'd put aside her biological family search. Jeremy was still working on that for her. He'd said that so far, he had no further information other than them landing in the Presidio in San Francisco.

"I'd love to see them sometime. I do give lessons in portraiture."

"I'm not from here. I live on the East Coast. I'm staying at the Four Seasons until Sunday's flight home." Hope paused. "I have a few pieces of my work in my briefcase." Why not? She could get some hints to improve her work. As she'd toured the facility, she'd seen many people showing their amateur work to the artists. Hope took out two of her charcoal and watercolors of the dramatic scenes from her office window in Boston and pencil portraits of Ernie and Mary.

"My apologies. I'm Lê Murray Linh. You can call me Linh."

"Oh, I'm also a Lê—Hope Lê Ketchum-James."

"We share one of the most common family names, don't we? Lê? Then, we must be related."

They both laughed.

"Yes, we're the 'Smiths' of America. Please call me Hope."

While Linh studied her works, Hope wandered through the studio, nervous about the talented artist's feedback. Without formal training beyond her high school art classes and Hope's ongoing hobby at the foundation, Hope felt silly even considering it. She hadn't come very far from those first sketches on the cardboard Cheerios box, but the instinct to create had been there from the beginning. Some kind of urge to express. She'd gone from pencil to charcoal to a watercolor and charcoal combination. There had been little time for the outdoor acrylic paintings she would love to create. Most importantly, taking a lesson would keep Hope's mind off Dominique, his mother, and the team.

"Do you have free time today to give me a lesson? Maybe later in the day? I leave tomorrow. I need to get the ferry back to the Four Seasons by five-thirty."

Linh returned from her worktable as a young man entered the studio. "I'll be right with you, sir."

She returned the artwork to Hope. "I'm sorry, Hope, I don't, but your works truly show promise. Not everyone can do good portraiture. And the . . . what shall I call it? The soul of your work is engaging. With a little technique, you could . . . listen, are you free tonight? I live in the Embarcadero area, walking distance from your hotel. Why not an evening lesson? I don't usually teach from home, but I follow my instincts."

Linh was just the person she needed to spend time with tonight—kind, calm, and creative.

"Won't I be disturbing your family?"

"We just moved into our own space. My American husband, John, couldn't adjust to Vietnamese American-style, multi-generational family living. We are down to two generations now. We have two sons. Brad is eight, and John Jr. is twelve. Their father is taking the boys to a basketball game tonight. Perhaps it's perfect timing."

"How did you feel leaving your family home, Linh?"

"I was conflicted. It was all I knew. Maybe you sacrifice privacy and some independence with a large family. Still, there are pay-offs that you don't get with many American single-family lives."

"Like what?" Hope was fascinated with how similar her own experience was with the Ketchums.

"You know you'll never be alone. You know that you will be taken care of no matter what. It's an unspoken promise you make to each other. You make that kind of promise to your ancestors' spirit. You are seen as selfish or unfilial when you break away from all that."

"You have no idea how I understand that multi-generational household. I lived with my adoptive mother's family when I was young, and it was wild and wonderful, surrounded by four generations of churchgoing, loving people. It's a culture unto itself."

"You were lucky, Hope."

"Still, I'm not sure I have the talent for art at this level. And I'm expected to work in the foundation. It's more than a job. It's my destiny to give back since I was once one of those babies."

"I understand, and the spirit of America's culture to find your own purpose battles with the past. *Lửa thử vàng, gian nan thử sức.* Fire tests gold."

"Excuse me, I'm not sure what that means?"

"Forgive me. It's an old Vietnamese proverb. You say you desire to explore your art, yet you are humble and perhaps reluctant to test yourself. The old saying translates to, *This is just a test. Believe in yourself; you will overcome this and shine bright like pure gold!* Have you ever seen a jeweler holding a flame to a gold piece to see if it is genuine? If it's real, it turns bright. If not, it turns black. Vietnamese parents often use that proverb to inspire their children to forge forth in their efforts to achieve."

"Linh, how can I resist finally knowing if I am gold as an artist? I hope I can accept the outcome." Hope felt she'd made a connection with the artist.

"We often know this answer if we are silent and listen. I believe you'll shine. Meet me at this address after dinner, at seven. Does that work?" She handed Hope a business card with an address written on the back.

Linh told Hope her story of the resistance she'd met from her entire family when she wanted to be an artist after arriving in San Francisco at fifteen. "I have met the flame and survived to shine and be myself," she said.

Moving closer to another of the paintings with a 1st place gold sticker on it, Hope read the price and her eyes flew wide open—fifteen thousand dollars.

19

THE MINIMALIST STYLE of Linh's condo allowed Hope to breathe. Neutral colors, simple, streamlined, popular style, Japanese furniture freed Hope's eyes to focus on the panoramic view of the harbor. She was grateful for the space in her life to enjoy her art unrelated to war. It struck Hope as she sat waiting for Linh to bring the tea that the cramped, viewless home of the Ketchums offered such an expansive, peaceful, loving environment. The expansive views and luxury she enjoyed in Boston had a price tag. Hope was lonely when her dad was traveling or when everyone was overseas working on a project.

Linh hadn't returned yet when Hope's phone rang. She didn't want to be rude, but it was an unusual time for anyone in her life to call. It must be something important. She had to answer.

"Honey, I know you must be worried sick." Shiloh's voice was both a comfort and a concern.

"I'm at an artist's home, so I can't talk long, but tell me, Auntie Shi, what's going on? Neither Jolie nor I have heard from

Dominique, and his mother's coming into Logan International tomorrow evening. Is everything—"

"Hope, listen, listen. I don't have much time. Our plane, filled with our last run of supplies, is ready for take-off." Shiloh explained that the border had been closed with Dominique at the distribution site with the others, leaving Shiloh and Michael on the outside looking in.

"Wait! My *dad* is with you? Oh, Auntie Shiloh, more to worry about."

"Hope, he's fine. We have no access to the country. No ability to bring in the supplies. Things are tense across the border. I'll keep you informed when I can. The current plan is to bring these supplies to another project in the region and head home."

"Tell Dad I love him, please. But Dominique and the others, are they OK? What's going to happen?" Hope trembled.

"There is no action in the area. All NGOs were told to evacuate. There is a helicopter ready to bring them out. Don't worry. Flights have been arranged."

"Don't worry? That's a tough assignment, Auntie Shiloh. What do I do about Jolie? I'll have to tell her, right? I can't continue to lie. She'll hate me for that."

"Let's see how fast we can get him home. You need to stay calm. I'll call you when we get to the next stop. We may be heading directly home from there, OK? Gotta go, honey."

Linh came in with the tea.

"I suppose you heard that?" Hope gathered her things into her briefcase.

"Only your side of the conversation, of course. Based on your face, it was not good news. Can I help?" She sat next to Hope. "What can I do for you?"

"Nothing, really. It seems my fiancé is in Bosnia with the border closed. I'm sure everything will be fine. May I use your powder room?"

"Of course, it's down the hallway to the right."

In the hallway, a framed newspaper article stopped Hope. It was the same photo that had drawn the attention of the Nguyen couple in Hope's office. The same one in which they'd identified their friends and neighbors.

Next to the photo along the hallway were five painted portraits. Hope examined the five familiar faces of the family climbing up the makeshift stairway that led to the helicopter on the tower above them. She had a blown-up version in her office. Hope knew those faces. When investigating the Frances Carlisle case, she'd studied each with a magnifying glass. Was this an art project Linh had won an award for? Some assignment from the government? The military, maybe?

Hope looked in the mirror after splashing her face with water to calm herself. She'd studied Post Traumatic Stress Disorder when her flashes of fear returned after taking the job at the foundation. Hope knew it was more common after traumas like combat and sexual assault. Still, she didn't realize it could come and go or even resurrect many years later like it had lately.

How much more could she take of the hatred in the world and the terrifying images that her job constantly brought into her life? Was the job she thought was so noble ever going to let her stop being that child running along the rice field with the roaring sounds of the plane overhead? Or contain the images of her mother's violent death she'd read about in Kate's journal? Hope already had the backdrop from her own experiences as a child. It wasn't hard to picture a beautiful woman in the same chaos. Would the same terrible happening take the man she loved away from her like Hope's mother was ripped from Michael's and her life? Some bizarre repeat performance?

She blew out a tense breath, gathered herself, and returned to the living room. "Linh, the portraits in the hallway? Was that an art project, or . . ."

There was a heavy silence in the room as Linh left the sofa and stood by the window. "Those are portraits of my family, the day we—"

"Your *family*? Lê?

She spun around to face Hope. "Yes, the famous photo that was spread around the news was the last military helicopter out of Saigon from the American Embassy. I was fifteen. We were lucky."

"And you came to the Presidio?" *Linh*, the name had seemed familiar from the start. Then, the Nguyen's list of the Lê family members as they climbed the stairs to the evacuation helicopter came back to Hope. The second oldest daughter, Linh. And yes, she was beautiful.

"Yes. My parents and two brothers. They were seventeen and twelve. Fortunately, my father had powerful connections, and we came directly to San Francisco. We weren't held in a refugee camp." Linh looked down the hallway. "I had another sibling, but she disappeared. We don't know where. She was a professor, and we lived in a village an hour from the University. Her coworker said she left one day and didn't return to her teaching job. We have no idea where she went. It was the peak of the war. Everything was in chaos, so we were never able to investigate properly. My family thought her boyfriend might have had something to do with it. But he left our area and was fighting in a hot spot, unfortunately. We had left, and we never heard from him again."

Hope ran her fingers through her hair and her lips trembled. "Her boyfriend?"

"What's wrong, Hope?"

"Michael? Was her boyfriend's name *Michael*? A Marine?"

"Yes, but how do you know that?" Linh put her hands on her hips.

"He's my . . . she's . . . I mean, she was . . . oh, God, you're my aunt." The emotion was too much. She'd embraced her romantic fantasy of finding her family for so many years. Now, it brought unexpected pain.

Hope felt like her stomach would erupt. Her elation was dampened by the loss of her mother and her fears about Dominique and the team's safety. Too much.

Linh was frozen in front of the casement window. "Who are you? Is this some kind of scam, a joke? Are you with the press?" Linh backed away and reached for the phone on the desk.

"Hằng, her name was Hằng. My mother."

"Hằng had *no* children. Who are you? How did you know my sister's name?"

"She was pregnant with me when she went to find my father on the battlefield. I was born only minutes before . . . I can't believe—" Hope dropped her face into her hands. "Wait." Opening her purse, Hope took out her wallet and removed the photo of her father and Hope when she'd first arrived at the Ketchums' home at nearly four-years-old.

"Michael. We loved Michael. He survived?" Linh went limp against the window. They both were overwhelmed by the realization. "I'm so sorry. It's just so unexpected." Linh threw her arms around Hope. "I can't believe it." Her voice quivered as she took Hope by the hand. "Come with me."

Hope followed. She was numb and weak, shuddering with the realization that she'd found her family.

At the end of the hallway, Linh turned left and led Hope into an art studio. On the wall was a portrait. It was like looking in a mirror for Hope, a self-portrait.

"This is your mother, Hằng, as I remembered her. I painted her when I arrived in San Francisco." Linh examined the painting and then studied Hope's face. "If not for your blue eyes, the resemblance is striking. She was quite beautiful. As are you. I'm . . . stunned. My family still holds on to the dream that she will show up on our doorstep someday."

They stood together, unmoving in their disbelief. Hope held back the news of Hằng's tragic death for a moment. She would have thought the family had discovered the truth somehow.

"Hope, you must meet our family, *your* family. It's not too late. They will all still be up, and it can't wait. Do you agree?"

Hope's words came out in a monotone. "But will I shame my mother's memory? The pregnancy? Won't it be too much for my mother's parents—my grandparents—to learn how she died giving birth to her illegitimate child? To hear of the terrible way in which she died . . . with no evidence of their daughter being left behind."

"Died? You know this?" Linh fell back against the wall.

"My father witnessed it minutes after I was born. He'd never discussed it, but I learned it from my stepmother. I'm so sorry. I thought you would have learned the truth by now. I know so little. Please forgive me."

Linh drew in a deep breath. The only sound was a grandfather clock ticking at the end of the hallway. Her voice was somber. "You are the evidence and very much alive. A miracle. A gift."

"I'm so sorry to bring the sad news. I had no idea. I'm so overwhelmed to finally find my family. But then my thrilling news is such sad news for your family. And add to that, I'm Hằng's illegitimate child."

"Oh, Hope it was not uncommon in the war. Emotions ran high. Tens of thousands of American soldiers left babies and pregnant women behind. There are more important things here. Your grandparents have received an unexpected gift from their eldest daughter from the beyond."

Hope was so conflicted. These weren't thoughts she'd ever considered before. The search had always been about finding the people to whom she'd first belonged. Why was she suddenly feeling ashamed about her start in life? She was illegitimate, a love child who was abandoned for three years. And with her came the news of her mother's death. Certainly, it had nothing to do with her. But she didn't want her mother or Michael judged either. It was knowing the Catholic culture and societal attitude about sex before marriage and pregnancy out of wedlock that shifted her perspective.

"I'll leave a note for my husband. Let's go. Tonight, you meet your family, four generations, all in one home. And tomorrow morning, I'll give you a tour of our family history before your flight." Linh moved closer to Hope. "I confess, I'm not a hugger type, but may I?"

Hope felt faint. She nodded. Her tears finally let go as they embraced. Hope had no words but a thousand questions.

20

WASN'T IT INSPIRING that Linh had met with such success as a Vietnamese American artist from a simple village in Vietnam, Hope thought. As they drove up Pacific Avenue in Linh's black Mercedes, Hope imagined the rural village family arriving in the US. How had they survived not speaking English and starting all over? Linh had said they were some of the earliest arrivals in 1975—the first wave. There had been no Little Saigon or Vietnamese community established back then for a sense of belonging. Only a few Vietnamese families were around to share their traditions and teach new immigrants about America. Did any of them speak English? Hope's early life had been so easy in comparison. She fidgeted with the lock on her briefcase. Had she ever been more nervous? Well, maybe when meeting Jolie. No, there was even more at stake here.

She had to keep her worries about Dominique, the team, and Jolie's arrival under emotional lockdown to survive the evening. Talking felt easier than thinking about the family's reaction to her. And had she dressed too fancy? Hope turned her diamond engagement ring around. She should have left it in the safe, but it felt like bad luck to take it off. "Linh, you said your family was against you pursuing art as a career?"

"Art wasn't what they wanted for their children after coming to America," Linh explained that her family had dreams for their children, fantasies of becoming a doctor or an engineer and for their only remaining daughter to become educated and settle in to expand their three-generation clan to four. "I must say my success was a surprise to them. Excuse me for saying this, but my income exceeds my brothers' salaries. I try to keep that under wraps." Linh glanced quickly at Hope, an edgy look that said, *please don't mention that price tag you saw on my painting today.*

Yearning to know more about her mother almost overcame Hope, but she held back. Wasn't it too soon for Linh? "You mentioned leaving the family home was difficult." Her conflicted feelings on the day Hope had left Glynn at six-years-old to move to the mansion in Boston invaded her body, and she hugged herself. "When my stepmother became successful, they wanted to give me the best schools, so we moved into an affluent area in Boston. It meant leaving my grandparents' home where I'd spent my first three years after arriving in the US."

"That wasn't my Grands' dream either, but we needed our own space. John . . . well, let's say he felt lost in the crowd, although he was accepted. Fortunately, he was the same religion. That helped. But, once we had the two babies, he wanted our own home and didn't think it suited our boys either." Linh glanced at Hope. "I believe the elders are used to our absence now."

"Was it a big deal to marry an American? And am I being too intrusive? I have so much I want to know about my family and birth culture. Well, and, of course, my mother." She turned to Linh. "I'll never forget how you stared at me and looked away when I arrived. I often get that response to my blue eyes. I never thought it was my resemblance to my mother. I admit, it's striking."

They stopped at a red light. Linh closed her eyes. Her moment of silence was unnerving for Hope. "If not for your blue eyes, you could be my sister. Your face, your size, your expressions. The way you bite back a fluttering laugh. It's uncanny. Makes me want to cry. At the same time, it makes me strangely happy." Linh reached over and touched Hope's hand. "I'm not exactly in the habit of bringing strangers home for lessons. But I wanted to get to know you. To keep my sister's look-alike with me for just a little longer. I thought I was being silly. Maybe her spirit was speaking to me."

Linh's profile showed her pain. Her lips were pressed together and quivering. "Your resemblance to Hằng is stunning. It's heartbreaking yet somehow comforting. Like having a piece of her back here with me again." She looked at Hope, and a warm smile won out in the tender moment.

Waves of realization swept over Hope, shining a light on her relationship with her father. Her understanding unfolded. The two sides of the way he looked at Hope now had meaning. The sentimental smiles, even joy that erupted on his handsome face, and the tears that sometimes edged his eyes when Hope came home from being away. She was a constant reminder of his true love. No wonder he couldn't let Hope go. No wonder he wanted her near and working for the foundation. Of course, he loved Hope for herself, but there was a powerful reason he'd cultivated that purpose inside her since childhood—to keep her nearby.

Gazing out the window, Hope noticed the area was changing.

They were driving through a less affluent area. The buildings were weary with age. People were hanging on the streets wrapped in blankets. It made her sad to think of Linh's family's early struggles. And wasn't Linh the successful "Kate" in the family? And Hope's mother, Hằng, was a professor in a simple village family. She must have made them proud to see her rise above like that.

"Many Vietnamese girls I went to school with married American guys, so that wasn't a shock." Linh took another turn. "I'm taking another route to the Tenderloin, Little Saigon. When we arrived in the US, only a few Vietnamese families were there. We'd met them on the flights and in the Presidio while we were being processed. The families still get together for holidays, like *Tet*." Linh turned again, driving through a street with a string of small Vietnamese cafés, noodle shops, and corner stores, all with Vietnamese names on the windows. Then she turned down a steep hill.

"So, let's see. You were three-years-old when you arrived in the US in nineteen seventy-three, and I was fifteen when I immigrated in nineteen seventy-five. So that makes me ten years older. And I'm your aunt. Funny. It feels more like we're sisters. You had a multi-generational upbringing. What was your household like, Hope? And why do I feel so comfortable talking to you?"

"We're family. I love how open you are, Linh. Is that usual in your culture? I mean, in *our* family?" The word "family" made Hope smile.

"From being in the arts, I guess. Years of deep conversation about our techniques and the emotions we were trying to capture in our paintings and complimenting each other's work. One artist at the ICB called everyone sweetheart and darling. That was strange for me. Discussions with other artists go deep. That caused even more excavating of myself. I was constantly asked questions like, 'What did you feel when you decided to paint this?' Things like that. In time, those years in the ICB enculturated me. In some ways, the more I adjusted outside the home, the less I fit in at home with my Grands."

"I like that expression, Grands. A good plural that covers all the senior generations."

Linh stopped at a red light. "Funny, sometimes I relate more to the younger generation in my outlook and cultural habits."

"Shoemaking didn't bring out deep conversations in the Ketchum family." Hope laughed.

"In our culture, when you break away from all the family traditions, you are seen as selfish or unfilial. Over time, I think they've forgiven me. Especially since I finished my education and became successful in my field. Oh, here's one. We still worship our ancestors. We light incense and pray to the generations long gone. That's to say, we talk to ghosts. We connected with the spirit of Hằng on holidays like *Tết*, our Lunar New Year, wherever she was. We didn't assume, but it left things up in the air. Just a little more insight for you, Hope."

"I suspect I have a lot to learn." Hope liked the unexpected openness that was developing between them. Was Linh to be another Auntie Shiloh in her life?

There was a span of silence. "Hard to believe I'm sitting next to my big sister Hằng's daughter. I still miss her." Linh turned toward Hope in the darkened car, and a streetlight illuminated her tearful eyes. "My family won't know what to say."

"I don't know what to say either. I'm worried that my coming into their lives will make the memory of their daughter an open wound again. And open mine deeper. But finding my roots is something I've dreamed of for as long as I can remember. To answer your question about my Ketchum family—lots of *doing* for you, not a lot of sharing of emotions. But you knew they were there behind the wall. They cheered me on through my education, though they'd never had the chance."

Staring out the window, Hope thought of her loving upbringing and acceptance. Grandma Cecelia, Uncle Jack, Ernie, Mary, all her aunts and uncles, cousins, and neighbors. "Thirty-seven relatives all living within two blocks, all pitching in to make life work. They were factory workers, skilled craftsmen, and cordwainers making handmade shoes and proud of it. It's hard to explain my own culture now that I think about it, Linh. Oh, and lots of kidding around."

Hope went on about her Vietnamese roots, the mysteries of her mother's death, and her father's reluctance to unfold those secrets until recently. "He still suffers from those memories of the war." Drifting off, Hope replayed the rare exchange with her father in the car outside Grandma Cecelia and Grandpa Kevin's home. The familiar kitchen welcome filled Hope's mind. "More like, *Sweetheart, how are you? Sit, and I'll make you a cup of tea* kind of love. Not many words like, I love you, but I felt deeply loved."

"Sounds familiar, without the 'sweetheart' part," Linh said. "I'm not sure I've ever heard those 'I love you' words at home, either. Although I felt loved. And humor is a different thing for each generation. You'll see. And we never talk about the war or the past. And we're only fifteen family members. Hope, that makes fifty-two family members you have now."

"Linh, I still don't know much about your sister . . . my mother."

"And I still don't know what my father was doing for the

Americans, but it did secure us passage on that precious flight out of Saigon in the final hours. Limited communication about the past."

"Are you sure you're not Irish?" Hope heard Linh's small pop of laughter and smiled.

"Funny. By the way, my grandparents only speak Vietnamese at home. In fact, my whole family does. So, I'll translate for you. Although everyone speaks English to varying degrees, we uphold the tradition. My nephew's and niece's generation won't speak Vietnamese. So, you're good there. It's the ultimate mix of cultures. Oh, and French works for the older gen, too."

"I speak French. That's a relief."

"Well, there's history there with the French, too. A political divide from the past. But not to worry."

The winding ride around the city's side streets from Linh's apartment building was only a few miles, but it felt like a lifetime. Hope imagined the four generations crowded into a small, run-down home near Little Saigon or some small enclave struggling to rise, which the Vietnamese apparently knew how to do.

She'd read about the Vietnamese neighborhood. It had seen better days. Of course, Linh would have helped her family. Or did the Vietnamese culture not want a daughter to contribute financially? She knew so little about the culture of her own people. It was awkward. She'd assumed they were Buddhist. It would have been surprising that Linh had met and married a Buddhist American. Hope felt her questions were getting too personal.

"Ketchum, you said. It's not a name I hear often. Are you re-lated to Kate Ketchum, by chance?" Linh laughed, singing part of Kate's hit song, 'Too precious to leave behind.' "Just kidding."

"Yes. She's my adoptive mother." Kate had worked hard to keep

Hope out of the news to protect her and give her life some privacy. In school, Hope had only used Lê James. And who would guess a Vietnamese girl would be Kate Ketchum's daughter? Later, it had leaked out and some of Hope's college and law school classmates knew about her relationship to Kate.

"Very funny." Linh held an imaginary mic and sang the lyrics again. "Too precious to leave behind."

"No, seriously." Hope giggled like a naughty child.

Linh's incredulous look was also precious.

"Oh my God, Hope. Michael is married to Kate Ketchum?" Linh nearly really ran into a delivery truck. "Oh, wait until my family finds out. They love her. I love her."

"I think we have enough shocking news. Let's hold off on that for a bit, OK?"

"I agree. OK, so this is the Pacific Heights area. You'll get to know the city soon. I mean, I assume you will be a regular visitor now that you are family."

They stopped in front of a magnificent Classic Revival Mansion on an upscale street in Pacific Heights. Hope stretched her neck to view the four-story sky-high corner residence.

"Where are we?"

"Home. They just finished a renovation."

Hope's face flushed with embarrassment from the stereotypic projections she'd been imposing on her family's situation. Poor Vietnamese immigrants struggling to survive in America. Not quite. Or at least not two decades later.

"It was built in nineteen-oh-six. My parents like modern, so imagine what it took. They hired the Decorators Showcase to make it their own. The designers called it 'timeless luxury' with modern living." Linh turned off the engine, and they sat looking up at the stunning home with its iconic front entrance and circular temple-style white marble portico.

"Hope, you look surprised. My father worked with the Americans for years as a cross-cultural adviser to the military, so he adapted fast here. He was a Sociology professor and a PhD foreign student at Harvard in his day. Then he made some, shall we say, *special* friends in the US government. He would never discuss it. Your mother was a Sociology professor. She loved to think all the students she put out into the world were helping people."

"That says a lot about her." Hope loved hearing about her mother's passions.

"We'll talk more, sweetheart." Linh reached over and touched Hope's arm. "Anyway, back to my father. Whatever he did to help facilitate the US was significant. As you can see, my father made some lucky investments when he arrived in America, too."

"I'm embarrassed to admit I made some naive assumptions since I arrived in San Francisco, Linh."

"Yes, that's a common American mistake. Like our family, the first wave of refugees were mostly the privileged ones who worked with the Americans—doctors, lawyers, and such. It was later the villagers arrived."

"Yes, I knew that, but my father said your family lived in a simple village."

"Our family lived undercover for a year when things got tough at the war's end. I don't know any more than that. We had a lovely home near the American Embassy, and one day, we were moved to that thatched hut. When Michael came along, we had to keep up the front. He never questioned why my sister was a professor from a poor village family. That made us smile back then. I don't know why my parents didn't stop her from going back to the city to work. My parents were not thrilled that Hằng had hooked up with an American Marine. But they loved Michael the more they knew him. He was so sweet and tried to learn Vietnamese. He always confused the language tones and said things he didn't mean to."

"Like what?" Hope had always assumed her father was fluent. But maybe he could only keep up with a three-year-old.

"He studied hard. Now we know he was driven by love, right? And by the way, we thought he was a simple guy from America. We had no idea he was affluent, either. His Vietnamese was good enough to communicate and bad enough to cause a lot of good-hearted laughter when he screwed up regularly." Linh smiled. "*Wrong tone, Michael*, my sister said once. *GI, you said butter instead of walk*. Hope, I cried when his orders took him away. We had no idea Hằng was pregnant. She was back at school teaching for the entire school year. We thought Michael was long forgotten."

Hope couldn't keep her eyes off the unexpected mansion.

"Let's go meet your family, Hy Vọng."

21

AS THEY WALKED up the long stone staircase, Hope thought she might have been more comfortable if the Lê family had been a simple middle-class family like the Ketchums. She was used to affluence, but this was fairy-princess-land, and the richer the people, the more complicated the dynamics, she'd found.

"Here's what you will see upstairs this time of night." Linh looked up at the top of the home. "The great-grandparents will be reading; my parents will be rustling through the San Francisco Chronicle; my siblings and their wives will be seated by the windows talking politics; and the kids will be watching some TV show that the elders disapprove of because it's either too violent or too mindless. They would rather they were doing homework or something productive. That's the big picture. Oh, and we still follow the tradition of removing our shoes when we enter the house."

"Funny. Some things are universal. Thanks, that helps." Hope admired the contemporary decor as they moved through the parlor—the glamorous period details from the home's rich design heritage remained, including wood paneling, beamed ceilings, wrought-iron balusters on the sweeping central staircase with a stained-glass skylight overhead.

"This is stunning, Linh."

"There are beautiful views of the Bay and Alcatraz from the top floor family room and terrace, too. Let's start there. Everyone should be up there now. It's tradition. My parents' bedroom overlooks the bay. The four levels work. Each family gets its own living space, but we spend all our meals and evenings in the upper main level together. That part that made my husband John feel uncomfortable and fenced in."

They rode the elevator in silence and exited on the fourth floor. Against the backdrop of floor-to-ceiling windows, the grand scale formal living and dining room were open to a beautiful eat-in kitchen.

Hope held her breath at the sight of the backs of the heads of her future family. They were seated right in front of her, the people she'd wanted to know her entire life.

Just as Linh had described, Hope observed the elders reading books in their comfortable chairs while listening to low-volume music. The emotionally charged sound was familiar—like the music she'd heard in a Vietnamese restaurant in Boston, light and lyrical with enchanting flutes and zithers. Linh's parents sat reading the San Francisco Chronicle, and the younger family members watched TV at the far end of the panoramic room.

Four adults who looked to be in their thirties or forties were chatting in a group of low-profile modern chairs. They were Hope's uncles and their wives, she assumed by age and process of elimination. On the balcony, spotlights shined on the dramatic

San Francisco Bay and Alcatraz backdrop. There was still time to escape.

As Hope scanned the group, she realized meeting them felt far more uncomfortable than her introduction to Jolie.

Linh cleared her throat. "Children, turn down the TV and come over here, please. Everyone! We have an important and unexpected gift."

"Who's *that*?" A young boy came across the room and stared at Hope. "Hi."

"Wait just a second, and I'll tell you." Linh signaled for him to sit on the floor with the rest of the children.

The silence was shattered by gasps and muttering among the adults as they turned and caught sight of Hope. The eldest of the family was caught by a younger man as she slumped to the floor, feinting from the apparition. Oh, yes, the generational split in their reactions made sense. How had Hằng reappeared at nearly the same age she'd disappeared?

When Hope lifted her gaze from the floor to their faces, there was a communal reaction to her blue eyes. Then the group of adults looked out over the glass view of the bay, the floor, the children, or their fingernails—anywhere to avoid eye contact with Hope.

Linh put her arm around Hope. It took Hope a few seconds to realize how surreal it must be for them to see the ghost of their beloved Hằng appearing in their home after two decades, unchanged, with no signs of aging. An awkwardness spread through the room. Hope would have to remember that when meeting someone who knew her mother in the past.

"Everyone, I don't know how to say this more gently . . . this is Hope Lê Ketchum-James, Hằng's daughter. She goes by Hope. She was born in Vietnam on the day our dear Hằng died.

She's Michael's daughter. There's a photo that might help you to believe this stunning news." Linh first passed the photo to the eldest couple, her great-grandparents, who'd both sat down after her great-grandmother's near-fainting spell. Each family member gave Hope a quick glance as they studied the photo, and a second stream of vocalizations in Vietnamese and French spread throughout the room. They moved closer to each other, hugging or holding hands.

"Hope, this is your family." Linh introduced Hope's great-grandparents, grandparents, two uncles and their wives, two nephews and a niece, and the children of Linh's brothers.

Hope's awkwardness from being on display and causing such emotional reactions made her want to run. The family's tension was palpable as they waited for Linh to continue.

Silence.

The group looked at each other, then at Linh as though searching for a sign of understanding or trying to absorb the double-edged news.

"Forgive me, but I just met Hope today myself. Please welcome your lovely new great-granddaughter, our new family member. I know the news has two sides, such sadness over the news of Hằng's death, but maybe for Hope and Hằng's sake, we should focus on our blessing. She is from Boston and works for a children's charity. You might know this organization, Uplift Children's Foundation. Michael is the Chairman of the Board. He started it in Hằng's honor."

It wasn't the first time someone had to sell Hope to someone. She suspected the reception would not be like Jolie's. In the background were continued murmurs in Vietnamese, muffled crying, and the familiar low soundtrack of Star Trek on the TV.

Appropriate music, Hope thought; she felt she was in outer space. Losing herself in the mundane to escape her apprehension, Hope eyed the clean, modern lines of the furnishings—stainless steel appliances, white marble countertops, and black cabinetry with an enormous refrigerator like the ones she'd only seen in restaurants. The scent of their dinner still graced the air. Unfamiliar but appealing. The distraction didn't work. The message seemed clear to her. Turning to Linh, Hope spoke softly. "Maybe this wasn't a good idea, Linh. I think I should go." Hope turned to leave.

"Hope it's not you. The family's overwhelmed with emotion, and they're conflicted. They're saying they're so happy to have found you, but honestly, the happy news comes paired with their loss." Linh lowered her voice. "They're having a hard time regarding Michael. They're angry and blame him for abandoning Hằng and their child. Without the nuance of the story, it's the easiest place to put their pain, it seems."

"Wait, please." Linh's brother stepped forward. "Hope, it's a pleasure. I'm your uncle. Please call me Tuân. We're just in shock. Forgive us, but it was as if Hằng had reappeared and was standing right in front of us. The resemblance is stunning. She was deeply loved."

"Uncle Tuân is a doctor at UCSF Medical Center," Linh said.

"It's wonderful to meet you, sir . . . Uncle Tuân." Hope wished she'd studied Vietnamese customs and manners when meeting and greeting family. She should have prepared for this so she wouldn't make a cultural blunder and offend without intent.

The group continued to respond, from tears to silence.

Uncle Tuán's youngest son snaked around his leg and Tuán again broke the tension that hung in the room. "This is my wife,

Anh, and our two sons, Long and Nam. Say hello to your Aunt Hope, boys."

They gazed up at her and then looked down with embarrassment. The youngest giggled. The older boy punched him. "Ow!"

Hope knew what was coming from their familiar expression. "Daddy, why are her eyes blue?"

"Don't be rude, Nam. And this is our daughter, Hong. She's embraced her American culture, as you can see."

Hong looked down at her black baby doll T-shirt and cargo pants, sighed, and shrugged, looking to Hope for support.

There was no way Hope would fall into that generational gap by weighing in on the teen's style. "Hello, Hong."

The teenage girl took over. "Why is everyone acting so weird? Lots of people have blue eyes. Hi, Hope, I'm Hong. Cool shoes, Hope. This is amazing. I have a new cousin."

"Thank you, Hong." The awkwardness still hung in the air, but Hong's relaxed all-American style made Hope slightly optimistic.

Linh crossed the room, and the older adults huddled together as she spoke in low tones in Vietnamese. Linh's gestures and body language told Hope she was sharing all the news with them—Michael, Hằng's death, and Hope's rescue. Linh's pleading gestures said she was trying to reason with them.

Hope had nowhere to look. The Grand's eyes were downcast all around her. Was it from their resurrected memories of Hằng? On the side wall, Hope saw a large crucifix with a sprig of palms propped behind it. A similar cross hung on the Ketchums' wall. "Excuse me, are you Catholic?" She addressed Uncle Tuân.

"Yes, we all are, for many generations. We carry on the tradition. And you?"

"Yes, I'm Catholic. My father and adoptive family are all

devout Catholics." Hope reached inside the collar of her dress and pulled out the gold cross she'd worn since childhood when Grandma Cecelia had given it to her for her first Holy Communion celebration.

"Would you join us for a nine o'clock Mass tomorrow if you are still in town? It might help us to bond." He winked and flashed his eyes toward the elders.

"I'd love to." Some of the family members overheard Uncle Tuân's invitation. With Hope's acceptance to attend Mass, the eldest woman stepped away from the others and spoke French to Hope as Linh had predicted. Linh had obviously led the way, telling them Hope could speak the official imposed language of Vietnam.

"*Bonsoir, Mademoiselle Hope. Voulez-vous une tasse de thé?*" The woman smiled hesitantly, then returned to her husband's side.

Linh nodded in encouragement, and Hope answered. "*Bonsoir, madam. J'aimerais une tasse de thé, Merci.* Good evening, madam. I would love a cup of tea, thank you." She repeated in English for the children's sake. Or had they learned French as well? Hope was at a loss.

Linh's second brother, Long, introduced himself and his wife, Bình.

An older man in a suit and tie approached Hope. "I'm your grandfather. Forgive us. We didn't mean to . . . it's just so shocking and perhaps hurtful for us to learn about Hằng's tragic ending . . . and her secrets. But maybe we can stay with the joy of meeting you."

Hope was woozy with emotion. "I understand. I'm sure it's awkward and painful for everyone." She was touched to know how much they loved her mother and sad that their shining memories of the Marine they'd embraced were now tarnished.

The Grands gathered around Hope.

Grandfather Lê took Hope's hand and turned to Linh. "Yes, you're right. Hope is an unexpected gift." Then, he spoke directly to Hope. "And I understand from Linh we are both alumni of the same institution. My unexpected granddaughter is not only a blessing to our family, but she's also a Harvard lawyer. Our alma mater's motto *Veritas!* seems appropriate to the situation. The *truth* finally comes out."

22

"STAY IN TOUCH. Maybe you can return for Tet in February?" Linh pulled up to the airport curb. "And Kate is welcome too, of course. I'm teasing. That would be a dream. You must always have to deal with people's adoration of your adoptive mother."

"Yes. Fading into the background when people find out she is my adoptive mother isn't fun. I'll try to come back as soon as I can. And maybe Dominique will join me. Thank you so much, Aunt Linh. It was magical, and I'm overwhelmed by your generosity."

"Oh, and I owe you those portraiture lessons."

"I'm excited to learn from you." Not just art. There are so many cultural norms to learn, Hope thought.

"You have something special in your art, Hope. It's in our genes. And here's something special for you." Linh handed her a large, stiff envelope.

"Can I ask?"

"No, it's a secret."

That made Hope laugh. "Another one?" They both understood their histories were filled with secrets. So many secrets.

"Don't open until you are on the plane. Oh, and I think you won some points with the family at Mass when you took Holy Communion."

"Thank you. St. Boniface Church was so welcoming. I didn't expect so many Vietnamese families."

They hugged. Hope grabbed her luggage from the back seat and closed the door. "Be well. Say goodbye to everyone for me." She'd become so connected to her aunt in such a short time—Linh's creativity, sense of humor, honesty, and courage in following her path, and Hope had found her biological family—*her* family. And her mother's past. It was too much to contain. Hope stepped up on the curb and signaled Linh to roll down the window. It was a spontaneous thing, kind of a joke referring to their earlier discussion, but sincere, too. She leaned into the car window. "I meant to tell you something."

"What's that?"

"I love you, Linh."

Her aunt's reaction was rewarding. She was taken aback, then nodded her understanding and smiled. "I love you too, Hope." Her gaze lingered. "Bye, dear niece. And I'll pray for Dominique's safety. We all will."

The airport security guard waved Linh on and Hope waved goodbye.

Hope's phone rang. Juggling her belongings and the package, she managed to get inside the sliding doors and sat on a bench. "Hello." The voice she wanted to hear. "Dominique. Sweetheart, where are you?" She couldn't understand his words through the crackling line.

"Are you OK?" The line cleared.

"Yes, yes, my darling. I'm headed to New York. I hope to catch the last shuttle to Boston. I miss you."

Her every muscle went weak with relief. "Is everyone else out?"

"Yes, they are all on their way back. Michael and Shiloh may already be home."

"I have to warn you. Jolie is on her way to Boston. I'm at SFO. It's a long story. I'm picking her up this evening at Logan."

"Jolie? I was hoping we would be alone."

"I'll drop her at your house around eight. Dominique, I need to warn you. I had to tell Jolie—"

The line went dead.

THE AIRPORT windows were foggy and wet. Waiting for Jolie's delayed flight left too much time to think. Hope hadn't been able to reach Dominique again. She'd checked the shuttle schedule, and if he made the last flight, Hope would be waiting with Jolie when he arrived. No running down the hallway into his arms. And if Dominique arrived about the same time, he would take Jolie home. So, no passionate bodies celebrating their reunion in private at home as she'd fantasized.

"Hope, my dear." Jolie tapped Hope on her shoulder. "You are far away. Thinking of my son, perhaps? I'm sorry we were delayed by this nasty weather." She handed Hope her carry-on.

The gesture made Hope smile. It was so Jolie. Not an act of rudeness. Jolie just assumed the world was there to serve her. And it did. "Oh, Jolie, how are you?" Hope's two-cheek kiss felt like a signal of betrayal. And hadn't Dominique put Hope in that terrible position to protect his mother by lying to her? "Dominique's flight is due any minute. Let's sit."

As Hope set Jolie's luggage on the seat next to her, the engagement ring flashed under the lights. She pulled it off and slipped it into her briefcase. Why was everything a secret lately? Secrets withheld; secrets revealed. Hằng's secret, the engagement, Dominique's secret adventure, and all that was withheld by Michael and her new Lê family over the years. It was exhausting being on guard all the time, Hope thought. It was against her nature.

"Here he is." Jolie stepped out in front of Hope before Dominique could embrace her. Was it inadvertent, simple excitement, or competition? There was no way to warn him that Hope had lied.

"Mother, what a wonderful surprise." He kissed her on both cheeks.

Moving on, Dominique swept Hope up into his arms and spun her around. "This is what I have wanted every minute for two weeks now."

The kiss she'd missed and the relief she'd felt having him home safe shuddered through her body.

"Hope has told me of your adventure." Jolie stroked Dominique's hair back into place.

Letting go of Hope, he looked at her questioningly.

There was no stopping the train that was thundering toward Jolie. The misunderstanding was steamed up and ready to leave the station, and Hope wished she weren't there to see the collision.

"So now you keep secrets from your mother? Tell me about your adventure, please." Her tone was teasing, not threatening. "At least now I know why you weren't returning my calls."

"I knew it would worry you, Mother, so I withheld it. There was no danger expected."

"Danger is never expected, my son."

"I'm sorry, but I thought I knew how you would feel about me going into the field, especially Bosnia, with the war just ending. The most touching things I can ever remember were the looks on those children's faces as we set up the food distribution tents. And I'm here now."

Waiting for the collision of the truth and the explosion of hurt, Hope reviewed the two other news stories that she was dying to share—the engagement reveal and finding her family. The timing was terrible.

It felt like Jolie was studying both of her betrayers. "*Bosnia?* Hope, I thought you said he went to a nature preserve for a conference with another NGO."

"I didn't want you to worry. I—"

Jolie turned her back on Hope and faced Dominique.

"A nature preserve? But Hope—" Dominique's confusion sent another message to Jolie.

"You both conspired against me? But it appears you two failed to coordinate your lies." She stared at Dominique. "Your strategy to protect your old mother's feelings failed since I was terrorized when you didn't return my calls day after day." Jolie spoke to Hope without turning to look at her. "And you, Hope. I obviously read you wrong. I put my entire estate behind your dreams. And for you to lie to me . . . it is the ultimate disrespect." Jolie grabbed her carry-on and walked down the hallway toward the luggage carousel.

"Mother, wait."

"*Laisse-moi tranquille.*" Jolie spoke without turning around. Her tone said it all as the glass doors slid closed behind her.

"Leave you *alone*? You're my mother."

"Dominique, I tried to warn you about the story I told her, but the phone cut off. This was what I was concerned about. You shouldn't have concealed your plans. What do we do?"

"You said you would not lie, just downplay. My love, this fantasy you contrived about some nature conference is an outright lie."

"You're blaming *me*?"

They'd never been so cross with each other. The few times they'd disagreed, they'd built a bridge quickly. Hope was at a loss. She didn't want to referee this one; she didn't want to take the blame either. "You know her best. You should go to her, Dominique. The company driver should be waiting for you outside. I'll go home. I'm exhausted. We'll talk in the morning." Hope's anger almost stopped her, but she kissed his cheek as a token gesture, grabbed her luggage, and left through the sliding door.

She didn't want them to say more damaging things to each other. They needed to cool off, and her startling news about her family couldn't be shared in the tension-filled environment of their untenable situation. One thing at a time. He had to work this out with Jolie.

Why did Hope feel like a child? Jolie's leverage over Dominique, Hope, and the future of the One Child division of the organization had complicated things. Wasn't Hope's resentment warranted? She was being disempowered and held hostage by Jolie. It wasn't the Ketchum-James way.

23

"DAD, SO GOOD to see you." Hope entered her father's office.

"Honey, you're here early." He swung around in his office chair, leaped up, bent over, and gave her his classic big bear hug. "The team meeting isn't until nine-thirty."

"Dad, I needed to see you. I missed you. It was tense for a while there." How much should she share? The usual stunning vista out the window was blurred by a swirling snowstorm, just like her swirling mind. She hadn't slept. It was a distressing message that Dominique hadn't called after he'd left the airport.

"I know you were worried, but we were never in danger. Shiloh said she'd reached you."

"Yes, she did. Do you have a few minutes? I need to talk to you, Dad." Hope felt ridiculous deciding in what order to share all the crazy news.

"I know when you rake your hair back like that, I'm in for a surprise, right? You know by now you're safe with me." He gestured for her to sit in the guest chair across from him.

"*Surprises*, plural." She started with the positive part, revealing her trip to San Francisco, her meeting with Janine about the whereabouts of Frances' adoptive parents, and the hopeful clues she'd gathered. "So, I'd like to follow up in Rhode Island this week if that's OK." Hope thought getting out of town alone might be a good thing to let things quiet down. Give some alone time for Dominique and Jolie.

"Don't we have our investigative team for that, Hope?"

"I know we have people to do that, and the leads I've received from them in my search for Frances have real potential. They found a recent address. But I'm excited to be personally involved in this case. I feel I owe it to the Nguyens and to myself."

"Well, you've been busy while I was away, Hope. That's fantastic. The Nguyen grandparents must be thrilled with your progress. How's Jeremy doing? We've got to reconnect." Michael sat back in his leather chair, laced his hands behind his head, and smiled. "That's why you're here, honey. I knew you would end up an integral part of this gang. Yes, go ahead and do your research. It's a quiet follow-up week for all of us here. No worries. By the way, I ran into Dominique in the hallway. He looks a little worse for the wear. Maybe the border issue was too much for him. But Hope, he wasn't in danger. I hope you had a good reunion last night. Or did you see him?"

"Yes, I did, at the airport." The story of Jolie and Hope's cover-up fairytale unfolded. Hope was concerned Jolie would pull her support for Uplift One Child. She wanted to be honest with her father. "So, we need to mend some fences, I'm afraid. Dominique and I, and Jolie and the both of us. And I confess I don't know Jolie well enough to know if that can be accomplished. But there is something even more important, Dad."

"What is it? But first." He leaned forward. "I will not let anyone leverage this organization through money or any other means. Though I know this is more complicated than that with your future mother-in-law."

"Thank you. I know, Dad. And honestly, that is a concern." But not her biggest, Hope thought. She handed him the large envelope that Linh had given her before her departure.

He slid the portrait out, studied the painting, and stared at Hope; an enigmatic, frozen, far-off look.

She couldn't read his reaction. Then his eyes watered, and supporting his head with one hand, he stared at Hằng's portrait.

What memories were going through his mind? Hope waited in the aching silence.

"Where did you get this? Is this your work? How did you know what she looked like? I don't understand. Wait. Did you do this from that old photo in my safe? How did you get it?" His eyes never left the watercolor as he released the string of questions.

Sharing the story without breaking apart took every bit of strength Hope had. As her father stared out the blurred window, she told him about meeting Linh, the art gallery, the family, and the entire story about what had happened to the Lê family and their rescue before the village was bombed.

"They *survived*? Living in the village *undercover*? I never—" He shook his head and looked down in the corner of the watercolor to read the signature. Lê Murray Linh. "I always loved Hằng's little sister. She's alive." His voice was flat and somber.

"She married an American named John Murray." Hope shuffled a photo from the bottom of the envelope and handed the Polaroid of Hope with the entire Lê family taken by Linh's friend after Mass at St. Boniface Church.

A sound came from her father she'd never heard before, like a wounded gasp for air. "Dad, do you want me to give you time alone?"

"No, honey, I just need to process this. Come here."

She sat on his lap and hugged him. "Dad, they really loved you."

"They must have been stunned to learn about you, and then Hằng's . . . her ending. What did you tell them?"

"I told them everything I knew. Dad, the older generations blame you for my mother's death. For Linh, it was like seeing her sister for the first time in two decades. I didn't know how much I looked like my mother."

Her father nodded. "Yes."

"Linh had a copy of the photo of the helicopter on her wall—the one where the Nguyens identified the Lê family for me. I shared the story."

Her father's confused look forced Hope's confession. "I read it in Kate's journal. The whole story, Dad."

"What? You read Kate's journal?"

"Dad, Shiloh knew I needed to know about my mother and what happened to her. She gave me the diary. I'm sorry. And I didn't want to cause renewed pain for you." Discovering her family was alive had been a dream, a fantasy. For others, it was not. Hope was helpless to comfort her father. It felt like a betrayal to celebrate finding the Lê family with him. And how would Kate feel? Wouldn't it be threatening to resurrect the wounds they'd healed together over time? "Dad, Kate wanted me to read it. She told Shiloh."

He dropped his head.

Hope felt there was no room for hesitation. It was time to be open and truthful. "The Lês had no closure, Dad. There was no gravesite, no place to honor their daughter. They didn't know if their daughter was still alive or—" Hope paused. "They've been suspended between hope and despair, waiting years to learn the truth. I had to tell them."

Her father answered in a low voice. "Of course they would hold me responsible. I was one of those soldiers who came in and stole a young romantic woman's heart and left a love child behind." He paused and looked down. "I let my emotions get the better of my good judgment."

"You must be happy to have found them, Hope." He hadn't come out of his daze. His flat tone didn't reflect the meaning of his words.

"Dad, I need to go back. You understand, right?" She wrapped her arms around his neck. "Linh is an artist, and she wants to teach me, and I need to learn more about the Lê family."

"I know you love your art, Hope. You have a special talent. I understand. And now a family."

"Dad, I have a *family* here, and now I have one on the West Coast, too. I think I'll go for Lunar New Year in February. It's *Tet*, right? Do you think you—" She couldn't predict whether he would want closure or if it would undo two decades of healing. And would meeting Hằng's family bring back all the pain for Kate?

A knock on the door broke the tension. Dominique entered. "Oh, I'm sorry to interrupt." He backed out of the door.

"Wait, don't go." Hope left her father and met Dominique at the door. "I know we need to talk. I'll come to your office right after the team meeting. OK?"

He nodded and left.

"Dad, I want to tell our family. It's wrong to sneak around leaving for the West Coast and making up stories."

"I understand, honey. Truth is healthier for everyone." He slid the portrait of Hằng and the photo of Hope and the Lê family back into the envelope. Casting his eyes down, he rocked his head like she'd seen him nod to the beat of a song and went silent. "I'm so over all the secrets and lies too."

"I don't know how you feel about seeing them, Dad. But I want to leave it to you to tell Kate, OK? I assume you'll see her before I will, and I don't want her caught off guard. I'm going to have dinner with the Ketchums and share it tonight."

"I agree. I'll join you." He crossed the room and hugged Hope. "I'm with you. But honey, my shame won't let me face the Lês, and I'm sure it's mutual. They wouldn't want to see me now and wouldn't want it to overshadow the joy of finding you." He took Hope's face in his hands. "Now, will I lose you too?"

"Dad, no! I don't know how this will all resolve, but I will always love you and want to be with my Ketchum family."

"Thank God." He gathered himself, straightened his tie, and pushed his blond hair back into place. "Let's go, honey. I have a team meeting to run."

HOPE WAS uplifted to see everyone together again in the office conference room, safe and sipping coffee. Across the room, Dominique was talking to Shiloh, his hands gesturing dramatically, his eyes intense. He constantly nodded as Shiloh spoke. Then he picked up the thread again with enthusiasm. Hope had never seen him so full of passion. What were they talking about, she wondered.

Dominique's experiences were clearly positive for him. It created yet another threat for her.

Michael leaned on the conference table against the backdrop of drifting white and charcoal clouds and the occasional flash of sun. "OK, everyone, let's start with the reports from the section leaders."

All five team leaders had nothing but good to say about the mission. They took turns talking about the supply chain, the medical tent, details that were gratifying. Uplift had serviced over one thousand families serviced with tents, transportation, and food. The border closing, though disappointing, was imposed with no violence, and the staff was evacuated safely. The team agreed there was a period of nervous concern, but the coordination was satisfactory.

"Dominique, why not share your experiences since this was your first overseas assignment on an Uplift mission." Michael gestured for him to speak.

The team applauded, and Dominique gave his personal report. He spoke of the impressive coordination, the team leaders, and the people on the ground who supported their efforts. Then he paused and cleared his throat. "For me, the most impactful part was the children."

He launched into a passionate soliloquy on the joy of providing for the kids, their eyes lighting up at the sight of the meals arriving on the mats in front of them. Their giggles and smiles amid the chaos. The fun he had handing out clothes, toys, and soccer balls. The tears of gratitude in the parents' eyes. Comforting crying babies while their parents ate. "I watched an entire tent city rise from the ground as the kids clapped. And handing out survival kits for the families to take to their tents. Yes, there was deep sadness when the medical team could not save an ill child," he said. "And the dire situation, of course, reflected the hatred in the world that you needed to constantly push away to stay focused on your work. But being there for those people, seeing the hope that shone in their eyes when we served their most basic needs, were the most joyous moments of my life."

An emotional silence was followed by applause, and the team members hugged. They shared a belonging that Hope envied but a responsibility she would not have wanted to share. She'd been that child. If only for her first impressionable three years, she'd suffered those fears. Never again. Hope didn't have to work in this field to care deeply for the fate of those children. It was a new perspective for her.

Shiloh finished the meeting. "And a big thanks to our entire team of Earth Angels, as Jolie has dubbed you."

24

BEHIND CLOSED DOORS in Dominique's office, they finally had private time to talk. The suspense was unbearable for Hope. "Please tell me how things went with your mother last night. I thought maybe . . . you would call." Hope went up on her toes to kiss him. She wanted peace between them. He did not respond in his usual loving way.

"Jolie did not speak one word to me. She went to bed immediately. I was so exhausted that I fell asleep in my clothes." Dominique held her face and put his forehead to hers. No kiss. An innocent intimacy for her romantic fiancé. "I'm sorry I didn't call." Dropping his arms, he leaned back on the desk and sighed. "She was gone in the morning when I woke up. She left a note that she was flying home to France."

"Oh my God, Dominique, I'm so sorry. Not even a fight? Not a chance to explain? That was cruel. It doesn't seem like the Jolie I met. I remember that first day when she talked about how emotionally accessible she'd become."

"She is Jolie of the past resurrected. You see how impossible she is?" He paced in front of the panoramic glass. "One false move, and she's gone." He put his arm around Hope, and they faced the clouded view. "I was wrong to lay any blame on you. I should have respected myself enough to tell the truth. I should have respected you. And I shouldn't have fallen for her show of support involving you. I was just so enamored with you—your loving heart, humor, intelligence, and so much to love about my beautiful fiancé. Jolie knew that *you* were the way to get to me. People who love you should accept you for who you are. This work is who I am."

The abrupt realization cast an unexpected shadow over their future. Jolie had played her. She'd used Hope to reunite with Dominique. To play up to him. Hope was teed up for it, having had all that rejection in her past, she thought.

If putting himself in danger, even for a noble cause, made him feel like his true self, then could there be any way for Hope to be happy with Dominique in the long term? Not with the constant threat to her peace of mind as he flew worldwide into war zones. It was hard enough with Shiloh and her dad, but somehow, Shiloh was like Wonder Woman and used to the fray. Her dad spent his time meeting with the government's leadership and the on-the-ground decision-makers, safe from the heat of the war and violence.

Hope thought of her engagement ring. Had they moved too fast? Their time together, all day, every day, had accelerated their bonding and understanding of each other. At least, she'd thought it had. She realized that Dominique was right. The passion in his speech did show her who he was. "Yes, it's who you are, Dominique." He wasn't the man who needed to be on the ground just once to see the children's faces. "Dominique, your words, your passion at the meeting made me realize . . . maybe this wasn't a one-time tribute to your father. Maybe you're more like your father than you thought."

His attention drifted out the window. For a minute, Hope thought he might argue her point.

"Yes, you are right. Even before I spoke, I realized I wanted to return. Even when the border situation occurred, I wanted to be a part of a mission like that again. Shiloh and I discussed changing my position with Uplift. I told her how meaningless I felt running around my office, making phone calls and copies of documents, and writing articles about things I'd never seen, compared to being on a mission."

His description of their work together stung.

"The only time I came close to feeling meaningful in my work was when I wrote those articles for our newsletter, but it wasn't enough. I'm going to accept a mission team leadership role."

Where was this taking them? It was a win-lose.

"Hope darling, I know how much this mission means to you. One child. As you said, it is the thought that haunts you daily. That one child out there. Now I know what you mean. And having your support means everything. The calm you showed me before I left for Bosnia was so supportive. We are the perfect team, no?"

She was split in two when he kissed her. The Hope who loved him wanted to be with him, to support him, and the vulnerable Hope who wasn't sure she could.

Where does she go from here? Ignoring his statement, Hope explained she would leave tomorrow for Providence for a few days. She'd received a report from their investigative people, and they'd had a lead on the whereabouts of Frances Carlisle's adoptive parents. A good start. Hope wanted to follow through personally.

"That's great. The Nguyens will be so thrilled. I hope it is a happy reunion. So proud of your work."

She wanted to shake off the day and return to her joy over finding her family. The miracle was lost in the dramas of Jolie and Dominique before she could share it with anyone. But dinner with the Ketchums would give her that chance. She couldn't leave him out after what he'd been through. "Will you join me at the Ketchums for dinner tonight? I have some exciting news to share." Could she adjust to his change? She didn't think so but wasn't ready to break things off, either. Where would she find such love again?

"More good news we need, darling. Shall I drive you?"

"I'll drive myself in case you want to leave early and get some sleep."

"Honestly, that sounds good." Holding both her hands, he kissed them. "I will never let my mother come between us again. I do not need her money or her approval. She has always been less than a positive influence in my life. Biology does not always translate to connection." He embraced her and whispered, "You, my dear, are my connection."

His words that only days ago would have planted the blissful seeds for her future happiness now fell on infertile soil. She'd set her own trap by being supportive of his dreams. Dreams that terrorized her.

THE WET snow had turned to rain as the day progressed, making the trip to Glynn easier. Hope pulled up in front of her grandparents' house. Dominique hadn't arrived yet. She thought of her father's favorite expression—between a rock and a hard place. This was a hard place. But despite the awkward situation, she knew Grandma Cecelia and the rest of the family would celebrate the discovery that her entire biological family was alive and had grown.

She thought of her new niece Hong and how she'd skipped all the awkwardness and welcomed Hope. She would model the wisdom of the teen. Finding her family was a blessing. A true miracle. A gift from God, as Cecelia always said, when unexpected, good things came into their lives.

Walking up the steps, Hope paused and observed the similarities. Despite the aging Ketchum home, the million-dollar Lê mansion, the lifestyle differences, and the educational divides, the patterns in her two families never changed.

The scene as the elevator doors opened in the Lê mansion was fresh in Hope's memory as she thought of the typical evening with the Ketchum clan. Grandpa Kevin in his Barcalounger reading the Boston Globe, Grandma Cecelia checking the roast in the oven, her aunts setting the table, her uncles playing Poker at the card table, and cousins watching TV. Thirty-seven relatives lived and loved within a few blocks, and her grandparents' house was Ketchum Central. Together, always together.

The hinges squeaked, and the scent of Cecelia's mouth-watering pot roast met Hope at the door. That was a sign in itself; it was a special occasion. Hope was home. Would she feel that way at the Lê's home someday?

"Hello!" Making her way to the kitchen, she passed her family just as she'd imagined. They stopped what they were doing to say a cheerful hello, except for her nephews and nieces, who were riveted to a favorite TV show and numb to what was happening around them.

"Grandpa, where's Ernie?"

"He's doing some fitting at the factory for some late out-of-towners. He should be here shortly. He'll be excited to see his favorite Ketchum."

In the kitchen, wearing her usual green plaid apron, Cecelia had her back to Hope as she checked the pot roast.

"Is it falling-off-the-bone tender, Grandma C?" The warmth of her grandmother's greeting always melted Hope's troubles. She was accepting and non-judgmental.

"Hope, I didn't hear you come in. Sit, honey. I'll make you some tea."

"I know you're busy, but before Dominique gets here, can I ask you for some advice?"

Sitting at the same table where she'd played with Cheerios as a child, Hope felt safe and loved. The world in which a new style of handmade shoes for a loyal client was the usual topic of discussion.

"It feels like the old days when Kate would come to me with that same look. You know, advice, that's something I've got plenty of. What's on your mind, dear?" Her grandmother wiped her hands on her apron, dropped tea bags into two ceramic mugs, poured hot water from the dented kettle, and sat across from Hope. "I'm all yours."

Sharing the story of Dominique and Jolie with someone who knew her and loved her lifted some of the weight of her burdens. Hope's dread of the violent and dangerous places where the foundation did its good work was a sudden realization that cast a shadow on her entire life—her job, Dominique, her relationships with her father, and Shiloh. It all came spilling out. When she'd finished the tale, Hope waited.

Cecelia's eyes searched the ceiling as though the answers were floating above her. She nodded. "Well, it seems you know the answer, Hope, in here." Cecelia put her fist to her stomach. "My advice is the same that I gave Kate years ago about her singing. Follow what lights you up. Often, it's there right in front of you from the start. You may not know what that is right now, but when you feel it, you'll know. Trust it. And maybe give your relationship with Dominique a little time to test how you feel. Let him see if this new direction fits him after the initial glow is gone. And honey, tell him. To be fair, he needs to know how you feel. Share your concerns. It's the beginning of an honest relationship. Informed decisions are important for Dominique right now." Her grandmother glanced toward the kitchen door. "Don't make the same mistake women of my generation made, saying, don't tell your father—trying to maintain some kind of martyred women's role. I've learned accommodating and protecting a husband is a fool's game. The truth is always better in the long run."

"One more thing, and this is big." Hope took out the large envelope and emptied it on the table.

Cecelia studied the photos. "Such a loss. I'm so sorry. Hope, Kate told me about what happened to your mother in the war during one of our kitchen talks when she was trying to decide whether she should go to Bangkok to reconnect with your father." Cecelia shook her head and stared at the photo of Hope's mother again. "She was beautiful, and you look like her blue-eyed carbon copy. How are you since all of this happened?"

"Frankly, there's been so much drama since I returned. I haven't been able to process all this. And honestly, I'm sad that Dad didn't show me this photo long ago. No, truthfully, I was really hurt. But I get it. He couldn't bear it."

"Tell me about your biological family."

"That's another thing, Grandma. I haven't been able to celebrate finding them. I've become close to my mother's one sister, an artist, a very successful artist. The Lês are close-knit like the Ketchums, and they're Catholic, too. That surprised me. Oh, and very successful financially."

Cecelia cleared the mugs, and they both turned when the doorbell rang. "Dominique, I assume. He's the only one who rings the Ketchum doorbell. Look, honey, you're still young. Your education is complete. Just keep your radar out for that special thing. You know the story of me getting pregnant and missing out on my singing career. There's nothing in your way, darling, and having two families is a blessing." Covering Hope's hand with hers, Cecelia leaned toward her. "Be honest and see where your love takes you. That's an old woman's advice. My life might seem boring and simple, maybe arduous, but being a part of this big, crazy family gave me that belonging I wanted. And didn't my own daughter live out her singing dreams?"

"With your loving support, Grandma C."

Hope rushed to answer the door.

A blast of chill accompanied Dominique into the hallway. "Your father is right behind me. He just pulled up in the driveway. Sorry, I was delayed while making travel plans."

"No problem, I'll take your coat. We're just starting now." Ignoring the subject of his next mission, Hope got everyone's attention as her father entered. "Dad, Dominique, please have a seat." Hope handed them glasses of champagne she'd brought for the occasion.

The TV went off, and everyone listened. Kids giggled as she poured bubbling grape juice into their fancy crystal flutes—the glasses Kate had bought to use for special occasions.

Ernie walked in at the last minute. "Hope! You're here. I missed you. What's the celebration?" With no brass hook available, he tossed his coat onto the floor.

Hope handed him a glass of the bubbly. "I have some wonderful, well, truly miraculous news. My mother's family, we'd all believed had died when I was just a baby, is alive."

"Wow! That's so cool, Hope. You mean they were dead, and now they're alive?" Ernie put his hands on his hips. "You mean like Jesus? Like they rose from the dead?" He tilted his head and squinted at Hope. "Wait, can that really happen? With regular people?"

"No, no, Ernie. We *thought* they were deceased, but it was a mistake." She'd tried to put it into terms the kids and Ernie would understand. Now, Hope had no choice but to say the entire village was destroyed by enemy bombs with no survivors. "My two grandparents, two uncles, and an aunt had left during the night. They'd escaped with the help of American soldiers." Hope knew she had to be specific to save a round of detailed questions from Ernie and the kids.

Ernie's shoulders dropped, and he looked at the floor. "So, you have a new family then? But you'll . . . still love us, right?" His lisp and squeaky voice made his plea even more emotional. He'd never had boundaries when saying exactly how he felt. It could be delightful or disconcerting.

"Absolutely, Ernie, you're my brother." She hugged him. In

his charming, naïve way, he always got to the point. "And you guys are my nieces and nephews. How could I not still love you?"

Taking her at her word, Ernie started the cheering, "Woohoo! Yay for Hope." The kids chimed in, and he led them in his traditional circle dance—like a Cha-Cha and a Rhumba combined, chicken-necking, feet thudding on the hardwood floor, his short arms with wrinkled fists rotating with the beat.

"Congrats, honey," Uncle Keith said.

"We're so happy for you, baby doll." Uncle Karl put his arm around Hope's shoulders.

"How amazing." Kevin clapped.

She was surprised and happy to receive rare hugs from Grandpa K, Grandma C, and her aunts.

"I'm happy for you." From the corner of the room, sitting on an oak dining room chair, Mary smiled as she hand-stitched a hem on a skirt. "I'm glad you found your other family, Hope."

It was a positive thing for the thirty-five-year-old former orphan to say, considering her history of abandonment. Despite their age difference, Hope and Mary had grown up as sisters after Kate had arranged for her aunt to adopt Mary from the institution. Mary hadn't spoken for years when Kate met her while interning at Rolling Hills. She'd come a long way working with Aunt Maggie as a seamstress. That was the Ketchums' way.

Hope had received the response she'd wanted—hugs, happiness, and congratulations. She made a toast through trembling lips. "Here's to family, the more, the merrier."

Dominique crossed the room and double-cheek-kissed her. "I'm so sorry you had to keep that good news under wraps while we dealt with the Jolie fiasco. And I'm so happy for you. Will I meet them soon?"

"I thought we might visit them during the Lunar New Year celebration. It's called *Tet* and falls on February nineteenth this year."

"That would be wonderful."

Hope wondered how Dominique would fit in with the Lês as a Frenchman. It would help to speak French with the Great Grands.

Shiloh arrived and slipped between them. With the TV on and Ernie playing with the little ones, she raised her voice to deliver the news. "The Bosnian War peace treaty negotiated in Dayton, Ohio, was approved in Paris today, December Fourteenth. We can go back to resume our work now. Dominique, did you book that flight?"

"I'm ready to go."

Shiloh turned to Hope. "I think you're pretty special to support his new direction."

How should Hope answer? She needed to update Shiloh. For now, happiness was in the air at the Ketchum's home.

25

SUNNY AND COLD, and the roads were clear—the perfect day to drive to Providence, considering New England's typical December trickery for welcoming in the winter. Hope was grateful.

Her father couldn't stop talking about his new Montreal metallic blue BMW 840 Ci sedan. He insisted Hope drive it while her car was in the shop. Speeding down Route 95, she struggled to reset her favorite radio station, 103.3 FM. Hope sang along with the hits. Aware that she had no genetic link to Kate when it came to singing, Hope only sang when she was alone.

Sometimes she felt uncomfortable with their affluent lifestyle while working to help people with so little. Her father always reminded her that every penny he'd inherited and every dollar he'd made selling his father's high-profile investment firm had gone to the foundation. He would say they deserved the life Kate had provided and should be grateful and enjoy. That was the arrangement Michael and Kate made long ago when she "hit the heights," as he'd called her success in the music business.

Kate also contributed to charity through her free music schools in inner cities in the US, Hope thought. Still, it was hard to fully grasp all that while driving her father's fancy car down the road to find a former refugee who'd been stolen from her country during a war.

Hope's call to Frances' adoptive parents was successful. Both doctors agreed to meet with her at the Southwest Pavilion, the main building of the Providence Hospital on 593 Eddy Street, at eleven thirty.

The two-and-a-half-hour drive down Route 95 went smoothly.

Hope entered the hospital. Looking for the right two doctors in white coats would not be easy. But Hope knew her description of herself as a five-foot-tall Vietnamese woman with blue eyes carrying a leather briefcase would make it easier for them to recognize her.

Seated in the reception area by the door, as promised, they waved and didn't seem the least bit concerned about identifying her.

They seemed nervous. "Please call us Brian and Rachael," the woman said. Introductions over, they shared their only knowledge about their daughter's whereabouts.

"Frances ran away when she was eighteen, right after her high school graduation," her father said. "She hadn't ever really adapted to life with us." He glanced at his wife.

"She was five when we got her," Rachael said. "Our friends who'd also adopted a baby had no problems, but Frances was . . . well, different."

The announcements over the loudspeaker and the busy reception room made it hard to have an intimate conversation. "Do you have any idea where I might start my search?"

"We've connected infrequently over the past two decades by phone. Frances wanted to let us know she was OK. She sends us a Christmas card every year. Here is the last address we had. She made us promise to let her live her life." Rachael handed Hope a slip of paper. "We've kept that promise, but not easily."

"Miss James, would you send our love if you locate Frances? And tell her we'd love to see her again."

Brian took Rachael's hand. "It was heartbreaking for us. We'd dreamed of how happy the little girl would be with us, to be safe and loved. She never adjusted. Always in trouble. We never dared to adopt again, frankly."

"And if her grandparents would like to meet with us, we're happy to share the years we spent with Frances. Only if that helps them."

"I'm so sorry." The optimism Hope had felt when she'd found the adoptive parents began to wane. But if she could find Frances, couldn't that result in two possibilities? The Carlisles and the Nguyens would have a chance to reunite with her. And wouldn't the two couples want to meet to learn more about Frances? She wasn't a rebellious or confused teenager anymore; she was a grown woman.

THE DRIVE to East Village through afternoon traffic was unnerving, with horns and cars swaying. New York City wasn't a place where she'd driven before. Trains and limos had been her transportation.

The address was in a middle-class neighborhood. That was

promising. Hope rounded the block four times before she found a parking place.

As she walked a block to the apartment building, a workman repairing a street pothole whistled and called out. "Hey babe, you are one sweet, tiny lump of Asian sugar. Gook candy. Give Daddy a kiss."

She ignored him. Racism wasn't a shock to her anymore. She buzzed apartment 3B.

A woman's voice sang out. "Who is it?"

What was the correct answer? What would Frances respond to? Too vague wouldn't get her attention. Mentioning the word, attorney, was always a mistake. Hope chose a straightforward approach. "I'm looking for Frances Carlisle. I have a message from her grandparents."

"She doesn't live here anymore." Her voice sounded agitated.

"Would you be willing to talk to me? I work for Uplift Children's Foundation. Her biological grandparents want to reconnect with her."

Hope waited a long minute. Long enough that she thought the woman had probably become suspicious and called the police. Big cities didn't exactly engender trust. Hope knew that.

She turned to leave down the brick steps when she heard the buzzer. The door unlatched, and the voice returned. "You said, Uplift?"

"Yes."

"Come on up. Third floor, second apartment on your left."

The articles Dominique had written about the foundation's work lately were hitting the major papers. The word about Uplift's good work was getting around, Hope thought, as she climbed three flights of creaking stairs.

Sitting with the young woman who introduced herself as Katrina, Hope explained the background without betraying the trust of the parties involved in the case. Katrina was fine-featured, pretty, blonde, and friendly, about the same age as Hope, she guessed.

"She used to live here, but she . . . well, we aren't together anymore. But I know where she works. At least she used to work there. The Strand Bookstore—Broadway and 12th. She tends to wander, it seems. I've never met anyone who's had more jobs than Frances. Sorry to say she's a quitter."

"Thank you so much." Hope opened the door to leave.

"Wait. Would you tell Frances that Katarina sends her . . . never mind. Thanks."

"I really appreciate your help." Hope could feel the woman's regret from across the room. She quietly pulled the door closed.

AT STRAND Books, Hope inquired about Frances. "She's in the back on a break. Who shall I say is looking for her? Oh, never mind, there she is." The young man at the register with a dragon tattoo down his neck pointed toward the back of the store.

The tall Vietnamese American woman was dressed in black jeans, a red crop top, and Black Doc Martens, with piercings up the side of her left ear and a small diamond nose stud. She had a suspicious gaze. "Can I help you?"

"Can we talk privately?" Hope handed her a business card.

The woman scanned the name. "*Children's* Foundation?"

They sat in the back of the store in the employee break room amid stacks of books. Hope gave Frances the background on her grandparents and her recent visits to her adoptive parents and former partner. "I'm not stalking you. It's my job to reunite families when possible."

The tale of Hope's own experience with the Lê family seemed to resonate with Frances. "We believe in trying to keep children in their own countries, by the way."

"I always wondered what would have happened if I'd remained in Saigon with the war exploding around us. The woman told me I'd be safe. Had I known I'd never see my family again—" Frances breathed in deeply and dropped her head back against the leather chair. "How did my grandparents ever end up in the US?"

"That I don't know, but I know they'd love to share that story with you in person. They live in Connecticut, as a matter of fact. New Haven. Not far from here."

"Unreal."

"Would you be willing to communicate with them?"

Frances stared over Hope's shoulder, then directly at her. "Look at me." Opening both of her arms wide, Frances invited Hope's inspection. "Do you think my conservative Vietnamese grandparents would want to meet *this*? This is why I had to leave my adoptive parents. I needed to be free. And I didn't want to shame them. Back then, that's what I thought. I'm more self-accepting now, but I'm not sure I've changed my opinion in that regard."

Her answer caught Hope off guard. The excitement she'd expected from Frances was replaced by a silent pause. "It's your call, of course. You would know what's best for you."

"I just don't see the purpose. So, I should tell my grandparents that I abandoned my adoptive parents, I've been bullied all my life, didn't finish school, and their sweet granddaughter is gay? I can't see the payoff for anyone. I don't want to be judged."

"I'm not here to convince you." Hope could see how Frances would feel. And she certainly didn't know how the grandparents would react. It could be the disaster Frances feared. "Well, I will leave you their address and phone number. Maybe you will consider calling?"

"You won't betray my confidences, will you?"

"It's not my job. But your adoptive parents have your grandparent's contact information. I can't say what they will do."

"I suppose that was your doing. You know how to stir up someone's life with your noble causes. Why don't you just let people be? I'm not a child anymore."

It never crossed Hope's mind that Frances wouldn't want to meet her grandparents she was ripped away from in a war. "I'm . . . I'm truly sorry. I didn't think—"

"No, you didn't think!" Frances grabbed her coat from a closet on the way out of the room. "You'll excuse me, but I need to quit my job and move on. Thanks a lot. And tell Katarina thanks too!"

The sarcasm in her tone was painful for Hope. Was she a naïve romantic, dreaming of the fairytale ending to her search? Finding her own family had brought Hope happiness and a sense of belonging. But Hope wasn't Frances.

26

"BEFORE YOU GO to San Francisco on Sunday, I want you to have this." Michael pushed his chair back, opened the office safe, and handed her a photo Hope had never seen—the Lê family with her father in the center dressed in his Marine fatigues, standing next to Hằng. She wore the traditional *áo dài*, a blue split long top with swaying white pants.

"Dad, how did you get a photo taken back in the war?" She studied the people in the faded shot.

"I was lucky. A Marine buddy gave me his camera for my last visit to Hằng's family before we moved out to another assignment. One shot left in the roll. After he got home and developed it, he sent that photo to me in Nantucket. Good guy to do that."

Hope recognized the younger versions of her great-grandparents, grandparents, Uncles Tuân and Long, and Aunt Linh.

"It's all I have of your mother. You should have it."

"Thanks, Dad. I heard you mention the photo in the safe before. I'll treasure it." Hope didn't want to push her father for his decision about reuniting with her Lê family. She was torn between his best interest and theirs. Being in the middle was threatening to her. She needed to stay neutral, yet she wanted to build a bridge. Looking at the photo, Hope got an idea. She imagined presenting a painting of the image to the Lê family. Maybe Hope could use it as a basis for her art lessons with Linh. She needed a distraction after the disappointment with Frances. Would it be an appropriate gift for *Tet*? Did they give gifts for *Tet*? I'll surprise them.

"Honey, I'm sorry about the outcome for the Nguyens."

"The disappointment in Mr. Nguyen's voice was so sad, and his wife sobbed, Dad. I wanted to do it in person, but they were visiting friends in Chicago, and then I leave Sunday."

"That was a tough case. You did a great job and are not responsible for the outcomes."

"I guess it's heartbreaking because it was from my own times and country. I should be grateful. It's the only case I've had without a happy face to capture for the wall. I never thought anyone would want to miss the chance to see their long-lost grandparents. Sometimes I feel so naïve."

"That's one of the things that makes you so lovable, right? No cynicism, tough, smart, with a big heart."

She didn't feel so tough, Hope thought. "Speaking of being a romantic, I'm late meeting Dominique at the Parker House."

"You two seem inseparable. I'm happy for you."

Tucking the photo into her purse, Hope hesitated by the door, then asked him the question that had been nagging her for weeks. "Dad, do you ever tire of all the wars? I know we do wonderful things for children and families in hellish situations, but after what you went through?"

"I can't get enough of it. Maybe I'd seen it all, you know. I look past the horrors and focus on the good we're doing. I think about Jeremy flying in to find you and—" Her father's gaze shifted to Hope's Harvard graduation photo on his desk. "And how you being here has changed my life."

There was no answer to those tender words. "Love you, Dad." She kissed his forehead. "Um. I don't think I'll see you at home tonight." These moments involving her relationship with Dominique and her father as their boss were awkward.

He gave her a smiling acknowledgment. "Say hi to Dominique for me."

SITTING AT their usual corner table at Omni Parker House drinking their Pinot, his red, hers white, Dominique took her hands in his. Leaning forward to give his words some privacy amid the clamor of conversation in the famous restaurant, he engaged her eyes. "Hope, I know we are moving forward on 'French time,' as you say, and it's less than five months that we have known each other. But I calculate that *is* nearly three thousand hours of intimate connection. Shall we make some plans for our forever?"

"My mathematician lover." She squeezed his hands. Cecelia was right. Hope wasn't ready to talk about marriage. They needed time to see how she could handle his new direction, and she was wavering in her commitment to Uplift. After constantly hearing about the atrocities in the world, the foundation's name wasn't something she was feeling lately. "Shall we talk at home instead of publicly? Do you mind waiting until three thousand and two hours?" A little humor to buy some time to think, she thought.

"That works for me, darling." He released a muffled laugh.

As Dominique reviewed the menu, Frances's words came to Hope's mind—stirring up people's lives for noble causes. The things they did at the foundation constantly stirred up *Hope's* life. But the outlooks of everyone in her world, her dad's, Shiloh's, Dominique's, and the team's, were significant factors weighing the scales toward her staying at her job. Maybe she just needed time, but her role did *not* feel like the passion Grandma Cecelia had described. It felt like the endless storm raging outside her office windows lately, with only short interludes of sunshine. Where had the all-day-long blue sky gone that she remembered from her first day of work?

Hope promised herself she would search for the light in the darkness when it came to her job. There was so much happiness in her personal life. Couldn't she reflect that light into her work world? Everything she did was filled with horror stories until she'd finished reviewing the adoption papers and was sketching the face of a child who'd found a new home or was saved from the terrors of war. Too much was happening out there—the First Chechen War, the Tajikistani Civil War, the Third Taiwan Strait Crisis, the Tuareg rebellion, the Turbot War, the Turkish Army winter campaign, Macedonia, Kosovo, and on and on. She would barely hang the children's portraits on The Wall of Hope, and another terrifying situation would arise. Hope wanted to stay in those moments with their happy faces. Her only power was to impose the smiles on those portraits, even if they weren't there. Even if the perpetual smiles were in her imagination.

Her days colored her nights with Dominique, too. After a

night of luscious lovemaking, she'd often reverted to a nightmare about her workday. He'd slept through the nights peacefully. She envied that.

And could she endure his absences when she knew they would be endless, not just a one-time reality check to honor his father? There was no separating the two—both being with Dominique and being in her job day-to-day held the same irony.

The skyscape outside her office window that she'd painted came to mind—constant floating clouds, dark and ominous, against a palate of gray with moments of bright, golden sun that never lasted. Love and joy in a dark world of war and violence. No peace for her heart.

"I meant to ask when I first saw you, do I have your permission to use one of your sketches for my next article? The one of the little Bosnian boy in his new blue shirt. His adoptive parents agreed."

His words brought her out of her reverie and back into the restaurant. Hope was touched. "Yes, of course. Use any of my artworks anytime." She picked up her menu, but Hope wasn't reviewing the list of delicious options.

"Maybe you should order for me, Dominique. I'm so distracted tonight."

The waiter arrived. "Are you ready to order? Tonight's special, perhaps. Filet mignon? I recall you both prefer medium rare?"

"Perfect, thank you," Dominique said.

"The other team members seemed to be able to balance those two worlds and stay on the positive side of the scale, too. José tells me to focus on the end results."

"That's good advice, darling." Dominique refilled their wine glasses.

They would need it, Hope thought. "I'm not sure I can focus on the end results. They are complex and not always as happily-ever-after as we would like to think. Right?" But what would she do with her law degree? She'd concentrated on social services and nonprofit work, she thought. If she went to work for an organization in the US, would that be any more cheerful? She knew it wouldn't, having interned at one. And how could she disappoint nearly everyone in her life, especially her father?

"Earth to Hope, come in Hope. Where are you, my love?" Dominique's gentle teasing was said with a haunting outer-space tone that made her smile. It was so unlike him. He'd become Americanized and less formal as he'd spent time with Shiloh and the team, and Dominique had stopped using French terms of endearment for the most part.

"What are you pondering, darling, the Nguyen case?"

"It was a one-time situation out of many, I know, but it was hard on me." Hope took a long swallow of her wine. "Most of my work has been bringing happiness to little cherub faces, but Dominique, doing this gratifying but emotional work against the backdrop of the hatred in the world, the wars, and atrocities, I'm finding it hard to stay in the joyful parts. Do you struggle with that?"

Their order arrived, and Hope tried to do the dinner justice, but she'd lost her appetite.

"Hmm. For me, it serves to put a context around our successes. When I write my articles and imagine the kids and their reactions to something as simple as a soccer ball, it puts it all into perspective. I feel regret and sometimes guilt when we have to leave. We can never do enough." Dominique got up and moved to the chair beside her. "Darling, you've had quite a disappointment that I don't experience one-on-one like that. Naturally, you'll have your downtime. The next smiling face will put you right. It won't be about the very war that traumatized your childhood." He kissed her temple, returned to his seat, and toasted her dedicated work.

"Maybe you're right."

"When you have a big heart, sometimes it hurts, darling. Only one disappointing one, a mission impossible to begin with, Hope. And it was too close to home for you. Frances wasn't a child—she was a woman with a life of her own. Let's celebrate all the kids you've placed on The Wall of Hope."

Yes, he was right, then why did it all feel so wrong for her lately?

"And maybe we should postpone discussing our future until you return from San Francisco."

"Dominique, how do you read me so well?"

"It's called love, darling. We can announce it to your West Coast family during—what was the Lunar holiday? Oh yes, *Tet*." Dominique's words melted into that alluring smile of his. "Let's go home and turn the night around, OK, Hope?"

Could they?

DOMINIQUE SLEPT peacefully beside her after making love, which was never a brief thing with her Frenchman. Was there anything about him she didn't love? Hope gently tucked the covers over his bare shoulder and turned on her small reading light.

Studying the Lê family photograph, Hope imagined how she would adapt it into a painting. The mood of it called for a watercolor, she thought. Linh would know best. Hope had everything to learn. But one thing she knew was that she could capture people's spirits, features, and personalities in her sketches. Everyone had confirmed that.

She no longer had to wonder where those artistic impulses had come from. Now she knew. It was Hope's lineage. Just like Cecelia had always said, Kate had inherited her Great-Grandmother Katherine's wanderlust, and her extraordinary singing voice came from her mother. Hope's great-grandmother on the Lê's side had passed her artistic genes down to her.

Linh had told Hope that her parents had never thought Linh would turn her harmless artworks into a passion and a successful career. They would have much preferred their children to achieve doctor or lawyer status, like her brother Tuân. Still, Linh's passion and a few convincing words from her great-grandmother to the family had opened the door to her satisfying life in Sausalito, capturing the scenes of her family's past. A sweet compromise.

Art was a hobby that had soothed Hope and given her joy. Maybe it would help to balance her life's work at Uplift. Maybe Hope could make it work with the stunning man beside her despite his desire for overseas missions.

27

BEING ON THE water in Sausalito again had its effect. Relaxing to the rhythm of the rippling waves as the ferry brought her to the shore, Hope spotted Linh waving. The big arcing arts building on the hill overlooking the Bay gave her chills. Like a refugee coming to a new land of freedom, she would spend every day becoming intimate with this new world—her art and her new family.

Linh took Hope's satchel of meager art supplies and hugged her. "Did you get into the house alright?"

"Yes, and you're sure John and the kids don't mind my staying with you for a few days?"

"Not at all. It's good timing. Next week, we'll all be in full Christmas mode."

"I get it. The Ketchums will be, as well."

Linh drove to the ICB arts building and led the way to her space on the second floor. Along the hallway, a dozen artists stepped out of their doorways to say hello, some covered in splatters of color and clay—sculptors, painters, potters, jewelers—so many ways to express that urge Hope knew so well.

"I will take you on an introductory tour tomorrow, OK?"

"Sounds like fun."

"And tomorrow, my Vietnamese women friends have their monthly luncheon. You're invited."

"Really, thanks."

"Don't worry. We speak English at our gatherings."

It was precisely the question Hope had. She was relieved.

They sat and chatted in the two chairs just inside the art space next to Linh's handcrafted wooden counter, where she completed her transactions with buyers and students. Sharing Hope's news about her engagement started them on a happy note. There would be no secrets or posturing with Linh. It was a fresh start.

"I look forward to meeting Dominique. He sounds like a wonderful guy."

"He is special, Linh. I had trouble finding someone who accepted my two sides, so to speak."

"I understand, but San Francisco seems more accepting and progressive. My problem was John's difficulty in accepting our family dynamics. He's an independent American guy. But we all adapted."

Books of Linh's award-winning works filled the Ashwood shelves behind the counter. A coffee pot and refrigerator were visible in the alcove by the bathroom across the thirty-foot-long gallery.

"You want a cup of coffee?"

"How did you know my addiction was calling? Sure. Thanks." Hope scanned the walls of art in the main gallery room. A second, large gallery room, a smaller classroom with walls filled with portraits, a supply closet, and a bathroom completed her aunt's rented art space. The bright white walls in the main gallery where they sat were the perfect background for Linh's large, dramatic landscapes of the Vietnamese countryside.

"Here you go. I remember you drink it black."

"Thanks. Why do I feel like a child on a playground."

"*The creative adult is the child who survived.* Oh, I meant that to be figurative, not literal. Sorry, Hope. You'll find I like to quote people. But that one was more apt for you than I'd meant."

"I love it. Who said that?"

"The author of my kids' favorite books, the *Catwings* series, Ursula LeGuin."

"Shall we start the lesson?" Linh locked the door and flipped the handmade sign over: "*Do not disturb, artist at play.*"

Hope liked that. She needed play.

They moved into the other room, donned aprons, and sat at a table. Linh put a large piece of handmade textured watercolor paper in front of them. "So, your works are from photographs, right?"

"Yes, almost always, unless I paint or sketch a family member or skyscapes." Hope was nervous. Even though she'd painted over a hundred portraits from photos in the past, she knew she could do better. She knew she had some artistic talent but didn't consider herself an artist. "I always admired the John Singer Sargent watercolor portraits and visited them at the Museum of Fine Arts, Boston."

"Based on your recent works of watercolor and charcoal, Hope, I think you have a unique talent. I don't want to interfere with that. We'll just work to refine and add techniques and tools to your skillbox, some color theory, and using washes. Agreed?"

The excitement electrified Hope's body. "Absolutely."

"Most importantly, let's develop your relationship with the medium and bring out the natural *Hope*. I do see Sargent's influence from the nineteen hundreds in your portraiture—that luscious bravura brushwork. I recognize his wet-on-wet technique of flowing blended strokes and soft edges you use. Those were based on the Carolus-Duran techniques. Am I right?"

"Yes. I didn't know I'd internalized all those museum trips."

"You've been emulating the best, Hope. Your loose, painterly marks look casual up-close. But notice from a distance they merge to create a precise portrait. Well done, Hope."

"I remember Singer Sargent's quote on the wall. *You can't do sketches enough. Sketch everything and keep your curiosity fresh.* I followed that now that I think of it. I never went anywhere without a sketch pad." Hope was encouraged. She straightened in her chair and ran her fingers over the thick, textured paper.

"So, let's focus on watercolor and charcoal since you like those media. Before we start, what are your first thoughts about your works?" Linh sat back to listen.

"I guess . . . maybe everyone looks at my portraits not as art, but to see the happiness on the children's faces as a reflection of the work the foundation does. Which is all I've ever thought about, too—those little faces." Hope took just a few seconds to realize her art was no longer her hobby or play; it had become work, her job. Where were her compelling nature scenes? There had been no time. "Maybe I've developed my skills without even realizing it because of the meaningfulness of the subject matter. Who can resist a child's smile?"

"Not me, especially when they are captured with such skill."

Hope had to say it out loud. "I need to be honest, Linh. In

the photos, those children weren't always smiling. Some looked traumatized, and some were crying. I understood. I wanted their lives to turn out like mine in loving homes with wonderful futures. I had to make them smile."

"A noble choice, Hope, and an artist's choice." Linh seemed to be sincerely captivated by Hope's work.

It was a relief to put her work in a truthful context. "I know I'm pretty good at capturing their expressions, but it's never been reviewed as art by anyone. Well, until you, just now. I'm flattered. I also often think of the adoptive parents and whether they'll like it?"

"*An artist discovers his genius the day he dares not to please.* I should say 'she' not 'he,' not to be sexist. The words are from André Malraux, a French writer and statesman."

"Another good quote, Linh. Good advice. The times I question where I'm going with my art are the times that I lose that wonderful feeling of escape and my signature style. Maybe I'm too much of a 'words' person after law school. And a nature girl."

"I suspect there's something else going on in you, but I will pretend you know nothing. Think of water as the main element in watercolor works, not the paint. What does it do? It flows. There's emotion and movement in the technique." Linh demonstrated painting a rectangle with plain water. "If you try to be the *painter*, you can't take advantage of the *partnership* with our flowing friend. I know from your children's portraiture works that you can express the spectrum of human emotions through your paintings by contrasting colors and light. Let's see if we can add to your instincts in that area. Let's start simply with wet on wet."

When Linh added blue with her paintbrush, they watched the

medium find its way across the paper. "A mind of its own, right? Now watch when I become its friend."

Hope worked her brush on her own paper, imitating Linh's technique, painting an identical rectangle with just water and adding blue paint. Watching the color spread, Hope studied Linh's brush techniques.

"You need to honor the color's journey as you take a journey of your own. You might discover your unique way changes with each piece, but the important thing is to be with the color and open to its messages as you impose your own."

WORKING THROUGHOUT the morning, Hope began to see the subtle differences between her methods and the clever brushwork and approaches her aunt took to imbue her portraits with drama and character while splattering herself and her clothes with paint. She found better ways to use her stubborn charcoal to add the contrast she'd seen in Linh's work and began to avoid the occasional muddy mess Hope had made of some of her pieces.

Hope was always pleased with the pencil sketches of the children's faces she did. They grounded her paintings. Still, Linh's watercolor strategies and subtleties of charcoal application began to expose new skill levels for Hope to explore.

By the end of the morning, Hope's wrists ached, and her intensity and bending over her artwork had left her neck and shoulders aching and tight. She stretched and opened her briefcase.

"Can I show you something, Linh?"

"First, let me do this." Linh leaned over with a damp cloth and wiped a splatter of blue paint from Hope's cheek.

"Thanks."

"Occupational hazard."

They laughed together. "What was it you wanted to show me?" Linh wiped off her hands and sat next to Hope.

"I think I want to do something special with this photo." Hope took the Lê family photo from her satchel and handed it to Linh. "Can you help me?"

There was the same long pregnant pause she'd experienced with her father when Hope had shown him Hằng's portrait that Linh had made.

Linh covered her mouth with one hand and studied the photo. "This is so precious. I remember the day our neighbor took this for us. I was fourteen the day Michael left for another assignment with his borrowed camera. And now we know it was nine months before we were swept away to the plane that saved us all. Where did you get this?" Linh's emotions showed in her shaking hands.

"My dad kept it all these years in his safe." Hope wasn't sure it was right to ask. "Do you think . . . I have the skill set to enlarge it into watercolor and charcoal. And maybe give it as a *Tet* gift for your family?"

"Let's go get some lunch, and we'll talk. There's a great Pho shop nearby, within walking distance."

HOPE LOVED having the chance to dine on their national cuisine together. The restaurant was located along a fashionable, charming Sausalito Street. There were only a few empty tables available in the popular place. The blend of English and Vietnamese echoing in the cozy restaurant was a metaphor for Hope.

The host led them to a table by the window, seated them, and handed them large, laminated menus.

Scanning the buzzing room, Hope ran her finger down the bi-lingual menu. "I'll have what you're having, Linh."

Listening to Linh ordering in Vietnamese again made Hope sad she hadn't learned her birth country's language.

The waiter turned to Hope with a questioning look. "Oh, you don't speak Vietnamese? We can order in English, no problem."

Wouldn't that give Hope a more profound sense of belonging? Maybe Linh would give her a few basic lessons as they painted. The thought of having access to an entire group of friends and family who shared that language inspired her even more. Wouldn't that make her feel closer to her deceased mother and Hope's new family?

The bone broth Pho soup was delicious—the rice noodles, thinly sliced beef, bean sprouts, and herbs. It wasn't something they'd grown up with in the Ketchum clan, but Hope had tried it in Boston several times and loved it.

"I love the distinct flavor the star anise gives the broth." Hope copied Linh as she leaned forward, chopsticks in hand, and constructed her favorite version of Pho from the ingredients served on plates—basil, mint, coriander, and chili. She chose a lime wedge instead of Linh's lemon and left out the bean sprouts. She was forming her own version. It made Hope feel far away from her Corned Beef and Cabbage home on the East Coast.

"Sriracha or Hoisin sauce?" Linh asked, pointing to the two bottles.

How could Linh have known that Sriracha was the village in Thailand where Hope had landed with Jeremy to meet her father? "I'll have the Sriracha."

"It's spicy, you sure?"

"I'm sure. I love it." It seemed like an omen. Hope would come to belong here like she had come to belong to the Ketchum clan. Or would her father's history with the family forever cause an awkward wall between the two trunks of Hope's family tree?

"I have one idea," Hope said as they enjoyed the soup. "I don't know if this is appropriate, but I think I might want to adjust my portrait of our family based on that old photo."

"Change your technique, or what? Just to be clear, I think my family would love a piece done by you, no matter the technique. They would be honored. Seeing the whole family twenty years in reverse would make it a keepsake, an instant heirloom. And certainly, you can give it to them when you return for *Tet*."

Hope added more hot sauce to the broth. "It's not about my art technique, Linh. It's something else. I want to be open, Linh. We need to start off right together, and since you were trained that way by your fellow artists in critiquing, we can practice that honesty together."

"You're right. We should be forthright," Linh said. "What's the concern?"

"Since you love poignant quotes, Picasso said, *Every act of creation is first an act of destruction*. The power of art is you can see the subject first, then feel it, then recreate it, he explained."

"I understand the quote, but maybe not the reference."

Hope put her hand on Linh's arm. "I know what I need to do to make the painting from the photograph right for the family. It just came to me, but it won't be easy for me."

"You have me suspended in your mystery, Hope." Linh put down her spoon.

"Michael doesn't belong in the new creation, does he?" Why didn't she think of that before? Hope was used to her father hiding the memory of Hằng out of respect for Kate, but Hope hadn't thought about how her new family might feel. "Linh, I wasn't thinking." Hope's perspective was spinning, and she settled on a positive one. "Well, as Picasso said, maybe I need to start with destruction to begin this creation. I'll challenge my art skills by painting a new version with just the Lê family members—minus Michael."

"I admire you for that, Hope. It's an artist's job to decide what to include in the frame and what to take out—what view and angle to approach a subject from, beyond mere replication."

"Thank you, Linh. Agreed." Hope was becoming more confident in her own vision. It felt good.

"Hope, I know I said we all loved Michael, and we'd love to see him someday. So many fond memories." Linh folded her napkin and set it next to her empty bowl. "But honestly, the news falls on tender ears for the older generations. And, yes, maybe having him in the family photo feels awkward. Not that anyone holds Michael directly responsible. And we know how much he loved Hằng. On one hand, you wouldn't be here without him." Linh hesitated. "On the other, my sister might be alive."

28

AS HOPE PRACTICED her art the next day, she realized she needed to find more time for her relaxing hobby when she went home. Linh's Vietnamese artist friends were all fascinating and in their twenties to forties. They'd all made similar tough choices to pursue their art. The empathy, laughter, and sharing stories were a breath of fresh air for Hope. It had been a long time since she'd been with a group of friends and not just family or work colleagues who regularly disappeared into the ether. Commuting from her home in Boston across the bridge to Cambridge and visiting Glynn on weekends had filled her life. A small and comfortable world but disconnected from the university's community except for classes. Looking back, because of that, Hope hadn't formed any close friendships at school.

She stopped painting and looked up at Linh. "Sometimes I feel spoiled and selfish when I take time for my hobby when it isn't related to work."

"Hope, maybe this isn't a hobby."

"What do you mean? I don't have your level of talent."

Linh looked into Hope's eyes. "Here's a quote for you that might be the answer. Because I take issue with your 'hobby' being the end of the line for the train ride of your talent. Well, that was a roughly posed metaphor."

Linh's intensity caused Hope to hold her breath.

"*One can fool life for a long time, but in the end, it always makes us what we are intended to be.* Perhaps it's in your genes, Hope. Like it is with me. After my first week at med school, I quit. I could *not* resist the call of my art, family pressures or not. Can you imagine my elders' reactions? My brother was a prestigious physician, my father a revered professor and financial tycoon, and my tuition was down the drain. Learning to negotiate between the *I* and the *We* was the most important lesson, a skill much needed to appease both cultures, especially when we'd first arrived. We were lucky we had the money and could have had separate homes, but my family is traditional. After the war's terrors, they eventually bought a house where we'd all lived together."

"I see that tendency in the Ketchum family, but it was an economic necessity. When they could, each family bought their own home, but all within blocks of each other. But still, they spend every waking hour together."

"Here's another piece of wisdom from André Malraux, *the truth about a man lies first and foremost in what he hides.* What might you be hiding, Hope?"

"What am I hiding?" Hope felt like a flower folding in from the cold. The question felt invasive. Her Aunt Linh had certainly internalized her artist friends' deep-dive culture. Still, it didn't take long for Hope to know the answer.

Stepping out of her comfort zone, she answered. "Yes, lately,

I'm conflicted about my legal job. The joy of arranging the adoption legalities and documents and the thrill of painting portraits had worked so well for me—at first. I was indoctrinated by well-meaning loved ones. I'm with family in a beautiful home. I'm in love with someone who gets me. But I'm surrounded by conversations of terror and endless stories of cruelty and rape, and genocide from the team members' experiences in the field. I hear it in the hallways, staff meetings, and even the ladies' room. I realize you can't cherry-pick a job like mine."

Every thought tumbling around in her head about her situation flowed out in the safety of Linh's openness. "I feel so free here, an innocence somehow. All we do here is play. Oh, don't misunderstand. I know it's your career. It's just so soul-fulfilling. Serious play. I never looked at my art in this way. The portraits come to me because a child has suffered or was terrorized like I had been. It serves a purpose, which I embrace, but I want to explore beyond what I allow myself to do in my East Coast world. Yet I belong there in every important way."

"Mark Twain said work and play are the same thing under differing conditions. I understand the play conflict. Not in the same way, but I had to fight and sacrifice to become an artist." Linh stopped washing her watercolors across the paper. "Would it bring you some relief to be a part of the artists' exhibit here when you come in February? I'll save some space. What if we did a theme? Something that would work for both sides of you."

Hope wiped her hands on a towel. "What do you mean?"

Lifting her brush, a drip of red paint hit the paper and flowed across the beautiful blue river Linh was creating. They both stared at the unintentional metaphor for the bloodshed of war that colored Hope's world.

Hope felt the energy behind the idea surge through her. The kind of feeling she got when she knew something was right. "Like 'War Babies,' or something like that?"

They both jumped up from their seats with the excitement of the idea.

"Yes! Maybe for the promo you could do a self-portrait as a child and one now as an artist and lawyer."

The idea gelled for Hope. "Then maybe we call the show 'War Babies: Then and Now.' So, I could exhibit some of my best portraits here at our open house and donate the proceeds to our foundation."

"Exactly, an excuse for you to visit again and get exposure for the benefit of Uplift."

"That would be when I visit for *Tet*, right, Linh?"

"Yes, and everything about *Tet* is related to a fresh start and renewal. A meaningful time to make a change."

"Six weeks. I think that's enough time to assemble the pieces." She pictured Dominique smiling off on the sidelines as she explained her process to a group of visitors. "Linh, I love that idea. Do you really think I'm ready for that?"

"More than ready. And if I can be so bold as to insert myself in your life, you could time your future visits when Dominique is out of the country if you'd like."

The ideas kept coming. It was meant to be, Hope thought. Yes, keep my sanity and calm through my art. "I could rent a studio." So rarely had Hope ever connected with someone so quickly as she had with her aunt.

"No, you can't."

The momentum stopped. Hope couldn't read her aunt's expression. Had she gone too far? "I don't understand."

"Of course, you couldn't understand. We should have discussed it, but I've been thinking ever since you showed me your pieces when we first met. I wanted to ask you to share my studio when you visit. I'm known for following my intuition. There's plenty of room, and we could do quick portraits at the openings when the public is allowed in. I've always wanted to do that." Pointing to the area just outside her art door, Linh closed her eyes. "Imagine the two of us, quick sketching out there. And we'll have a photographer taking photos for future portraits we can paint for our customers. What do you think? Hope, we're family. And, of course, we would sell our portraiture and my landscapes. And think of how happy our Lê family will be?"

"You mean they would be happy to have me around? I didn't get the feeling . . . well, I wasn't sure how they felt about me."

"They love you, but I meant how happy they would be since I'd live in a three-gen family home."

They enjoyed the joke together. "You're funny. They get their way, after all. But what about John?"

"I've already talked to him about the possibility. It's been bubbling in my brain these past weeks. As long as it's an off-and-on basis, he's fine with it. He's constantly traveling for work anyway. Our boys will love you."

Was Hope in touch with reality? She looked at her watercolor-stained nails and wiped them on her black jeans. This way, Dominique could have his passion; Hope would have hers. It might be the only way she could get through, and they could stay together as a couple and spend time together in between. They would figure it out somehow.

Buried in her art with the support of her West Coast family here, Hope wouldn't be as stressed when he was away. There were no constant reminders like in the office. There would be no daily updates about the war—its conflicts, killings, and atrocities. On her previous visit, Hope had already experienced the calming difference. Yes, she would worry about Dominique, but there were long periods when she was working on art or enjoying the family and scenery in nature when she could forget for a while.

What about her dad? she thought. Hope would need to work it out with him. But didn't she have the right? She could work from anywhere when it came to reviewing documents. It was hard when the executive team was traveling. Hope was lonely there with just the administration team. The space beside her at night in her bed was achingly empty. The idea of quitting flashed through her mind. No, maybe this hybrid plan Linh suggested was the answer to juggling her love, job, belonging to two families, and her art. Hope couldn't predict the outcomes. Her life had always been mapped out from the beginning, planned and preconceived. She'd never let herself stray far from her father, Shiloh, and the Ketchums. It was a loving, safe place. This direction was spontaneous and came from inside her. Her first actual decision. She wasn't following Auntie Shiloh's path or her dad's path.

"This is crazy, Linh, but I'm in."

29

THIS IS WHAT Hope needed: to be in Dominique's arms. The trip back to Boston had been filled with fantasies and anticipation. The decision came quickly. Thinking it through, she'd unraveled all the complications of her decision. "Honey, it's a win-win. I'll be near my Ketchum family when you're in Boston. I'll go to California with the Lês when you go on a mission. For me, those are the times the office hallways echo with loneliness. And the 'waiting' was painful. I think I'll be able to handle the fear and separation anxiety if I'm away, busy, doing my art with Linh. She has a great circle of artist friends." Hope kissed his shoulder. "So, you can follow what fulfills you without worrying about terrorizing me. What do you think?"

She could almost feel the heat in his body rise. "What about future children?"

Dominique's curt tone was surprising. "I can paint their portraits in Linh's studio and bring them back when I return or ship them. I don't see the problem."

His silence unnerved her.

He shook his head, sighed, flipped back the covers, and headed for the window. Pushing back the drapes, he put his hands on his hips. "Not the *Uplift* children, Hope." He turned toward her with a posture and a manner she'd never experienced with her lover. "I meant *our* children. How does that work for *our* children?"

Hope was unnerved when Dominique put his palm to his forehead in frustration. "Please tell me what's going on, Dominique."

"You realize you are recreating precisely what you criticized Kate for, putting her singing above you, her adoptive child. And these would be *our* children by choice."

"Dominique, I hadn't . . . it's so far in the future, isn't it? We aren't even married yet. We've never discussed having children."

"I just assumed from your love of kids you would want to have a family with me. Am I right?"

"To be honest, yes, I love children, but I'm not sure I can handle the fragility, the responsibility, and the vulnerability after what I've seen. And should that time come, how would the children handle you going off into war zones? How would I? Would *you* stop following your passion? Dominique, we'll find our way. You seem so different. What happened while I was away?"

Pacing in front of his bedroom fireplace, its flames having dwindled down to a row of red embers, he finally shared his news. "Jolie is returning tomorrow. She said she wanted to talk with Michael and the two of us. She asked for a meeting at ten a.m. in the office conference room."

Hope was right. Something was going on beyond Hope's announcement about her art plans. She hadn't said it was a forever plan, just a way of giving them both what they needed at this time. Of course, Hope wouldn't leave their children behind if they had them. This theoretical argument shouldn't go any further. She wanted to be the one to bridge this unfamiliar distance between them. Crossing the dim room, she put her arms around his neck. "Honey, this whole thing has spun out of control. It's a short-term plan that benefits us both. We'll work things out with love. What did Jolie say? Let's sit."

The white linen loveseat was a symbolic place to work it out, she thought. Dominique sat and pulled her in close with the protective arm she was used to having around her. The gap, that moment of distancing, was frightening to her.

"Darling, I'm sorry, I don't feel like myself when she gets in my business. I'm afraid she'll withdraw the funding, try to leverage me or you, and even destroy us. I love you. I want to marry you, care for you, and have a family of little Vietnamese American French kids with brown and blue eyes. And I shouldn't have made assumptions. I should have talked to you. I don't want to subject you to this woman." He sighed. "It's ironic. My mother wants me back in her life, yet she pulls this drama scene. You don't know the damage she's caused her so-called friends over the years." Dominique held Hope's shoulders. "I'm so afraid you will find it to be all too much with her in our lives. I can't lose you. Tell me you won't let her come between us, darling?"

"Of course not." Could she keep that promise? Hope wanted to believe so.

He pushed her long hair back, kissed her neck, and took a deep breath. "I'm sorry. She has me so unnerved that I overreacted to any threat to our relationship. Of course, you wouldn't leave our children behind or jeopardize their happiness or security, moving them all over the country like Kate did to you. I mean, if we decide to have children. We would, wouldn't we?"

Hope didn't know the answer.

Fortunately, Dominique continued. "And the idea is quite brilliant to give you a support system while I'm away. I'll feel less worried about you if you are with your Lê family, especially with all those studly American men around Boston."

His newly developed humor was her fault, and he was looking to her for a smile to break the tension. She delivered.

"Finally, you can learn about your original culture and create art for your first *Tet*. I will join you there to meet your family at your first official exhibit."

"Exactly. Dom, I feel safe and happy doing my art and being with family. That will help lower my anxiety about your safety. I can still support the foundation with my art. We're creating a gallery exhibition to raise funds and spread the word. It's called 'War Babies: Then and Now.' Linh is interviewing Vietnamese people from her church in San Francisco—refugees from the time of Saigon's fall. I'll sketch a portrait from an early childhood photograph and one from adulthood that shows their life's path. It's inspiring. A special series to mark the twentieth anniversary of Babylift and Uplift. I can honor my father's charitable work, as well."

"Hope, I wanted to surprise you. It seems my next article will be syndicated nationwide."

"Oh, that's wonderful, honey. Congratulations." She'd always hoped Dominique would focus on his writing. He was good, and it might give him more time away from the heart of the chaos.

"I think I know just what to write about. But I'll surprise you."

Hope snuggled into his chest. "How intriguing. My mysterious man."

"Hope, I'm sorry, truly. I don't ever want to feel like that again.

We're good together, and we have the same values. Forgive me for making assumptions."

"And now we take those values and face your mother together and see if we can make things right for all of us," Hope said.

"I have deep doubts, darling, very deep. She has left a trail of cadavers in her wake as long as I've been old enough to be aware of her manipulations. Countess Dracula and her victims. I will not be one of them." He hugged Hope tight. "Nor will you."

"Keep your collar closed, monsieur."

DESPITE HOW good it felt to see her father, Shiloh, and her Uplift colleagues, being back in the office at the staff meeting only reinforced Hope's decision.

Linh had sent the photos and background stories for the portraits, and Hope had arrived at 7:00 a.m. to start her paintings for the exhibition. Once Christmas was over, she would work early and late before bed until she left for the exhibition in February. Hope had a schedule and a plan.

As they sipped coffee against the backdrop of the awakening city, Michael shared a report by the Human Rights Watch outlining The First Russian Chechen war actions. "Indiscriminate bombings and shelling by Russian forces are being carried out," Michael read. "They're targeting civilian populations by ground forces causing an 'unimaginable catastrophe,' that German Chancellor Helmut Kohl described as 'sheer madness.'"

"The destruction of three hospitals, one orphanage, and numerous market areas was reported," Michael added. The buzz in the office among the team caused a flash of heat across Hope's face as her father added the final details.

"At least three hundred and fifty thousand people were forced to flee the region due to the conflict. I'll have a conference call later today with the other NGOs and the usual governmental people to determine our role. Thanks, guys. You know the routine. Let's get ready."

Just before 10:00 a.m., as the conference room emptied, each person in their rush to exit and get to work on the phones quickly welcomed Hope back and congratulated her on finding her biological family. There was no time to celebrate when children were at risk; she understood that.

Dominique stood at the world map and stabbed a pushpin where the new conflict was—his assumed assignment.

Hope felt nauseous.

"I see why your plan to leave for California makes sense to you, Hope." He turned around to face her. "It makes sense for *us*. But I look forward to meeting your family at *Tet*. I need to be able to picture where you are. To keep those happy images in my mind while I face these tragic situations." He glanced at the clock at the other end of the large room. "So, now we face another conflict. Jolie should be here at any moment." He checked around the room to ensure they were alone and kissed her forehead. "That is the way it's done in your family, no? On the forehead? We will soon be family."

"Yes, you are culturally correct, my love." The gesture and lighthearted moment only postponed the wave of disappointment that came with the news. Her familiar fear gathered force in her stomach. Fear over his imminent departure rose, and the danger and fear of facing the other more imminent war with his mother.

Hope was ready, but the woman was an unknown— hard to read and understand. Now, her father, Shiloh, and the foundation were intimately involved. Hope was sure she knew what was coming at the meeting with Jolie. A disaster of a different kind.

Shiloh and Michael returned to the room with Jolie. "Let's all sit and listen to Mrs. Bonchance. The floor is yours." Michael directed them to the conference table. In keeping with her metaphorical mind, Hope sat facing the rainstorm outside the wall of windows—an appropriate backdrop for the drama.

As always, Jolie was wrapped in her gracious demeanor and draped in her fashionable garb. She was an attractive woman in her early fifties. Just like Kate with her stylish fashion, Jolie seemed far too young to be Dominique's mother. His older sister, maybe.

"How can we help you?"

Hope was amazed that her father showed no hint that he knew exactly why the meeting was called. A class act.

Shiloh moved quickly to sit next to Hope as if to provide protection so that Jolie had no chance of having an unpleasant, close encounter.

Jolie kept her gaze on Michael. "Monsieur James, I have unfortunate news for you. Based on my recent experience with your daughter's lying and the unacceptable office romance she and my son are carrying on, I'm afraid I need to withdraw my support for the foundation." She glanced at Hope. "She may not be as honest as you might think looking at her innocent face."

"I will not allow you to disrespect my fiancé. Hope is not—"

"Dominique, please. Let's allow your mother to finish." Michael nodded a signal that seemed to say, I've got this.

"Regarding the funding, that is unfortunate, Jolie, especially considering the children in our Uplift One Child safe schools.

Would you please give me more details about Miss Lê Ketchum-James's dishonesty?"

"I wanted to help her to save face, considering she is your daughter." Jolie lifted her chin. What did that gesture signal? Hope wondered. To indicate dignity?

"In this room, she is my employee," Michael said.

Hope almost wanted to laugh at Jolie's lack of self-awareness, but it was sad and impossible to think of this woman as her future mother-in-law. She had to be so damaged to be so unkind.

"Is there anything else, madam?" Michael began to stand up.

Dominique's expression of shock and confusion permanently hung on his face. Hope observed his head turning from his mother to Michael and back as though he were watching a French Open tennis match.

"Perhaps you don't understand. Due to your daughter's unprofessionalism, I am withdrawing millions of dollars from—"

"Forgive my interruption." Michael stood and put his hands on the table, leaning toward Jolie.

She pulled back at his sudden move.

His voice rose as Michael began to lose his intended cool. "No one, no matter how rich or powerful, will *ever* leverage or threaten—"

Shiloh held out her hands and dropped them slowly to calm Michael like a conductor at the end of a tender symphony. "Excuse me, maybe I can help, as Vice Chairman of the Board and someone who has known Jolie for decades. Jolie, as you said when you first met Hope, she is a charming, intelligent, quality woman. And you asked her one question. What is the one thought that haunted her, that lingered and influenced her actions?"

Everyone was caught off guard.

Shiloh's forward approach was unexpected.

"You said you'd become open and expansive, Jolie. I have a question for you to ponder in the safety of this room filled with people who care. What is the driving reason you manipulate people with your money, time and again, losing friends and, on more than one occasion, your son's admiration? Take a moment or an hour. But the answer might be the key to your future happiness."

Hope didn't know where to look. Had she ever experienced such tension and weighty silence—while observing contentious court cases, in school debates, or even upon meeting her Lê family? No. It was palpable. Her father appeared dumbstruck, and Dominique's eyes had never been so wide.

Jolie drew in a breath that tremored with emotion. She didn't make a move toward the door. Rubbing her right hand with her left thumb, her downcast eyes appeared to be sincerely searching. Then she nodded, keeping her gaze on her hands. Her voice was barely audible. "Since I am likely to lose everything that matters to me through my actions today, yours is a bold but fair question, Shiloh. One I never have been forced to consider."

Shiloh's bangle bracelets chiming was the only sound in the room as she put her hand on Jolie's shoulder and studied her eyes. "Please be your new open person with us. There is everything to gain."

Hope remembered that moment when Jolie had put her in that awkward position where she'd had to connect with her vulnerability. She almost felt sorry for the poor woman.

Shiloh tried to keep the channel of communication open with another question. "You are not alone in having a past you might regret. But do you want to suffer in the same way going forward?"

Jolie dropped her head and spoke into her lap with her hands folded in a tight grip. "Ever since my husband died . . . I think, well, perhaps I have on occasion—" Jolie turned to take in the view. The expanse of the sky seemed to change the look in her eyes. "No. The truth is, I have always used my money to attract people to me, to lure them to care about me, and to get people to love me. But Shiloh, you just made me aware it has never worked. My money never lured your mother and her compassionate hippie self. She's the only one who knows me and still cares. Perhaps I was lost with no purpose. I was afraid to lose you, Dominique."

"Mother, I—"

"No. This must be said. I have never found a purpose, and I've tried to buy love and attention." Jolie turned to Hope. "I'm sorry, dear. And I love you, Dominique. Someday, you'll forgive me. As you might imagine, I feel quite pathetic right now, so I'll be leaving."

"Wait." Michael had a look Hope had never seen—serious and confident, but with a slight, enigmatic smile that seemed out of place at the poignant moment.

"Please sit. I want to propose something that might seem invasive. I hope not. Suppose your one thought is that you have no purpose. If you cannot find a way to be valuable for simply being you, would you consider removing your donation and joining our board so that we can go back to square one? I have a position that might suit you well. Director of Events. Rumor has it that no one can plan a social event better than you. Our annual donor appreciation event is coming up in the summer. There are several other celebrations—smaller private events with other NGOs and receptions for government officials."

As Michael went on about the various gatherings that needed

leadership, Hope watched her future mother-in-law's excitement rise. Shiloh was something else using Jolie's own strategy on her. Yet, it was done with love. Had she and Michael planned for this moment?

Dominique moved next to his mother. "Do what is right for you, Mother. But you will never come between Hope and me."

Did they have a more transparent window into the real Jolie at this fragile moment? If so, could Hope ever again resent or fear her future mother-in-law? Was this version of Jolie going to stay? Hope wanted to believe it. Or was it another manipulation?

"I would love to accept—that is, if you are comfortable with that, son?"

"As long as I am near the woman you are right now, Mother. I didn't realize what was behind your manipulations."

"I apologize, Hope. Please forgive an old, damaged fool?"

Hope couldn't be unkind. Hesitating, she searched for the right words to show strength and compassion. "Jolie, I'll work on forgetting that former woman desperate to be loved—as we all are—if you will forget the well-intentioned liar you once knew."

30

PACKING FOR TET was important. As she took out the luggage for their trip, Hope practiced the traditional *Tet* greeting, struggling to use the correct tones. *Chúc mừng Năm Mới!*

Linh had explained that one error in a tonal language meant she could say something unintended. But it could also cause a lot of laughter, and everyone would still understand what you were trying to say, Linh had said. Depending on the tone she used for Nam, the word for "new," she could mistakenly say "male" or "five." Well, Happy Male Year was appropriate with Dominique in her life now. Hope laughed at the trouble mispronouncing the word for happy, "mung," could cause. Misspeak the tone, and you'd be talking about mung beans or mosquito nets. Thankfully, her Lê family spoke English and French. Linh would translate when they were at the family home, where tradition called for speaking Vietnamese.

Opening her luggage flat on the bed, Hope thought about some of the Lunar New Year traditions she'd learned from Linh.

One long-held practice was to wear all new clothes on the first day of the ten-day celebration the Catholic Vietnamese adhered to, depending on the family. No black or white clothing should be worn. They were colors for a funeral.

A fresh start, she was counting on that with her new plan in place. Folding the new blue plaid blazer, light blue dress shirt, and navy slacks, she placed them on one side of the suitcase. She added the new socks she'd bought for Dominique, new underwear, and the leather toiletry bag he kept at her house.

Linh had a new *áo dài* for Hope to wear, a colorful red satin long tunic with a mandarin collar and flowing pants. Hope's new dressy suit, a little red print dress, and pearls Hope had bought would work for other events. Hope had kept the price tags so she could confirm they were new if that was somehow part of the tradition.

Luckily, Uncle Jack and Grandpa K had recently made Dominique a pair of handmade Owl & Shamrock men's navy leather dress moccasins with pewter medallions across the instep. She thought they would work for both church and casual.

Of course, Hope had several pairs of shoes she hadn't worn yet—gifts from her Ketchum clan. At least she didn't have to worry about religious customs at church. She was happy both of her families were Catholic.

The thought of introducing Dominique to her Lê family was exciting. He was so polished, respectful, and kind, and she could hear him speaking French with the Grands. Hope loved the word Linh had made up for the elders in the family.

On a recent call, Uncle Tuân said the family would not view Dominique negatively simply for being French. Hope just had to ask so she could prepare. She didn't know the politics. Moving to

Boston from his life of Parisian affluence to help war babies was all that needed to be said about her fiancé, Uncle Tuân had said.

She would arrive a day before the holiday to plan the exhibit with Linh. There were complications. Following tradition, the family did not work during *Tet*, except for her Uncle Tuân. He was dedicated to his job at the prestigious hospital.

Hope would describe their exhibition and foundation fund-raising plans to the elders. Linh said the portraits from the past could be seen as modern ancestor worship. Her family wanted to honor the spirit of Hằng, but they didn't all adhere to the old ghost traditions as much as some families still did.

The idea of *ghosts* intrigued Hope. Linh gave her insight into ghosts in Vietnamese culture. She'd said they were known to take on many forms. They could be good and kind-spirited or evil and dangerous. Most elders in their family believed ghosts were people who'd undergone unnatural, premature, painful, or violent deaths, especially when they died away from home, unlike ancestors who died a good death in their homes, honored by proper rituals.

Since the Lê family didn't know where Hằng was, they held out hope and kept her in their thoughts and prayers. Linh had shared more about the traditional beliefs.

Hope was fascinated that the souls in their afterlife needed the same things to exist as the living. This was why families made offerings of things like paper money, food, clothing, shoes, or even a house. Only souls that had received the proper rituals, were buried in a good location with a proper tombstone, and had their tablet installed on the family's ancestor altar would become ancestors. They would be nourished by the family, Linh had said. It was thought that the dead would reciprocate by continuing to help the family members prosper. Those who don't have these rituals and circumstances would become ghosts and were thought to roam the countryside in hoards stealing. In this sense, they're seen as the supernatural equivalent of robbers. They were also called "hungry ghosts," *ma đói.*

Hope could now see why not knowing if Hằng was deceased or alive meant the family would just hold out hope and pray. If they assumed she'd died in the war and did the usual honoring of the dead and Hằng returned, it would be awkward, rude, and bad luck. They would put her photo on their altar and make no offerings like they would for a deceased family member, Linh had explained. This gave Hope an idea.

My mother is dead, but she has no grave, Hope thought. There was no site to visit or to decorate with flowers to honor her as an ancestor. She knew who would be the perfect one to create that sacred place for her mother so she would no longer be a ghost.

The portable phone rang. Hope pulled up the antennae. "Dominique, I have you all packed. You'll love your new clothes."

Her father's voice was loud, a signal he was on his way somewhere, calling from an airport or limo. "Sweetheart, I have some not-so-good news."

"Sorry, Dad, I assumed it was Dominique. What's happening?" Did she really want to know? She held her breath and wrapped her arm around her middle. "Go ahead, Dad. I can hear you."

Her father explained that the team was ill and was in a Red Cross temporary hospital. Shiloh and the others were down with high fever and congestion.

"It's not life-threatening, honey, but we needed Dominique to help. We have two planes filled with supplies and food, and Dominique knows the distribution system and logistics and can fly in medicines. The Uplift private jet has just departed with him on board. Dominique will call you shortly once he's in the air. He was on calls with the people on the ground in Chechnya."

"Dad, what is the war situation near there?" She squeezed her fist so tight her nails were digging into her palm.

"There's no threat by the Russians in that area now. Just the spread of the illness. Two people have already recovered, no deaths, don't worry."

Michael's words didn't comfort her.

"I'm so sorry, sweetheart. Have a great time. My guess is Dominique won't make the *Tet* festivities. If some of the other team members recover quickly, there's a slight chance he will."

Besides her concern for their safety, it was her worst fear. Hope slumped into her chair, heavy with disappointment. She immediately experienced the familiar emotional conflict between the greater good and her desires and plans. "Thanks, Dad. I understand. I'll wait to hear from him. Our flight departs in four hours. I'll cancel his reservation."

ON THE flight to San Francisco, Hope tried to think of things to be happy about and focus on the good, an exercise she'd once learned at a self-help seminar. She was glad to be flying first class with no one beside her. She could spread out and review her artwork after take-off.

With the captain's good-weather announcements blaring overhead, she read her weekly letter from Kate. Although her missives were always about the fascinating cities she was touring and nothing personal, Hope still loved getting them. Her dad had given Hope reports, too, when he'd often met up with Kate on her tours. They'd managed to make it work.

Over the most recent years with Hope in college and law school, she'd mainly seen Kate on school breaks at the Ketchums in Glynn. Summers, Hope had traveled. It was an annual reward for her accomplishments from her dad. She did catch that recent concert with her dad and Grandma Cecelia when her schedule and Kate's touring had intersected. Hope tried to accept the long-distance relationship with Kate as she'd become an adult. It was both distant in miles and emotion, limited and unsatisfying. Hope tried signing her letters *With Love, Hope*, but the return letters were simply signed, *Kate*. She still hadn't finished Kate's journal. Hope was too busy with her painting, but she'd read a section here and there about her meeting Michael, his troubles, Kate's passion for her music, their spontaneous wedding at the Embassy in Bangkok, and the conflict she felt loving Michael but not wanting a traditional married life.

Turning to her portfolio of portraits, thick with her works for the exhibit, Hope was proud. She'd finished the last one yesterday. Linh had sent her a dozen people's written stories and two photographs for each testimony. The first photo was taken in childhood, many around their evacuation to San Francisco or at one of the refugee camps before transferring to California. The second picture was taken recently, twenty years later. The stories that accompanied the photographs were diverse and touching.

"Care for anything?" The stewardess offered her juice or coffee. "Is this your work? The child in the box is an odd thing. She's adorable."

"That was how they transported the infant orphans on the

evacuation flights when Saigon fell." Hope pointed to a photo. "This is her all grown up. It's part of an exhibit I'm working on."

"May I see quickly? There's only one other man in first class. I have some time before breakfast."

Hope showed her the first painting of a smiling baby in a cardboard box being loaded onto a Pan Am flight. "Refugees from the Vietnam War."

"Oh my. So sad." The stewardess put the tray down and bent over for a better view.

"And this is the child all grown up." The updated photo captured the waitress in a San Francisco diner. "She'd been adopted by a teacher and her husband and had become part owner of his diner. Now, she also hosts charity tables for the homeless to eat free."

The stewardess put her hand to her chest. "That is such a good ending."

"Here's a young Vietnamese pilot from the US National Guard. He'd worked his way through college and ultimately had become a mechanical engineer, designing award-winning appliances," Hope read aloud. She related his story of being on a mission in Vietnam and being told to surrender. But instead, he flew out, nearly running out of fuel over dangerous territory before he landed in Laos. Once on the ground, he'd crossed the Mekong River to Thailand and safety by breathing underwater through a reed. An American Embassy official in Bangkok found a sponsor for him in San Francisco.

"What a heroic young man. I'm Kristen." She glanced toward the captain's door. "Thank you, I better get breakfast ready. You made my day. And your artwork is amazing. It makes them come alive."

"Thank you, Kristen. Your response makes me more confident."

From highly successful to simply grateful, from doctors to landscapers to Pho café owners, the gratitude showed on nearly all the faces. They were survivors.

Hope and Linh hadn't wanted to over-romanticize; they wanted to reflect the truth. But the fact was, everything Hope had read indicated that the Vietnamese people as a group had adapted and worked hard and were family-bonded, fun-loving, dedicated souls. Not everyone had achieved that elusive American dream, but everyone she'd captured in her art had led a respectable life over the two decades since they'd arrived.

When Hope had read one refugee's story after another while sitting at her art table at home, she'd been inspired. She'd diligently captured their spirits in her watercolor and charcoal portraits. One photo had stopped her. A young boy in jail for stealing food from a grocery store. His story was heartbreaking, having endured so much as a child in a refugee camp. But the follow-up photo showed him with his college diploma in hand. After nearly a month of working on the project, Hope was proud to be Vietnamese.

The second section of the portfolio held the surprise she'd planned for the family. A portrait of each of the primary Ketchum and Lê biological family members for four generations. She'd made a family tree, two branches, the working-class American Ketchums and the world-class wealthy Vietnamese Lê family. Hope had an idea to paint a sprawling tree on one of the studio walls and hang the two families together. It would represent the blending of two cultures, the joining of good people, with Hằng's and Hope's portraits in the middle and branches for Ernie and Mary.

31

"HURRY, OPEN IT. I'm dying to see your work." Linh closed the door to her studio. "I'm so excited you found the time with all your legal work."

Opening the portfolio, Hope experienced a strange combination of elation and anxiety. She flipped through the paintings and took out a portrait of Linh. "Have you seen my beautiful aunt?" Her decision to focus on the positive was the right one.

"Oh, Hope, I've never looked so good." Linh held up the watercolor next to her face. "You took away all my flaws, warts and all. You're such a kind artist."

"Very funny. I just painted what I saw. I focused on your beautiful fine features and long swaying hair like mine, except the true color without the genetic glitch of highlights from my father's family. Seriously, Linh, will it do?"

Holding it up on the wall, Linh smiled. "I admit it shows off all the positives. Thank you. But I never expected you to have the time to do both projects."

"Let me show you the rest." Dealing the portraits out on the table brought such a satisfying reaction from Linh, one after another, gasps and words like, wow, and love that one, oh, and that one's sublime.

"And not to brag, but I did two of each, so I can give one to each family member."

"You are quite the productive one. This will be the most amazing exhibition. I've lined up an advertisement in the local Vietnamese magazine and newspaper and have a connection at the Chronicle. Oh, plus I arranged an insert in the church program for the bi-lingual, English-Vietnamese Mass on *Tet*. My friend Minh designed it. She's talented at that kind of thing."

Linh shook her head as she studied the portraits of her mother and father, the Grands, and the Ketchums. "Love the red hair on so many of your relatives. Seriously, Hope, this project is a masterpiece." She hugged Hope. "It will appeal to the Amerasians, as well. They need some acceptance, even twenty years later. And my kids will love it. They'll want a family tree of John's family and ours. You're on to something."

"Let's get started on the tree and The Wall of Hope." Linh pointed to the portrait of Hope as a newly arrived child. "Oh, the painting of you as a toddler at the piano is so adorable, and the portrait of you as an adult must have been challenging. Self-portraiture is the toughest. Hard to be objective, but you know what?"

"Wait, before you say it. I just painted what I saw in the photograph, trying not to think of it as me."

"That's why it works. You allowed yourself to be as beautiful as you are. That is an art form." Linh ran her hand down Hope's hair, which had grown well beyond her shoulders in the past months. "Silky, like Hằng's. You look so much like my sister, I could cry."

"Well, everyone who sees us thinks you and I are sisters. So, you must be good-looking too."

"Amazing. Please tell me more about these two branches?" Linh pointed to the portraits of Ernie and Mary.

"My adopted brother and sister. A long story, I'll tell you over wine some night."

"How about a synopsis now over a coffee? Then we'll get started hanging them. I'm intrigued."

They sat in their usual chairs, and Hope gave her the summary. "It was a rescue with as much drama as any," she said. "I read it in Kate's diary. Mary had been dropped off at a state institution for people with disabilities by her mother to save her from an abusive stepfather. Her mother told Mary never to speak, or they might send her back. Mary pretended for years to be mute or incapable of speaking. But eighteen-year-old Ernie, a resident at the facility since birth, overheard her reading in the classroom closet before class."

Hope continued, "My adoptive mother was interning at the institution for her graduate work before she chose to sing for her life's career, and long story short, she found Mary's mother who released her parental rights so my great-aunt could save Mary from her fears. Mary was nearly raped at the institution too, but Ernie saved her. He was seriously injured in the struggle with this perpetrator." Hope caught her breath and stopped. "You're sure you want to hear this, Linh?"

"Let's finish it up. I'm learning about your history, Hope."

"Well, Kate feared leaving him there where the boy involved with the rape would be living in the same housing unit. And she'd developed a deep connection to Ernie. Anyone would. He has more physical disabilities than you can count, but his heart is always in the right place, and he is so comical. He was my first friend. My grandparents adopted Ernie, and I grew up with Mary and him. I hope you meet Ernie someday. He's extraordinary and was a big part of my adapting to life when I came to America at three. Mary is sweet. She's a seamstress in my Aunt Maggie's dress shop."

"Good for her. And Ernie sounds so loving. And no wonder you're so accepting."

"Yes, sadly, he was abandoned at a hospital after he was born to two young teen parents. He wasn't expected to survive and ended up in the state institution."

"Kate must be a compassionate person to do that, too."

Hope hadn't often focused on that part of Kate before. A frequent glimmer of understanding for her adoptive mother had flashed through Hope's mind lately. "Let's start painting a tree. Is that wall a good place?"

"The main display will be in the gallery out front, and we'll put the family tree here in the studio. I'm picturing my family in this room with some privacy when they first see it. They will need that. Will any of your family be able to come?"

"I guess, based on the family's feelings about my father, they wouldn't want Michael to show up. And he may never be able to face them, Linh. He holds a lot of shame over his past. And wouldn't his presence forever remind them of my mother's death?"

"I think if he came, they could build a bridge. The timing is the question."

"So complicated and painful." Hope hesitated. She had to share what was going on. "I avoided bringing it up this morning so I wouldn't kill our joy. But there's a crisis with the foundation team in Chechnya, and unexpectedly, Dominique is orchestrating the mission. Everyone has taken ill. I was packing when my father called to tell me. This is what I was telling you about. Always the unexpected."

"I'm so sorry. I noticed you had a certain sadness when you arrived. I thought you were just tired. I know you were excited for Dominique to meet the family. It will happen at the right time, honey." Linh picked up a portrait of Hằng. "Tell you what, let's do this project for Hằng, your mother, my big sister, and let the world go by for a few hours. Your father said they were recovering. Let's hold onto that."

"Yes, Linh, that's the beauty of art. Let's get lost in it. How about we sketch out a tree on the wall to accommodate the family portrait part of the exhibition?" Imagining the family tree, Hope remembered the Sokan Split-Tree concept. She'd seen it in Japan when Bonsais were cultivated to have twin trunks, designed after trees, split by lightning or bombing disasters during the war. Survivors. It was the perfect metaphor for the display. She would write a description for the wall to give the viewer poetic insight. Diverse intimacy, the Japanese guide had called it, when the roots were one, but the tree trunk was split into two. "Linh, I have the perfect concept. It's called the Sokan Split-Tree Trunk."

Hope explained her idea. The bomb that had taken Hằng's life had split Hope away from her Vietnamese family. The growth and rise of the family members had brought diverse intimacy into their lives. And the creative connection of their art had survived through Linh and Hope. Talking about the metaphor brought them to tears as they silently began to outline the tree that would bring their lineages together. Time had turned tragic circumstances into smiling faces.

Hope used her marker to design the split in the tree trunk.

Working her way up her side of the tree, Linh drew a spray of branches, counting them to match the number of portraits in her family. "This will be an expansive painting, Hope. It will fill this entire wall and embrace everyone when they come to the exhibit." Linh stepped back. "I'm reminded of Picasso's painting, *Guernica* from nineteen thirty-seven—the immensity and the impact."

"I saw that enormous mural in Madrid, Linh. But I couldn't linger. The imagery was so graphic and violent—mutilated people, the woman with her head thrown back screaming with her dead child in her arms. I know Picasso painted that with a noble purpose, capturing the horrors of Hitler's bombing of Guernica. Still, it was too much for me." Hope had to change the subject. "Linh, I haven't had time to read everything about how traditions among immigrant families in the US have evolved. I'm sure everyone is different. What does our family do to celebrate *Tet*?"

"We have trimmed back many of the traditions over the years. My mother has a team come in to clean the house beforehand. Traditionally, you don't clean during the week of *Tet*."

"Why is that?"

"It was believed that the good luck would stick to the dust and be swept away. I think today it's just to prepare for guests and our dinner. It's a feast. These days, we have it catered. Some things we still embrace and believe in; some things maybe we're afraid to let go of lest we bring bad luck. And our Catholic faith makes things slightly different from our Buddhist brethren."

Turning to Hope, she lowered her voice. "Honestly, I don't miss the old days of all the tedious preparation. It used to take several of us ten hours or more just to prepare the *banh chung*. They're square, sticky rice cakes wrapped in bamboo leaves. The rice turns green from the leaves when you boil it. It's got glutinous rice, pork, and mung beans inside. Delicious, but tastes better from the caterer." Linh laughed. "I'm too lazy and too busy now."

It was intriguing listening to Linh describe all the foods and their symbolism. Families prepared boxes of colorful candied fruits called *mut* to give visitors, friends, and family and offer to ancestors. Hope loved the idea of *Li Xi*. Linh explained that money was given to children by the Grandparents and adults in red envelopes.

"Oh, Linh, I would love to do a little something for the kids. Is it appropriate?"

"Absolutely, only if you wish to. It's not necessary."

"I want to be a part of the tradition. I'll prepare the envelopes. And I know you told me all about ghosts and ancestral worship. Does your family do anything special to worship the dead?"

Linh assessed Hope's side of the tree and continued sketching the smaller branches to complete her portion. "There's the altar I mentioned at the house to honor the dead and the ancestors, where we have the traditional five-fruit tray—watermelon, mango, papaya, pineapple, and coconut."

The thought of the altar made Hope think of her mother. She only had Kate's diary sharing her father's description of Hằng's horrific death. Hope stopped drawing until the weighty sadness passed. Maybe hearing about her mother from the family would help to change that and give her some dimension in Hope's mind beyond her mother's death.

"I mentioned to you that we wouldn't have arranged a gravesite for Hằng to decorate with flowers since we had no knowledge of her fate. In hopes she would return. But we dedicated a pew to her years ago at St. Boniface church. We all sit there when we go to Mass for *Tet* and every Sunday. Sometimes, I often feel her presence there. We didn't have time to discuss that the first time you went to Mass with us."

"I thought about her while I sat there, but I look forward to learning more about my mother so I have more images of her." Would Hope ever experience her mother's presence? What would that feel like? "Linh, would it be appropriate to put my portrait of my mother on your home altar for your family?"

"Gift it to our great-grandmother when you arrive. She is the one who passed down this irresistible art gene to us. Then, she can place it on the altar to invite Hằng to return for a *Tet* visit. I mean, now that they know she's gone."

32

WEARING THE NEW blue *áo dài*, Hope entered Linh's living room. She admired Linh's rose-colored version with silky pants. "You look great, Linh. No, stunning."

"This is my once-a-year tribute to the culture." Linh spun around.

"Welcome. And you look very traditional, Hope." Dressed in his suit and tie, John sat with their two sons against the expanse of windows that framed the scenic backdrop of the Embarcadero, the ferry terminal, and shimmering blue bay water in the distance. The shine on their shoes showed her they were new.

Linh's husband introduced their two sons, Brad and John, Jr., eight and thirteen, wearing matching blue suits. Brad looked like his fair-haired father with Linh's features. John Jr. resembled his mother with sparkling eyes and little influence from his American genes. Both were lean, sprouting boys. John Jr. was already challenging John's medium height.

"You look pretty, Cousin Hope."

That was unexpected for a boy of twelve. They were both handsome boys. Seeing them in person was fun after painting them from their photos. She handed them their portraits, wondering how they would react to the images.

"Wow, these are cool. You did these? You're an artist just like my mom?" John took Brad's portrait and examined it. "Yeah, you look like her, too. But awesome, you have blue eyes."

"Cool, but weird," Brad said.

How had their Amerasian heritage impacted them socially and emotionally? Hope wondered. Had the prejudice been the same in San Francisco as it had been for her in Glynn and Boston? Although they'd had the benefit of an extended Vietnamese family, Hope thought. So much to learn and understand. In Boston, she could pull off her sophisticated lawyer image. Her limited cultural knowledge of the new environment made her feel like a child again. This was more complicated than learning what fork to use.

"OK, the meal with the family is at noon. Shall we go?" John opened the door for Linh and Hope.

The boys squirted ahead of them, tossing a basketball Brad had picked up from the closet by the front door. "Yay, red envelopes today!"

HOPE CARRIED her folder with the portraits and climbed the stairs to the stunning family mansion. This visit was so important. It would set the stage for their future, she thought. The portraits would break the ice. Linh was kind enough to let her have a day to adjust before visiting the family. With the family tree finished and the exhibit ready to open, Hope was elated as they reached the front door. "Wish me luck, guys."

There were a lot of traditions regarding how to address people and relatives, but Linh said they would forgive Hope since she didn't speak Vietnamese. Still, it was so easy to offend or miscommunicate through behavior, body language, or tone of voice. Hope knew that from her work.

"Wait. In the old days of the 'first footing' tradition, 'ladies first' wasn't the overriding tradition on the first day of *Tet*," Linh said.

"What do you mean?" Shivers ran down Hope's arms. Avoiding a faux pas in such a landmine of unknown traditions would not be easy.

"In the old days, my grandparents would have chosen the first guest to enter since, traditionally, everyone would emulate that person's qualities for the entire year."

Linh put her hand on Hope's shoulder. "As our long-lost and found family member, we would all see it as a good omen if you went in first. From what I know of you, Hope, your qualities would certainly be worth emulating."

"I'm honored." Hope felt humbled by Linh's words and was grateful when John turned, took her arm, wrapped it in his, and led her inside, with Linh close behind.

Uncle Tuân was waiting inside to greet her warmly.

"Uncle Tuân, good to see you. I thought you had to be at the hospital."

"I did an early shift so I could be here for your first *Tet*."

The early part of the event had gone smoothly. Hope distributed the portraits to her great-grandparents and the one of Hằng to her great-grandmother. The gifting went well, and Hope received a gracious reception and lavish praise for her work.

Great-grandmother Lê was surprised. "I had no idea Hope had inherited the family's artistic gift." She crossed the room and placed the portrait of Hằng on the altar. "Now, our beloved Hằng is here with us again. *Merci beaucoup*, Hope."

Everyone had gathered in the living room, enjoying an incredible, sunny view; no clouds or fog obscured the spectacular vista. Traditional Vietnamese *Tet* music and delicious scents from the catered *Tet* feast, unfamiliar to Hope, filled the room. "*Chúc mừng năm mới*. Happy New Year," Hope sat next to her grandfather.

"Oh, look at you, speaking Vietnamese already. That was quick," her grandfather said, laughing good-heartedly.

"Oooooh!" The adults and kids clapped.

After the elders and adults had given the excited kids the anticipated red envelopes with undisclosed amounts of money, Hope presented her little *Li Xi* packets, too. That gesture was a big hit with the cousins.

Hope's body settled into relief as she nibbled on the candied fruit and sipped her tea amid the family chatter. She belonged. Had she ever felt so happy after a day lost in her art and family portraits? Two families, one tree, she thought. A family that had risen from the dead. Her art had spoken for her. No language was necessary, she thought.

"You are the best, cousin Hope." Her teen cousin Hong, who had broken the ice for Hope on her first visit, sat beside her. "Anything you want to know, I can tell you."

"Thank you, Hong. You were the first to welcome me into your home. Do you like the portrait?"

"Yes, I like that you dressed me the way I really dress, even my ear studs."

"How does your family feel about your American ways? Just curious."

"One day, when my grandmother was criticizing my style, my great-grandmother took me aside and said, 'When we moved here, my husband told me a secret: you must learn to speak English, dress like an American, eat the same food that Americans eat, and above all, learn to think like an American. Then you will be successful.' Oh, I think your phone's ringing in your bag."

"I better answer it in the hallway." Was it Dominique?

"Hope?"

"Cecelia? What's wrong?" She'd never received a call from her grandmother.

"Oh honey, I'm so sorry to interrupt your day. Are you painting?"

"No, I'm with my West Coast family. It's their Lunar New Year. Are you OK? What's going on?"

"I'm fine, sweetheart, but I thought you should know immediately. Ernie was taken from the factory to our hospital by ambulance just now. He collapsed. We think maybe it's a stroke, but we are not sure. I'll call later and let you know when we get news."

"Oh my God, send him my love. Will you be going there now?"

"Your father is coming to get us. We just left the factory. He'll be in touch from the hospital. Oh, there he is now. I need to go. Pray for your brother, darling."

"Love you, Grandma Cecelia." Dialing Michael's phone, Hope looked down the hallway to the room buzzing with their celebration. The children were huddled around each other by the window, shuffling through the cash from their red envelopes. The adults surrounded the altar, their muffled words directed at the portrait of Hope's mother. The table was laid out with a colorful feast. There was no way Hope could leave; there was no way to stay. The exhibit, Mass for *Tet*, her new sense of belonging, weighed against her brother? Impossible.

"Hope, is everything alright?"

Uncle Tuân's voice startled her out of her thoughts. She explained the situation. Hope needed to know more to make the decision to stay or leave.

"I can help. What's the name of the hospital?"

"Glynn General. My brother's name is Ernest Randall-Ketchum. I think he's still in the ER."

The wait was dizzying as Uncle Tuân went through several connections to reach the right staff member. It did not sound good. But most of the med-talk went over her head.

"Uncle, I need your advice. Do I need to be there with him? I mean, is he . . . how bad is it?"

"Hope, depending on the test results, diagnosis, and treatment, it could go either way. You might be more comfortable being with your brother than celebrating *Tet* here. What do you think?" The look on her uncle's face was enigmatic.

"I feel terrible either way, Uncle Tuân, but worse if I weren't with him. He was always there for me in my childhood."

"You handle your travel arrangements and say your farewells; I'll handle the family."

His kindness touched her. Hope hadn't even thought about the exhibition. The disappointment flushed through her body. "I'll talk to Linh, OK?"

Hope's head was spinning. She dialed the airline to make a

plane reservation from the alcove and left a message on Cecelia's landline. She could see the family's reactions as her uncle notified each group. They seemed sympathetic.

The gang of three teens, led by Hong, was the first to approach. Linh's two sons were sincere. "Is your brother gonna be alright?" Brad said.

Hong answered for her. "Of course, he is. Tell Ernie that Brad, John, and Hong said Hi. And our Great-grandmother sends this." Hong handed Hope a box of traditional *Tet* treats. "They're for your brother when he feels better."

It was touching, though she prayed he'd be there to receive it.

Grandfather Lê approached with a newspaper. "I wanted to surprise you with this for your *Tet* happiness. I discovered it this morning." He handed her the San Francisco Chronicle with a yellow post-it, marking a page. "Quite impressive. Wait until you're on the plane. And we are all sorry about your brother. We will pray for him at Mass."

When Linh came out of the kitchen, Hope explained the sad situation.

"Darling niece, I will handle the exhibit. I know how close you are to Ernie."

"Thank you, Linh." The unexpected had become the expected in Hope's life, she thought.

"We'll run another of the same exhibit when you can return. Keep us in the loop."

As Hope rushed out the door, her lingering thoughts hung heavy in her chest. There would be no sitting in her mother's pew at the *Tet* Mass to feel her loving presence.

33

READING THE NEWSPAPER article was the only thing that helped Hope through the long, tense flight. Dominique's work was finally syndicated, and his first article had been about discovering that the Lê family was alive. The photo of Hope with the mission team in the foundation office was a good choice for the article. The story focused on Hope's dedicated work with adoptions and the chance discovery of her family's existence. With discretion, there was no mention of Hằng. A loving gesture. Dominique would never reveal the family's details without their permission.

Grandfather Lê had seemed proud of the story. Hope was touched.

In the article, Hope's father was only positioned as the Chairman of Uplift and the force behind their excellent work. Was this a good time to advertise her job with the foundation when Hope was on the verge of quitting? She knew Dominique had good intentions. She missed him terribly.

The hours suspended over the country in the jet and the car ride from the airport to Glynn made Hope numb. Would Ernie still be there when she arrived? His condition had sounded so severe from Grandma Cecelia's description. Why was there always something good against the backdrop of something terrible in her life?

Cecelia was waiting for Hope at the hospital door. "How was the visit to your West Coast family?" her grandmother whispered.

"Oh, it went well. The Lês were gracious about my leaving. But how's Ernie, Grandma?"

"I'm afraid he isn't doing very well. There is little news so far. They haven't let us see him yet."

"What? It's been ten hours." They entered the old hospital. The ER check-in room was empty, except for a young man in jeans and a hoodie holding an ice pack on his eye. The area had dulled, tan walls, a small waiting room to the right with a dozen chairs, a water cooler, and a TV with the sound turned off. The environment didn't give Hope confidence in the quality of the treatment Ernie would receive. She'd seen Boston's immaculate, well-equipped big city hospitals.

Hope's father, Grandpa K, Great-Uncle Jack, and her triple-K uncles were gathered around a nurse in the hallway as Hope approached with Kate.

Cecelia explained that Hope's aunts, Kendall, Karen, and Kelly, finally had to leave to care for their children.

"What is going on here? This is absurd. It's been ten hours now! What's being done? We have a right to know." Michael addressed the nurse.

"Sir, please, we are doing the best we can. The doctor's orders had been no visitors due to his condition. You can see the patient now. Please stay in here and visit, two at a time. Please." The nurse welcomed them into the dingy waiting room. "The doctor will have to give you the patient's status. It's against the rules for me to say. Try not to overstimulate the patient. The doctor will be right in to brief you. My condolences." She swept out of the visitors' waiting room in a hurry.

Condolences? That's confusing, Hope thought. She talks as though he were about to die. Releasing a shuddering breath, Hope entered the waiting room. It was so hard to have Dominique working in the field when things like this happened.

The seven family members stood in silence amid the scent of antiseptic that failed to cover up more than a hint of urine.

"Shiloh and Kate should be here shortly." Michael put his arm around Hope and pulled her close. "You must be exhausted."

A gray-haired older doctor arrived and whispered to Michael and the Ketchums.

They stepped outside the door.

Launching into his diatribe, the doctor didn't bother to introduce himself. "Young disabled Down Syndrome people with Ernie's multiple birth defects often have a limited lifespan, lucky to survive at all, and rarely beyond their twenties. He's thirty-nine." The doctor stood tall with his white coat swept back, flipping through the chart. "Appears he's had a severe stroke. He is lucid for the first time and can communicate a little, but he's confused and paralyzed down his right side. Unfortunately, he's complaining of a severe headache. We'll wait and see."

Hope put on her lawyer's voice. She had little patience waiting for hours in suspense. "*Down Syndrome people?* Wait, and *see?* Is that a *medical* strategy, sir? It's morally wrong and illegal to withhold treatment because he has disabilities." Standing up to a towering, tall man was difficult for a petite woman. It was hard to be taken seriously. Hope had faced that challenge before. "Ernie is a person with disabilities, a person *first*, doctor!"

Hope was good at reading people after dealing with a dozen countries and cultures and arranging adoptions and child services. But this doctor wasn't hard to read. The older doctor's demeanor screamed more than a hint of arrogance and discrimination. If nothing more, he displayed social ignorance about people with disabilities.

"I suggest you calm down, little miss."

"Little miss?" Hope resisted responding to his rude comment. It didn't deserve an answer.

"This *little miss* is a high-powered Harvard attorney, doctor." Uncle Jack jumped in.

Hope wished he hadn't. But it was sweet that Uncle Jack had such an opinion of her having graduated from law school less than a year ago.

It was hard for her to believe that the "Shoe Elf" could ever leave the Ketchum clan. Hope held back tears at the nickname Ernie had given himself to charm little kids when fitting them for handmade shoes. "And your point is, doctor?"

"There's nothing we recommend. I don't typically use life-saving procedures for Down Syndrome patients. Not to mention all his other disabilities." He turned to Grandpa K, Ernie's legally adopted father. "You must have had a tough life caring for him all these years. My condolences."

Grandpa K put his arm around Grandma Kendall. "*Condolences,* doctor? It's been our honor and joy to have Ernie in our lives."

The entire family was silent. They shared the same incredulous look.

"A stroke like this has likely caused irreversible damage. The patient could also have an aneurysm. At thirty-nine, he's gone years beyond his life's expectancy," the doctor said.

That made Michael join Hope in her fury. "Who's expectancy, doctor? Why not expect more? So what if Ernie was thirty-nine? What if he'd expected less all these years that he'd survived?" Michael stepped closer and read the doctor's nametag. "Doctor Gordon, I can't help thinking of the Hippocratic oath."

Restraining herself, Hope let her father take the lead. She thought if anyone was "abled," Ernie was—his humor, wisdom, compassion, and kindness. "So, you mean if he weren't a 'disabled Down Syndrome' person, as you inappropriately label him, sir, there would be some available avenues of treatment, rehab, maybe? At least you'd ascertain if he does have a life-threatening aneurysm?"

"Calm down, mister. I could put him through several scans, and then it may be just the stress that ends things here. I suggest you spend time with him while you have it. OK, fine. I'll have the nurse hook him up with some oxygen."

Hope interrupted. "This is the mid-nineteen-nineties, and might I remind you the federal anti-discrimination ADA nineteen ninety law is on our side on this, doctor. It's been five years since it became illegal to withhold treatments based on disabilities." She could see the muscles in her father's jaw tighten. He clenched his fists at the doctor's prejudice. Hope knew there were many decades in which treatment was withheld from people deemed 'not worth saving.' But she'd thought those days were over. Could any doctor still feel that way? Her frustration was hard to keep in check. It was so ignorant.

"Well, it's my professional opinion that he's lucky to have come this far." The doctor turned to walk away. It was clear he wasn't used to being questioned. "We have limited resources at this small hospital and must set priorities. I suggest you spend these last minutes with him. Other doctors may be willing to waste their time and your money." The doctor hung the clipboard in the holder at the foot of the bed.

"We need to take action, get Ernie tested, get another doctor, or transfer him to a decent hospital in Boston." Michael stepped in front of the doctor.

"I'm very sorry." He threw the words over his shoulder like he would a wet towel in the locker room and left.

"Well, I'll be damned if we're going in two at a time, though. Let's go, everyone." Michael led the way.

Shifting behind a curtain, Hope quickly called Linh and shared the sad and frustrating update on Ernie's status. "I need to go, Linh. I'm sorry. Will you tell Uncle Tuân and the family?"

"Honey, he should be arriving shortly. He left right after you did. Tuân didn't like what he heard on the phone call to the hospital."

"What? He's coming to *Glynn*?"

"Yes. Our uncle was concerned about the level of care. I wasn't sure what was going on. Now I see. Good luck. Let me know, OK?"

When Hope joined the others, the nurse had finished adjusting Ernie's oxygen mask.

"My Uncle Tuân is arriving any time now. Maybe he can get them to take some action."

Ernie lay in bed motionless, but his delight in seeing them was evident even through the foggy plastic oxygen mask over his face. "Where's Kate? I want . . ." Ernie drew in a breath. "Please." His face was slack and expressionless, and his voice was cloudy and strained as he seemed to search for the words. "Mr. Michael? Can . . . this thing off . . . Mr. Michael, please? Can you?"

Michael understood his slurred, muffled request and reluctantly pulled the mask down. Should he remove the only treatment that was being provided?

"Sweetheart. We're all here. Look who flew from California to see you." Cecelia held his small, wrinkled hands.

Hope moved to his bedside. "Hi, buddy."

"Woohoo! Hope! When am I . . . out of here, Hope? Sandra's new shoes . . . coming tomorrow . . . her fourth birthday party. Shoe Elf . . . must be there . . . won't be the same." He struggled to speak with his squeaky voice and twisted, thick tongue. "Mrs. Ketchup's coming?"

Sentimental smiles swept across the relatives' faces at Ernie's nickname for Kate Ketchum, formed when she'd interned as his teacher.

"Kate and Shiloh are on their way. They'll be here any minute." Hope leaned over and put her head on Ernie's chest. "She's coming. It won't be long, buddy, it won't be long." No, it wouldn't, Hope thought. Without some intervention, she feared it wouldn't be long. Life would never be the same without Ernie.

Shiloh pushed the curtain back on the other side and revealed Kate's presence. "Ernie, look who's here."

"Hi, Shi."

With her arms spread wide like an airplane's wings, Kate repeated the entry she'd used to cheer him when he was hospitalized after the attempted rape. "Guess who flew halfway around the world again to see her best buddy?" She buzzed like an airplane, landed beside him, and kissed his forehead.

"Woohoo! My teacher, Mrs. Ketchup!"

"I loved the pictures you sent me of your new shoe designs, Ernie," Kate said as she pushed the sweat-drenched strands of hair from his forehead.

"I missed you, Miss Ketchup." His words were strained and barely audible.

Hope knew Ernie's message was loud and clear despite his struggle to speak. He loved Kate. They had history. She'd changed his life dramatically, bringing him into a life of acceptance among the Ketchums. Who would have thought he would find a place working in the skilled world of the Owl & Shamrock factory? Why hadn't Hope been able to focus on Kate's passionate kindness and let go of her not being there for her as a child?

There was a pause between Kate and Hope.

"Missed you, honey."

Hope kissed Kate's cheek, hugged her, and stepped back to give her and Ernie more time to reunite. The gesture surprised them both.

Disappointment in Kate's mothering was melting with Hope's maturity as she watched Kate comforting Ernie. And Michael's loving support of Kate was a painful reminder that Hope could never be sure Dominique could be there during challenging times.

"Missed you too, sweet Ernie. And you are going to get better, buddy," Kate said.

"Yes, he is."

Everyone turned to see who'd spoken. "It's a pleasure to meet you. I'm Hope's uncle, Dr. Lê Phạm Tuân. I wonder if I can be of help?"

"Uncle Tuân. You are too wonderful to come." Hope introduced her family. "Ernie, this is my uncle from California. He's a renowned doctor at the University of California at San Francisco. He came all the way here for you."

"Excuse me." Dr. Gordon entered the room and pushed aside the curtain. "I'm told you are here to see my patient. Visiting hours are over, doctor."

The family froze in place, waiting for the conflict.

"No, Dr. Gordon, I'm Dr. Lê Phạm Tuân, Ernie's personal physician. Sorry, I'm late for rounds. I was traveling. I have some tests to order on an emergency basis. But not to bother you, doctor."

THE VIGIL through the night was harrowing. Once Ernie was checked into a room after the tests, the family members took turns sitting next to him, reminiscing, re-telling stories of good times and the funny things he'd done.

A twitch of a smile and Ernie's hand moving to his mouth got the entire family's attention.

"He moved his arm. Oh my God, Ernie, you moved your arm." Hope kissed his forehead.

"I have good news for you, Ernie." Dr. Tuân arrived with a clipboard in his hands. "Do you mind if the family hears the results of your tests?"

Ernie nodded his permission.

"I've checked his CT scan, echocardiogram, and ultrasound. You've had a Transient Ischemic Attack or a TIA. Big words, huh?"

Ernie could puff out a laugh for the first time since he'd been admitted.

"It's a blockage of the flow of blood to the brain. And it's temporary, Ernie. It's also called a mini-stroke. Didn't feel so *mini*, did it? The symptoms of TIA are the same as a full-fledged stroke. But here's the good news."

The family encircled the bed.

Hope took Ernie's hand and felt him squeeze hers.

"It doesn't cause any permanent damage. Not to say it isn't still a serious condition. But let's not go beyond the good news." He turned to Ernie. "You have already begun to recover. I heard it in your speech. Your arm moving was a great indicator. Usually within hours, at the most a day, we typically see a full recovery."

The entire family gasped and brought their hands to prayer position at their chests.

"We need a few more tests early tomorrow morning, then I think you just might be ready to go home to continue your recovery. I'll do everything to quiet things down. And get you back to the shoe fitting room again, making kids smile. Hope has told me about your talent with kids."

"Thanks, doctor. Hey, why does Hope look like you?" Propped up in bed, Ernie put his hands on his hips as though it were an accusation.

"Ernie, you're back to your old joking self," Hope put her hand on Tuân's shoulder. "You were distracted when Dr. Tuân arrived. He's my uncle."

"Wait." Ernie sat up, dangled his legs over the side of the bed, and dramatically spread his arms wide above his head. "You mean you are one of Hope's family who rose from the dead? That is so cool."

"Young sir, you are the one rising. Look at you." Tuân clapped, and everyone followed, thrilled with his sudden ability to move.

"OK, tomorrow you'll be back to your old self, and I'm making your favorite spaghetti and meatballs for the celebration," Cecelia said.

"Woohoo! Thank you, Grandma C."

WHILE WATCHING the Ketchum family say their sincere and emotional goodbyes, Hope thought they couldn't thank Dr. Tuân enough. She could never have imagined connecting her two families in this way.

Hope's father had stepped aside. She imagined their old connection when Dr. Tuân was Hằng's little brother, looking up at the handsome, uniformed Marine who'd visited their village home often. But Hope could only pray that the elders would someday accept her father. Still, she understood the pain Michael had caused them through his love affair and pregnancy with their eldest, accomplished daughter. Without his uncontrollable love for Hằng, Hope would not be here to remind them of their painful loss. And the Lê family would have their daughter in their lives. Insurmountable barriers to their acceptance of Michael, she thought.

Once everyone had expressed their gratitude to Dr. Tuân, Michael finally approached. "Tuân, I couldn't have imagined you'd show up in my life decades later as a prestigious doctor who would save the day. Thank you." His sunken posture spoke of his discomfort and shame as Michael turned to leave.

"Michael, wait. Please know that time heals all wounds." He put his hand on Michael's shoulder to comfort him. "Let's put it all out in the open. I know how much you and my sister loved each other. There were so many losses in that damn war. And you were so good to me when I was a kid. Nothing but good memories, buddy. My family will come around in time. They really cared about you back in those horrific wartimes."

"I'm not sure I could ever face them, Tuân. But yes, I loved your sister. And my loss cuts as deep as my guilt."

"We all need some healing time, Michael. It's a miracle we've reconnected."

It was a rare situation when her father was at a loss for words.

Tuân broke the silence. "Michael, I've heard about your foundation. I've been on missions with Doctors Without Borders. Maybe we can discuss a collaboration considering Hope's history and in memory of my sister? I'd love to help."

Hope loved witnessing the light in her father's face as he rejoined Tuân. It was a gift. Maybe Tuân was right. Maybe there was a chance to reconnect with the Grands in time. Hopefully, someday, her father would open up about her mother without triggering his pain.

"WE HOPE you enjoyed the little breakfast celebration." Cecelia and Kevin shook Tuân's hand.

"I apologize. I'm needed at the hospital. My flight leaves in two hours, I should go. It was my pleasure to share Ernie's happy outcome. I'll get in touch with your primary doctor and give him my assessment for a diet and exercise plan going forward. He can do some further blood work." Dr. Tuân held up the post-it note

Grandpa Kevin had given him. "I have a few other ideas, too." Tuân turned to Hope. "As for Dr. Gordon and the legal issue, I'll submit a report about his unprofessional behavior. He won't be withholding treatments anymore. I'll go up and say goodbye to Ernie if that's OK?"

"I'm here, look." After cautiously negotiating the stairway holding the railing, Ernie did a conservative version of his jig in the living room. He plopped down into Grandpa Kevin's lounge chair. "Thank you, Dr. Tuân."

"Take it easy, Ernie, you've been through a lot. You're doing great."

"Thanks for checking me out this morning. But your stethoscope was so cold." The word stethoscope didn't translate easily with Ernie's usual lisp.

"I'll take that under consideration." Dr. Tuân smiled. "Maybe I'll give you a one-hundred percent discount on your bill, Ernie. Let's do the math. One hundred percent of zero equals what?"

"You are funny, Dr. Tuân. Wait. If you're Hope's uncle, you're my uncle, too, right?" His words were slurred, but Ernie was speaking better. "Cuz she's been like a real sister to me."

"I guess that's right, Ernie."

Hope's triple-K uncles shook hands and patted Uncle Tuân's back. Their wives and a swarm of Hope's younger cousins chimed in. "Thank you for helping Ernie."

"Uncle Tuân, you can see from our faces we're having a hard time containing our gratitude."

"Hope, we're family."

Family. She had so much family. As always, moments like this brought her to the question of what would have happened to the orphan she was had Jeremy and her father not been rule-breakers.

In the living room, the TV was on, as always, with the sound turned down. Barbara Walters on ABC News was showing scenes of refugees lined up at the border of some country. The camera flashed from women holding crying babies to men receiving food packages from an NGO when the group came under fire, scattering the people. The horrifying scenes changed to an interview with a group of weeping women in a tent cuddling children. As the last sequence flickered on the screen, Hope spotted Shiloh and Dominique getting in a truck with an Uplift logo on its side. When the scene ended, trembling, Hope crossed the room and turned off the TV.

It was the first time Hope had seen Dominique in action rather than a story told at a meeting in a conference room. It was real—her loving man and her beloved Shiloh in the flaming chaos of war.

She pictured the future children Dominique had always alluded to watching cartoons and the scene switching to a news flash of a war somewhere with their father in the chaos. How could she ever protect them from that? The tremors shaking her body told her it was doubtful she wanted children of her own with Dominique.

Did Kate see her reaction? She signaled for Hope to join her in the kitchen.

Sitting at the sentimental table, it was strange to be talking to Kate and not Grandma Cecelia. "How was your tour? And by the way, seeing Ernie's face when you arrived was so sweet."

"Love that guy. But let's talk about the clip we just saw on the news. It must have been tough."

Talking about anything but her tours and general questions about what was happening in the family was a first for Kate.

"Seeing Dominique and Shiloh in that scene was terrorizing for me, of course." Hope closed her eyes and sighed.

"Too close to home for you, Hope. Seeing Shiloh, my best friend, running through the fire made me shiver. I can't imagine if I were watching Michael, too."

Hope felt her anger toward Kate surface. Why now? Maybe because it took twenty-six years for Kate to have a real conversation.

"You're angry at me, aren't you?"

"The truth? I guess I'm operating from resentment, yes, and anger. But isn't anger really hurt?" Hope was not going to pass up the opportunity to understand her stepmother.

"And I'm operating from guilt," Kate said.

"Can I ask why it took so long for you to be real with me?" Somehow, seeing that TV clip made Hope want to be upfront. The curtain was pulled back. No more people pleasing. She wanted to know. "Was it because I rejected you when my dad first brought me to Bangkok?"

"How do you know that?" Kate studied Hope's face.

There was no sidestepping the truth. "I read your journal. Shiloh insisted you wanted me to read it so I'd understand you."

Kate shook her head. "That would be Shiloh, the rule-breaker. But she usually knows what's going to help a situation get better. Well, years ago, I did say I wished you would read it to understand. Still, it feels more than a little invasive."

"I felt that way too every time I opened it, but it was too tempting. Sorry, Kate."

"And who could blame you?" Kate inhaled deeply. "I certainly have a lot of guilt over that. You're not a child anymore. I need to embrace that. Maybe you do need to read the whole thing. Hope, it's time we formed a real bond." Kate leaned toward Hope. "We both deserve that."

Hope squirmed in her chair. She was afraid to get close to Kate only to have her gone again.

"Hope, I was afraid to get close to you back then. You captured my heart in those early days. And yes, you rejected me. You were a newly traumatized toddler. I understood that." Kate looked off into space. "I was afraid of how I felt about you. I fell in love with your little self when you arrived with Michael. I never really wanted children. I feared a child would get in the way of my dreams."

"What do you mean? You wanted to get close to me? You resented me and my relationship with my dad. I remember your words in your diary. You said the arms that used to hold you were now engaged."

"Quite the contrary, Hope. I didn't want to get close to you."

"Well, that's being honest." Hope could relate. She wasn't sure she wanted children either, but for different reasons. She feared she couldn't protect the child from a world of dangers. There was too much responsibility, too much vulnerability.

"You misunderstood. I was afraid my connection to you would be enough to stop me from doing what I love. I was afraid I wouldn't have followed my passion if I got close to you. As Grandma Cecelia says, what lights me up. It was bad judgment on my part. But if I'd stayed home with the people I loved, I would have . . . I would have missed being *me*." Kate's eye contact was new.

Hope mumbled to herself. "I understand. When is it selfish, and when is it self-love?"

"Exactly, the constant battle. I'm so sorry. Grown-ups don't have a corner on wisdom. Forgive me if I hurt you with my choices, but I do love you. I guess my feeling love for you isn't enough if *you* don't feel it."

The door creaked open.

"Dominique!"

"*Bonjour.* How is Ernie?" He bee-lined to hug and kiss Hope.

It had felt like months, not days, since she'd been in his loving presence. But there was a shadow over their relationship now. The truth about her ability to tolerate his work had to be discussed. Hope had to find time to be alone to talk.

They returned to the living room, and Hope made the introductions. Everyone said their farewells as Michael rushed Uncle Tuân out of the house to get him to the airport on time.

34

AFTER A DAY spent with family watching Ernie's improvements, everyone had gone to O'Leary's to celebrate and have dinner. Kate had left early to get extra rest before her next tour in a few days, and her sister, Hope's Aunt Kendall, stayed behind to keep Ernie company. He'd gone to sleep early after his day-and-a-half ordeal. Hope needed some privacy tonight.

It was not a good idea to get into bed with Dominique, no matter how tired she was. Hope wanted to have a conversation to share her true feelings with him. It would never happen in bed with a man like her fiancé. And the scenes on the TV still haunted her.

Being at Dominique's home would have meant having Jolie present in the house. It was better in Hope's sitting room, where it had all started. Neither Dad nor Kate would ever come to her wing of the house without calling first, anyway. Hope realized she was an adult still living with her parents. "Honey, I need to talk to you about something important. Can we sit on the loveseat?"

Sitting beside Hope, Dominique stroked Hope's hair—one long, slow, calming stroke. "I assume this is not about how much you missed me." He smiled, and his blue eyes started that cobra allure she feared would pull her off track.

"Yes, I missed you. No, I ached for you, especially when this terrifying drama with Ernie happened." Hope was determined to find the right words.

"The outcome was so wonderful, Hope. To see Ernie recovering before our eyes. A frightening thing, that TIA. So, what is it that's concerning you, darling?"

Dominique hadn't been there to hear the terrible doctor's disrespect. She had more important things to discuss. Finding the starting point for her complicated thoughts was difficult. "I think I've found what lights me up, as Grandma Cecelia always says." Hope wanted to start with the positive, the main point of it all.

"Yes, of course, your art. It is so clear you were meant to do that. Such joy, and darling, you are so talented. What puts that dark look on your face when you should be thrilled? Do you have doubts?"

"Not about the art, but about . . . us. Our future." Releasing that haunting thought suspended her between relief and regret.

His response was expected—he looked incredulous, caught off guard. "Darling, I'm confused. We've found a compromise: your lawyering and art split between California and here in Boston. I will follow my passion to serve. And now, with Jolie settled down—virtually a changed woman—what about us is troubling you?"

Starting with her mistrust of Jolie's magical overnight change into the dream mother-in-law would only derail the main point of the conversation. Hope was cynical about Jolie's transformation.

"I've been less than honest with you." A woozy feeling melted her resolve. She wanted to take him by the hand, move to the bed, and lose herself in their loving connection. He'd spoiled her, charmed her. But would this situation ever give her the peace she needed? She pictured herself comforting their future children if they'd had them while Dominique missed all the highlights of their lives. Again, Hope imagined their fears when they were old enough to see the news of bombs and destruction on TV where their dad was working. And her fears.

"Is there someone else? I'm so confused . . . is that it?"

"*What?* Dear God, no, Dominique. You know me better than that." She hugged him, then sat back. "But I'm struggling with the separation, the repeated trauma of you leaving, never hearing from you for days, seeing the news on TV, and knowing you are in the midst of all the fighting and hatred."

Sitting up straighter, she was determined to get it all out, to be honest, brutally honest. Finally, the door to her truth had opened. "I'm experiencing such fear and worry when you're away on missions. Even when you're here, the office conversation always turns to horrifying subjects. Although, you know, I believe passionately in what we do." She'd started the impossible conversation, but she had to finish. "I can never escape it. Even when I paint the children's faces now, I'm thinking of their trauma like mine."

"But, Hope, there are so many happy endings for those rescued children, including yours."

"Yes, there are happy endings for us, but still, they will struggle inside. I know. My concerns are more about our futures, yours, mine, and our children's if we decide to have them. Even when I'm happy painting and learning my art with Linh, which is pure joy for me, I'm constantly pushing away fears about your safety, and it often resurrects my own trauma."

"I don't mean to be intrusive, but perhaps some therapy is warranted." He shifted closer to her.

Anger raged in her face, red and hot, but Hope controlled herself. "Yes, I went to therapy as a child for years for my night-mares and PTSD. It was very beneficial, but the stability and love of the Ketchums were the keys," Hope explained. "This is the real concern, Dominique. Tonight, while we were all saying goodbye to Uncle Tuân, there was a news flash on TV. Seeing you in those violent scenes made it more real. The terrors from my childhood that had receded into the background with therapy came alive again." Hope sighed and tried to convey her internal experiences. Would she ever be able to express how her inner child felt while running along the rice fields with the fearsome growling of the plane overhead or the boom of the bomb shat-tering her orphanage? The flashing lights, the tremble of the ground beneath her feet, and the scattered children's bodies along the path.

"What are you thinking, Hope?"

"I don't know if you understand how much I need the constancy of *you* in my daily life, Dominique. How would you handle things if I were the one working in a war zone and you saw me fleeing into a truck under fire on TV? Would your days be unbearably filled with worry? I saw that at my grandparents' house as we were getting ready to leave. I imagined our kids watching that and seeing their father surrounded by such chaos and violence."

She waited for Dominique's response.

"I'm so sorry you saw that. I didn't want to share that since I knew it would terrorize you. But honestly, we were safe."

"Safe?" Hope explained that in the early months, when she'd fallen in love with him while spending all day and all night together, her new terrors had faded into the background, even evaporated at times. Sharing deep emotions and dreams together had kept those memories and fears at bay. In fact, she'd almost thought she'd be able to leave them permanently behind. Hope told him their love had been so healing, just what she needed, like the stability of the Ketchum family, predictability, as predictable as this capricious life could be.

"What about our own children, Dominique? You were concerned about my being in San Francisco part-time. I would make the changes so I wouldn't ever leave them abandoned. My art is portable. Isn't a father being in war zones, endangered, and out of touch with them far more untenable?"

"Hope, what are you saying? You want to end our relationship?" He put his hands on her shoulders. "We can work it out. Whatever it is, we can find a way. Didn't you say that? Look at me."

She lifted her head and forced herself to engage his worried eyes.

"Our project in Bosnia is finished. Let's celebrate your exhibit together, the one you missed that Linh said you could reschedule. Ernie's fine now. He got up and did his dance. That's proof enough. Dr. Tuân confirmed that his prognosis is good. We can visit him to say goodbye tomorrow. Darling, give us a chance."

They undressed in silence and got into bed.

"We'll talk tomorrow, I promise, Dominique. Let's try to sleep now. It's so late. We're both too exhausted to make sense of anything right now."

"You're right. This makes no sense. We love each other." He punched his pillow and turned away from her.

Tucking in behind him, Hope attempted to normalize things a bit. "Dominique, sleep, darling. We'll figure it out."

Hope thought of the portrait she'd given Ernie today as she drifted off. "He said, you should be an artist, Hope. You wouldn't be sad anymore. I'd be happy for you. You'll come back. I know. You always come back to see me."

How had Ernie seen through her illusion of happiness?

HOPE KISSED Dominique as he slept, and then she left for the office. Despite her desperate need for rest, Hope had a long night of constantly waking to the sound of Dominique's gentle snoring.

On her way up the elevator, Hope decided to talk to Shiloh to clarify her thinking before she shared her thoughts about leaving her job with her father. Auntie Shi had always been a reliable sounding board. She would put Hope's best interest first. As she exited at the penthouse level, Hope nearly bumped into Kate. "Oh, Kate, you're here early."

"Just had an early breakfast with your dad. He's in his office. Hope, you look like you lost your best friend. What's going on?"

Hope closed her eyes and sighed.

"Maybe we should talk again, Hope."

It would be their second *talk*, beyond the cheerful greetings and updates whenever Kate came home. "In my office, OK?" Hope slipped down the hallway and led Kate to her office.

Kate settled into the chair across from Hope. "Go ahead, honey, I'm listening."

Sitting at her desk, studying the aura of the morning sun around Kate, Hope opened, like she'd never done before. "I feel trapped by my love for Dominique—with his constant travels, the threat of his possessive and previously malevolent mother, whom I don't trust, and his love of a job that terrorizes me. Is love enough?" Hope propped her elbows on the desk and put her face in her hands.

"Hope isn't your art like my singing, joyful, the real you? Couldn't you work things out like we have?"

"It's not like you and Dad. You never had children, and singing and your concerts are uplifting things for both of you. And you get to live in that world and escape the trauma and hate? Even my art has been associated with the foundation. And I know Dad would be disappointed if I quit. In some ways, I think he depends on protecting me for his own security. I'm only coming to this realization now. Does that make sense, Kate?" She didn't want to mention that looking so much like her mother might also play into Michael's obsession with keeping Hope close by.

"I think you're right. Michael lost you once. He never wants to risk that again."

"I can't imagine life without Dominique, but I can't deal with the thought of his job in my life forever, either."

Kate's eyes flashed left and right as if deciding whether to share her thoughts.

Her expression confused Hope.

"Honey, we are more alike than you might think." Kate leaned forward. "We don't talk openly enough, do we? I'm sorry, sweetheart. I haven't been there for you. It was my own survival."

"I've missed that connection, as I said before." Hope surprised herself. Once the door was ajar, she blew through it, letting out all the pent-up frustrations and anger. "I've been angry at you for a long time. You put your singing above Dad and me as I interpret it. The time away was one thing, but your emotional distancing was another for a child. You were fun, yes. But loving? I missed having a mother. Twice." The release shocked Hope. It felt good; it felt terrible.

Hope was surprised to hear Kate's story. She admitted she'd stayed away all those years, to avoid Michael's foundation work—the negativity of it all, surrounded by talk of wars and lost children. "Even my best friend, Shiloh, lived for her work, too busy to find someone to love her. Naturally, she'd talked about the wars and her dangerous escapades constantly. Granted, her lifestyle truly fits her, but it's not me. All the money in the world can't change how a sensitive person with an artist's soul can handle the violent things in the world, Hope. And now I see that you and I both fall into that category. I misjudged. I'd always thought you were headed to a hard-hitting lawyer's life."

"And I always thought only your singing kept you away, Kate."

"I so wanted to help the kids in the institution. And the director said I had a talent for getting through to kids who were different. But honestly, I couldn't survive the sadness, the dreariness of that place. After studying to be a special education teacher and investing in all that hard work, I couldn't deal with it. Even though I was doing something good. I couldn't save them all."

"I never understood why you left. I get it now. Your institution was dreary and depressing. My foundation job is in a gorgeous fancy high-rise with beautiful décor, but still, I'm disturbed by the endless war stories and the terrors the little kids go through."

"Honey, as I said before, maybe it's too close to home for you with the past you'd endured." Continuing her confession, Kate explained when the foundation was much smaller with its limited staff and security resources, it had seemed that things were so dangerous. But she was learning, as visible targets in the news and internationally recognized, Michael's work today was even more worrisome.

"I imagine how Dad's terrorizing work compared to the high you felt touring and singing at your concerts," Hope said.

"The happy faces of the audience, the adulation, and frankly, the financial rewards after growing up with limited resources. It's all very alluring. I could finally help my parents like I'd always dreamed." Kate made eye contact.

Something was changing, Hope thought. "Well, I'm not sure my art will have financial allure, but I feel alive and peaceful when creating with my Aunt Linh. Doing portraits for immigrant families who have created new lives here in the US gives me purpose. It's uplifting. Not to use an obvious term. But I'm truly happiest painting nature scenes—skyscapes, sunrises, and sunsets on the water."

"I've never seen those. But that part, I get," Kate said. "Hope, Dominique is such a wonderful person. Go forward cautiously. I can't tell you what to do. He's a French version of Michael, so lovable, complex, and inspired."

They heard Michael's voice in the hallway.

"I'm so sorry, Hope. I know I fell short of being a good mother to you. Forgive me?" Kate reached across the desk and covered Hope's hand with hers. "But now you know the nuance of the whole thing, except my new plan I haven't even fully shared with Michael."

"What plan is that?"

"I'm retiring but not coming home to live in Boston. I just can't."

"Where will you go?" Slumping in her chair, Hope regretted the irony of it all. She finally felt close to Kate, and she was leaving.

"No, from your reaction, I think you've misread me. I'm building a home near your Grandma Christine's lake house. A place where everyone can visit and enjoy nature. A place where I can escape the terrors of your father's work."

"Oh, how wonderful. You'll only be an hour away."

"And a world away. I'll do one annual overseas tour, sing for specials in Boston, and do a fundraiser or two."

"Sounds perfect."

"Well, I'll really miss the touring, to be honest. Just so you know, I told your father I'm tired of the hustle and bustle of cities and travel and want to be in nature. This is true, but honestly, I think it would be good for Michael to be in a place that he's always loved, in nature, where he can spend time with his mother, as well. At a certain point, we are going to have to retire anyway. I want to be near my family in Glynn. As my lawyer daughter would say, the truth, but not the whole truth."

"True enough." They shared a humorous moment amid the confessions. Hope had a flash of a memory, kayaking with her father on the lake when she'd first arrived. Holding onto the rhythmic oar as the ducks scattered with their approach to the pier.

"Your dad said life on the lake is a good compromise. He so loves it there."

The intimacy Hope was sharing with Kate was healing.

"Maybe you can find a way to be with the man you love and still be true to yourself. I hope so." Kate's words were so genuine and caring.

"I'll try in every way I can. Thanks, Mom."

35

SHE'D CALLED KATE 'Mom.' The word had come out naturally. What had just happened? They'd connected like the wall between them had just crumbled with their intimate conversation. Had it been Kate's wall? Hope's wall? Or both? She shook her head. Hope would have laughed at the irony if it hadn't been such an emotional moment. From Kate's reaction, watery eyes, and suspended hug when she left, it seemed their new connection had also moved her. And Kate's advice felt right.

At nearly twenty-six, Hope had found the mother she'd needed, who'd been there all along but just out of reach. And Kate was right. Just because Hope didn't have the answer to her future with Dominique now didn't mean she shouldn't try to find a way to be together that worked.

Facing her father was the first step in distancing herself from her foundation work. Then, she had two phone calls to make—to her aunt Linh and the airlines. She wasn't a child, she thought. Hope had the right to direct her own life. Maybe for the first time, she more fully understood why her dad had kept her close by, with college and law school just up the road. No dormitories or wild parties. But it was time for Hope to do what was right for her. Following her own dreams, not everyone else's. Love was complicated, but Grandma Cecelia had been right—follow what lights you up.

Today had to be her last day with the foundation, Hope thought, shuffling through the stack of mail on her desk. She could finish up any document reviews without being in the office. It was best to leave on a Friday. That would give Michael the weekend to recover from the news. And Kate was still in town to support them both.

Thanks to Hope's people-pleasing personality, her father would have no idea she wasn't thrilled to be in her job. Where did that come from? She'd always been deeply loved and accepted, even celebrated by her father and the Ketchums. They were her safe place. But maybe until she tested herself out in the world, she would never truly feel safe. Couldn't she learn to use their secure foundation of love to take the risks that would make her happy?

Why hadn't she felt safe enough to find her own path? Even when deciding on a career, she'd followed Shiloh's suggestion. And she'd even gone to the same schools. Was she afraid they wouldn't love her? Hope could never remember making any major decision based on her personal desires. Her only wish was to be loved, she realized. That strengthened her resolve. She needed to catch up with her grown-up self.

There was never a doubt she would work for her father from his viewpoint or hers. All good intentions, but Hope felt like an adult for the first time today. Delayed maturity, she thought. But honestly, it's better late than never. Maybe the safety of always knowing where you were going was what she'd needed then, but not now. She wanted to embrace the joy and freedom of her choices, the unknown, and to be her true self. It was her responsibility to rescue herself now. Wasn't Hope that *one child*?

Hope picked up the phone and dialed her father's extension. As it rang, she scanned the view she loved, boats and buildings and mother nature painting those stunning sky scenes outside Hope's office windows. She would miss that wide-open view. Being up high. There would be no dramatic view from her art studio inside the old ICB building. But she could create her own high with scenes on canvas and paper and still impact people's lives with her artwork. It felt right.

"Hey honey, how are you?"

Her father's voice inspired her resolve. "I'm good, no, very good. Can we talk? Are you busy?"

"Is this a conference room talk or an 'in my office' chat?"

"I'll come there, Dad." Walking down the hallway, she passed all those darling faces smiling back at her—The Wall of Hope, Dominique's loving gift to her.

She would always have those hopeful faces in her mind. Remembering that first day when she'd come alone with two dozen balloons, she opened the door to enjoy the expansive view of the conference room, then closed it. She was proud of what they'd accomplished during the time she'd been there. Hope tapped on Michael's door. After today, she could get back to calling him Dad.

"Come in, Hope."

She sat in the leather guest chair across from the man who had been her rock. "Dad, this is a hard conversation to have."

He leaned back and laced his fingers behind his head. "I'm ready, sweetheart."

She wanted to stay in a business mode so she wouldn't weaken, and "sweetheart" wasn't helping. Launching into her pre-planned speech, she explained her dilemma. She loved doing the children's portraits. Hope's art had become more than just a hobby. It was her purpose.

"Are you saying you don't want to do your law work? The adoption reviews connecting lost children? Honey, after all your efforts to go through Harvard Law and pass the bar? I don't understand. It was all you'd ever wanted."

There was no use in arguing that point. It's what Hope had always told him. How could he know when she hadn't known herself until she'd experienced the terrors of being involved in their work, day after day, hearing stories of war and devastation? What others wanted for her is what she'd embraced. She now realized that truth at an even deeper level. "Dad, I want to pursue my artwork."

"Honey, you can do both. You've been doing both, haven't you? I'm confused."

"For the first time, I'm not confused. I want to follow a passion without being restricted by the war and loss themes."

"OK, I thought the art was just a way of supporting our work, not a career. So, you're telling me you want to quit your real career to paint and sketch?"

"Yes, although I wouldn't use the same tone or words to say it." This was the moment things could turn hostile and ugly, Hope thought. "I want to get away from all the terror, Dad. The announcement of a new war or crisis is in nearly every meeting and conversation here. It's depressing and hard on me, and it resurrects images that interfere with my happiness. I know that's not how others on the team process this. My PTSD is raging now. When I compare how I felt in Sausalito doing my art to how I feel at work each day, my decreasing happiness quotient, if that's a thing, is making my decision clear. I'm asking you to let me go."

"I didn't realize I had you in a trap. Had I known—"

"Had *I* known, Dad? I'm so sorry. I'm just realizing it myself. And I'm trapped not knowing how to be with the man I love and somehow escape his world that makes me suffer."

She studied her dad's every reaction. He looked over her shoulder at the view to think. The silence would have terrorized her in the past, but something had changed. She was voting for Hope. She could still love her father, but she couldn't be the solution to ameliorating his past pain either.

His silence was disconcerting. "Honestly, I've had this conversation before. My dedication seems to cause trouble for the women in my life. I have to respect your desire to fulfill that in yours. I did that for Kate."

"And I respect you for that. It must have been tough, Dad."

"Tough, and the best thing I've ever done. The concerts and seeing Kate shine like that were rewarding for me, too. It wasn't easy to be in the background of Kate's life while she was touring. But it made me a better man. As I told her on stage in Ireland, prioritizing her singing dream had turned me into a feminist." He tried a brief laugh, but it diminished into a sigh.

He picked up the photo of Kate holding a Grammy with him by her side. "I'm afraid to ask what this means for you and Dominique."

How could she answer the question?

"Hope, I never meant to put you in this position. I can reassign Dominique to the offices again. Or he can assist me in my meetings if he needs to be more involved directly with our overseas missions."

"No, Dad. That has to be his decision. He would hate me interfering with his life. A power play through my father would be the end of us, anyway." Moving around his desk behind her father, Hope put her arms around him. It was easier to talk without looking into his eyes. Cowardly but effective. "It's not just Dominique's job."

"There's the complication with your West Coast family, right? You will have to bridge that, too."

Hope wasn't even considering that issue. She was focused on Jolie. The Lê family was a positive new part of her life, except for the elders' feelings about Michael. But she wasn't going to go there. "Jolie is a concern, as well. I don't trust her, Dad. Her change was too sudden." Hope imagined Jolie as her mother-in-law. Wouldn't she be held hostage, caught between Hope's love for her husband and Dominique's love for his mother? "Now that you have brought her into the fold . . . well, I'm afraid she'll always be a potential hand grenade in our lives."

"Honey, I always say, keep your enemies close. And she's been wonderful in her job and well-behaved. I'll keep her busy and out of your business."

"She used me once. Will she use me again? I have to deal with that fear." Stepping back around the desk, she faced her father. "Dad, I'm formally handing in my resignation. I know it's the only way there is any potential for my long-term happiness and maybe a chance for Dominique and me. How that would work, I don't know."

"I understand." Her father glanced up at her, then looked down at his folded hands on the desk. "I wish you well, love you, and respect your decision. I'll announce your resignation at the staff meeting today."

They were the right words but the wrong tone again. Her father's usual eye contact and uplifted spirit were absent. They'd never had a negative word between them that she could remember. That should have been a suspicious fact. What teen doesn't experience some element of rebellion and conflict in her effort to find her path? Still, her father was such a positive force in her life. A grounding. And she understood she'd played a role in his healing. Guilt is an ugly feeling, Hope thought. But if it was the price for her freedom and the chance for a new start, she would pay it. She would take her father at his word. "Thank you for understanding, Dad."

FEELING THE freedom like a child let out of school for the summer, Hope swung around in her office, her arms wide open, like Mary Tyler Moore's opening credits. She laughed at the image. It was only step one. She would have to see if there was a way with Dominique. Hope would still have to face the team. Shiloh was no problem, and now Kate was her strongest advocate. Hope's life, which had always been so stable and planned out, was spinning with change. Her life's map, which Hope's father had followed with an intense finger to keep her safe and close, was now in her hands.

What butterfly had fluttered its wings in some foreign place, causing the hurricane in Hope's world? Chaos theory. It was the exact word for what had been happening—her Lê family rising from the dead, as Ernie had humorously labeled their appearance in Hope's life. Meeting the perfect man in an imperfect world that didn't suit her. The possibility of a future mother-in-law who changed like a fairytale character from a good witch to an evil witch and back again. Discovering a new passion for art had swept her away to find herself. Inspiring, exhausting, and confusing all at once.

36

IT WAS THRILLING to finally have the exhibition open. The enormous central lobby was filled with a hundred artists' tables welcoming guests outside each gallery door. They came to meet the artists, view their works, and find something special to take home. Painters, sculptors, jewelry-makers, and fashion designers were all showing their talents to the world. Hope was lit up. Yes, Grandma Cecelia, this is what lights me up. And Dominique was here to share it.

"OK, we're ready, Linh." Hope made her way to Linh's side. "Our photographer is set up in the back room with a great back-drop of the Split Tree. He'll take photos of the guests if they don't have one of their own with them. The ads all explained the theme. 'War Babies: Then and Now.'"

"You did a great job, Hope. This is our dream. People are already lined up to meet with us to tell their stories." Linh was beaming. "And your lover boy is captivated."

Staring at the enormous portrait tree on the wall, Dominique studied the dozens of twelve-by-eighteen paintings of each member of the two families.

Hope joined him. "What do you think, darling?"

"Fortunately, you don't have bigger families; you would have needed more than a fifteen-foot-high ceiling. This is a magnificent work, Hope." Dominique took a photograph of the tree. "It's an apple tree, no? Clever. The fruits of your ancestors."

"Thank you. I'm excited you like it." The energy in the room filled with people was beyond what Hope had expected.

"I see a little space remains for a certain gentleman from France right here." Dominique pointed to a small open area next to Hope's portrait in the tree's center.

The arrival of Linh helped Hope to avoid a response. If only, she thought. Why was he so confident it could work out? Why was she so doubtful?

Focusing with his Nikon camera on the opposite wall, Dominique flashed a shot of the Lê family painting with their daughter Hằng, minus Michael, and returned to Hope's side. "A precious memento, no?"

Amid the chatter of the attendees at the exhibition, Linh was beaming. "What a turn-out. Dominique, are you enjoying Hope's creative genius?"

"It seems she has found her niche."

Hope was taking it all in. She'd found her true passion, hadn't she?

Excited voices of the dozens of Vietnamese American customers huddled around Hope and Linh's artwork.

"I think you'll be doing more than one of these trees," Dominique said.

"I suspect so." Linh took Hope aside. "I have so much to tell you. This morning, when I first opened the gallery, a woman called inquiring about buying one of the enlarged prints of the tree. She also wanted to donate to Uplift—a surprisingly large donation, ten thousand dollars. She is coming in the next few days to make the donation in person."

"Seriously? This is so beyond my expectations, Linh. Your marketing friends outdid themselves. I'm in heaven. I'm nervous but ready."

"Love yourself first, and everything else falls into line, Lucille Ball said. It seems like you are in line with yourself, Hope."

"Now you're quoting Lucille Ball? Well, I better put on my chef's hat and start wildly eating chocolates from our conveyor belt." Remembering the hysterical classic scene from the TV episode, Hope gathered up her art supplies.

"Hilarious image, Hope, but speaking of 'being in line,' we need to start quick sketching and interviewing. Look at all the people waiting."

Dominique put his arm around Hope. "I'll wander through the other galleries before I leave for the airport. I still have a little time."

"Honey, I wish I could see you off." Hope tried to keep her mind on the positive things happening around them.

"Don't be silly. This is your moment, Hope. I'll enjoy the art, then get a cab. I'm sorry my visit is so brief, darling. I'll be back right after our annual meeting in time for the dinner and award ceremony in two days." He kissed her and lingered with his warm cheek against hers.

Hope would miss those tender moments.

"I saw some beautiful handmade jewelry across the way that might look good on a certain woman I know." Dominique kissed

Hope, said goodbye to Linh, and wove his way out through the growing crowd.

"OK. I see what you meant about your guy."

"What's that?"

"A wonderful, loving man. Let's get started, my dear." Linh gave her manager, Jean, the signal, and she began collecting the fees and handing out numbers to the customers. "Numbers one and two, the artists are ready," Jean announced, swinging her waist-long hair over her shoulder.

"Oh, I love it, Hope. Thank you." The reaction of the first woman to sit for her portrait was gratifying.

Hope watched Linh laughing and sharing stories with her client on the opposite side of the double-wide door to the studio. It was as much fun as Christmas with the Ketchums, she thought. Clips of customer inquiries about custom family trees floated through the din, reaching Hope's ears as Jean fielded them at the register.

"How much is an original of—"

"What is the cost if we have twenty-two family members?"

"Can you do one where the tree splits twice?"

"Would the artist come to our home to—"

Catching Hope's attention through the crowd, Linh shrugged her shoulders, flashed an incredulous look, and nodded. "Why not?"

Any shyness Hope felt evaporated with the smiles and stories her models shared.

"After he helped our entire family to evacuate, my grandfather came over on a boat that had capsized in a storm, and he was the only survivor. He's turning ninety next week. I brought my whole family to get portraits and a tree done for his birthday. There are twelve adults and sixteen children."

"My sister and I are the only ones who came to America in April of seventy-five. We each have two children now, so we want to send these portraits to my parents in Vietnam. That's my sister in line with our four daughters—all successful businesswomen." The four women, who appeared to be about Hope's age, were dressed in matching, traditional Vietnamese-style áo dài, ready to pose for their grandparents' gift sketches.

The stories were emotional and inspiring. Fast-forwarding the immigrants' lives who'd embraced the importance of family and education and had found successful lives in their new country was different from hearing about people in the heat of wars and trauma. Seeing the blossoming of families over the generations made Hope emotional and gratified.

In the clamor of conversation around her, Hope heard no sounds of charcoal or pencil rubbing along on the textured paper in the din. The silent flow of the watercolors made it seem like the portrait was painting itself. She worked on a painting based on one of the photographs as she interviewed each guest.

AFTER TWO days, the line of people who wanted to order a portrait hadn't ended, and commissions for family Split Tree paintings had rolled in. The word had spread, and Hope was thrilled that families of different ethnicities had begun to arrive. Not just Vietnamese Americans. The art form was colorblind, she thought, as she dragged a charcoal stick across the background of a sketch. The final touch.

"How do you do that? It looks exactly like me. Thank you."

The woman hugged the painting to her chest. "The portrait is a special gift for my daughter in Chiang Mai. She will love it."

"I'm grateful. Thank you so much for your support. You can check out at the counter inside. Enjoy." It meant so much to Hope, with her own history of discrimination, that the people sitting for the photographs or submitting their own photos for portraits were as varied as the United Nations, as Linh's husband John had said yesterday.

Hope's artwork would hang on a wall in a home in Northern Thailand. She'd given up thinking she could guess the nationality of her customers. Still, she'd speculated the woman might be from Southeast Asia. It was a game Hope had played with herself and often lost. Labeling people was senseless when focusing on the subtleties of skin tone, the lines of a profile, the angle of a nose, the fullness of lips, or the texture of hair. With her artistic lens zoomed in close, it was all simply beautiful shapes, lines, and colors to Hope. It was pure humanity, pure art.

"There is someone here to see you and Linh." Jean nodded toward the inner room where the Lê-Pham—Ketchum-James Split-Tree had been painted on the wall.

It was almost time to close, but Hope would make time for the final two customers. Excusing herself, she promised the next guest in line she'd be right back. Hope signaled Linh and went to the inner studio door.

Along with a packed room of fifty people, a tall, dark-skinned man with wavy black hair in a blue suit with a folder in his hand was studying the painting on the wall.

Linh joined her at the doorway. "Hope, that's the president of San Francisco Artists Association's board of directors. His name is Gregory Sanford. He's a sculptor and has been here for over thirty years. A good guy." Linh nudged Hope's elbow. "Let's see if we placed in the New Art Contest."

"Seriously? I forgot about that. I've had my reward, Linh—two days of pure heaven."

"Still, it would be wonderful to be recognized statewide. More proceeds for *Uplift* and *One Child*."

"True, it would be the *paint on the palate*—an artist's version of *icing on the cake*."

"Cute, Hope. And tomorrow night's dinner and award ceremony will be fun. We've reserved two tables for the family."

"God, I hate that Dominique's missing all this."

"Gregory, this is my niece, Hope Lê James. She has recently joined my gallery."

"Pleasure. Seems it's all in the family here at your gallery. This is a profound work of art." He flashed a look across the painting that filled the fifteen-by-thirty-foot studio wall. "I've been listening to the conversations around me. The Split Tree pulls everyone in and makes us think of our families. Please, follow me." He pointed in the direction of the outer gallery door.

With her hand on Hope's shoulder, Linh whispered, "I omitted the Ketchum name so you wouldn't get the 'Are you related to Kate Ketchum?' question."

"Thank you. I appreciate it."

Gregory stopped outside the door where she and Linh had set up to do the portraits. "Let me be the one to share the good news." He opened the folder, peeled back the tape on the back of the large, blue, and gold first-place ribbon, and pressed it on the Lê Gallery door. "Congrats. The work is genius, and every artist here at ICB benefited from the crowd of art aficionados you attracted."

"Yes, and the genius was all Hope's."

"I don't deserve all the credit, sir. It was a collaboration between Linh and me—a duet."

"Winner of the best exhibition in the Northern California New Art Contest is the Lê family Gallery." The announcement was loud enough to draw the shoppers' attention in the crowded central lobby. Surrounded by applauding customers, he hugged Linh and shook Hope's hand. Then he lowered his voice. "I suspect you'll be at the special dinner tomorrow night to accept the award from Mayor Johnston. It's the new mayor's first time here at ICB. San Francisco's proud to finally have a black mayor. Things are looking up."

"Yes, they are. Thank you, Gregory." Linh put her arm around Hope.

"I'll wager when the mayor sees that Split Tree, he'll want his family tree done. His wife is from New Delhi. A silver jewelry maker whose studio is right across the hall." Gregory nodded toward the opposite side of the building. "Wouldn't that put you even farther into the stratosphere?"

THE ATMOSPHERE at Linh's house after dinner that night was upbeat and relaxed. Hope's two young cousins, Brad and John Jr., were playing a video game on the coffee table. Linh and John sat by the windows discussing investments and upcoming tax time.

Hope knelt on the floor next to Linh's sons. "Oh, Super Nintendo. That's the new one." She'd seen it at the Ketchums'

Christmas being played by her nephews. "What's this game about?" She hadn't had much time to spend with them since she'd arrived, and it was important to Hope to build a bond with the younger generation in the family. They were friendly and bright. She liked that Linh and John's boys, like Tuân's daughter Hong, were so relaxed with her. Having no memories of Hằng or the war, they had less baggage from the past and were the bridge to the older generations.

"It's Yoshi's Island. See, Hope, this friendly dinosaur is on a quest to reunite baby Mario with his brother Luigi, who's been kidnapped by Kamek. He's a Magicoopa."

"Magicoopa?" Hope studied the bespectacled wizard Kamek in a blue robe and watched Yoshi run and jump to reach the end of the level while solving puzzles and collecting items with Mario's help. The whole scene felt like a metaphor for Hope and Dominique's relationship—working to reunite babies with their families and the dangers of the quest.

She looked forward to seeing him tonight and prayed his flight was on time for the awards dinner. Sharing their success would be fun. She loved how Dominique's face lit up when she shared any good news about her art.

"So, this friendly dinosaur is out on a quest. Do you know what a quest is, Cousin Hope?"

Brad's innocence made her smile. Did she even know what a quest was? "Oh, yes. I was on a quest to find someone."

"Who were you looking for in your quest?"

Hope connected with Linh's glance. "Myself."

"You're funny. You're right *here*, Hope." Brad fell back on the hardwood floor, laughing.

His innocence was endearing.

"Then, I guess that means I fulfilled my quest, right? Tell me more about this quest."

"It's the newest Mario game. Really cool. This dinosaur wants to reunite baby Mario with his brother Luigi—"

"Yeah, he's been kidnapped by Kamek. He's the bad guy." His brother John chimed in as he manipulated the game. "See, the bad Kamek attacked a stork delivering baby Mario and his brother Luigi, and Luigi fell out of the stork's sack and then—"

"Good luck with the game, boys. I'm going to get some coffee in the kitchen, OK?" It was like being in the office at a staff meeting again. Hope didn't need to hear more.

"You have a choice, Hope—taxes or kidnapping." John teased her from across the room.

"I think I'll take the taxes, John. And honestly, I need some sleep before my artist's hands cramp up. I feel like I did a hundred portraits in the past two days."

"I'm turning in too." Linh gathered up her papers. "Boys, let's call it a night. We have a big day tomorrow, and you're going to the movies and pizza with Leila while Daddy and Mommy go to an event."

Linh turned to Hope with a smile. "Well, Niece Hope, you know how to launch your career with a bang. First prize. I'm so happy for you. I'm happy for me. I love working together. Tomorrow, the entire family will see what a precious gem they've added to their family."

"Thank you, Linh. What would I do without you?"

"Let's not find out." Linh held Hope in a suspended hug. "Sleep well. Your lover boy arrives tomorrow."

"Let's hope so."

DRESSED IN her *áo dài*, Hope opened the Lê Gallery door. Had she ever been happier? The news was comforting. Shiloh and Dominique had sent a message late last night through her dad that they were about to depart from the small airport in some Bosnian town.

Despite the peace treaty, ongoing ethnic cleansing by small groups of Serbs was still occurring as the Yugoslavian wars were ending. Hope protected her sanity by not watching the news or reading the papers. It helped her to not create images in her mind of what might be happening to the Uplift team. But now that their annual meeting was over, Shiloh and Dominique would be coming to enjoy a fun night of artists celebrating their creations at the ICB. Wouldn't that be soothing after what they were witnessing overseas? The Uplift teams had made such a difference in the lives of the refugees from the violent wars. The issue of how things could possibly work with Dominique and Hope was unanswered. Still, Hope just wanted his arms around her.

Linh and John were picking up the extended family in two limos to see the Split Tree exhibit before the dinner. They hadn't come to the first opening since it was the night of *Tet*.

From the studio's doorway, she could see all the artists turning on the lights and preparing for the celebrations in the three-story building. There hadn't been much time for Hope to get to know her fellow artists with all the work Linh and she had been doing. When she'd taken a break to tour the other galleries, Hope enjoyed meeting the other artists working in every creative effort she could imagine. Sonya, the weaver; Toma, the collage creator; Olive, the landscape painter; Petra, the Greek sculptor; Chinh, a Vietnamese man who made unique men's accessories; and the mayor's wife, Maya, the jeweler. The silver and pearl masterpieces Maya crafted for Indian brides to wear on their wedding day were stunning. Dominique had said he'd bought Hope one of those in solid gold and pearls. The complex masterpieces filled the bride's neckline and were complemented by matching earrings and bracelets. Hope questioned if her slender neck could support them. And she was weary of wondering if that day would ever come.

The artists had made Hope feel so at home. Nearly one hundred studios. She looked forward to meeting them all. They had one undeniable thing in common with Hope—their irresistible creative urge.

Turning on the lights in both studio areas, Hope smiled at the Split Tree. She could live in this building, she thought. Just bring me my meals. She laughed at the memory of saying that when she'd first visited the Harvard Library. Learning and creating, she was happy in those worlds.

37

GUESTS FLOODED IN and registered for their reserved tables in the main event room overlooking the Sausalito waterfront, sparkling with lights. The dozens of masts on the sailboats in the harbor and the outline of two tall palm trees against the hills of Marin could still be seen in the distance as night settled in. A breathtaking backdrop for the evening's start.

Linen tablecloths, candles, and handmade pottery place settings on the countless tables for ten weren't the only beautiful décor. Along the walls of the expansive room, the winning artworks in all categories for the Northern California New Art Contest were lined up on display tables. Hope stopped. A full-size print of the Lê-Phạm—Ketchum-James Split Tree provided the backdrop for the band whose instruments had been set up on the stage for the evening's entertainment. Section by section, the enormous print of the piece had been constructed and put together. Hope thought the event committee must have been busy all night like Santa's elves. What an unexpected thrill. There was no describing the chills that showered over Hope's body. The sense of belonging wrapped around her as she scanned her own Wall of Hope. Her quest was over.

JUST AS Hope saw the Lê family enter the double doors to join the festivities, her phone rang. She slipped into the nearest hallway to answer it. "Hello?"

"Hope, darling."

The tone of Dominique's voice told her more than she wanted to know. "I'm guessing you won't be coming tonight if you haven't left yet. Or are you at the airport?"

"I'm in Sarajevo. I'm so sorry, sweetheart, but I know you will understand this above all people."

As always, he gave her too much credit, assuming she had the same priorities. Of course, she'd put people's lives before an awards event. There was no question. But weren't there other people who could take on his role? It wasn't something he was suited for. There was no point in discussing it. Either she accepted him the way he was, or she had to end it. He was so perfect for her. They were so perfect.

A sadness swarmed inside her as Hope peeked around the corner and watched the Lê family shuffling around their two reserved tables, deciding who would sit where. The contrast between her two worlds was blatant.

"Are you there, darling?"

"Yes. What's happening?"

"The child whose final adoption papers you just reviewed

before you left—she and three other children have been captured by a group of Serbs."

"Oh God, Dominique."

"The adoptive parents are devastated. She was due on a flight next week to Boston. I was assigned delivery to her new parents in Maine. It makes me feel such a responsibility, darling. We're going back to work with the government to find them."

"Isn't that beyond the scope of Uplift's work?" She closed her eyes and sighed. This was getting to be a crisis in their relationship. Images of the baby girl she'd sketched flashed in her mind. She was only nine months old. "Ask my dad to keep me informed, please." She tried to hide the desperate plea in her voice.

"Of course, darling. Hopefully, they will be successful in the rescue. I won't take unnecessary extra risks, Hope, I promise. I love you."

Extra risks, she thought. It was already beyond what she could handle. Was this the authentic Dominique, or was he trying to live up to some standard his father had modeled for him, just as Hope had wanted to please her father? "Be safe, honey. I'll see you soon." It took every bit of effort to keep the terror and maybe anger from her voice.

"I love you. I'll be in touch." He hung up.

This was not the authentic Dominique from every indication. Hope loved that he was gentle, loved the peace of nature, and lit up when he was writing. She'd observed him when he was composing a piece for a newspaper or magazine—his enthusiasm, his interest in getting every word right to touch the reader, his kindness and empathy were reflected in the Dominique, Hope thought she knew well—the parts of the man that had made her fall in love so fast.

The articles had resulted in more donations and support than any other promotion they'd done. Couldn't Dominique contribute in that way, as she was now doing with her art? But it wasn't her place to fix him or correct him. That was no way to start a lifelong relationship. Hope was on Jolie's side when it came to wanting Dominique to stay out of the fray.

She crossed the room to join the celebration.

"Congratulations, Hope. We are so proud of you." Her grandfather Lê waved, pulled a chair out, and gestured for her to sit. It was a seat of honor facing the stage next to Linh.

"And we can't thank you enough for the portraits." Hope's grandmother Lê had spoken directly to her for the first time.

Their warmth and welcoming smiles made Hope feel accepted. She was a Lê. But would she ever truly be a Lê Ketchum-James with the rift between her father and the Grands? She wanted that.

There was an empty seat on the other side of Hope. "Linh, who's sitting here?"

"I'll tell you, but first, why do you look like you've seen a ghost?"

Leaning close, Hope whispered, "Dominique called. He's off to coordinate the rescue of four children from some Serbian kidnappers. I can't talk about it. Let's try to enjoy ourselves. I don't want to ruin our special night."

"Oh, sweetheart, I'm so sorry. Look who just arrived." Linh nodded in the direction of the entrance. Shiloh waved and hurried over to the table. Her bangles announced her arrival. Linh made the introductions to all the aunts, uncles, and Grands.

"I feel like I'm with the Ketchums. Wonderful to meet all of you. Happy to meet the other trunk of the split tree."

The conversation was lively with Shiloh at the helm, and dinner went smoothly. She spent a lot of time singing Hope's praises—a welcome boost for Hope. The looks on her relatives' faces conveyed they were impressed and maybe a little surprised to hear Shiloh's accolades about Hope. It was the first time Hope was socializing with them outside of the Lê family home, and all was going well. Most of the exchanges were in English out of respect for Shiloh. That helped. Could they be more different from the Ketchums? Could they be more alike? Other than the difference in education, affluence, and dress, the feeling was the same. Trade flannel for fine wool and cotton for silk, and the two families were so similar when it came to giving Hope a sense of belonging. But wait, didn't they both wear soft Italian leather shoes? She laughed to herself.

Grandfather Lê stood and made a toast to Hope, holding his water glass high and speaking loud enough for both tables to hear. "We are not just celebrating Hope and Linh's award, but we're celebrating finding the great-granddaughter, granddaughter, niece, and cousin we never knew we had. We are blessed. Welcome to the family, Hope, and bless you for your portrait gifts to all of us."

Bowing her head, Hope brought her hands to the prayer position at her chest and was speechless. She fought hard to keep her quivering shoulders still and to prevent a total breakdown in front of the group. She was touched and grateful.

Gregory pulled the microphone from the stand at the front of the stage. "I'm Gregory Sanford, and as the president of the ICB Artists Association, I would like to welcome our new Mayor, Rory Johnston, and his lovely artist wife and ICB member, Maya. And a warm welcome to our honored guests, ICB artists, families, and friends." He interrupted the suspended applause. "Tonight, we recognize the winners of the Northern California

New Art Contest. But first, we have a special guest who would like to make a dedication to our first-place winners from the Lê Gallery, Hope Lê Ketchum-James and Lê Murray Linh. Our guest had asked us to make this performance a surprise. Direct from Europe, here she is! Enjoy!"

Hope wasn't the only one to recognize the band members who scurried onto the stage and took up their instruments. The drummer pulled the cover back on his base drum, and the crowd cheered at the sight of the famous logo—Riverrun.

"Hope, your *mother*. Were you expecting her?" Linh had to yell to be heard in the clamor.

The crowd leaped to their feet. The energy had its way with Hope, as it had with all three hundred guests. She was lit up. It was a first. When Hope needed her the most, Kate had come through for her.

"Kate, Kate, Kate." The spotlight and the familiar chant brought Kate Ketchum out onto the stage in her leather mini skirt, high boots, flashing, long red hair, high cheekbones, the famed Irish beauty with engaging green eyes—an Ann-Margret look-alike as everyone had said about Cecelia and Kate. Her fame had bridged the generations from teens to seniors. Each concert had something for everyone, Hope thought.

It was awkward to watch the reactions of each Lê family member. Kate Ketchum was her world-famous beloved mother and the wife of the man they'd held responsible for losing their eldest daughter, Hằng. They hung their heads at first and exchanged flashes of eyes. Then their eyes shined, and they smiled when she dedicated the evening to them.

Kate shaded her eyes and peered out into the audience. "This special performance is dedicated to my daughter Hope, her business partner and aunt, Linh, and the entire Lê family. I love you, Hope. This song's for you."

Kate sang the Grammy-winning lyrics with a tenderness that shared her truth with Hope, "Too precious to leave behind."

WHEN THE private concert ended, Kate signed autographs. Even the mayor appeared captivated by Kate's fame, kindness, and charm. After giving the mayor and his wife autographed shirts for their children, Kate took Shiloh by the arm and accompanied the couple to the Lê Gallery to view the first-place-winning creation.

"It's stunning. Hope and Linh, you have captured something unique here." Mayor Johnston and his wife exchanged looks. "My wife and I would like you to create one of these for our extended family. Would that be possible?"

"We'd be honored, truly. Would you like it to be created on a portable backing or permanently at your home?"

They stepped aside to consider the answer.

Hope found humor in the excited reactions of some of her Lê family aunts and uncles as they stood in the same room with Kate Ketchum, mouths agape. She was always so attentive and genuine with her fans. There was no egoic aspect to her presence. No one dared to mention Michael, but Hope knew from Linh that the family was torn.

"We'd love it to be portable if that's OK. In case we move in the future. Would you be willing to add portraits if we add new family members? Would the tree have that capacity?" Maya studied the portraits on the tree. "It's so lovely, and each person is so different. Would it be possible to have it completed by next Christmas?"

"If we can make a baby in nine months, I think we can work that timing out to do your Split Tree." Hope's humor made them smile.

Linh discussed the number of family members to be included and set up an appointment to discuss the details and cost.

The crowd drifted off, and the gallery emptied, leaving the Lê family, Shiloh, and Kate to enjoy the exhibit.

"Miss Kate and Miss Shiloh, would you care to join us for Mass tomorrow and breakfast afterward?" Hope's grandfather extended the invitation with a pleading tone that Hope had never heard him use. "Our teens would be thrilled, and we would be grateful."

"*Bà ngoại* and *Ông ngoại*, I'd be delighted." It surprised Hope when Kate used the right words of respect—different appropriate titles—to address Hope's maternal grandparents, Grandfather and Grandmother Lê. Kate was very impressive, and her manners had certainly charmed the elders. "I'd be so delighted. It's wonderful to get to know Hope's Lê family."

Everyone said their good nights and headed for their cars.

Hope rode with Shiloh in Kate's limousine. One of Hope's favorite views was crossing the Golden Gate Bridge at night to return to San Francisco—the famous ruddy bridge strung out from Sausalito to Marin like illuminated strings of pearls against the blackness. In the distance, the hilly coastline was dotted with tiny waves of light. They rode in dark silence to Linh's house.

Were Kate and Shiloh feeling as high as Hope was? She couldn't stop grinning. But her ache for Dominique was always in the background. Would she ever learn to manage that conflict?

"Hope, I totally understand your choices. This is so you. I've never seen you so happy. And your art is beyond meaningful. Subtle, positive, powerful, political," Shiloh said.

"Your alliterative support means everything." Hope laughed.

"You two clever ones," Kate said.

"I thought you would be disappointed in me, Shiloh. Making such an outrageous shift in my career path."

"Maybe we never gave you a chance to choose that path. Maybe *I* should be apologizing. But I believe everything has a purpose, even our so-called mistakes."

"Thank you, Auntie Shi." This was what it felt like to live your own life. Hope looked at Kate. This was what it felt like to have a mother. This was what she'd craved her entire childhood. As a woman in her twenties, she'd thought Kate's connection had every bit as much impact had she been a child. Maybe more when your adoptive mother stood before an audience to announce her love and dedication. She wanted that song to come on the radio so Hope could sing along, knowing what the lyrics meant now. "Mom." Hope loved saying that word. "I can't thank you enough for coming." She squeezed out her words through her throat, tight with emotion. What a touching gesture for her mother to change her touring plans to attend her daughter's award ceremony. "When is your flight back?"

"I'm here for as long as you need me. I've rearranged my last tour."

"Last tour? I thought retirement was a long-range plan." Hope wondered why Kate thought she would need her.

"Honey, I want to be here for you."

Shiloh's phone rang. Hope knew that calls at odd hours never brought good news.

The headlights on the passing cars sent pulsing lights across Shiloh's face as she spoke.

"Hope, that was Michael. Dominique made him promise not to share any news of his assignment with you on your special night. Well, his self-imposed assignment. Although I'm sure he didn't anticipate this would happen." Shiloh's sigh sent a warning to Hope. This was not a sound you often heard from confident, cavalier Shiloh. "A few hours before the award ceremony, Michael got a call from José."

"I already know Dominique's working with the government to help find the children. He called me from Sarajevo." Hope didn't like Shiloh's pause. It told her there was more to the story. "I'm dying here. What happened?" Hope sat on the edge of the leather seat. "Please."

"Dominique broke his agreement to work through the government to free the baby girl and three kidnapped boys. He tracked down the kidnappers, using informants who were happy to help the man who had delivered food and shelter to them months before. Dominique did escape with the children."

"Oh. Thank goodness. Where is he now?"

"Hope, wait. Before Dominique could get to our Uplift plane, he was retaken hostage by the same group, under fire between the Serb kidnappers and the government troops. The kidnappers knew Dominique was a valuable asset."

"And the children?"

"The children were released. The team is working to reunite them with their families."

"And the little girl?"

"The orphan girl Dominique was bringing back for adoption is being transported back to our Boston headquarters."

Kate moved to sit next to Hope and took her hand.

"Dominique is all they wanted anyway. The children were only trouble for them."

"Oh, God, Auntie Shi." Dropping her head back against the seat, Hope went silent. "Where is he now?"

"Just outside of Sarajevo."

"Do we have any word? Is he . . . unharmed?"

"It appeared they want him alive." Sitting facing Hope, Shiloh put her hand on Hope's knee. "Honey, he would be no good to them otherwise."

"Does Jolie know?" Hope put her hands over her face.

"Yes. She's with Cecelia," Shiloh said.

"And my dad? Where is he? Wait, Mom, you don't think Dad will try to be a hero for me, do you?"

"I'm not sure where he is, but he's not in Sarajevo. He said he was working on a special project in the States unrelated to a rescue mission. I asked him specifically."

Kate pulled Hope close. "Let's not assume the worst. After I drop you off at Linh's house in Embarcadero and get back to the Four Seasons, I'll call Michael again. But he promised me he would not go over there."

38

STARING AT THE patchwork quilt on Linh's guest bed, Hope sat propped up against the feather pillow, trying to clarify her thoughts amid prayers for Dominique. She refused to imagine what was happening to him or the children. There were too many real stories. They were fodder for fear, but she wouldn't feed her imaginings. Instead, Hope focused on positive memories of Dominique—his charm, their loving moments, driving through the park every day, watching nature transform through the seasons, and the stunning articles he'd written. Whenever any terrifying images invaded, Hope took Dominique to the park in her mind, their favorite restaurants, or stood with Dominique in his home looking out over the gardens. She let herself take an imaginary walk down the office hallway to see The Wall of Hope with four new children's portraits joining the other children who had new lives. It wasn't about whether he was suitable for Hope. Given his chosen work, that conflict lived on. It was about his safety as a loving human being.

Linh's colorful family quilted heirloom was constructed of squares of fabric made from generations of traditional dress—women's *áo dài* and men's traditional *áo gấm*. The embroidered fabric with plum blossoms and Mulberry designs was made of every subtle and bold color. Scraps of history, Linh had said. She'd gathered them from generations gone by and her Lê family's unwanted, outgrown, or well-worn dress clothes. She'd sewn them together to preserve her family's history.

Why had Linh used this precious heirloom as an everyday coverlet for Hope's guest room bed? She'd said she wanted to symbolically link Hope with her ancestors. It made Hope sentimental as she rubbed her fingers lightly across the sleek, silky quilt patches, fragile like her.

Life without Dominique would be unbearable; life with him as her husband and lover would be endless torture.

Hope made her decision as the morning sun rose, illuminating the shades in the room. The answer was in the quilt. She couldn't constantly live patching their lives together, with no consistency, no plans, at the mercy of the whims of wars, never having the complete picture. It was an unbearable thought that she could not plan anything in her life or give their children the stability she knew was important for their happiness. She had to face that truth. Short of some miracle, their relationship had to end unless he came up with the solution himself. The timing was the issue. But there had to be honesty on Hope's part once he was safely at home.

She prayed an unthinkable fate wouldn't complete the terrible task for her. No, she couldn't let herself think of that. "Please, God, bring him home." She wept into her pillow.

LAST NIGHT, when Kate had left for the Four Seasons Hotel in her limo, only a few blocks away, and Shiloh had left for the airport, the darkness had descended. Being with the family for Mass might help, Hope thought.

In the depths of her fears and possible loss, Hope dressed to attend Mass and looked in the mirror. Her red eyes reflected her long, painful, sleepless night. How many more would she have to endure? Her emotions kept swinging from fear to anger to compassion to love. She knew some NGO volunteers had suffered years in overseas prisons or were never heard from again. This had been her greatest fear. This was why she didn't want him to go on overseas missions.

She slipped her ballet flats on and dressed for Mass. One foot in front of the other, Hope told herself. Time will heal. He'll be OK. She was anxious to know the kidnapper's demands. These kidnappings of humanitarian workers were becoming all too common. But this small rebel group knew they'd caught a big fish now. Son of an heiress, leader of the world's wealthiest charitable organization, and connected to Kate Ketchum.

She would call Jolie after church. That was not a call Hope wanted to make.

Flipping through the outfits in her closet, Hope couldn't focus on the clothes she'd unpacked upon arrival. Had Kate told the Ketchum family about Dominique's capture? Certainly, the Ketchum family would know. But the Lê clan would always have the joy of last night and Linh's award, uncontaminated by the troubles Hope had brought into their family's lives. She'd resurrected painful memories for them—Hope's mother's death, her father's resurfacing, reminding the Lê family of their long-ago loss. Now, the terrors of Dominique being held captive with four innocent children were added to the list. Could the children be innocent now after what they'd seen?

Throwing her leather jacket over her arm, she followed the voices downstairs.

LINH MET Hope at the bottom of the staircase and hugged her. "How are you holding up?"

Hadn't her cheerless face and slumped body said it all?

"Oh, honey, never mind. I know the answer to that. Just know we're here for you. We're all going to the bi-lingual, eleven o'clock Mass at St. Boniface, OK? The Grands like that one—it's the Mass many Vietnamese Catholics attend. They love hearing the service in their own language. Let's have breakfast."

"OK, but I just need coffee, Linh. Badly."

The boys were already dressed and playing video games on the floor in front of the large-screen TV with the sound turned down. A news flash came on—a silent clip of a man holding a baby being shoved into an open military vehicle along with three young children. At the bottom of the screen, the words scrolled: *This just in from Sarajevo: Children released. Ransom demanded for the release of NGO executive. Stay tuned for the update.*

"Let's go, boys." John bolted up from his chair, nearly knocked over his coffee cup, flashed a look their way, and nodded his head toward the table. "And turn off that TV, please."

Hope gasped, and everyone followed her wide-eyed gaze to the television. "Dominique, oh my God." The story had finally hit the news. "But what's the update, Linh?"

"He has to be alive." Linh covered her mouth.

"Mom, what do you mean? Who was it, and what happened to him?" John Jr. rushed over and turned up the volume.

It was too late. A commercial came on, preventing them from gathering any details.

"Dominique is in another country, and he got lost." Hope didn't regret the lie. The boys shouldn't be burdened with the whole truth.

"We didn't know he was in trouble," Brad said.

"Your dad and I didn't want you to worry. Everything will be fine." Mouthing the words, "I'm so sorry," to Hope, Linh turned off the TV.

Chills still showered down Hope's arms as she stared into space, replaying the scene in her mind. Was that when he was first taken hostage, or was it when they were transporting him somewhere? He looked healthy. As far as Hope could see, Dominique wasn't injured, and the children seemed OK, too. They were alive.

And now there would be a ransom.

"A ransom. Isn't that encouraging? Doesn't that mean they won't dare to—" Linh stopped. She put the ham and cheese omelets she'd made at Brad and John, Jr.'s place settings.

"Boys, come eat your omelets. Everything's fine." John's no-nonsense tone immediately brought the boys to the table.

Not wanting to frighten the kids, Linh signaled Hope to follow her, and they moved into the study to talk. "Sit for a minute, Hope."

They sat on the leather sofa. "I can't believe this. A ransom.

We need to call someone and find out what is happening. It appeared that the kidnappers weren't being aggressive toward their captives. Thank goodness, right, Hope?"

The whole thing was surreal, Hope thought. It was like a staff meeting tale that had come to life. "I hadn't thought of that. I need to talk to my dad. I'm sure he knows more. Last night, Kate called late to say she couldn't reach him. He was probably en route to a meeting." Hope leaned into Linh's arms. "I'm sorry the kids had to see that."

"They'll be fine. John's out there talking to them. They've seen worse playing their fantasy games. Let's go back and eat, or at least finish your coffee. We'll go to church and afterward call Michael."

"Oh, poor Jolie. It's already afternoon there. She must know. But you're right. At least we know Dominique is still alive."

They returned to their dining seats.

"We saw your boyfriend and some kids going into a big jeep. Where were they taking them? That was mean. They were tied up." With his palms up, pleading for the answer, Brad's eyes were riveted on Hope.

"They won't hurt him. The bad guys just want money. Then they'll let him go," John Jr. explained.

Brad put his hands on his hips. "Oh, that's just like our Mario game."

WHILE JOHN waited by the curb to help the elders when they arrived, Linh and Hope stood at the top of the stairs under the massive arches of the entrance to the beautiful St. Boniface Catholic Church. To pass the time, Linh shared the history of the Romanesque Revival edifice as the boys ran up and down the stone stairs. "An earthquake and a fire destroyed the old eighteen hundreds church in nineteen-oh-six, then it was rebuilt. So much history here in the Tenderloin district for the Vietnamese people who'd settled here."

Hope stretched her neck to admire the arches of stained-glass windows and two tall bell towers that flanked the sprawling church. The distraction wasn't working.

"When we'd first arrived, this is where we'd met the few other Vietnamese families who'd immigrated during those early days. It gave us our first sense of belonging. Here comes a sight, Hope. Look."

As Kate arrived in her limousine, the Grands pulled up from the opposite direction in an entourage of six cars with the entire family in tow.

Hope, Linh, John, and their sons gathered at the top of the stone stairs beside the double doors to the church, waiting for the family.

"Good morning, sweetheart." Climbing the deep stone stairs, Kate embraced Hope in an unusually long hug. "Oh honey, you look so tired. Let's keep the faith." She kissed Hope's forehead.

"Thanks, Mom. You've seen the news, then." Kate's new title was becoming more comfortable for Hope. It was even more meaningful now as the ache of worry over Dominique's safety became more real after seeing him on the news clip. Flashes of her private loving moments with him resurrected one after the other without intention. Hope just wanted him to be OK. That one thought overtook any decisions about leaving him. She just wanted him to return alive and uninjured with the children. Then they would talk.

"I couldn't reach Michael. We'll call him after Mass and get to the bottom of this." Kate drew Hope close to her.

The Lê family created a crowd outside the imposing church. As a flow of other parishioners entered the church, they greeted a young-looking Franciscan Friar in his brown robe and rope belt. "Good morning, Father Lawrence."

Uncle Tuân and his wife helped great-grandmother Lê up the stairs. She was the family source of Hope's creative genes. That fact had endeared her to Hope, Linh had said.

"Good morning, Hope, Kate?" She'd greeted them in English. Where had Kate learned the Vietnamese greetings? It made things go smoothly.

"*Xin chào bà ngoại*," Hope and Kate responded in unison.

Hope realized that after all her travels, touring, and meeting people overseas, Kate would have learned the social basics in many languages. She'd especially liked learning the tonal languages like Thai and Vietnamese, Kate had said.

When Hope's great-grandmother extended both hands, a sign of intimacy, Hope held them, gazed down humbly, trying not to cry, and repeated, "*Xin chào bà ngoại*."

There was an extra warm tone in everyone's greetings as they said good morning dressed in their Sunday best. Had they seen the news?

They greeted Father Lawrence, and led by Uncle Tuân, they walked down the center aisle. Halfway to the altar, they divided into two lines, filling one of the long pews. Each side of the shiny wooden pew had a brass plate engraved with a dedication to Hope's mother.

Would the commemorative pew comfort Hope? Would she feel her biological mother's presence, like Linh had said she would? Was the calming feeling Hope experienced as she knelt to pray, the presence of her mother's spirit, or simply the result of being surrounded by more than a dozen relatives and Kate—the woman she now called Mom?

The congregation began to sing the first hymn.

"Be not afraid

I go before you always

Come follow me

And I will give you rest."

Hope could read the comforting words in two ways, she thought. The song lyrics were perfect for what she needed. She pleaded that it meant Dominique's safety and not *rest in peace.*

Throughout the service, the lyrics ran through her mind repeatedly as Hope prayed for Dominique's safe return. Coming out of her coma-like state, she heard Dominique's name spoken by the priest from the pulpit. The congregation prayed for him in one humming voice as the sun pushed through the stained-glass windows, casting colorful crystals of light on the cathedral walls. Was it a good sign, Hope wondered.

During the final hymn, Kate took Hope's hand, and they sang the poignant lyrics, "Let There Be Peace On Earth, and let it begin with me."

WITH MASS over, the Lê family, Kate, and Hope remained and prayed for Dominique. Dressed in his ivory and gold vestments,

Father Lawrence came to the pew and whispered, "May I see you all before you leave?"

Outside, the sun lit up the sparkling marble church steps where Father Lawrence waited until the entire family had gathered around him. "I'd like to invite you to share a private prayer of thanks in the church garden. Someone has prepared a very touching gift for your family."

Whispering with confusion, the Grands tried to guess who might do something special for them as they followed the priest to the garden side of the church property. What was the occasion? Who was their benefactor?

Father Lawrence stopped as they walked along the path under an arc of Crepe Myrtle trees still dormant in the April sun.

An area had been cleared for a new stone bench with an engraved marble sign on the ground beside it. *In memory of our beloved Lê Phạm Hằng Am. April 9, 1975.* A few feet from the bench, a headstone was surrounded by freshly planted flowers. It was engraved with a longer message in Vietnamese. Hope assumed it held a similar meaning. The date was painful for Hope—her birthday and her mother's demise. Could Hope ever celebrate her birthday without connecting to that loss? Hope saw her father in the shadow of the thick border of dense arborvitae trees.

Michael approached hesitantly.

"I will leave you to your private moments. God bless you all. And God Bless your daughter's memory." Father Lawrence left and entered the church through the side entrance.

It was evident to Hope the family's reaction to Michael was mixed and went along age lines. The teens stepped forward. "Hey, I'm finally meeting you. I'm Hong. You know my dad, Dr. Tuân."

"Yes, he's a great guy, and Hope told me about you, too."

"I saw the news where you got the award from Vice President Al Gore for your charity work with kids. Nice to meet you, Mr. James."

"Thank you, Hong. And the pleasure is mine. And Tuân good to see you."

Linh's two sons stepped closer, and John Jr. introduced them both.

Tuân pointed to his brother Long. "Michael, of course, you remember my little brother Long."

"Long, I can't believe it. You were just a tyke."

"Oh man, buddy, it's been too long, right? I have so many fun memories of your visits to that village where we were undercover those two years."

Michael glanced at the group of elders who had separated from the group.

Hope knew her dad felt awkward speaking with the young people and his peers before acknowledging the elders. He knew the customs.

Tuân broke through the awkward moment and turned to the Grands. "It was so kind and thoughtful of Michael to arrange the memorial for Hằng, wasn't it? We've lamented that we didn't know where she was, and we had no gravestone to honor her yet."

There was a silent moment. The two pairs of grandparents and great-grandparents turned to walk away. Kate moved beside Michael. "Forgive me, but I understood that you all loved Michael at one time. I'm confused. I, of all people, was threatened by Michael's undying love for Hằng. I'd fallen in love with a man dedicated to the memory of a past love. We worked through that. I moved past it because he loved me too and suffered a loss beyond my comprehension."

Hope's emotions were surfacing, about to erupt. It was her turn to express herself. With a supportive hand on Kate's arm, Hope spoke. She had to; it was time. "If she were here, what would Hằng say? We all need to heal our hearts to move forward. I didn't know my mother, but I believe Hằng would say, we can't just walk out of Mass and then not live by our beliefs."

Linh faced the Grands and supported Hope. "Michael deserves our compassion. He lost his first love. He risked everything to rescue his child. Our Hope. How many American military men left babies behind to suffer discrimination and have no family? Literally, tens of thousands." Linh's audacity surprised Hope. She was grateful for her aunt's support.

Tuân turned to his father. "Dad, we need to do the right thing here, and we all finally need to know the truth. Please? Hằng took a risk for love when she followed Michael into danger. And she was an adult, not a victim when she became pregnant with Hope. She didn't know the war would shift suddenly to that area. And Michael didn't know she was coming. It wasn't the plan. Imagine Michael watching as his true love . . . I can't even go there." Tuân put his arm around his wife.

"Maybe we need a little time to process, Michael. Will you give us that?" Hope's grandfather looked at the gravestone. "We were always holding out hope that Hằng was still with us. But our hearts are so heavy that we never had the chance to create a place to honor our beloved daughter. And now—"

Hope loved that her grandfather had tried to build a bridge.

"Please give us some time," he said.

"I will, *Ong*. I understand. I want you to know I had once

planned to cherish Hằng for a lifetime." Michael bowed slightly and turned to walk away.

Hope was impressed with her grandfather's solution to the tense moment. Take a little time to process as a family. She wanted to speak up. "Maybe this is a lot to ask, as the newest member of the family. Can we find a way for Michael to be just my *father* in the future?"

Uncle Tuân added, "Yes, for the sake of your granddaughter and your great-granddaughter? Our lineage?"

Hope couldn't resist adding to Uncle Tuan's plea. "That's all Michael truly is now when it comes to the Lê family—he's my father. I've learned that in the past, he was a man who made your daughter, my mother Hằng, feel deeply loved."

Michael wrapped his arms around Hope. She felt his body trembling.

"We've all suffered in our own way from war. Please, no more wars. Not in our family." The perfect lyrics came to Hope, and they spilled from her lips. "'Let There Be Peace On Earth.'" Hope paused. "And let it begin with *us*. We need to live those lyrics, not just sing them."

39

AS SHE RODE the elevator with Linh, John, and their sons, Hope thought brunch with the family would be, at best, tense or awkward. Still, she was determined to build peace within her Lê clan. Had she gone too far? She wasn't used to speaking her mind so boldly. "Linh, did I sound like a lawyer arguing in the courtroom back at the gravesite? I hope not."

"Don't worry. It'll be alright, Hope. You were amazing and courageous. I was worse than you in that case. Things needed to be said."

Being open and upfront when issues got difficult in her personal life had never been Hope's strong suit. She may have caused irreversible damage. But right now, there was no room for the past. As the elevator door opened at the top floor, Hope realized Dominique and the present time needed her full attention.

With the familiar sounds of the TV and kids chattering in the background, Hope looked out over the Bay with Alcatraz in the distance. Yes, imprisoned was the right word. How much longer could Hope hold it together? Thoughts of Dominique were excruciating.

She was trapped now between her elder relatives' feelings and her father's gesture of love. How could she be loyal to her father and respect the Grands, too? Had Hope damaged the beautiful connection she'd begun to build with the family she never thought she'd have? And her bond with Linh was beyond the art they shared. With only a decade between their ages, Linh seemed more like a sister than an aunt. They were on equal terms and on the same page about art and values. She would help Hope to keep her connection to the family.

Hope heard a familiar voice in the family room. The priest was headed to the elevator. "Father Lawrence, good to see you again." She had an ally. But was it necessary? Across the room, framed in the expansive windows as if floating with the clouds in the blue sky behind him, was Hope's father.

With Bloody Marys in hand, Kate and Michael were toasting the adults who had gathered like old friends in front of the serene bay view. Michael's words weren't audible in the buzzing of the socializing in the room, but the message was clear to Hope. They'd built a bridge.

She knew it was an effort for Michael and Kate to lose themselves in the moment with Dominique on their minds. But the emotional and encouraging moment was a respite from tension for everyone.

"I believe your work is done here, Father." Hope's humor conveyed.

Father Lawrence released a muffled chuckle. "Thank you, miss. But I believe I should be saying that to you. Your words sparked Mr. Lê to call me after thinking about what you said. And the lyrics, 'Let There Be Peace On Earth and let it begin with me,' were powerful. Perfect timing. Perhaps you missed your calling."

Hope listened to the priest's story. He'd come to talk to the elders at her grandfather's request. Father Lawrence explained that Grandpa Lê had called Hope's parents at the Four Seasons and invited them to brunch. Uncle Tuân had tracked them down. Father Lawrence glanced over his shoulder at Kate. "Honestly, I can't believe I'm here with Kate Ketchum. I know that's getting out of my vestments, so to speak, but it is exciting."

Seeing the young priest so taken with Hope's adoptive mother brought back memories of her friends in college screaming when Kate picked Hope up in her limousine. Back then, it had made her uncomfortable. Now, the enthusiastic response of others to Kate brought a light note to the day. "I understand. I've lived with that my entire life. She's magnetic. But as for everyone's interactions at the cemetery, they were so caught off guard by my father's gift. It was understandable."

Discovering how her biological mother was so violently killed in the war shocked the Lê family. Questioning Michael's role in bringing her to that moment was inevitable. Who would want to blame Hằng?

The priest cast his eyes down and paused. "This is my first year at St. Boniface. I'm afraid I didn't handle things right. I thought your father was a current family friend who wished to make a beautiful gesture."

Hope followed Father Lawrence's gaze as he looked around the room. No one would interrupt their conversation, Hope thought. They would assume she was confessing. They would never guess the reverse was true. She felt compassion for the young novitiate.

"I need to study and garner some insight into the Vietnamese cultural norms and beliefs if I am to officiate the Sunday bi-lingual Mass. These parishioners are an integral part of the congregation. I wonder if I was acting with selfish motives. I wanted to seem responsible for your father's large donation to the church. Sharing the news with the Monsignor was a great beginning to my position here at St. Boniface."

"Your intention was good. And Father, the outcome was good. Had the family been forewarned, I'm not certain the result would have been this honest and open. Look." She gestured toward the family, talking and sharing.

"When I arrived at the house here, the youngest boy, Brad, began singing, 'Let There Be Peace On Earth.' The family started smiling at the boy's innocent yet profound message. It broke the ice. So, I'm guessing the message will live on. I should go. I have another service to officiate. I hope the family is forgiving when it comes to my bad judgment. As a priest, I should have the wisdom to ask more questions and be better informed."

"As a lawyer, I should be more skilled at arguing my case. We'll earn our wisdom in time, Father. I'll help them understand if it becomes an issue."

The ache over Dominique's situation was ever-present for Hope. Like a physical weight she'd carried. A sadness. Loneliness even when she was with the people she loved. She knew it was hard for her dad and Kate to stay focused on the reunion unfolding with the Lê family.

"Father Lawrence, may I ask you to pray for my fiancé? This is not the normal request." Hope felt the clenching of her stomach that had accompanied her since it had happened.

"Unusual is my specialty. I'm honored to pray for your cause."

"He's been captured and held for ransom in Sarajevo."

"Of course, and his name is?"

"Dominique Bellamy Bonchance."

"I will add him to the special prayer list for our Masses this week. I'll slip out now." Father Lawrence turned to the crowd, raised his voice, and made the sign of the cross. "God bless your entire family."

"Thank you, Father." A chorus of voices answered him.

From across the room, Michael waved Hope over to join them.

Her great-grandfather's quivering voice caused a sudden silence around the table across the room. He spoke in English. "Hope we owe you a debt of gratitude."

An unusual consideration for Michael, Hope thought. Or it could have been done so that even the young children could understand. She wasn't sure.

"We were faced with a flood of sad memories, the bench dedication, the unexpected gravestone, and seeing Michael after all these years. It was easy to blame Michael for Hằng's disappearance. And maybe we suffered from some disappointment that we hadn't the chance to build a memorial for Hằng ourselves, not knowing for certain our loved one was . . . we want to remember her; yet we don't want to remember her ending. Do you understand? We've asked Michael for forgiveness, and he's graciously offered the peace pipe—to use an American expression."

"But Great Grandpa Lê, you told us we shouldn't smoke." Eight-year-old Brad struck his usual pose with his hands on his hips.

Hong's cackle echoed through the room, and the relieved family laughed, evaporating the tension.

The norm resumed as a wave of animated conversation and sentimental stories from the past flowed through the room. The usual low volume of the TV went on again. The most healing cacophony of sounds Hope had ever heard. She could see it brought tears to many eyes, not just hers. She crossed the room and thanked her great-grandfather for being so gracious.

Michael signaled Hope and offered her a drink. "Let's quickly talk about Dominique before the meal starts. We don't want to burden the moment with discussions of his capture. Tuân will inform them later."

"Dad, it's been terrorizing for everyone." Hope recalled the news update they missed on TV before they left. "A ransom? Is it true? I've been going crazy waiting. What's going on?"

Her father nodded. "I was contacted by some group of rebels outside of Sarajevo. Bottom line, they want five million dollars."

"*Five million dollars?* Seriously?"

"They've done their research, and the news stories of Jolie's donations to Uplift, Kate's fame, my recent history in funding the foundation, it all adds up to an assumption about our ability to pay."

"But how long would it take to pay the ransom and get him home? I should be there with Jolie. I've booked the earliest flight I could get. It leaves on Wednesday morning. I'm traveling back with Mom."

"Mom? Honey, you called Kate 'Mom' again?"

"I know. Things have changed."

After refilling her coffee in the kitchen, Kate joined them in the corner by the altar with Hằng's portrait. "What are you two conspiring about?"

"Mom, I can't believe the ransom is five million dollars. Jolie needs our support. I want to be there when Dominique arrives. We will get him out, won't we, Dad? Should it take long? How do these things work?"

"Yes, we will get him out. I'll be damned if we won't. And we have lots of supporters in-country to help. But it may take some negotiating. We need to move fast. And I'll be honest. There is danger in the actual exchange. We—"

"What, Dad?"

Hope didn't like her father's slight hesitation.

Kate linked eyes with Michael. He shrugged, pursed his lips, and nodded.

"What did that exchange mean?" Hope wished she had that level of communication with Dominique.

"Brunch is ready," Linh called across the room. The family filled their plates from the breakfast buffet and settled into seats at the two large round glass tables for twelve.

"We'll talk after we eat," Kate said.

"THE NEWSPAPERS are here." Just as they finished their meal, Brad brought in an armful of the Sunday San Francisco Chronicle. He distributed them to the adults.

Pulling out the Arts and Entertainment section on the front page, above the fold, Hope saw a photo of Linh and herself sitting outside the door to their Lê Gallery, painting portraits for the Northern California New Arts Contest. "Linh, did you *see* this?" Hope moved to sit next to Linh on the velvet sofa at the far end of the windows in the corner of the great room. The spread introduced a new columnist, Dominique Bellamy Bonchance. "He must have submitted this before he left." Together, they read the explanation of the art effort to capture the lives of

Vietnamese and others who'd immigrated and created new lives in the US—the diversity, the successes, the love, and dedication it took to rise.

Linh took Hope's hand. "This is so well-written I want to cry."

"His stories are always crafted with emotion—classic Dominique." Hope wanted to revel in the article and not think about what was happening in Sarajevo.

After reading the general explanation of the purpose of the Split Tree art project, they studied Ernie's portrait and read his story.

The world-renowned singer Kate Ketchum had rescued him from a life in a depressing institution. With Ernie's eye for detail and empathetic heart, he'd found his place in the handmade shoe factory, charming children as he measured them for their new handmade shoes. The article spoke of his humor and kindness growing up with Hope. And Ernie's role in helping Mary with her new family as Hope's aunt's adopted daughter.

The syndicated article included a few quotes from Ernie that showed his heart and humor.

"Linh, this is amazing." Hope read more. The Ketchum family's role in his adoption and Grandpa Ketchum's teaching Ernie the family trade was inspiring. She smiled, imagining Grandma Cecelia, Grandpa Kevin, and the entire clan gathered around to see their lives honored in the Boston Globe. The moving story of Dr. Tuân flying in to save the day for Ernie when discrimination in the hospital threatened his life made the connection between the Ketchum and Lê families even more dramatic.

The photo of the Split Tree on the Lê Gallery wall was surrounded by miniature portraits that Hope and Linh had painted during the contest. Short stories of more immigrant families in San Francisco they'd painted were sprinkled throughout the article. The whole idea for the featured article was genius.

A section of the two-page article showcased Michael James, the Uplift Children's Foundation's founder, and his important work for children in war-torn countries. The story of Hope discovering that the Lê family had survived and finding her work with her art partner, her Aunt Linh, at her gallery at the ICB Arts Association Building was powerful and made them both tear up.

At the bottom of the spread was the Lê family portrait, painted from the photo Michael had entrusted to Hope, minus Michael. She thought of her father. What had he felt when he saw his daughter had deleted him from the precious sentimental portrait, Hope wondered. Across the room, his smile and Kate's delighted look calmed Hope's concerns. After all, Michael wasn't a member of the Lê family.

The wound in the split tree of Hope's family seemed to have begun to heal, and hadn't that partially come from Dominique's moving article? Had she ever been as surprised as when Hope had opened that newspaper expecting to read about the latest plays, concerts, and movies but instead found her new life's work, her new family connections, and the powerful stories of immigrant families of all ethnicities rising?

Above the fold. Hope loved that expression. The article continued below the centerfold to complete the story with photos and mini memoirs of immigrant families. What more could you ask for a start-up artist? Such a loving gesture by Dominique. It deepened her inner conflict—the right man, the wrong environment for them to thrive in.

FINALLY, HOPE had the privacy and time to call Jolie. Next, she needed to connect with her father and Kate to hear what they seemed reluctant to tell her.

Maybe Hope had been avoiding the conversation with Jolie. She shared Dominique's mother's terror. Hope thought Jolie's worst nightmares must haunt her now—spinning images of her husband dying on the streets so long ago. Nearly three decades wouldn't erase those memories of the photos and stories on the front page of the Paris Papers. Hope knew that experience from her own PTSD.

And now Jolie relives the terrors with her son.

Stepping out on the balcony by the kitchen, Hope called Jolie at her grandparents' house in Glynn. Grandma Cecelia answered.

"Grandma C. Hi, it's me."

"Oh, honey, this is terrible. I'm so sorry. I'm praying for Dominique and the children. We're all praying for their safety and a happy outcome. But Dominique's a clever man. And Michael understands these things. They'll find a way out."

"You're right. Dominique is a brilliant and convincing man. And Dad has so many relationships with people who know how to deal with these situations. It will all work out, and they'll be home here safe and sound soon."

"Glad to hear you are your usual optimist, Hope. Let me get Jolie for you. She's in the other room watching the news. I wish she wouldn't, but who could blame her." There was silence and the sound of a door closing. "Hope, I'm in the pantry. I needed privacy. Just to tell you, Jolie isn't staying here at night. She's at Dominique's house with her new beau. I just wanted you to know she is not alone during these difficult days."

"Really? Do you know him?"

"He owns the commercial real estate company your father engaged to rent out the other forty-three floors of the Uplift building. His name is Peter DeHaven. He's Dutch and quite handsome and kind."

"Wow. That's wonderful that Jolie has his support."

"Hope, I was brought to tears by Kate's generosity regarding the ransom. What did you think?"

"What did she . . . you mean Mom's paying the ransom? I didn't know . . . I thought Jolie had to sell everything?"

Was that what had caused the flicker of communication between her parents?

"Hope, you call Kate 'Mom' now? When did that happen?"

"Well, ironically, Grandma, it seems it took my growing up to embrace her as my mother. We had a long talk. We have more in common than I thought."

There was a muffled silence on the line. "Grandma? Are you still there?"

"Yes, sweetheart, just having a moment. I'm so happy for you both."

"I was going to come home Tuesday. I should be with Jolie, but now, with Peter in the picture, maybe I'll stay here until we get word. It could be days or weeks, and I am more comfortable creating here in the studio, with all our supplies and space. I do want to be there when Dominique gets back."

"Focus on your work, honey. You're just a few hours' flight away. You have lead time once the news of his release comes in. Shiloh is already in-country, safe in Sarajevo."

"Oh, that's so comforting. You're right, Grandma. We have so many orders and deliveries for paintings now. I can create here rather than try to set up a studio in our house."

"Dominique's surprise article in the Boston Globe is so wonderful. You and Linh must be thrilled. Ernie is going around showing it to everyone at the factory. He's so proud. And your artwork is a gift to the world, Hope. You've found that spark. It's so perfectly you."

"Yes, you were right. I love painting. It's not only painting that's purposeful. I love to paint for the joy of it. Soon, I'll have more time to capture the water scenes here and the amazing sky over the bridges. And this idea we came up with focuses on the successes and positivity and the joining of people in a family. Grandma, I just can't take the wars." Hope sighed. "And now Dominique is right in the middle of it all. My greatest fear. Honestly, I can't imagine us ever being together now—"

"I hear what you are saying, honey. So, you understand Michael's stand in support of our country's refusal to pay ransoms?"

Hope's head was reeling with the sudden change-up. She looked across the room at Kate and Michael, who were in deep conversation alone in the corner by the wall of windows, intermittently glancing her way.

"Grandma, I thought you said Kate had offered to pay?"

"Honey, yes, she *offered*, but your father and Kate agree it's not right and could make things much worse than if they handled it personally with the help of the governments, Uplift's allies, and other NGO loyalists."

"I don't know anything about how these situations are handled. I'll say goodbye now, Grandma. I need to talk to my dad."

"I'll pray for Dominique, sweetheart. And we will see you soon. Just a minute, Hope. Jolie's here in the kitchen now, and I know you want to speak with her."

The conversation with Jolie went as well as could be expected.

They were both emotional but held it together. She said it comforted Jolie to be with the Ketchums, and she was looking forward to seeing Hope. The gratitude she expressed for Kate and Michael's offer to pay the ransom was passionate. But as a French citizen, she disagreed with the US and UK's "no ransom" policies. "We should pay and get Dominique out right away." She was angry at Michael's stance, she said. France had no such restrictions. "Often, it's the case that ransom money is recovered after the exchange, anyway. I admit I am no expert in these matters. I'll see you soon then. I must go, Peter's waiting. He's been so wonderful. And should your father change his mind, Peter is also willing to pay the ransom."

Hope was happy for Jolie. During this horrific time, she had someone to care for her. Hope didn't want to hear any more details, just like she didn't want to watch the news. There was no point in discussing strategies; it was all beyond her pay grade. She trusted her father's judgment. She just wanted Dominique to come home.

"Wait, Jolie."

"What is it, Hope?"

"I wanted to say I understand your feelings about Dominique being in the fray. He's sensitive and a creative writer, and he belongs here with us. You and I both lost a loved one to conflicts. I wish I'd listened to you. I wish I'd asked him not to go. I didn't want to interfere with his passion. I know how you feel about him volunteering to help in the war zones."

"Hope, I thank you for understanding my perspective," Jolie said. "The thought of losing him is beyond terrorizing. I would have nothing."

"It's not going to happen. We *will* see him come through the

Uplift door. We need to believe in that. But you wouldn't have *nothing*, Jolie. You would always have Peter now. And, Jolie, you would always have me."

"We would always have each other, Hope."

40

HOPE NEEDED QUIET. Only a few artists were working at the ICB galleries at 6:00 a.m. She needed to be alone to finish a series of portraits for a Laotian immigrant family. They had several family members from Guatemala and two from the US who'd married into their extended family over the years.

Hope was captivated by the unique faces that were easy to look at or enchanting or striking, like the two silky, dark-haired children with soulful, penetrating eyes looking back at her. The more subtle the variations of curves that shaped their faces, the happier or more pensive their expressions, the more excitement Hope experienced in her painting. The first child's face drew Hope into her work.

She stopped.

Thoughts of Dominique made her set up a new piece of her best paper. She began to transfer his face from her mind to the page—his Mediterranean blue eyes, his kind smile with a dimple on one side.

Her enthusiasm was boosted by her decision to return to Boston with Kate to meet the plane carrying the little eleven-month-old rescued girl. Two team members had made a stopover with the child to have her checked out by a medical team before allowing the orphan to travel to Uplift Headquarters.

With the three older children safely returned to their biological families, Dominique would want Hope to be there for the young orphan, Tara. He'd risked his life for the little girl and promised to bring her to the new adoptive family in Maine. Hope would keep that promise. If the unthinkable happened to Dominique, this baby would be a legacy for his work.

The Millman couple had been through enough. They'd already been officially notified by Uplift's placement coordinators. Of course, Hope's father had informed her that the dramatic rescue had been on the news for the past week.

While Hope reviewed the adoption documents, she imagined the child's life on a lake in Maine with the Millman family. She'd told the adoptive parents she'd have the child checked again by the Uplift doctor when she arrived. Hope planned to call the Millman couple again to make plans as soon as she confirmed the child's estimated arrival date and time in Boston.

The baby would be safe and happy in nature with a charming small town nearby. With a bit of luck, the child had not been traumatized. She was young and wouldn't have been as aware as the older children. Hope clung to that thought.

At nine o'clock, while Hope waited for the office coffee maker to finish brewing, she locked the gallery. She craved one of the famous homemade pastries from the snack bar down the hall. When she returned, a woman was looking through the gallery's front window. She was lean, tall, and well-dressed in a light blue, skirted business suit with a floral blouse. Bits of silver highlighted her dirty blonde hair, which was fastened in the back by a tortoiseshell clip. The woman's demeanor, her blue eyes flickering from Hope to the doorway, was a strange reaction to her arrival at the gallery.

Hope went on high alert. It didn't take much since Dominique had been captured. "May I help you?"

"I called about buying a print of the original Split Tree painting. Was it you I spoke to?"

With a quiet sigh of relief, Hope unlocked the door. "No, I believe you spoke with my aunt Linh the other day on the phone. Come in, please. The coffee I made might be ready now. Would you care for some?"

"No, thank you. I'm fine."

"We had several prints made. What size were you thinking about?"

"Just a small one would be fine, or is it possible to purchase just half of the tree? I'm interested in the, um, Ketchum side."

"Oh. That would be my family. I could arrange that, no problem. Please have a seat." Hope sat next to the woman, waiting for her to share her name, but she didn't. "My name is Hope Lê Ketchum-James. I am one of the artists for the project. May I ask? I'm curious. What's your interest in the Ketchums?"

Still, the woman's behavior was unusual. She crossed and uncrossed her legs, flipped her hair back, adjusted her glasses, and shifted her purse on her lap. "My name is . . . well, I'm specifically interested in one of the portraits. But I would like to have the whole Ketchum family."

"Come with me, and we'll go into the studio. The entire project is on the wall, and you'll be able to see exactly what you'd like."

Hope led the way into the other room, where the enormous project took up the entire wall. She turned on the art spotlights.

The woman stared at the portraits and focused on the one of Ernie. "Miss Lê Ketchum-James, was it? My name is Allison Randall." She took a tissue out of her purse. "And I believe I've found . . . my son."

As she pointed to Ernie's portrait, Hope's legs melted under her as she grasped the edge of her painting desk. "You're Ernie's *mother*?" Hope could see the woman was emotional and had clearly responded similarly to her admission. "Please, sit down. We'll talk."

Allison relayed the story of being seventeen and pregnant by her eighteen-year-old boyfriend. Immediately after Ernie's birth, the doctors had told her that their new baby was severely deformed, had Down's Syndrome, missing vertebrae, and severe life-threatening health issues, and would undoubtedly not survive the night. "I'm ashamed to say, I didn't want to see him. You understand. It would be too painful, and I felt like a child myself at the time. We were petrified. We named him Ernest Randall and signed the papers to give up our parental rights. We both had fake IDs for access to alcohol, so the hospital personnel thought we were of age. As soon as I could leave that hospital, we did. My boyfriend, well, he wasn't really a boyfriend, just a mistake, but he took me out in a wheelchair, and we got in his old junker-of-a-car and left town. We were both traumatized. I'd run away from home the previous year. My family had no idea that I was pregnant. A sordid past for sure."

Allison walked up to the tree and gazed at the picture of Ernie. "What's he like? Truthfully, I read the article in the Chronicle but was left wanting to know so much more. Would you be willing to share since you grew up with him?"

"He's my brother, best friend, and the most compassionate, funny, loving human I've ever met. That's the truth." Picturing Ernie's face, if he'd had the chance to meet his mother, Hope took a chance. "Would you . . . have any plans or interest in meeting him? I could call and ask him if he would like that."

Hope held her breath in the silence. Was it a good thing? For Ernie, it would be, she thought. She knew him well, but it had to be up to him. "I want to be open now to help you make that decision. He always felt his parents left him behind because he was ugly."

"We never saw him, dear. And I can't say I might not have run from the responsibility anyway because of my lack of money, maturity, and education. At seventeen, I didn't have a clue about raising a child. But I would like to meet and tell him it was not about him being ugly. It was about me being young and afraid. He deserved more than a young, confused alcoholic for a mother. And I'd lost track of his father shortly after that."

Hope imagined Ernie having closure on his past. She thought of Allison telling him just what she'd told Hope. She wanted it to happen for Ernie. He wasn't a child who needed a mother but a man who needed closure.

"I'm leaving tomorrow to go home to Boston to see him. This is a difficult time for me. My fiancé is being held hostage near Sarajevo. He works for the Uplift Children's Foundation. You've read the article in the paper." It made it even more painful to say it out loud to a stranger.

"Yes, I read the article. That's how I found you. When I heard you say your name, I thought it insensitive of me to bring up the subject of your fiancé, Hope." Allison glanced up at the portrait of Ernie. "He seems like such a wonderful little soul. Well, I know he's a man now. I teach preschool. I wonder if my career choice was me trying to make up for what I did. The doctor told me my baby wouldn't survive the night. At the time, I thought it was my punishment for being immoral. I'd always assumed he'd died. I'd never considered for a minute he was alive in an institution."

"If I call Ernie and he approves, would you like to travel home with me to Boston? You can stay at my home." Hope offered. "We'll visit Ernie. He lives with my grandparents, less than an hour away from Boston. What you just told me would mean the world to him. And if I can be so bold, it would also be a good thing for you." Hope hadn't stopped to consider that the woman was a stranger. But she was good at reading people. Allison was a good person.

Allison stared off at the Split Tree painting. "I confess, I would have left him even if he'd survived." She made no eye contact with Hope but spoke as if sharing her confession with the world. "Truthfully, even if the baby had been healthy, I'd planned to give it up for adoption."

Hope sat quietly listening. She understood that need from her work with adoption cases.

"The fear of that first experience repeating itself kept me from trying to have another child. An experience like that weighs heavily on your soul. My husband left me because I refused to try. I realize I was a child myself in so many ways."

Hope handed Allison a mug of coffee. "Black, cream, sugar?"

"Sure. Just black, please. Before I leave, I want to make a donation to Uplift. Ten thousand dollars," Allison said.

This story gets stranger by the minute, Hope thought. "That would be wonderful. You can write a check to Uplift Children's Foundation. There's no rush. Let me call Ernie first and see if he agrees. If so, I will ask my mother about you traveling with us. She has a private plane booked. I'm sure she would be thrilled to meet you."

"Your mother?"

"Yes, you must have read, Kate Ketchum is my adoptive mother. If not for her, Ernie would be back in the institution."

"Yes, I read the entire tree article. Amazing, but travel on Kate Ketchum's private plane? Yes. If that works, I'd love to. I love her music. I hoped I could thank her in person, but I never imagined I'd ever have the chance. And by the way, from the quotes in the article, it seems that Ernie has his father's sense of humor, not mine."

"Well, you never know, Allison. Once you meet Ernie, it might come out in you, too. It's contagious." Hope was delighted to draw a smile and a slight release of air from Allison that could almost have qualified as a laugh.

Hope dialed the Ketchum's home. Ernie hadn't returned to work yet, and she assumed he would be home. Everyone had insisted he enjoy some time off.

"Hello?"

"Ernie, it's Hope."

"Woohoo! Hi, Hope. Grandma Cecelia's at the factory."

"Ernie, I called for you. I have an important question for you. And I know you're always honest."

"Yes, I like to be honest. We shalt not lie. It's a commandment, right?"

"Yes. Your mother came to see me today. She saw the newspaper article with your story and wants to meet you. Would you be OK if she came to Glynn to meet you?"

"My *mother*? I thought she left me because I was too ugly?"

"Buddy, no way. Where did you get that idea? Your mother never saw you. She was only a young teen. She ran away from the hospital, afraid to be a mom after she gave birth to you. She wanted you to have a good home. And look, you did!"

"OK. My mother was nice to do that for me, right? But I had to be in Rolling Hills. I did make friends there, and now Mary's here. Oh, and I met Mrs. Ketchup there. So that's cool. I've been a Ketchum for twenty-two years now."

"She read your story in the newspaper, and she's seen you all grown up, and you weren't ugly enough to scare her away."

"Yeah, so that's cool. I want to meet her, yes! It was the portrait you did, Hope. The portrait got me a mother! I have a mom. Oh, sorry, Hope. You lost yours."

"I have a mom. She's Kate."

"Woohoo! I love Kate."

Hope smiled at Allison and nodded.

"OK. So, Ernie, we will be there soon. And Kate's coming home to Glynn, too."

"What's her name? Oh, wait, do I have a father, too?"

It was hard to tell him they didn't know. "Your mother's name is Allison, and I'm sorry, but she doesn't know where your father went."

"That's OK. I have a mom. Woohoo! Allison!"

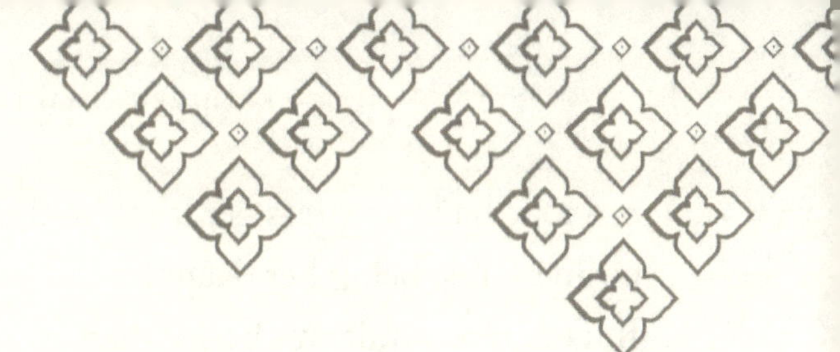

41

THE CROWD THAT blocked the doorway to the private plane terminal entrance at SFO was easy to explain. Hope could find Kate wherever she was by the buzzing crowd that instantly surrounded her stepmother. The word always got out.

"There she is, buried in her adoring fans' arms." In the past, Hope would have had a different feeling about Kate drawing the adulating crowd. She knew this would happen when Kate had to meet her agent ahead of departure time. Now, Hope saw how kind her mother was to her fans and what it meant to them. "Allison, she'll sign whatever they ask for—their tickets, their shirts, their bald heads—it'll be a while. I'll introduce you on the plane, Allison."

"Oh, Hope, that's so funny. Don't you just love Kate? I can't imagine being her daughter. How about the charity concert she did for school supplies for underprivileged kids in Northern California last year? I teach in a public school in Oakland. We were so thrilled to get those supplies."

Hope had to repress her laugh as they stepped out of the limousine. "Yes, being her daughter has been a unique experience." In fact, recently, it was better than ever, Hope thought. She had no complaints. Kate canceling her tour to stay with Hope during this traumatizing time while waiting for news about Dominique had been transformative for their relationship. The intimate thoughts and emotions Kate had shared with Hope had been healing. Hope had felt loved and close to her adoptive mother for the first time.

Allison and Hope sat in the private waiting lounge and watched the chanting autograph frenzy through the window. "Kate could have avoided her fans and gone straight to her private jet, but she doesn't want to disappoint."

"She's just like everyone says." Allison took out a camera and snapped a shot. "I have so many questions for her about Ernie."

"Well, she's the right one to ask about Ernie. Without Kate's audacity, I wouldn't have had the best brother ever."

"Audacity?"

"That's the word her graduate school director used when Kate implored her to include her, a music major, in the special ed master's program. Kate tells the story better. Dr. Goodman said, 'Miss Ketchum, I see all you brought with you was your audacity,' when Kate also asked for a scholarship on the way out of the office. Grandma Cecelia always says, 'You don't ask, you don't get.'"

"Kate's very special." Allison's nervous gesture of spinning her ring around on her finger was an obvious tell.

"What's troubling you right now, Allison? Can I help?" Asking the question of a woman she'd just met made Hope aware of how much Linh and her artist friends had influenced her in such a short time. Hope was more open, confident, and aware of others than she'd ever been.

And now, with Dominique being held hostage for more than a week, Hope was practicing compartmentalizing her life—Dominique in one hidden place, everything else in the foreground. How else could she endure it? Who knew how long it would take to get him released? Especially now that paying a ransom was out of the picture. She'd been more terrified than ever after learning that. Wouldn't violence be more likely now that paying the ransom wasn't an option?

"I was just thinking of how much harder this would be if Frank, my deceased husband, were alive. I'd never told him about leaving that little baby behind. He couldn't have handled visiting Ernie. And I'm so grateful Ernie led a loving life with your family."

A woman in a flight attendant's uniform, flanked by two security guards, approached them. The gathering of fans had finally thinned out, leaving Kate ensconced in a small cluster of admirers as Hope and Allison were ushered out to board the plane.

Once on board, the attendant stored their carry-on luggage, and they settled into the luxurious ivory leather seats around a table set for four with a floral centerpiece. Lavender roses—Kate's favorite, Hope noticed. Two seats facing two seats was the perfect conversational for the long flight.

"Sweetheart, I'm here. Oh, Hope, sorry for the delay. I should have worn a disguise." Kate laughed and huffed into one of the seats across from them. "You must be Allison. This is such a surprise. Ernie will be thrilled to meet you."

"Miss Ketchum, can I get you a drink?" The cabin attendant, who'd ignored Hope and Allison as she prepared for the flight, didn't hesitate to cater to Kate.

"Hope, Allison, what about you? You've been waiting longer than I have." Kate winked at Hope.

There was an example of true class, Hope thought. "Black coffee, please." Why not take advantage?

"Water is fine. Although if I ever needed a drink, it's now." Allison laughed, scanned the cabin, and clipped on her seat belt. "This is so luxurious and surreal. I've just been adding it all up since I arrived." Allison counted on her fingers. "I never imagined I would be a widow at fifty-six, on a private jet from San Francisco to Boston, sitting across from one of the most famous singers in the world, to see my abandoned, thirty-nine-year-old son, whom I assumed had died the night he was born, whom the singer had saved from a dreary institution, and had given a home and a job in a handmade shoe factory." Taking a deep breath, she turned to Hope. "Now that's a movie script. You can tell I've been going over my life story lately."

A man wearing sunglasses and a suit peered through the curtain separating the cockpit from their cabin. With all the attention at the airport and the places Kate went, it was understandable why Kate engaged security guards and a private plane and pilot for her travels, Hope thought.

"We're ready for takeoff in a few minutes, Miss Ketchum. There is only one flight ahead of us."

"Thank you, Edward." Kate focused on Allison. "I recognize Ernie's humor in your storytelling, Allison."

"Seriously, I do feel a bit awkward about meeting Ernie. It's been thirty-nine years since I fled that hospital. I'm surprised that my feelings of shame still linger. To be honest, they do. My perspective has changed dramatically these past few days. For all these years, I'd never known he'd survived."

Even from her profile, Hope could see the sadness in Allison's face as she spoke softly to herself. "I can't imagine what a burden it would be to think your parents abandoned you because you were *ugly*. Does he really think that?" Allison closed her eyes and shook her head.

Kate reached across the table and patted Allison's arm. "Yes, and I can't speak for Ernie, but he usually doesn't have room in his heart for grudges. But this is an emotional and complex situation. Let's hope for the best. You'll love meeting him. He's one of a kind. I suspect there's a lot of you in him. He is blond and has blue eyes like you."

"That's so kind of you, Miss Ketchum."

"Oh, no, I have to be Kate for this situation."

"Thank you. It's my honor, Kate."

Sharing funny and touching stories about Ernie went on through the meal.

"Do you both agree a nap is in order?" Kate reached for her silk sleep mask.

"I do," Hope said. "You'll want to rest up for this reunion, Allison. He'll want to know everything about you."

Kate put on the mask, reclined her lounge seat, and settled back. Within seconds, the cabin attendant had tucked a blanket over Kate, handing one to Allison and Hope.

Whenever there was a quiet time lately, Hope had spun off into thoughts of Dominique. The Barbara Walters 20/20 news show photo had made it so real, with Hope's fiancé shackled on a dirt floor, his head hanging with dark locks of hair over his eyes, and two men armed with oversized weapons squatting next to him. Her emotions vacillated between fear, aching love, and anger that he'd changed his pledge not to participate in overseas missions. He had the right to do what he wanted, but it would surely be the end of them.

Why hadn't he kept his word? In her misery, Hope drifted off to sleep.

"IT'S LIKE a little town out of the past," Allison said as they drove through Glynn. "I love the attention you're getting, Kate. Look, everyone is waving. Even the old man on the hardware store steps is applauding. The little churches, old homes, and general store look like they've been here for centuries." Allison sat quietly, staring out at the streets. "Hope, it's a good distraction for me. I'm so nervous about meeting Ernie. I keep telling myself to breathe."

"That's a good idea." Kate smiled.

Hope spotted Ernie's face in the front window. They parked the car, and she stepped onto the curb.

Would it be pressure, awkwardness, or pure joy for Ernie and Allison? Hope wondered.

Ernie opened the creaking Ketchums' front door, stumbled down the stairs, opened the back door to the limo, and swept his welcoming arm toward the house like a valet. "Welcome to the Ketchums, Mom."

Hope grinned as the "Ernie charm" took over.

THE LATE afternoon was filled with getting-to-know-you conversations. Hope was glad everyone was working at Owl & Shamrock, giving the mother and son a relaxed time together. Watching their uninterrupted interactions was heartwarming. Hope honored Ernie, letting him sit in their grandfather's Barcalounger. Allison sat next to him in Grandma C's rocker.

Ernie immediately clarified that he didn't want to leave the Ketchums. "Just so we both understand."

Hope was taken aback by his boldness.

Allison said she understood and had no intention of disrupting his beautiful, loving life with the Ketchums. She shared her difficult childhood with no siblings, no grandparents now, the loss of her parents, losing her first husband to conflicts, and her second to cancer.

"Grandma Cecelia says your family is anyone who makes you feel loved and safe, Mom."

"Your grandma is wise, Ernie," Allison explained that she was a teacher and had to return to Oakland to finish the school year.

"You're coming back, right, Mom? Now that you know I ain't ugly." He laughed.

"I'd love to return for a few weeks in the summer. Would that work for you? Do you get a vacation from the factory, Ernie? We could go to the beach or whatever you like. Or just stay here, and I'll get a hotel room."

"Woohoo! Yes, I'd like that."

"And Ernie, beauty is on the inside, not the outside of us," Allison said.

Ernie thought for a moment and stood. He spread his arms above him. "That means I'm gorgeous like you, Mom!" Then he dropped like a marionette in hysterics.

Kate chimed in from across the room. "Allison, anytime you want to visit, you are more than welcome to stay in the house next door. We own it, and it's used for guests. And there's no point in you going to Boston tonight. You can stay here and get to know the family. I'll give you the key. They would all love that. What do you say, Ernie?"

"I say, Woohoo! I have a real mom. And can I take you to the factory before dinner to measure you for new shoes? Then, every time you look at them when you're gone teaching, you can think of your gorgeous son."

Allison laughed and crossed the room in tears to hug Ernie. "It's a deal. You're my Shoe Elf."

42

HOPE'S PHONE RANG at five o'clock the following morning. She sat bolt upright and answered. "Dad?"

"Sorry to call so early, sweetheart. I just spoke with Kate."

Hope was disoriented. The sitting room came into focus. I'm in my own room, she thought. "Is there news?"

"I'm in Sarajevo at a hotel. Just so someone is nearby for Shiloh and Dominique. I had a note delivered just now from Shiloh. She's got someone on the inside working for her."

"She always has her creative ways. But what's the update? Please?"

"They made an attempt during the night to free Dominique but . . . it failed."

"Oh, Dad, no. Is he . . . and Shiloh?"

"Honey, he's OK. Shiloh's note also said, *I've infiltrated. I'm safe. Give me a little time.* We'll get him out of here."

"What does that mean, Dad?"

"I have no details. But the way things go in these situations,

Shiloh elicits help from someone she can trust to help her. That's all I know, but it's big in my estimation. And no ransom, but the undercover guy will get some kind of payoff, I'm sure."

"Like what?"

"You know Shiloh. Hope, I feel awkward saying this. But I imagine Shiloh would have used certain *personal skills* when things got desperate in this special case."

"Personal skills? Oh God, Dad. I hope she's safe. If anything happened—"

"Sweetheart, don't go there. It serves no purpose for you or any of us. We have to trust and pray," her father said.

"You're right. Shiloh has pulled off so many rescue missions, even without notice, when she was simply there to distribute food and supplies to refugees. She's smart. I need to have faith."

"Next subject. A little more upbeat. Baby Tara arrives today."

Hope got out of bed and started to dress. She'd learned to shower at night since everything seemed to happen at dawn. "What time? Oh my God, something good for a change, Dad."

"Shane and José are bringing Tara." Her father's mention of the team leaders made Hope smile. Tara was in good hands. He continued, "She's perfectly healthy. Can you meet them at Customs with copies and originals of all the appropriate docs? Two p.m. at Logan. And can you take care of her at our house, honey? I know you're busy, but Dominique wants to deliver her to the adoptive parents. It's important to him."

There was silence on the phone. "I must admit that brings back memories for me."

Hope waited for her father to gather his emotions. "If not for you, Dad, and your rule-breaking soul!"

He laughed. "OK, thanks for saving me that time. We can't

afford to be emotional. Little Tara has so much in common with your story. An American soldier for a father. Her mother and family were all killed in a bombing. Let's not go there, honey. Tara's a lucky girl. Sorry, I've got things to do. Got to go."

"Love you, Dad. Everything's in order. I'll be at the airport early with Kate. So good to have her support. And if you communicate with Shiloh, tell her I love her. Oh, and I'll stop by Glynn first. Grandma has all the baby things I'll need." Hope quickly told her father about Allison and Ernie's meeting.

"So happy for the guy. I'll keep you up to date. Got to go, honey."

"Thanks, Dad. Be sure to give Shiloh my love."

"Of course, and if we have direct contact with Dominique, I'll do the same."

Just the sound of his name made the heat of worry rage in Hope's chest.

TARA'S STORY had been the inspiration for Dominique. He's risked everything to rescue the child from the start. Dressed and ready to go with the required documents in her briefcase, Kate did some research in their home library. Michael had gathered numerous books on the areas where Uplift worked, and Hope had moved them into her bookcase in her sitting area. Tara was just outside of Belgrade when he'd first found her, Dominique had told Hope.

Flipping her finger along the titles, Hope pulled out a book on Serbia. Quickly researching the culture, she discovered they were among the tallest people in the world. That made her smile. "We're a pair, Tara."

The child belonged to the Dinaric people, a mix of a Northern and Mediterranean race. She already knew the Serbians, most commonly, had dark brown to dark blond hair. Their eyes were typically a wide range of colors, from brown to dark blue to light blue-green. Serbians were known for their long legs and arms and often a prominent nose. Hope read that the child's name had its roots in the Tara Mountains in the Dinaric Alps in Western Serbia. There were rivers named *Tara* in Montenegro, Bosnia, and Herzegovina—places so familiar to Hope from her Uplift work over the past years.

Hope imagined doing her sketch of Tara for her adoptive parents. Thank goodness Kate would be with her when they picked up Tara. Hope knew nothing about caring for a baby. She'd always been the baby.

What trauma had little Tara endured? Hope couldn't avoid this child. She had to do it for Dominique, the childless Millman couple, Shiloh, and everyone who'd risked their lives to save this little girl.

KATE AND Hope met Shane as she disembarked the Uplift plane, followed by José. Taking Tara into her arms sent a duet of emotions through Hope—a deep ache for her lover and relief that caused a lightness, a joy to think of the child's new life—an outcome so like her own rescue—a bit of hope.

"Good to see you both. Tara was a good girl on the flight. So sweet," Shane said. "I'm so happy she has a good home to go to. Thanks for meeting us."

José handed Kate a diaper bag. "We're going to grab a cab for a meeting at the office."

The name Tara meant solid, firm, and steadfast. Hope wished the light-skinned, green-eyed girl with her wild, head-full of brown hair would live up to the meaning of her name. She was happy the Millmans were keeping Tara's name. Her identity. So many adoptive parents changed the child's first name if it was foreign sounding, as though the baby were a puppy from the pound, Hope thought. But maybe that helped the child to feel a belonging when they grew up. Would Hope's experiences have been different had she remained Hy Vọng?

Hope submitted Tara's documents to the agent at the Customs desk while Kate held the baby.

The agent kept flashing looks at Tara and Kate. If he argued, Hope was ready to defend her work. She had every detail covered in the legal documents, including her temporary custody.

"So, her legal name is Tara Rachael Millman, correct?" The agent was acting strange.

"That's correct."

He wouldn't look at Hope. What was his problem? He could read Tara's legal name right in front of him. Was she missing a document? Was this another racist situation? Was it Hope being an "Asian" woman lawyer? What would Hope do with Tara if he rejected her entry? She would need a passport or visitor's permit to return to Serbia. Then what? Where would they go? Hope had to make it work. "Here, I'll take her, Mom." Putting her briefcase down, Hope took Tara from Kate.

Hope held onto the baby tighter. The agent's words brought

her back to the story her father had told her about trying to get Hope into the country through customs illegally over two decades ago with a forged birth certificate. Everything had been illegal, including how he'd rescued her from a war zone in Vietnam using US military property. The stress of Dominique's situation, then meeting Ernie's mother, and now this. It was all too much lately. She leaned against the booth.

Whispering, Kate calmed Hope. "Don't let him spook you. We have everything in place. Sometimes it's just a power play."

"Excuse me, could you step out of line for a moment." He put a CLOSED sign on his window.

Holding Tara on her shoulder, Hope nervously patted her back as they followed the agent to the corner of the room. "What's the problem, sir?"

It was one of those moments when everything overwhelmed Hope. With Kate's arm through Hope's, she took a deep breath and tried to find her confidence.

The agent's behavior was enigmatic. He kept glancing over his shoulder at the security office door. Taking Hope's documents, the customs agent stared at her, then down at the passport, studying Hope with a confused look. "Really? Your *mother*?"

"Yes, she *is* my mother."

The baby became fussy, squirming, and whining. "It's OK, honey." Hope jiggled Tara to the rhythm of one of her mother's hit songs and hummed the tune.

"I thought so!" The agent startled the baby, and she started to cry.

"Hope, I believe this gentleman needs to talk to me." Kate rescued Hope's briefcase, kissed the baby, and gave Hope a look that said, *don't worry, I've got this, but come with me.*

The customs agent pulled back the curtain to a private booth and signaled for Kate to go in.

Was he going to frisk her? Why? Hope listened through the crack between the curtains.

"I'm sorry. I didn't mean to scare the baby. You're Kate Ketchum, aren't you?"

"Yes."

"I hate to interfere with your personal life, but . . . my wife never stops talking about you since we went to your Madison Square Garden concert. I know I'm crossing the line here and might get in trouble. But would you be willing to sign this customs declaration brochure for Christine Judith Cohen? She's such a fan, and it might go a long way for me." He looked over his shoulder and scanned the windows to the security office. "I almost didn't recognize you without your leather mini skirt and boots. Oh, and with your signature red hair pulled back in a bandanna." He laughed awkwardly.

"I try to be inconspicuous when I travel. Let's hurry, though. I don't want you to catch any flack. And I've got to get little Tara some food."

Kate knew how to take advantage of her fame when she needed to, Hope thought.

Kate emerged from behind the curtain, customs agent in tow.

Hope followed with Tara. "What's going on, Mom?"

"Just follow me."

The documents were stamped and approved as Kate personalized the note and drew her flaring signature on the paper. "Say hi to Christine," Kate said.

He cleared his throat and stood straight as another agent passed by. "Welcome to Boston. Enjoy your evening, ma'am."

HOLDING TARA'S tiny fingers and watching the familiar scenes coming into Glynn was comforting. The agent had been acting strange. It wasn't Hope's imagination. It was fan insanity. Hope had seen it before.

"There are times my success is a benefit, and times it's a liability." Kate pulled Hope close in the back of the limousine and kissed her forehead.

"Mom, I don't know what I would have done if I'd been alone with Tara in customs and something went wrong with the paperwork. Imagine Dad with everything on the line, bringing me into this country. He lost his job."

"But he didn't lose you, honey."

When they arrived in Glynn, the welcoming committee made Tara squeal with giggles. Everyone in the Ketchum clan knew how to handle babies and kids. Even the kids themselves had the knack of the Ketchum's kindness and playfulness.

"I'm so glad you brought her here before you went home, Hope. She's adorable. Look at Tara in the car seat with all the kids around her," Grandpa Kevin said.

"Grandma Cecelia, it warms my heart to know Dominique was behind her having the chance for a good life. But admittedly, I'm exhausted, and we still don't know what's happening with Dominique or Auntie Shi." Hope sat on the green sofa next to Grandpa K's Barcalounger.

"Hope, when will you bring Tara to her new parents?" Grandma Cecelia made cooing noises for Tara.

"I'll give her a few days to acclimate, Grandma, then set it up for next weekend. But I'll call them as soon as we get home later tonight."

Watching Ernie clowning around entertaining Tara, just as he had with Hope, made her sentimental. "I'm going to ship her some *pitty wed soos* when she turns one, Hope. And I'm working on my mom's new shoes with Grandpa K, too." Ernie reached up and put his arm around Allison's waist.

"Hope, take this with you. Tara's the perfect age. You might need it over the next few days. Especially if you're painting." Grandma Cecelia handed Hope a contraption she didn't recognize. "What is it?"

"A Jolly Jumper. Remember your nieces and nephews bouncing around in it? Well, maybe not. You were away at college and law school most of the time. I pulled it out when they were visiting. And Grandpa K dropped off a crib and highchair earlier today when Michael called. We still have your house key Michael gave us."

"Wonderful, thanks. I was going to ask for those. I'll take all the help I can get."

"Listen, everyone. My mom and I need to get going. It's been a fabulous but exhausting day. I'll bring Tara back tomorrow. OK? I have some legal work to do at home in Boston for her. Thanks for everything."

"Hope, I put the car seat in the limo for you."

"Oh, good, thank you, Grandpa."

"MOM, I could get used to this limo, especially with the baby. I can stay close to her."

"You should have it when you take Tara to Maine. It's a long trip and challenging with a little one, Hope."

"Really, I'll take you up on that. I can't wait to hear the Millmans' voices. But I think I'll call tomorrow. It's getting late. I had a surprisingly good time tonight. I've never taken care of a baby before. I wonder how I'd do without two dozen relatives pitching in." Hope tickled Tara under the chin. She couldn't hear the baby laugh often enough.

HAD ALL the travel made Tara cranky? She hadn't slept all night. Hope had set the crib next to her king-size bed and covered Tara with her blue satin coverlet. As soon as Hope had drifted off to sleep, Tara's screaming began. Repeating the comforting words, "It's all right, sweetheart. It's alright." Hope finally calmed her down. But as soon as Hope put her in the crib, Tara would begin sobbing, accented by occasional shrieking screams.

Hope was so tired and helpless with no baby experience. Holding Tara tight, she too began to cry from frustration and sadness for what Tara must have been through. Finally, little Tara fell asleep next to Hope just as dawn glowed around the edges of the velvet drapes that Kate had installed years ago when she'd renovated the rooms with fancy antiques.

Hope was grateful for the heavy solid wood doors so Kate couldn't hear Tara's crying from the master suite downstairs at the far end of the house.

Hope wanted to handle Tara herself.

Kate had said she would come to help later in the morning after she returned from some early errands. Hope felt silly that she knew nothing about taking care of a baby despite having been raised in a big family. "Good morning, angel." Tara's smile was the perfect start to the day and such a relief. Then, battling with her kicking legs and squirming, Hope managed to change Tara's diaper and clothes amid the little girl's outbursts of crying. She strapped the child into the highchair and fed her a scrambled egg, applesauce, and some of the fruit Grandma Cecelia had sent. Well, at least some of it managed to reach Tara's mouth. The rest was splattered on Hope's clothes. That part didn't go well, either.

Hope pinched open the blueberries so Tara wouldn't choke on the little balls. For a few minutes, Tara became engaged in chasing them around the tray with her finger before stuffing them in her cheeks.

Hope was anxious to call the Millmans. What if they heard the screams? What if Tara cried hysterically when she saw her new parents?

With Tara and Hope finally dressed, Hope wanted to do some artwork before calling the Millmans to give Tara time to settle down.

While Hope worked on fine watercolor paper, Tara quieted for a moment and scribbled on printer paper with a colored pencil. They worked on a blanket that Hope had spread out on the floor. She couldn't wait to sketch Tara's strong features and wild, curly hair that framed her happy face. Her big sparkling green eyes and regal nose brought Shiloh to mind. Tara's heart-shaped lips and sweet smile made Hope want to take the child in her arms. But whenever she did, the screaming resumed. There had to be a solution. An idea came. Looking through the baby things that Grandma Cecelia had supplied, she spotted the Jolly Jumper. Would she even let Hope put her in it? The last thing she wanted to do was to traumatize Tara any more than she had been.

She put Tara in her highchair and grappled with the Jolly Jumper that lay twisted on the floor by the settee. Hooking the clamp securely to the bathroom's upper door frame, Hope read the instructions outlining how the apparatus would help a child's body to become strong, build leg muscles and coordination, and keep them safe in your sight while a mother was busy. All Hope prayed for was a little quiet to make the phone call. She didn't want the couple to be held in abeyance any longer.

Struggling with squirming Tara, Hope slipped her into the navy-blue canvas diaper-like seat. Hope wrapped the child's tiny fingers around the two cords that blended into one thick cable clamped on the door frame overhead. Tara's eyes widened and sparkled, and her mouth pulsed from *oooo* to *ahhh*. She panted with delight, then squealed before breaking into an unbridled dance. Suspended in the doorway by a rubber stretchy cord—Tara's excitement became Hope's.

As Hope showered, she watched Tara explore her new joy toy. Like an Irish step dancer, she thudded her feet on the hardwood floor and soon learned to spring into the air. She giggled, jumped, twisted, and turned with vocalizations expressing her ecstatic delight.

Springing from the floor, Tara launched into the air and freed her hands, pumping them like an orchestra conductor. The fun factor was a ten. Watching her revel in pure bliss was more exciting than had Hope been in the sling herself. It was contagious. The vicarious excitement lifted both Tara's and Hope's spirits.

At nine o'clock, Hope slumped into her chair and dialed her phone. Tara began to scream again. Even the pink bunny had no effect on the child's mood. Hope quickly hung up and sighed.

It was a struggle, but between Tara's crying fits, Hope finally had the chance to update Mrs. Millman and suggested a few days of respite for the baby before traveling again.

There was silence on the phone, and Mr. Millman came on the line. "Miss Lê or is it Ketchum? We have been discussing the situation. Maybe you can understand as a lawyer who deals with adoptions . . . we are very concerned." He paused. "Well, my sister is a child psychiatrist, and she has reviewed the issues we might be dealing with by adopting a child traumatized by war. The news has been horrifying. Maybe if we hadn't seen all those news clips. If we are going to adopt, we . . . well, we are withdrawing our application. But are ready to find a child. Perhaps a baby from the US is better for us."

"I see. But the documents are already in place, and the child's name is now Tara Rachael Millman."

"I'm so sorry. We'll pay for any inconvenience, of course."

Mrs. Millman's sobbing could be heard in the background.

Hope was numb. It was shocking news after all the trauma the child and the Uplift team had endured, including Dominique. She'd never considered they would cancel the adoption. "Mr. Millman, I don't know what to say. This was not a typical adoption situation, and—" Hope stopped.

Mentioning Dominique and the circumstances would turn things personal. It was unprofessional to contextualize the situation for them when they'd already made a tough decision. "When I have the paperwork or any other requirements in place, I will be in touch, sir."

"Thank you. We're so sorry for all that everyone suffered to rescue the child. Although, I guess that was going to happen in any case. Our hearts are broken over this, but I'm sure you understand. Goodbye, Miss Ketchum-James, and good luck. We hope she has a happy life going forward."

Pay for any inconvenience? No currency could compensate. Numbed by the news, Hope lifted Tara from the floor and rocked her in her arms. Which child was she comforting, Tara or herself?

The weight of the news immobilized Hope. She had to investigate how to legally handle this unexpected twist.

Hope researched re-adoption and looked through her files to find other potential adoptive parents. Who would want this damaged child? She'd obviously been traumatized. That wasn't the right thought. Hadn't Hope been a lovable child herself? According to her Ketchum family, she was. And today, Tara seemed different. Hope recognized that irresistible spirit. Although Tara was nothing like him, looked nothing like him, and was not even a year old, she had that indescribable, uplifting personality everyone loved about Ernie as she danced up and down in the Jolly Jumper.

There was no way to describe what that short interaction with pure, unadulterated happiness had done for Hope's spirits. Inspired to find the family who deserved this darling child, Hope finished getting dressed and made a pot of coffee in her bedroom kitchenette.

She placed a blanket on the floor next to her desk, surrounded Tara with the toys the Ketchum family had given her, and pulled out her file on potential parents again. Hope had a lot to learn, but she'd seen her aunts and cousins care for their babies. She would manage, Hope told herself, if she kept Tara fed and clean until she had a safe and happy placement for the sweet girl. It shouldn't be long.

After what had happened with the Millman couple, Hope went through the file quickly, eliminating one couple after the other on the social workers' list. But she did find one Connecticut couple who looked like a good match. They were the right age, and she liked what they had to say in their application. The mother was an author of children's books, so she worked from home. That was a good thing. The father was Native American and worked for a company Hope didn't recognize. She would have to investigate that. Hope wanted to find a stable situation where one of the parents wasn't always traveling for their job. Hope knew that was her own prejudice.

The rest of the applications had one thing or another that didn't work for Hope. But she had to admit her standards were high right now after what the child had been through—and maybe what Hope had been through as a child. She would have to coordinate with the social worker in her organization to conduct the investigations. But Hope took this personally now that the child was in her care.

Kate arrived, tapping at the door. "Hope, you look like a natural work-from-home mom, with Tara—all happy and playing, with you deep into your research."

"Mom, this child would make any parent look good right now. But we had a rough night. And I have some bad news. Well, in hindsight, maybe it's good news. The Millman couple has backed out and put Tara up for re-adoption." Hope read Kate's reaction. "I know I felt the same way when they told me, and after all this. But if she's not the right child for them, I'm glad they were honest with themselves. She'll be the right child for someone else. Watch this, Mom."

Hope lifted Tara into the Jolly Jumper and shared the experience with Kate. "Have you ever seen a happier child? I'm so grateful she wasn't emotionally damaged. At least doesn't appear to have been."

"Hope that is the cutest thing. Have you found an alternative family that will commit yet?"

"No, but I have one in mind."

"Won't you have a challenge getting the name changed and the adoption figured out? Well, I guess that's what you do for a living. I admire that."

Hope appreciated Kate's support. "There are no complications. Re-adoption is handled the same way as any adoption."

"The car is outside waiting," Kate said. "We're due for lunch. Let's take off for Glynn."

"And Mom, whatever you do, don't let me forget the Jolly Jumper."

43

WITH TARA BOUNCING in the doorway to Ernie's bedroom just off the living room, the family enjoyed the same uplift that Hope had experienced. There was only a brief lunch break for the family members to enjoy a visit with Tara. The uncles and aunts all took turns encouraging Hope as they stopped by the house to see Tara on their breaks from the factory. The child had more than fifteen forehead kisses by the time the visit ended. Hope didn't share the news about the Millman couple's announcement. She wanted everyone to just enjoy the moment.

"Well, we know what lights *her* up." Grandma Cecilia laughed and kissed Tara's forehead as she finished her lunch and left for the factory.

"If it were only that easy for the rest of us to know what lights us up," Hope's Aunt Kelly said. "Hope, I'm so sorry about Dominique. I'm sure Michael will figure out a way. Good luck."

Everyone meant well when they brought up Dominique and the situation. Still, Hope was trying to escape it, to put it off somewhere in the far reaches of her mind so she could survive the day, secure committed parents for Tara, get back to her sketching and artwork, and pray for Dominique's return.

As she updated Linh on the phone, Hope saw Ernie and his mother through the kitchen door. Allison was clapping and cheering while Ernie did his classic jig, thudding his club feet in his handmade orthopedic shoes on the floor—a version of Tara's Jolly Jumper dance routine. The child responded, squealing and stomping her feet. Last night must have been her re-entry adaptation. Maybe she would be OK. Maybe she would fit in anywhere, Hope thought.

Once the team investigated the prospective couple, she would contact them to arrange Tara's adoption. When Hope researched re-adoption and fortunately found it was no different from any legal adoption, she was relieved. There were no legal glitches to delay her placement. Hope would draw up the new paperwork as soon as she had things in order and hopefully have Tara in a stable home soon. Her caregiver responsibility weighed heavily on Hope.

Of course, in Hope's phone calls to Linh, her aunt told her not to worry. She would fill in when Hope couldn't finish the portraits or the Split Tree orders. Linh still couldn't believe the news that Ernie's mother was the one who'd called to order the reprint and that they'd been reunited. "Hope, I will talk to my family, and we'll have another special Mass tomorrow to pray for Dominique and Shiloh. Father Lawrence said he would arrange it. Again, Hope, don't worry about the Split Tree orders. We'll get them done. We love you."

"Thank you, Linh. I love you too."

Hope's world had been spinning since she'd found the Lê

family. It was a blessing to have their support. She'd received a card of encouragement in the mail from a different Lê family member every day since she'd returned to Boston. The weight of worry about Dominique and Shiloh was heavy. How did mothers do it? How did they handle the stress, the emotions, the riveted attention it took to care for a little child?

"Hope, shall we go home? Everyone is back at work for the day. I think you need some rest." Kate pushed the curtains aside and waved to her chauffeur through the front window.

"Yes, and Tara needs a nap after her performances." Humor was the only thing left, Hope thought.

On the way home to Boston in the limo, Kate's phone rang.

Hope overheard her father ask Kate if Hope was there with her.

"Michael, honey, why don't you just speak directly to her." She handed the phone to Hope.

"Dad . . . just tell me quickly, please."

"We received news that Shiloh is now also being held."

"But just yesterday, Shiloh had sent a message that she had a plan and that things were going well. She was optimistic. She said, and I'm quoting here—'do what you have to do. I've got this.'"

"I'm not sure what *being held* means. That's all I know. We have a group of locals whom we've helped significantly over the past several years, and based on what they've seen, they want to do a hit on the camp where Dominique is being held and—"

"What, Dad?"

"I approved it. I just wanted you to know. I think from Shiloh's message, it's the right thing. Originally, the kidnappers gave us until tomorrow to pay the ransom. And they know we're not going to pay it. Somehow, it leaked all over the news today. We need to do something now. And this pro-US group has been watching the kidnappers since the whole thing started. They were the ones who managed to get the children away. The longer we leave Dominique there, they said . . . well, I think it's time, let's just say that."

Hope relayed the news to Kate.

"So, we'll all pray and trust that Shiloh will have the smarts to figure this out, as she always has in the past," Kate said. She put her arm around Hope's shoulder.

Hope was conflicted. But what else could they do? And if she was going to trust anyone, it would be Shiloh. But she was just one woman in an insane, violent situation. "Thanks, Dad. We'll get the entire Ketchum clan and the Lê family to pray. Please keep us updated if you should hear anything, anything at all."

THERE WOULD be no answer regarding the adoptive parents until after the weekend. Hope kept herself busy with Tara while working on the Split Tree paintings in the new at-home art studio she'd set up in the bedroom next to hers. The baby fell asleep on the blanket beside Hope's painting table. It was quiet in the house, finally. There was space for Dominique and Shiloh's situation to invade Hope's mind.

Kate arrived. "You two doing OK in here? Your art studio came out great, Hope. I'm glad you could use the table from the back porch. No one's ever out there. The bookcase and the containers are all so neat."

"Thanks for getting the movers, Mom. You must be so worried.

Shiloh's your best friend. Yet you are always supporting me. What about you?"

"Hope, just like you are losing yourself in caring for Tara, I'm losing myself in making up for lost time with you."

Hope put her paintbrush down and rushed into Kate's arms.

"I have a feeling things will work out, Hope. Trust. There is no other option."

"I know. It's so crazy, Mom. I'm engaged to a man I love, yet I'm prepared to break things off when he escapes. It feels so wrong, but I can't live in his world. And I can't find a way like you suggested. It's in his hands—*if* he escapes. And who knows how this trauma has affected him."

44

THE BABY CRIED out at the sound of the phone ringing.

"Dad?"

"Hope, the camp has been destroyed—"

"No, *Dad*!" Between Tara's crying and the crackling overseas phone line, Hope could barely hear Michael.

"Wait, honey, we don't know if they were there when it happened. There's a good chance Shiloh and Dominique got out, and *then* our supporters took the kidnappers captive. That was the plan."

"Did you say they got out? Oh, thank God."

"No, we aren't sure yet. This happened minutes ago. Stay by your phone. I'll be in touch as soon as I hear. Sorry honey. I promised to keep you in the loop."

"I'm here. Call me on my mobile as soon as you hear anything." Hope snapped the phone off.

"Kate, it could be days. How can we just sit here?"

"Honey, would you let me hold you? It's something I wanted to do from the start?" Kate sat next to Hope on the settee and put her arms around her. They embraced in silence. It was calming for Hope, but she had to do something.

Tara called out.

"It's OK, sweetheart." Hope fed Tara a bottle and was rocking her when she realized she needed to go to church and pray to make it through the day. "Kate, would you watch her for a while? She cried all night, and honestly, I'm a nervous wreck. I need to get out. I thought I would walk a few blocks to church to light some candles for Dominique."

"Of course, honey. Go. I will handle things here."

"There's food in the fridge. Tara loves blueberries, but I always pop them so she doesn't choke."

"No worries. I've got things under control."

THE CHURCH was empty except for one older, bundled-up woman who knelt at the left side of the altar in front of the statue of the Virgin Mary.

Hope genuflected in front of the massive crucifix that hung over the altar. The stained-glass windows, telling the story of the life of Christ, filled the dome that arched above the altar, casting shimmering crystals of color on her. She knelt before the wrought-iron stand that held six rows of red glass candle holders.

Pulling some change from her purse, Hope slid the coins into the slot in the bronze offering box. The clink of the quarters against the metal box echoed throughout the church. She lit a candle for

Dominique and one for Shiloh, two of the most beloved people in her life. What would she do without her one true love? And Shiloh was her mentor, her friend, her substitute mother, Kate's best friend, and Michael's right-hand person. Their loss would devastate her and so many of the people in Hope's life.

Hope stared at the flickering flame in a daze. "Please, God, keep them safe," she whispered.

She dragged her slumped body home, not bothering to button her coat against the bitter winter wind.

At home, Kate sat with Tara, rocking her back and forth. "She gets upset easily."

Hope placed her in the Jolly Jumper, and Tara giggled and bounced immediately.

For three days, they worked together to keep Tara happy and distract themselves from the terror of what was happening. They traded off doing brief errands to pass the time—grocery shopping, filling the car with gas, and calling family with no news to share. Hope sketched a portrait of Kate with the baby. It only served to make things worse for Hope. There had been no response from the new adoptive couple either. Perhaps they were out of town?

Together, Kate and Hope watched the evening news, praying to hear Barbara Walters announce the good news. Instead, they endured war and more war, and pictures of the devastation.

As Kate changed Tara's diaper on the afternoon of their third endless day of waiting, she encouraged them both. "Let's keep the faith, Hope."

The phone rang.

"They're out."

"Oh, thank God, Dad. Are they OK?" Hope kissed the baby over and over and wept.

"The Uplift plane has Shiloh and Dominique. I'm on my way to the airport to get on the flight with them. We want to get out of here before the news hits."

"When will you be here?"

Kate ran into the room. "Is that Michael?"

Hope nodded. "They're safe. On the plane."

"It will take us around fifteen hours with the time change. They'll bring them directly to our house. Have Kate send the limo to the airport. You stay there with Tara. I estimate we'll arrive around eight o'clock tomorrow morning."

"Are they OK, Dad?"

"As far as I know. I have to go, honey. See you tomorrow."

"Travel safely. I love you. Tell Shiloh and Dominique I send my love."

Kate signaled for the phone and spoke to Michael. "Be safe, darling. My arms are waiting."

"I can't believe it, Mom."

"We have to believe." Kate shuffled through her bag and retrieved a journal. She handed it to Hope.

"What is this? I already have your journal."

"Not this one. I confess I helped your dad. A little encouragement, and he was ready. I was ready. He entrusted it to me in case there came a time that you really needed it. Now is that time."

Hope recognized the handwriting immediately.

"I'll take care of Tara while you read about what you always deserved to know." Kate walked to Tara and knelt. "Are you having fun, sweetheart?"

Tara's giggles faded into the background as Hope read the opening lines of the journal.

Sunlit mornings always bring my thoughts back to when I

first saw Hằng. Her slender shape as she leaned against the old Tamarind tree—its branches dripping with long, copper-colored seed pods. Its wide arc shaded her from the blazing sun like the umbrellas the women held overhead as they padded by me, barefoot, on the path to the market.

I could picture the small herd of baby goats huddled under the tree's cool protection near the beautiful young woman. The traditional village woman had a book spread open in her hands. As I approached, I saw the title, The Great Gatsby. No way. In English? Fascinating. I was sure she didn't fail to feel the heat of my riveted stare as I passed her.

She glanced over her shoulder. "Hello, soldier. Do you like to read?" And then the smile like a wild jungle vine snaked around me and squeezed my heart. It was a new feeling, unlike any other response I'd had to a girl before. "Oh, uh, yes. But how is it that you . . . "

"You are surprised a village girl reads English novels?" She leaned her head back against the tree and laughed. "Oh, it's the clothes that fooled you. Am I correct?"

"Well, yes . . . and speaking English."

She shared her name, Hằng. She pronounced it for me, "Hahng." She was no village woman. Not wanting to forget her roots, she liked to wear traditional garb for her family while visiting at home. She'd only been visiting her parents on break from her position as a professor at the university in the city.

The moments I stole with her over the summer months I'd spent assigned to her village area had made me never want to leave. Her classroom English was no barrier. We felt the same way about so many things. I remember talking while watching a young child in the distance riding on the neck of a water buffalo beside the rice fields. Strange a small boy could tame such a beast, we'd said in harmony.

I remember not talking, too—our instant, irresistible, electric attraction bridged our cultural divide.

I see us squatting, sipping tea with her parents and three siblings in their small cottage—translating, laughing, as Hằng dropped her head against my shoulder. After two years, my Vietnamese was good enough to communicate and bad enough to cause a lot of laughter. It was those damn six tones I screwed up regularly.

"Wrong tone, darling." I can see Hằng's smile. "GI, you said butter instead of walk."

Before I returned to my unit each night, those special times were the most family I'd ever felt.

How had I found such peace in the chaos of war? How hard it had been to leave her when my company pulled out after such a long time together. She'd wanted to follow me. It made no sense. We both finally agreed she would wait and continue her teaching. With my discharge date only ten months away, I would return to get her, and we'd be married with her family in attendance and then return to the States. I slipped a crude ring on her finger I'd twisted from lime-green grass.

I try to stop the memories—Hằng dropping into the mucky hole where I'd hidden. She was not a village woman; she was my woman, disguised, dressed in her country woman's attire. Hằng, my love, was bursting from her clothes with our child about to come. I don't know where she got the information about my location. It had been nine months. Why did she risk it? I can still hear her words: "It's crazy, I know, but I had to be with you." We embraced and kissed and couldn't let go. My arms wrapped around her trembling body.

I told her I dreamed of our life in Vietnam. She'd dreamed of our life in the US. There could be no dreams of living near my family. It was something she couldn't understand. "But they are your family, Michael," she said.

My mother would have loved Hằng. She would have accepted Hằng as her own—the daughter she'd never had, but my father wouldn't have such open arms. And I wouldn't have subjected her to that. As different as Hằng and my mother looked, they were a lot alike—strong, with a loving nature, and that laugh. They would share that laugh.

My arms still held the memories of holding Hằng, whispering soothing words, making promises I couldn't keep as her breaths of childbirth came faster. "We have to have hope," I said. "Breathe, darling, breathe!"

Echoes of Hằng's screams in the foxhole when the fire came down on us still split my skull. I can still imagine her running through the flashes of the unexpected conflict. I cursed the cruel moonlight that had escaped the shadow of a cloud and spotlighted her against the dense green. Every detail is still alive: Hằng's muffled screams when I guided our newborn daughter from between her legs; Hằng running from the crossfire in slow motion, one arm bolting upward, shrapnel pummeling her arching back, the other arm desperately gripping our child; my true love lifting her near lifeless arms from around our baby girl. I wondered if I would re-live my loss in living color forever—the red on Hằng's blue and white áo dài.

I failed to protect her. I failed our little girl, too. Failed the Marine's pledge—honor, courage, commitment, always faithful... Semper Fidelis.

Would it be a betrayal to let memories of Hằng fade? Would it insult my love to stop suffering over her? I fought to remain loyal to my wartime love when I met Kate. How could I love someone else so soon? At the Ketchums' Thanksgiving dinner, I felt Hằng standing behind me as though giving me permission to love again. I promised I would honor Hằng's gift. I would never let those haunting memories invade my life with Kate. I would never share that violent ending with little Hy Vong.

"That's not the man I know." Kate was the one who said those words when she learned I'd left Hope behind to be with her family. Those were the words that brought my beautiful daughter into our lives.

IT WAS a long, restless night as they waited, caring for Tara, keeping the Ketchums and Lês informed, and trying to get some sleep despite the revelations in her father's journal. The images haunted Hope. Knowing the truth was a relief and painful. Now she knew her mother had died on Hope's birthday, April 9th. The number nine had appeared again. Good fortune indeed. Soon, Hope would be in Dominique's arms again. And soon, she would have to face the most profound decision of her life.

Had Tara sensed Hope's tension? She'd awakened crying three times.

At 7:00 a.m., Hope changed Tara's diaper, dressed her, and put her in the Jolly Jumper so Hope and Kate could dress before the team's arrival.

No matter what was happening, despite the drama of the situation, watching Tara bouncing and hearing her giggles and happy vocalizations broke through Hope's fears and lifted Hope's and Kate's moods.

At 8:01, there was a welcome tap, tap-tap, tap at Hope's door.

Shiloh and Michael walked into the bedroom with Dominique behind them. Shiloh hugged Hope, and Michael embraced Kate. "Oh honey, that was hell, I'm sorry."

"Were you looking for us?" Shiloh held Hope's face in her hands, kissed her forehead, and quickly stepped aside to let her reunite with Dominique.

The bandages on Dominique's wrists and forearms surprised her. He held his arms out so she could hug him. "What happened?" She kissed him and buried her head in his chest. "I never thought I'd . . . Shiloh . . . how did you do it? Dad, I can't believe you're all home and safe."

"You know me. I used my personal skills." She laughed.

"God, that is so you. You're laughing? What personal skills?"

Michael and Kate shook their heads, shared a knowing glance, and smiled.

"Think about what Auntie Shiloh might do to convince a guard to conspire with her," Kate said.

"Oh, my God. You didn't?"

"She did. And I'm alive because of her sinful creativity." Dominique sat on the settee. "Do you all mind if Hope and I have some private time together? We can tell our tales around the breakfast table later."

"Of course." Michael herded Kate and Shiloh toward the bedroom door. "Hope, we've had eleven hours on a plane with awesome tailwinds to decompress. You deserve some time alone. Come down when you're ready."

Hope glanced around the corner where Tara was bouncing

slowly, suspended in the bathroom doorway. As though she knew it was time to be quiet, Tara's eyes fluttered, then closed, and she hung in the doorway in her sleepy silence. Perfect timing.

Hope wanted to reunite with Dominique before discussing Tara's new adoptive parents. She sat next to him.

"Are you alright? I can't believe you're sitting here."

"Yes, where it all started. Hope, I'm a little bruised from the shackles and, to be truthful, more than a little traumatized worrying about how you were dealing with all this."

"You were worrying about *me*?"

"And what I put you through."

Hope didn't argue. "I have so much to tell you. But first, *you*, Dominique." Hope stroked his face. "You've lost weight, but you look good."

"There was no torture. Hope, before we discuss the kidnapping, did you see the article in the Chronicle?"

"Yes. And it brought Ernie and his birth mother together. So much has happened." Sitting next to Dominique, Hope shared the amazing story. Feeling his warmth wasn't something she thought would ever happen again. Now what?

"So, his mother found him through my article. That's so wonderful. Oh, Ernie. Is he thrilled? I'll go to see the Ketchums tomorrow and talk to him. I'd love to meet her and interview her about their reunion." Dominique's look turned serious. "Darling, how do you feel about us *now*?"

His direct question stunned Hope. How could she answer? She hadn't expected to have to tell him her decision so soon. How could she decide without talking to him first? She'd been alone in her own mind without him, and Hope hadn't found a way to be together or to marry and have the family they'd discussed.

"I find it hard to say right now."

"Please, I want to hear it."

Despite the tenderness of the moment, it called for the truth. "Doesn't this horrific experience only confirm my fears?" Hope lightly ran her fingers over his bandages. "Look what happened to you. I find it impossible to think of my life without you, Dominique. But I had to face reality while you were being held by those terrorists. I couldn't go through this again or have you out there, even if you were safe."

"Even after the article, Hope? I confess I'm shocked."

"I can't change my feelings just because you wrote a great article. Dominique, you nearly died. That would be so wrong. I don't know how to have you in my life without having constant violence coloring my days, our days."

"But what about the article and Ernie." Dominique turned Hope's face toward his. "Don't you see how it can work?"

"No, I don't. The article was wonderful, but . . . nothing has changed. I can only see us together if you are not constantly in danger. I just can't. And I love you. It's an impossible choice."

"Oh, darling, I see you didn't read my byline?" Dominique picked up the newspaper from the end table where Hope had unpacked it the day she arrived home.

"I know you wrote it. And it was a touching and obviously effective piece. It convinced Ernie's mother to reconnect. So powerful. But still . . ." Hope was confused by the absurdity of his idea. It wasn't about the portraits or the article. It was the terror of his job. Why couldn't he see this? Didn't his horrifying experience make him see? She couldn't subject herself or their future children—if they had them—to this ongoing nightmare, could she?

"Hope, darling, read the byline." He handed her the copy of the paper that sat on her coffee table.

She wasn't sure what difference it would make.

Dominique pointed to a fine print byline off to the side of the final page. He read it aloud. "Dominique Bellamy Bonchance, Former Director of Overseas Operations for the Uplift Children's Foundation. Currently, The San Francisco Chronicle's syndicated journalist for the new Sunday family column, Split Tree."

"Former director? Split Tree? I don't understand."

"Do you mind? I borrowed your theme for my new column. You once said I could use anything of yours. Darling, I need to recover and get things in order, but it will all work out. You're everything to me. I wrote my resignation to Michael *before* I left. Then, I submitted Ernie's story to the editor. I was supposed to start my new journalist job last week. I planned to be with you when the paper came out. But you know, I was, shall we say, otherwise engaged." He held up his injured wrists. "I wanted to surprise you, but not in the way I did."

Hope re-read the byline. Tucked up in the next column, she'd missed seeing it the first time, and so had everyone else. An eruption of emotion overcame her. Breathless and immobilized, she listened.

"I'm so sorry to have put us both through this ordeal to try to *find* myself. We can celebrate the Split Tree families coming together. It's so moving. Or follow my writing and your art wherever they take us. Can't we? Hope? What are you thinking? Are you OK?"

She blew out the breath she was holding. "I understand now. You had to find your way, Dominique. As did I, darling man. As did I." She finally understood.

Dominique pulled Hope closer. "Sweetheart, I have found the true me."

"Yes, you have." They were back in the familiar settee. Things could work.

"Hope, my work is portable, and so is yours. Visits to the Ketchums will be a breeze."

One odd placement of a byline, she thought. One formatting issue and the butterfly had fluttered again, causing a hurricane in Hope's life. But the storm had calmed. She knew what she wanted to do. "When I return to California, maybe I should do a little house hunting?"

"Wonderful." Dominique kissed her. "I suspected you would want to be in California, and it's fine with me. Better than fine."

She threw her arms around his neck and then pulled away. "Wait. This is all too much. We're moving too fast. What about Jolie?"

"No. Jolie will not be a problem. She loves her new job. And she and Peter are getting engaged, she says. I haven't met him yet. Sounds like she has reason to stay. And, you know she hates to fly." He laughed and put his arms around Hope.

"Careful, Dominique, your injuries. You decided this *before* you were held hostage? So, that means no more wars and violence in our lives? I need to know this, Dominique."

"I cannot promise you that."

The surprise brought her to her feet. "What do you mean? I thought you said—" Hope shook with anger and confusion. The constant whiplash of their relationship was overwhelming.

"No, wait." Dominique joined her, standing beside the settee, rubbing his hands up and down her arms to calm her. "Hope, there will *always* be wars, violence, and hatred. But you've opened my eyes. You had the wisdom to find your *Guernica*—in your healing art . . . the Split Tree of survivors, joined in one trunk with roots in their new soil. I can picture the original on your gallery wall. Picasso's Guernica was twelve feet wide by twenty-five feet tall. The same size, except yours is a horizontal masterpiece of spreading branches. And your Split Tree is just as powerful. Do you realize that? You share Picasso's goal. He wanted to stop the pain and suffering of war to reject war as *heroic*. The real heroes are in your portraits, the smiling survivors. Just a different approach. A healing intent looking forward with hope. And I'm looking forward with *Hope*."

Even in his solemn soliloquy, Dominique had stopped to smile. Hope wasn't used to being compared to Pablo Picasso. Still, she was flattered by Dominique's point about her art's intent. "I'm still confused. What direction do you and I share?"

"Remember the French saying I quoted about lovers looking in the same direction? You were right. The price was too high. We would lose *us*." He brushed strands of hair from her face, his hand lingering. "But it was about more than *us*. It was about finding a way for us both to live our true selves and do something for that one child in the constant wars. I didn't need to be in the heat of war to honor my father and myself. I needed to make a difference like Picasso did. But I'm no Picasso."

"Neither am I, Dominique. But writing that article brought peace, healing, and a new perspective to Ernie and Allison. And that was just your first effort."

"Will you forgive me? I was slow to know what you knew the minute you sat in Linh's studio and created your art, free of the traumas and violence of war. Our arts are about the future, the rising of people after loss and devastation, or soothing the sufferings they'd endured from the prejudice against them, simply for their differences. I have more to say."

"On this point, I have no doubt." She managed a laugh. Hope loved how his romantic tendencies launched him into sharing his inner thoughts in a deep stream of consciousness and oration. She was back in their team debriefing, imagining when Dominique had told the story of his first mission. With every word he spoke back then, Hope had realized she was falling in love with this expressive, emotional Frenchman with his Spanish tendency toward tears.

"Hope, did you know that Picasso's enormous, frightening painting, *Guernica*, went on tour around the world raising money for the refugees of the Nazi holocaust?"

"I didn't know that."

"I'm picturing the impact you can make with 'War Babies: Then and Now' through Uplift if you toured your Split Tree works worldwide."

"And Dominique, you can complement each one with the story of their journey."

Hope was caught up in the dream.

"These will not be war stories with uncertain endings. They will be historic tales of rising. No mystery, we will already know the uplifting outcomes."

His brilliant idea sounded like the key to their connection. Hope felt the thrilling light that Grandma Cecelia had described. She relaxed into Dominique's chest. "Oh, sorry, your arms. Are the injuries painful?"

"They're healing as we speak." He kissed her forehead. "And I assume we'll live in Sausalito near your studio. We'll love the view. Perfect for a writer, no? I see in today's Chronicle that

I picked up at the airport there's a houseboat for sale, or am I being too romantic?"

Hope pictured the view from Janine's living room across the water to the high arches of the Golden Gate bridge peeking over the Marin hills. After visiting her, Hope had told Dominique it would be a fantasy to live there. The long walk to the ICB along the water, her time with Linh and her Lê family. She listened to her true self as Grandma Cecelia had always said to do. "I cannot live in a *houseboat* in Sausalito."

"But Hope . . . when you visited Janine, you said you loved—"

Tara called out, interrupting their poignant moment.

"Oh, Tara! I didn't see her over there in the doorway. What about this sweet little one? Did you find alternative parents for her adoption?"

"I have two strong potentials."

"Wonderful! What's the next step? Can I help? I'd do anything to give this little one a happy life after all she's been through. Another portrait for The Wall of Hope?"

The tears threatening the edges of his eyes made Hope pause with a new thought. He'd said he would do anything. Could she make this commitment? Yes. Would he? The only thing in their way had been his job, and his career aspirations had changed. She imagined them making a healing difference through their art. And family. She had so much family in her own Split Tree, and now so would he, an only child.

Then Hope imagined something else. Her response was spontaneous and natural. "I think Tara needs swimming lessons."

"Swimming lessons? I'm confused. Do the prospective parents live by the water or have a pool?"

"Not yet, Dominique." Hope directed Dominique's glance to

Tara, suspended in the Jolly Jumper. The happy child pumped her little legs and smiled, her eyes wide with excitement. "But I think, if all goes well, they're moving to a houseboat."

Dominique's expression was suspended, too. His eyes widened with a noticeable shift from confusion to clarity. It seemed Hope's meaning had finally been conveyed to her lover.

"Hope, darling. . . I don't know what to say. It's not . . . what we planned, and so soon to begin our life together with a child." He glanced back at Tara. "Darling, I don't think I can . . . aren't we moving too fast?"

"Maybe I've become a little French lately. Didn't we both say we'd do anything for this little girl? Maybe she's the reason this all happened."

Dominique stared at Tara and took in a deep breath.

Hope listened for the fearsome roar of Jeremy's rescue plane overhead that had haunted her days since childhood. Silence. Only Tara's happy squeals could be heard as she bounced freely in the doorway.

Crossing the room, Hope lifted the smiling child into her arms, then moved next to Dominique. The metaphor wasn't lost on her. They would uplift this one child. "Was *any* of this planned, Dominique? We love each other. And it's not called a *houseboat*. It's called our *floating home*. Or am I being too romantic?"

He nodded and smiled. "Is there such a thing? I'm all in."

Hope kissed Tara's forehead. "Dominique, she's just *one* child."

EPILOGUE

HOPE PEEKED OUT of the heavy church door, searching for Dominique. Wearing their colorful Vietnamese wedding garb and Sunday best, the Lê and Ketchum families were gathered around Hằng's gravesite. A dozen of the younger kids were running in and out of the group, playing some spontaneous game, making a natural Lê Ketchum connection, oblivious to their differences.

Hidden in the group of fifty-two family members, Hope spotted her beloved talking with Jolie, her fiancé Peter, Grandpa Lê, and Grandma Cecelia. Had Hope ever seen such a glow around Jolie as her beau wrapped her arm in his and patted her hand?

Hope's throat tightened at the sight of Dominique's Vietnamese wedding fashion—a red brocade *áo gấm*, a groom's tunic, with gold dragon patterns symbolizing good fortune for their marriage. Would any other man do that for his soon-to-be bride?

Wearing a full-length matching red crepe *ao dai*, its bodice accented with gold lace and an embroidered dragon on the front,

Hope swept up her dress's sheer red train. They'd planned to surprise each other. The plan had worked.

In the St. Boniface cemetery, the lavender Crepe Myrtle trees were showing off their early full blooms, scenting the beautiful spring Saturday morning. It was a perfect day for their wedding. Hope listened to the soft sounds of the group mumbling prayers in unison led by Father Lawrence in honor of her mother, Hằng.

When they'd first arrived ahead of the guests, Hope and her father had made traditional offerings of flowers and lit incense at her mother's headstone. She felt at peace inside knowing so much more about Hằng. How can you feel close to someone you'd never met? Hope did.

Her father joined her at the church door and looked over Hope's shoulder at the crowd outside. "You're looking for Kate, I assume."

"Dad, I'm not. Kate is where she's supposed to be. I trust her."

"Better come inside, Hope. Everyone's getting ready to come in for the ceremony."

Watching the group line up behind Dominique as he led the traditional French wedding procession, Hope closed the church door. She wanted to have her father bring her down the aisle after everyone was seated; she did not wish to join the end of the procession as a French woman would. The hybrid Catholic-Vietnamese-French-American wedding would be a potpourri of traditions. That was intentional on Hope's and Dominique's parts.

"Let's go into the side room here, Dad. I don't want the groom to see me before the wedding. It's bad luck. And just to tease you, Dominique and I have a surprise for everyone."

Hope noticed her father's faraway gaze as they stood in the quiet room. "Dad, what are you thinking?"

He sighed. "I'm thinking about how much I've learned from you, Hope."

"From me? Really? About what?"

"Freeing yourself to follow your art, in some way, freed me. The secrets are out, and I've made peace with your Lê family. I would never want you to be torn between the two families you love on opposite coasts." He hugged Hope. "Thank you, sweetheart. I can still do what I do at the foundation, but not out of guilt or to make up for my sins. I can simply do it for the children and in your mother's honor."

MICHAEL WALKED Hope down the aisle. The closer she came to Dominique, who stood by the altar with tears edging his eyes, the more she felt gratitude shiver through her. The choir sang hymns with the music of the enormous pipe organ filling the cathedral arches. The ceremony, the vows, everything, was as Hope had imagined. And then there was the first kiss and the surprise.

Father Sullivan entered from the sacristy holding Tara, dressed in her new, white lace Christening gown.

"Father Sullivan!" Michael looked around, confused, as Shiloh and Uncle Tuân followed close behind the priest. Hope knew from all the stories in Kate's journal that the priest had played a powerful role in Kate and Michael's college life and connection. He was wonderful to come across the country from UConn to officiate the holy occasion.

The Christening ceremony was a delightful surprise for their fifty-two member family. Hope was in a daze, holding onto Dominique's arm.

"Where's Kate? Did she know Father Sullivan would be here?" Her dad was confused.

"Dad, Dominique and I planned it for you and Kate and for Tara. But Dad, it doesn't matter that Kate isn't seated with the family at the wedding. She's where she was meant to be."

"I'm confused and disappointed." Michael continued to scan the crowd.

"Be patient." Hope took his arm.

The godparents, Shiloh and Tuân, stood up for Tara and, along with the congregation, made their commitments to love and support the child in her Catholic faith.

Tara let out a chirp as the holy water trickled down her forehead.

"I Christen you in the name of the Father, the Son, and the Holy Ghost. Ladies and gentlemen, family and friends, may I introduce you to the newest member of our family and our faith." Father Sullivan held Tara up and said each of her names one by one: "Tara Lê Ketchum-James Bellamy Bonchance." Father Lawrence joined him, and they walked down the aisle and delivered Tara to her new parents. The all-inclusive six-part name elicited smiles and happy utterances from the family.

Dominique cuddled his new daughter and put his arm around Hope. "Darling, we did it."

Hope leaned in and whispered, "And we didn't need to be Picasso." Staring up at Dominique's profile, Hope smiled. My husband, she thought.

The organ began to play, and the church echoed with Kate's unmistakable solo in "Let There Be Peace On Earth."

"Like you said Dad, Kate's voice is like velvet, a bell, like a smooth glass of fine wine," Hope whispered, then squeezed her father's hand. "*Surprise.*"

Everyone spun round in unison to see the singing superstar standing above them. The scene in the choir loft was reminiscent of the place in Glynn where she'd gotten her start. A story everyone knew from magazine articles, Grammy acceptance speeches, and TV interviews over the years. Beside Kate was Grandma Cecelia.

At the sound of Kate's celebrated voice resonating from on high, everyone sang along, ". . . and let it begin with me."

The End